He halted at the bottom of the passageway. Before him stretched the hall of an ancient Hindu temple. The walls and pillars celebrated every conceivable erotic posture in voluptuous reliefs; the flames of ornamental sconces made them seem almost alive.

Although he himself could not see the musicians, and saw only the shadows of the nauch dancers, he was sure that Magus Rex could see them all very well in the room beyond the arched portal. And Zenobia probably sat at his side, helplessly watching their performance. The great wizard had secreted her here in one of his pleasure-domes until her suitor gave up and went away. But he, Valorius, had not gone away. No matter how stormy the interview, he was determined at least to see her. Taking a deep breath, he started across the erotic, torch-lighted hall.

And suddenly he was running for his life. Never had a mere hundred feet seemed so far. At the last possible instant he left his feet, diving headlong past the open monolith just as thousands of tons of rock crashed down from above, completely sealing the passageway behind him. . . .

JACK LOVEJOY

# MAGUS REX

A TOM DOHERTY ASSOCIATES BOOK

MAGUS REX

This is a work of fiction. All the characters and events portrayed in this book are fictional, and any resemblance to real people or incidents is purely coincidental.

Copyright ©1983 by Jack Lovejoy

All rights reserved, including the right to reproduce this book, or portions thereof in any form.

A TOR Book

Published by:
Tom Doherty Associates, Inc.
8–10 West 36th Street
New York, New York 10018

First TOR printing, September 1983

ISBN: 48-532-8

Cover art by Stephen Hickman

Printed in the United States of America

Distributed by:
Pinnacle Books
1430 Broadway
New York, New York 10018

# CHAPTER I
# THE NOME

A band of naked troglodytes stood watching from the base of the escarpment as the golden-haired youth in the shimmering blue cape and tunic strode through the ruins in the valley below. Some broken walls still showed vague traces of a gridiron pattern, but a thousand generations had passed since their long-forgotten ancestors had lived in cities.

They were flesh-eaters, devourers of their own kind. Yet, though the troglodytes outnumbered the youth in the shimmering blue cape and tunic thirty to one, they made no move toward him. Degenerative evolution had resulted in brutalized minds and bodies, but their instincts of self-preservation were unimpaired.

It was day, but there was little daylight. The great red ball of the sun rarely broke through the clouds any more. When it did, the troglodytes were driven into the depths of their squalid caves, for its heat was unbearable. Twilight and night was the normal diurnal cycle.

Beyond the ruins the valley opened out onto a

broad rolling plain, its barren surface scarred hideously
with canyons and erosion gulleys. At the very heart
of the plain stood a palace of white marble. Only on
the rare days when the cloud cover thinned could the
troglodytes make it out in the distance. Their ancestors might have classified the great structure as Byzantine; they themselves had no idea what it was, nor
who or what might live there. It was just one more
mysterious entity to fear in their primitive existence.

There were no natural barriers of any kind. The
ancient ruins petered out toward the mouth of the
valley, gradually giving way to the scarred and eroded
plain beyond. And yet there existed a point beyond
which no troglodyte ever ventured, a barrier thrown
up across their savage minds by the accumulated
experience of countless short-lived generations. Physically, any of them could have just strolled right out of
the valley. Instinctively, they knew that if they did
they would never come back alive.

But the youth in the shimmering blue cape and
tunic strode without hesitation directly toward this
invisible barrier-line. The troglodytes shifted uneasily
back and forth on their squat, hairy legs. This was not
in the normal order of things; like all brutes out of
their familiar element they were restive.

There was one of them, however, who continued to
watch steadily. He was even more squat and ungainly
than the others, a dwarf in fact. But his eyes glittered
with intelligence. Not the low cunning of savages, but
real intelligence — and intelligence of a high order. He
stood somewhat apart from the others, so that none of
them could sneak up behind him with a rock and
smash his skull in. He was a stranger, and the troglodytes usually had only one use for strangers.

They began to jabber exitedly. The youth had crossed
the barrier-line as if it did not exist. And nothing
happened. Their tension became acute. Some even
began to urinate where they stood, forcing those
nearby to hop out of the way. This would certainly
have led to a squabble, but one of them grunted

and pointed to an object far out on the plain.

It was barely visible in the perpetual twilight, but was moving rapidly toward the youth in the shimmering blue cape and tunic. The troglodytes had seen this creature before. It was one of the Guardians.

This was more in the normal order of things. They jabbered and danced back and forth in happy anticipation of seeing the tall golden-haired youth destroyed. They saw him leap lightly over an erosion gulley and begin to stride purposefully up the slope of a broad, swelling hill. The hill screened his view of the rapidly approaching Guardian, a fact not missed by the troglodytes. They bleated with savage laughter.

The youth was now a mere splash of shimmering blue upon the scarred, shadowy terrain. He had reached the top of the hill. Any moment now he would see the Guardian thundering toward the hill from the opposite direction. The creature was over twenty feet high, with a monstrous head and jaws; although it weighed several tons, it moved with amazing speed on its two powerful legs. It gave the troglodytes great satisfaction to know that they could see the Guardian and the youth could not.

The monstrous lizard had now reached the far side of the hill. Bent almost parallel to the ground, its huge tail held straight behind it for balance, its disproportionately small arms—hardly bigger than a man's—reaching forward to clutch its prey, the Guardian charged up the slope.

The troglodytes howled with delight, raising an abominable stench as they danced up and down. The youth had suddenly become aware of the enormous lizard thundering toward him. He could not hope to dodge the monster, and there was no place to hide. The troglodytes expected to see the youth turn and run, be caught from behind and crushed in the jaws of the Guardian. But the eyes of the dwarf, standing somewhat apart from the others, only narrowed in calculation.

The youth did not turn and run. He stood unflinch-

ingly in the path of the charging monster at the very
summit of the hill. And suddenly the Guardian lurched
to a halt only a few yards away. Then it settled comfortably back on its haunches, as docile as a puppy. If
its tail had not been so huge it might have wagged it.
The youth circled it and strode down the far side of
the hill.

The troglodytes were furious. They shrieked with
mindless rage, grimacing and gnashing their mossy
teeth in frustration. Seeking some outlet for their rage,
the whole band turned as one toward the stranger. If
they had been cheated of their savage spectacle, at
least they would not go hungry. But the dwarf had
vanished without a trace.

Meanwhile, the youth continued to work his way
down the trellis of erosion gulleys covering the slope
of the hill. He found an arroyo at the bottom which
ran more or less in the direction of the white marble
palace. He followed it for over a mile, ready for any
contingency. The giant lizards were by no means the
most formidable of the Guardians.

His movements were those of a young athlete. But
there was something in his eyes, which were the same
shimmering blue as his cape and tunic, that somehow
belied his otherwise youthful appearance. He stood
well over six feet tall; his hair was thick and golden;
the handsome symmetry of his face was marred only
by an unusual breadth of forehead. Although he was
without weapons, he did not give the impression of
being defenseless.

As he turned into a blind canyon he suddenly froze.
What he saw was the one contingency he was not
prepared for—at least, not so soon.

A man in decadent violet robes sat voluptuously
on an overstuffed violet cushion at the top of a
white marble pillar. He was a stunning contrast
to the starkness of his surroundings. Except for
a distinguished touch of gray at the temples, the
man's neatly-trimmed hair and beard were silky
black. So poised and distinguished looking was he

that even his long violet fingernails seemed somehow
appropriate.

"Ah, Valorius," he said, "so you've come to visit me.
And uninvited too!"

The white marble pillar was about ten feet high,
glistening at the very center of the gloomy canyon like
a beam of sunlight. The youth approached it gingerly.
He could only address the distinguished looking man
with the long violet fingernails by looking up at him
like a suppliant before an idol.

"Magus Rex, my lord," he began nervously. "First
permit me to say—"

"No preambles! Stop maundering and explain yourself. What do you mean by popping on to my nome
uninvited, you insolent young snippet?"

Valorius had expected this inevitable meeting to be
difficult. Decades of rigorous schooling had given him
control of even his unconscious somatic processes.
But he had to concentrate now to subdue the wild
fluttering of his heart, the ringing in his ears, the
watery wobble about his knees.

"I had to come uninvited, my lord," he said in a
voice that sounded too loud even to himself. "You
wouldn't have invited me, even if I had formally
requested an audience."

"Of course not! What have I to do with poppet-
headed pipsqueaks like you? Now go away, and I may
consider vouchsafing you an interview, let's say, sometime about the middle of the next century. In the
meantime I'll try and think nice thoughts about you—
which will tax even my powers."

But, shakily, Valorius stood his ground. Although
he had not expected it to take place in the middle of a
gloomy canyon, he had prepared for this interview
with a set speech.

"With the approach of my first centennial and the
completion of my formal studies," he recited, "I have
come to you, Magus Rex—"

"Uninvited!"

"Uninvited," Valorius nodded, "to present you with

my qualifications and to request that you consider
me—"

"An impudent half-baked sniveler. That's what I
consider you. Your qualifications indeed!" he sneered.
"Bah!"

"I would never dream of comparing myself to you,
Magus Rex—"

"I should hope not, you pandering incompetent!"

"But I maintain," Valorius defended himself, "that
I have worked long and hard, and, three years in
advance of the minimum age, have met all necessary
qualifications for a Master Wizardship. The title will
be awarded to me on the date of my first centennial.
And though you choose to disparage me—"

"I justly censure your impudence, nothing more. In
this nome a Master Wizard doesn't qualify to clean
the birdcages. However," he added magnanimously, "I
will do you the justice of saying that your schoolboy
exploits have not gone unnoticed. But that you've
learned to juggle a few of the coarser vibrations does
not excuse your gatecrashing onto my nome. Now tell
me why you want to see me, so I can tell you why you
can't. I've already wasted enough time with you."

"Well, my lord," Valorius stammered. "It's like this.
You see," he coughed and lowered his eyes, "uh, how
shall I put it—"

"Come, come. Don't shilly-shally! You are under-
standably nervous in my presence. But do try to relax.
After all," he complacently surveyed his long violet
fingernails, "it is only I, Magus Rex."

"To be frank, my lord," Valorius said as firmly as he
was able, "it's not exactly you that I've come to see.
Although," he added quickly, "we—that is, I—would
most assuredly have sought, uh, I mean, requested. . . ."
He broke down, and before he could rally, a sneering
voice exclaimed from the top of the pillar:

"So that's it! You've come tomcatting after my
daughter. How dare you, you presumptuous punkie!
Is there no limit to your impudence? Next you'll be
telling me that you love her."

"With all my heart," replied Valorius with manly firmness. "Long have I repined in silence, neither complaining nor outwardly fretting, whilst I dutifully pursued my studies. But I can remain silent no longer. Oh, my lord, if I could only make you realize the depth of my feelings for your daughter. Zenobia, the fairest bud that ever flowered in all the realms of wizardry. And I have reason to believe that my love is not unrequited. How could I have gone on, loving her as I do, and not have made some attempt to make her mine? Zenobia, the guiding star of all my hopes—"

"Oh, stop it, will you!" Magus Rex impatiently flicked his long violet fingernails. "Spare me your puppyish yammer. Whether you love my daughter is beside the point. You can't have her, and that's that. Now get off my nome, you maundering mooncalf!"

"But Magus Rex, my lord—"

"You are trying my patience, Valorius. What you hoped to accomplish here I don't know. Can even you have been so fatuous as to believe that I'd simply hand over my darling daughter just because you think you love each other? What could two infants like you possibly know of love? And surely you realize that you couldn't have Zenobia unless I chose to give her to you. Am I not the most powerful wizard who has ever lived?"

"Yes," Valorius had to admit, "that's undeniably true."

"All right, then," said Magus Rex, somewhat mollified. "And of course you know that I'd pounce on you within minutes if you ever had the temerity to try and elope—no matter how far in time or space you fled."

"Yes, my lord," Valorius had to admit again. "I have no illusions about that."

"Well, then we're back where we started. And you're nothing but an impudent trespasser, a mooning suppliant, a beefwitted blunderer, a muddleheaded mummer, an empty attic, an oafish dotard, a twitterpated tyro, a caterwauling catechumen." He paused, smacking his lips. "Rather good, that."

"But, my lord—"

"Don't interrupt me in the middle of a diatribe! Now where was I?"

"Caterwauling catechumen, I believe."

"Ah, yes." And he continued to abuse Valorius for another ten minutes without once repeating an epithet. Then he smoothed his voluptuously violet robes and settled himself more comfortably into his overstuffed violet cushion. "Now that you have my judicious opinion of you, have you anything to say before I have you chased off the grounds?"

"Only that I love Zenobia with all my heart, and that she loves me. If you were to let her make her own choice—"

"Which I have no intention of doing. Now I've put up with your nonsense long enough, Valorius. Here is my final word on the matter. You'll never call Zenobia your pigsney while I can still twist a single vibration. And I can twist more than a few, as you well know. And since I'm barely into my second millennium, and hence likely to be around for at least a few more centuries, I suggest that you take your tomcatting elsewhere. You're yowling on the wrong fence."

"You underrate me, Magus Rex," Valorius replied, his jaw muscles tightening. "I remain firm in my purpose, and cannot be dissuaded."

"You can't be dissuaded, eh? Then how about a bit of overwhelming force? I'm beginning to think that what you really need is a good lesson, you impudent puppy. Have you any conception of the power I'm capable of wielding? Perhaps you're not familiar with the saying: 'The Earth is a vast storage battery charged with psychic energy, which those wise in the ways of wizardry can bend to any conceivable purpose.' "

Valorius racked his schoolboy memory. "That was one of the sayings of Tellian Magus, if I'm not mistaken."

"Well!" cried Magus Rex disgustedly. "That certainly won't get you anywhere. What are they teaching you acolytes nowadays? Tellian Magus, indeed! That was one of my sayings, nincompoop! If you don't know the ANALECTS OF MAGUS REX, what do you

know? Baboon! Perhaps you'd like to tell me about
your qualifications again? Or how long and diligently
you've worked? Bah!"

"My apologies, Magus Rex," Valorius winced. (What
a time to muff a quotation!) "The saying is of course
from the ANALECTS. The Earth is indeed like a vast
storage battery charged with psychic energy, in the
manipulation of which there is none more skillful
than Magus Rex. As you once memorably observed to
my late father: 'Matter is thought, and my thoughts
are all that matter.'"

"Now that's more like it, Valorius. If you had any
chance at all in this affair—which you haven't—it
would be through just that kind of obsequious flattery.
Your father was a pudding, but at least he knew how
to show a proper deference to his superiors, among
whom I head every list. And though he could never
quite decide whether to approach me as a fawner or a
lickspittle, I magnanimously forgave him this little
inconsistency because it showed the proper spirit. In
fact, were he here now instead of you, he would have
been reduced by this time to clinging to the foot of the
pillar, blubbering for my forgiveness."

Valorius knew that this was probably true. His
father had been a studious and highly respected wizard.
Moral courage, however, had not been his strong point.
In fact, the mere mention of the name Magus Rex was
enough to set him trembling for hours. The epithet
"pudding" was, alas, not inappropriate (although
Valorius would never have admitted such a thing in
public).

"Magus Rex, my lord," he said with a fortitude that
did him proud, his shoulders thrown back, his tall,
slender form erect. "I know how powerful you are—"

"Do you really?" Magus Rex studied his long violet
fingernails through heavy-lidded eyes.

"But I love your daughter with all my heart. And
I know that she loves me. When she sent . . . uh,
that is, when I first determined to come here, I
felt that nothing could stand in my way. I'm sure

I can make her happy, my lord."

"But she is happy. It has been my good pleasure to spoil her outrageously, to provide her with everything she could possibly want, from all times and places. And as to nothing standing in your way, that's just more of your impudent drivel. I stand in your way, and never in the two million years of man has there been a more formidable obstacle. There is literally nothing I can't do. There is literally nothing I can't say to anyone and have them take it. And that's why I'm so jolly."

"But Zenobia, my lord—"

"Remains with me, for it is my good pleasure to have it so. No other reason is necessary. For the sake of your father, who was my sycophant, I've chosen to overlook your impudence on this one occasion. But be warned: even my sublime patience is not unlimited. If you persist in making a nuisance of yourself you face the dire possibility of arousing my wrath. That is a fate I wouldn't wish even on a snotnose like you."

"I'm sorry, my lord," Valorius said firmly. "But I cannot turn back until I've seen and talked with Zenobia."

"So you would defy me, even me, Magus Rex, for the sake of your true love. How sweet! Just like in an old storybook, isn't it?" he sneered. "Well, since you've cast me as the ogre, I will play the part. Pacifying a giant lizard did show some trifling degree of skill. I'm sure your average troglodyte couldn't have done it. But I've got all kinds of beasties roaming about, and it will soon be night."

"My lord, I would be craven indeed if I were to allow such obstacles to stand between me and my love for—"

"You're not going to start that again, are you? But I see that you are. Well, then there's nothing more to be said. I dislike wasting good psychic energy on a mere pest. But I will not be bearded in my own nome. Proceed if you dare!"

And with that he began to fade, white marble pillar,

overstuffed violet cushion and all. But then, just before he had completely vanished, he began to reappear, like an afterthought.

"By the way, Valorius," he said mockingly, "I notice that you're walking. It's a good twenty miles to the palace, and night is falling. Even a bumbling tyro like you should be wizard enough to transport himself."

"I have indeed acquired some skill in transportation, my lord."

"Then why don't you dematerialize, and save yourself a pair of sore feet? Not to mention a night of ungodly harrassment." A sardonic twinkle appeared in his heavy-lidded eyes. "It might be fun to see just what you rematerialize as. No? Ah, well. Then I suppose you must take your chances on foot."

This time he disappeared completely. Valorius found himself alone at the bottom of the gloomy canyon. Dense rolling vapors obscured the sky only a few hundred feet overhead. It was darker than before. Night was falling.

# CHAPTER II:
## CARNIVAL NIGHT

The power of the great wizard was astonishing. Valorius felt at times like a helpless mouse being toyed with by a cat too powerful even to imagine. The white apes and centaurs were the worst, but the number of Guardians seemed endless. Over and over again he was driven, almost herded, away from the path to the white marble palace. He slogged his way doggedly through the night, determined to reach the palace by morning.

The first structures he encountered, however, were not Byzantine. They were unpretentious two- and three-story buildings of brick and stone. The cobblestone streets were alive with throngs of merry-makers, dancing and laughing and singing. The entire population seemed to have abandoned itself to this night of revelry; freed briefly from the drudgery of their everyday life.

The costumes were gaudy and imaginative. Jugglers and acrobats entertained at street corners; the wine-shops were full to overflowing; the tinny throb of drums and trumpets blared from the dance-halls, where bright chains of dancers bobbed and whirled in time to the gay music. It was carnival night in ancient Paris, a living kaleidoscope set in the midst of a barren, nightmarish plain.

Valorius had no idea why Magus Rex had created all this. Certainly not for his benefit. It was not an illusion. These were real people, going about their business with no more knowledge of their creator than people have ever had. Nor were they at all aware of the void surrounding them.

There was no trouble entering the town. He simply walked right in. But when he looked back, the sterile plain was gone. Like a kaleidoscope the colorful patterns of the streets seemed to repeat themselves endlessly through space. Foot-sore and weary, he picked his way through the crowd.

In his shimmering blue cape and tunic he might have been just another merry-maker in search of a night's happiness. The crowd ignored him, and he ignored the crowd. Only when he reached the pantomime theater did he stop. Mimes were popular in ancient Paris, and a crowd had gathered to watch a free preview of the show inside. Valorius watched with them.

It was a makeshift stage, supported by wooden trestles and lighted by the orange-red flames of torches set on poles at either side. A troop of young girls, dressed all in feathers, cleverly mimed a flight of birds while a pierrot told of the even greater wonders inside for those discerning enough to buy a ticket for tonight's performance. Odalisques and Red Indians stood shoulder to shoulder with lions, dwarfs, and giant eagles at the back of the stage. But it was a young ballerina standing in the shadows at the back of the stage that had really caught Valorius' attention. She reminded him curiously of Zenobia.

The sight of her was just enough to tip the balance. After a long night of struggle and harrassment an hour's respite could do no harm. The ticket-seller was doing a brisk business, and Valorius could not resist the temptation to get in line.

A moment's hard concentration was all he needed to reproduce the coin of the realm, a silver franc. The energy tapped from his immediate environment was hardly missed by those around him. He made no resistance against the surge and jostle of the crowd, allowing himself to be carried along like driftwood on the tide. Never had it felt so good to sit down.

The rough terrain, shattered by erosion gulleys and dead-end canyons, had forced him to double back again and again. Abominable white apes had dogged his steps like the creatures out of a nightmare. He had lost sight of the palace about two hours ago during an especially savage attack by a band of centaurs. He was wizard enough to fend them off, but only after he had been driven into a weird, silt-choked depression, hundreds of feet below the level of the plain and far out of his way. It was at the very center of this depression that he had stumbled into ancient Paris on carnival night. He bought a raspberry ice from an old catering-woman and sat back to watch the pantomime.

The little bandbox theater was jammed. Whistles and catcalls echoed down from the gallery above; staccato clapping and the impatient stamping of feet arose from the main floor below. The theater manager soon took the hint. The grubby little orchestra struck up the overture.

He had a perfect view of the stage from his front-row seat in the very center of the first balcony. The pierrot he had seen outside in the street was the principal mime; his ability to convey emotion without dialogue was extraordinary. Magus Rex had probably recreated him from a classic mime who had once actually lived. But the young ballerina seemed some-how out of place. Her figure was much too voluptuous for her profession. From a distance she did indeed look remarkably like Zenobia.

She and the pierrot were making their way through a forest of pasteboard trees. Their progress was con-tinually interrupted by dancing dwarfs, Red Indians, and comic gendarmes. It took them nearly fifteen minutes to cross the little bandbox stage. Then a two-legged bear popped out of the pasteboard forest and terrified the poor ballerina by dancing all around her. Fortunately, there was a slapstick lying ready at hand (the ideal weapon against two-legged dancing bears), and the brave pierrot, to the delight of the packed house, drove the beast offstage with sundry loud thwacks on the rump.

Valorius good-naturedly joined in the applause. He knew that he should be on his way. But he could not bring himself to leave. Here there was light and laughter, the warm camaraderie of a carnival crowd. A major part of his work at the Academy was study of the two-million year history of mankind, and had he racked his brains for the ideal relief from weariness and anxiety, he could have found no better one than a pantomime on carnival night in ancient Paris. He decided to stay for just one more act.

The young ballerina was now alone on stage. A grubby little violinist with greasy white hair hanging to his shoulders stood up in the orchestra pit and began scraping a mournful air. With a great deal of hand-wringing and pleading looks toward the balcony, the ballerina danced a solo expressing her concern for the safety of the pierrot and her fear of being alone in a pasteboard forest. Suddenly her worst fears were realized. Out of the wings leapt a two-legged lion and a giant eagle with buttons down its back. The orchestra erupted in a wild dance as the solo became a trio. Finally the gruesome pair carried off the poor ballerina. She hardly had time to drop her handkerchief before the curtain fell.

Valorius stretched and yawned. Catering-women began circulating through the crowd again. A number of people left their seats for the foyer. There was a lot of raucous badinage among those who remained in their seats. Sounds of skylarking rumbled down from the balcony above. A fistfight between two big beefy women broke out in the gallery, but it was quickly suppressed.

He bought another raspberry ice, and let his eyes wander over the crowd. The yellow glare of the gaslights made everything seem strangely lurid.

He had noticed earlier that the box overhanging the right side of the stage had its curtains drawn. But now he suddenly became aware of someone in the box watching him through a slit in the curtains. The moment he turned in that direction the curtains were yanked shut.

He glanced suspiciously at the raspberry ice in his hand, but then shook his head. Magus Rex never did anything underhanded. His equitableness was legendary. He might be ruthless and all-powerful, but he had an Olympian scorn of anything mean. Valorius finished his second raspberry ice with confidence.

The grubby little orchestra began the overture to the second act, and the carnival audience came tumbling back to their seats.

The curtain opened onto an empty stage. The scene was still that of a pasteboard forest. Then the pierrot skipped triumphantly out of the wings, his slapstick over his shoulder. His victory dance recounted his successful offstage encounter with the dancing bear. All at once he realized that something was missing. The ballerina! Up and back he raced, flapping the loose sleeves of his costume like a demented goony bird. His chalk-white face was twisted into a look of excruciating loss. Then he discovered the handkerchief. After dancing around it for several minutes, he at last picked it up. It was the ballerina's! Instantly he surmised that she had been ravished by a two-legged lion and a giant eagle with buttons down its back. Several woodland creatures (including that well-known denizen of pasteboard forests, the walrus) pranced out of the wings to help the poor pierrot celebrate his grief.

At that point, Valorius caught another movement out of the corner of his eye. He turned toward the mysterious box just in time to see its curtains yanked shut again.

His suspicions were now fully roused. Was the

ballerina's resemblance to Zenobia more than mere
coincidence? What if it were Magus Rex himself sitting in the curtained box? It seemed unlikely that he
would go to so much trouble for somebody he regarded
as a mere nuisance (Valorius had no illusions about
his status here). This whole wonderful creation was
merely a pleasure-dome built for the great wizard's
own amusement, just as ancient Russian aristocrats
had set up gypsy villages on their estates. And like an
ancient Russian prince in a gypsy village, Magus
Rex's enjoyment of ancient Paris would probably not
be confined to watching pantomimes.

Perhaps that explained it. Magus Rex had carried
his daughter away from the palace so that she would
not be there when he, Valorius, arrived. After all, he
had stumbled upon this pleasure-dome by the merest
chance. It could not be seen from the plain above, and
it was not on a direct line to the palace. In any case,
he had to get a look at the occupants of the mysterious
box. There was no point in continuing on to the palace
if Zenobia was right here.

The curtains of the box obviously would not be
drawn across its front. From the far left corner of the
balcony he might just get a peep inside. He tried to
avoid people's feet and shins, but was cursed more
than once for his clumsiness.

Then he noticed that the scenery on stage was also
moving. Invisible machinery smoothly shifted the pasteboard forest into one wing while a park scene, complete with pasteboard pond, statues, and benches,
glided in from the other. The mime in the pierrot's
costume, although not actually moving himself, looked
so wonderfully like a disconsolate lover walking with
head bowed that he seemed to be wandering out of
the forest and into the park, rather than the scenery
shifting behind him. The audience applauded.

Valorius used his hands for other purposes. Brac-
ing himself against the railing, he leaned out of the
balcony as far as he dared. He could just make out the
back of a woman's head. She had the same auburn

hair as Zenobia (and the young ballerina), but he could not quite see her face. To have leaned out any further would have resulted in a great surprise for the clarinet player directly below.

There was no constraint to silence for the pantomime, and the audience commented freely on the performance. Many of those nearby also commented freely on Valorius, although in less flattering terms. He pondered his next move.

On stage, the poor pierrot had discovered a rope with a noose tied at one end lying conveniently at hand. With his head tilted to one side and his tongue lolling out of his mouth, he showed the audience exactly what he had in mind. Then he tossed the noose over the limb of a pasteboard tree, ominously adjusting it around his neck while the grubby little violinist with the long white hair played another mournful air. But just when the pierrot was ready to end it all, a little girl came skipping out of the wings and asked to borrow the rope. Reluctantly, he loaned it to her, and she did a clever rope-skipping routine, accompanied by various nursemaids, flower-girls, comic gendarmes, and the inevitable walrus in a kind of gavotte.

Since he could not see into the front of the curtained box, Valorius had no choice but to try the rear. Before the act ended he started working his way toward the exit.

The red carpet of the mezzanine was threadbare and patched in several places. It opened into a dusty, dimly-lighted corridor behind the boxes. Garish paintings were luridly illuminated by gaslights in sconces of red glass. The walls and heavy maroon curtains muffled the sound of the orchestra, but the rhythmic thump-thump-thump of the bass drum seemed as loud as ever.

Drawn curtains hung all along the corridor. The mysterious box lay at the very end. Beside it stood a narrow wooden door, evidently leading backstage.

Valorius hesitated. Magus Rex was already angry.

It might not be a good idea to barge in on him again—assuming of course that it really was Magus Rex in the box. And Zenobia. Nervously, he awaited the fanfare that would end the second act.

It came in less than two minutes—a tinny crescendo, followed by the muffled applause of the audience. Curtains all along the corridor shot open, and an occult miscellany of carnival costumes and formal evening dress spewed forth, with a babble of talk and laughter. A few people tried to imitate the facial expressions of the pierrot for the amusement of their friends.

A rotund gentleman with thick lips lit a fat cigar, pretending to listen to the chatter of his rotund wife. His somewhat less rotund daughter tried to catch Valorius' eye while they were not looking. But he was interested only in the box at the end of the corridor. Those curtains alone were still drawn.

He waited impatiently for several minutes. At last, still hesitant, he edged his way through the crowd of boxholders. Taking a deep breath, he very deferentially drew the maroon curtain aside. The box was empty.

Perplexed, Valorius ran his fingers through his long golden hair. That he should encounter some weird and formidable obstacles crossing the nome of Magus Rex was to be expected. But he had not expected a mystery.

He examined the compartment for a clue of some kind. But there was nothing—not so much as a single loose strand of auburn hair. There was only one way its occupants could have left without passing him.

But just as he started toward the narrow wooden door leading backstage he saw a flash of red. He quickly drew the curtains. Above his head, hovering in mid air, a phantom blaze of large red letters slowly took shape. It was several minutes before he could read them:

> Our only love has beckoned,
> And instantly we start;
> Forgetting in that second
> That transports of the heart
> Prepare a cage apart.

It had been Zenobia! It was by just this means that she had first contacted him at the Academy. To create blazing red letters out of thin air was no mean feat, even for a Master Wizard. He had no idea how Zenobia had learned the trick. But then she was the daughter of the greatest wizard that had ever lived, and love has devices of its own.

They had loved each other since childhood, since the days when his father had been Magus Rex's personal secretary. In fact, he had always suspected that his early enrollment in the Academy had been, in part at least, to separate them. They had been strictly forbidden to communicate in any form whatsoever. But their love had endured over the years. When the cryptic verse had suddenly appeared three days ago in his quarters at the Academy, he had known at once that it was from Zenobia. He still had no idea why she had contacted him at this time, or used this peculiar means for doing so. But he had wasted no time leaving the forests of Antarctica and rushing to the nome of Magus Rex.

He read the cryptic verse through again. It was obviously a warning of some kind. The first two lines probably alluded either to his coming here in answer to her summons or to trying to follow her after having seen her in the curtained box. The key word in the third line was "second." It was probably meant to warn him of something occuring next in order, rather than simply referring to a brief unit of time. A second what? Or perhaps it alluded to a double. The young ballerina? The last two lines seemed less ambiguous. "Cage" could only mean a trap of some kind, and "transports of the heart"—unless it had been thrown in for the sake of the rhyme—meant their love. Was Magus Rex planning to use their very love as some kind of trap?

But he could not spend the whole night mulling over it. He had to act—and fast. He quickly memorized the verse, and hurried from the box.

The rotund gentleman's somewhat less rotund

daughter had apparently been lying in wait for him, and he nearly bowled her over. She blushed and rolled her cow's eyes at him. But her maidenly confusion did not keep her from strategically pinning him into a corner.

French was a dead language. He could read it, but had no idea how it was pronounced. And this shrinking violet had ten clinging tendrils which seemed to anticipate his every move. When he finally shook her off — literally — he was thoroughly perturbed.

Tearing open the narrow wooden door, he rushed down a narrow wooden staircase backstage. At the bottom of the stairs a golden-haired young man about his own size leaned against the wall, complacently flipping a shiny new silver coin. He had been the inevitable walrus in the pantomime, and his tusked headpiece lay on the floor beside him. Valorius dashed past him and out into the narrow alley.

The alley was dark and deserted. At its far end he could see the seething lights and colors of the carnival. Just as he reached the street, a black fiacre pulled away from the curb. Its rear window was curtained, but as it plunged through the crowd into the middle of the cobblestone street, a head appeared at a side window. It was Magus Rex!

The great wizard glared angrily back at him, then shouted something to the driver. A whip cracked, and the black fiacre's four black horses raced down the street, sending scores of merry-makers scurrying for their lives.

# CHAPTER III:
## A CAGE APART

By the time Valorius had jostled into the middle of the street, the black fiacre had turned a corner and was lost from sight. He looked desperately about for some means of following. And there stood an open landau at the opposite curb, which seemed almost to be waiting just for him. He pushed toward it through the carnival crowd.

It was a private vehicle, evidently waiting for its owner (perhaps the rotund gentleman with the fat cigar in the corridor behind the boxes?) to leave the pantomime. Some quick financial arrangement would have to be made with the driver. He wondered how much coin of the realm he would have to create—and how much time he would lose creating it. But to his surprise, the instant the landau's driver spotted him he jumped down from his box and held the door open.

Valorius was sure he had never seen the mustachioed little man before. It was as if somebody had ordered him to look specifically for a golden-haired youth wearing a shimmering blue cape and tunic. Valorius hesitated, recalling the word "second" in Zenobia's message. The second carriage? Was this the "cage"? He also recalled the golden-haired youth he had seen flipping the new silver coin backstage. The youth resembled him almost as closely as the ballerina in the pantomime had resembled Zenobia. Surely this was not a coincidence. Perhaps "second" meant *double*. And who had given his "double" the new silver coin?

Before the driver got a good look at him, Valorius turned and plunged back into the crowd. The youth was still backstage flipping his new silver coin. Within minutes he was flipping a new gold coin, dressed in Valorius' cape and tunic, headed for the landau outside. Valorius himself, rejecting the walrus costume as too bulky, grabbed the only available one that fit—a tropical bird suit with a long beaked mask.

The driver of the landau noticed no difference. He held the door open for Valorius' double just as he had held it open for Valorius himself. The double gave the directions he had been paid to give; the driver whipped the horses in pursuit of the black fiacre.

Valorius stood watching about twenty feet away, the long-beaked hood of his costume pulled down over his face. He was no longer worried about the black fiacre escaping. If the landau were indeed the "cage," Magus Rex would not let himself get too far ahead.

His own problem was not to get too far behind. Somehow he had to keep both carriages in sight. And the very means of doing so lay conveniently at hand. An ordinary bicycle leaned unattended against the wall of a nearby pastry shop. Its high front wheel was a good five feet in diameter, and its tiny rear wheel about one-fifth that size. Nor did it have brakes of any kind. It would be tricky to ride; but it was high enough to see over the heads of the crowd, and probably fast enough (once he got it going) to keep up with the carriages. It also had a horn, which he was careful not to touch until he was well away from the curb. Then the chase was on.

*"Voleur! Voleur!"* sounded behind him, and the

cry was quickly taken up by the crowd.

Valorius, squeezing the bulb of the horn like mad to warn those in front of him, quickly outdistanced those behind him. The landau had opened a path through the crowd. He followed in its wake, pedalling at breakneck speed.

At the first corner he turned he learned his first lesson about ancient bicycles: they work best on the straightaway. Had the pie wagon been a foot farther out from the curb, or had the fat man dressed as a pirate reacted a split second slower, the lesson might have been a painful one.

With the pedals attached directly to the hub, Valorius had no choice but to keep pedalling. He felt ridiculous each time he squeezed the bulb of the horn, perched several feet above the cobblestone street. What a way for a Master Wizard to travel! But Magus Rex had already hinted at what might happen to him if he dematerialized. No, he would risk transportation only as a very last resort.

Suddenly he felt an overwhelming urge to turn back. Had there been brakes on his ungainly vehicle he would probably have tried to stop. He seemed to be rushing headlong into a mirror image of the street behind him. The urge to turn back was almost overpowering. All at once he saw a huge tropical bird mounted ludicrously atop a bicycle rushing right at him. He tried to swerve out of the way, but the other bicycle seemed determined to collide with him.

The next thing he knew he was out of Paris. The street could not have ended more sharply had it been cut with a guillotine. There had been no warning. One moment he had been weaving crazily through the carnival crowd, headed for a sure collision, and the next he was back in the weird, silt-choked depression.

He could still see the lights of Paris gleaming behind him, but he had not been able to see out. Somehow the recreated quarter of the ancient city stood self-contained within its own panorama, a vague mirror image that somehow discouraged people from approaching too close. The wizardry of Magus Rex was indeed awesome.

Valorius was now certain that he had stumbled purely by chance into a pleasure-dome created by the great wizard for his own amusement. There was no telling how many other such pleasure-domes lay scattered about his vast nome. Like this one, they would certainly be found in natural depressions, where psychic energy was easiest to focus and manipulate. He had read that ancient parapsychologists could create hazy images out of their "auras" or "psychic fluids." Magus Rex could recreate whole societies, perfect to the last detail. Despite nearly a century of rigorous study, Valorius knew that his own abilities did not reach much further than the creation of a silver franc to pay his way into a pantomime. But his beloved had "beckoned," and he had no choice but to follow.

He could just make out the rear lanterns of the black fiacre and those of the landau racing to overtake it. Concentrating, he widened the pupils of his eyes. The nightmare landscape was still dark and murky, but he did not dare produce a light. He seemed to be flying through the night like an ancient witch on her broomstick.

The black fiacre was now racing directly toward the edge of a canyon, with the landau right behind it. Then he saw that there was a road leading down into the canyon. The black fiacre turned onto it and disappeared from sight. But just as the landau started to follow, the night erupted in a bedlam of cries and screams. White apes and centaurs, scores of them, overwhelmed the landau. The mustachioed little driver and the golden-haired youth in the shimmering blue cape and tunic were trussed up like a pair of capons.

Half jumping, half tumbling, Valorius got down from the perch of his brakeless bicycle. He had been battling white apes and centaurs all night, but even he would have been overwhelmed by such numbers. The "cage" had meant an ambush. But even without Zenobia's warning, he would probably not have been

caught unawares. The landau had been just a bit too
obvious.

But was this really what Zenobia had warned him
against? This was certainly the work of Magus Rex.
The driver of the landau had passed easily through
the mirror-image, while he himself had almost been
brought to a stop. But if the great wizard had wanted
to take him prisoner he could have done it without all
this trouble. He went over the cryptic verse again in
his mind.

What did the word "prepare" mean? Prepare what?
And the "cage," apparently the landau, had stood ready
at hand, not "apart." Or had Zenobia just thrown that
in for the sake of the rhyme? He threw back the hood
of his tropical-bird costume and ran his fingers through
his hair.

Just then the black fiacre emerged from the far side
of the canyon. Its lanterns jiggled wildly as it sped
across the depression toward the palace of Magus Rex.

Helplessly he watched it disappear into the night.
Then he noticed that his double was also watching it.
In fact, the double had no choice. For some reason the
white apes and centaurs had stopped terrorizing him
and deliberately turned his head in that direction.

It came to Valorius in a flash. Magus Rex and
Zenobia were not really in the black fiacre. After all,
the "cage" had been shut. There was no longer any
need for Magus Rex to travel so uncomfortably. Why
spend half the night jouncing across a dismal plain
when he could instantly transport himself and his
daughter back to the palace? That had to be it! They
had gotten out of the fiacre somewhere in the canyon.
Of course! The white apes and centaurs were only to
delay him until Magus Rex could "prepare" something
"apart" from the palace.

But what? An underground refuge of some kind?
Perhaps such a refuge already existed—another of
Magus Rex's pleasure-domes.

Valorius refastened the long-beaked hood of his
tropical-bird costume and started for the canyon. Nei-

ther the white apes nor the centaurs noticed him. It was too dark for any eyes except those of cats and wizards.

The canyon was deeper than he had suspected. He had no trouble finding the road used by the black fiacre; but following it downward was like descending into a river of ink. Even with the pupils of his eyes widened to their utmost he could hardly see a thing.

But the "cage" had been sprung. There was no longer any reason why he should not have a light. Concentrating, he created a scintillating globe of fire just overhead. Then he sent it flashing up and down the canyon like a tiny meteor. But there was no sign of them. He followed the ruts left by the black fiacre; the scintillating light followed him like a pet star. The ruts went straight from one side of the canyon to the other, ascending the steep, narrow road on the far side without a break.

Then he noticed a place where the hoofprints of the horses clustered together. On closer inspection he saw that the ruts were slightly deeper here. The carriage must have stopped. For what other reason than to let out its passengers? There were no footprints leading away, but Magus Rex could easily have covered their tracks. They had to be here! And they could not have gone far in the short time he had lost sight of them.

Systematically, he began to explore the canyon. Its jagged basalt walls rose for over two hundred feet on either side. There were no fissures or caves of any kind, not even so much as a large boulder to hide behind. But if they were here he would find them. He had worked hard to master his craft; by any absolute standard of wizardry his powers were formidable. Not the faintest clue would escape him.

And then he saw the handkerchief. It had been wedged into a tiny crevice in the rock wall—clearly not by accident. It was just below eye level; he had been so intent upon looking for footprints that he had nearly passed it by. He held it to the light. It was a delicate white gossamer handkerchief. He knew that it was Zenobia's because he had a handkerchief just like it in his quarters at the Academy, a childhood keepsake he had treasured for decades. Standing alone with the handkerchief of his lost love in his hand, he felt just like the poor pierrot in the pantomime.

He began searching the rock wall. The door was less than five feet from where the handkerchief had been wedged; its joints were virtually invisible. They looked like they had been cut into the living rock with a precision razor. Had Zenobia not dropped her handkerchief he might have searched the canyon for a year without finding the door. The next problem was to open it.

Psychokinesis was the most difficult skill for a young wizard to master. There was no point in looking for secret springs or mechanisms. The psychokinesis of a rock door would be child's play for Magus Rex. His own psychokinetic powers were less by a couple powers of ten, but he could not go away without at least trying.

Concentrating until the light overhead began to dim, he tried to move the door. It did not so much as quiver. But he had the residual psychic energy of two million years of mankind upon which to draw. Nor had he spent decades studying the occult classics of wizardry for nothing. He threw his full occult skill against the monolith of rock.

He began to concentrate, to unify all parts of his mind toward a single purpose; becoming one with the psychic energy lapping all about him, unifying it, controlling it. But even now he was almost defeated. The rock door turned out to be over six feet thick. Only by extending his psychokinetic powers to their utmost was he at last able to force it open.

Weird sensual rhythms rose toward him out of a steep passageway. Exotic perfumes enveloped him, caressing his senses with the fragrance of a temple garden. He could see a light at the far end of the passageway, a hundred feet below. He started toward it, leaving, perforce, the great monolith open behind him.

He halted at the bottom of the passageway. Before
him stretched the hall of an ancient Hindu temple.
The walls and pillars celebrated every conceivable
erotic posture in voluptuous reliefs; the flames of
ornamental sconces made them seem almost alive.
The hall itself was deserted, but through an arched
portal directly across from him he could see the
shadows of nauch girls swaying lasciviously as they
danced.

Although he himself could not see the musicians,
and saw only the shadows of the nauch dancers, he
was sure that Magus Rex could see them all very well
in the room beyond the arched portal. And Zenobia
probably sat at his side, helplessly watching their
performance. The great wizard had secreted her here
in one of his pleasure-domes until her suitor gave up
and went away. But he, Valorius, had not gone away.
No matter how stormy the interview, he was determined at least to see her. Taking a deep breath, he
started across the erotic, torch-lighted hall.

But then he hesitated. He was about to plunge into
the most important interview of his life dressed like a
tropical bird! Even the poor pierrot in the pantomime,
capering pathetically about the ballerina who looked
so much like Zenobia, had not cut a more ridiculous
figure. Like the poor pierrot he too had lost his beloved.
Like the poor pierrot he too had found her handkerchief.
Like the poor pierrot. . . .

And suddenly he was running for his life. Never
had a mere hundred feet seemed so far. At the last
possible instant he left his feet, diving headlong past
the open monolith just as thousands of tons of rock
crashed down from above, completely sealing the passageway behind him. Like the poor pierrot in the
pantomime, he had been given enough rope to do
himself in.

Valorius angrily slapped the dust from the feathers
of his tropical-bird costume. Without a backward glance
he turned on his heel and headed purposefully toward
the road leading out of the canyon. What had Magus

Rex called him, a "caterwauling catechumen"?

It was all too clear now. Magus Rex had nearly succeeded in making a complete and utter fool of him. What else he might have made of him was not pleasant to think about. Perhaps the word "cage" in Zenobia's warning had been meant literally. He knew that his tropical-bird costume was no accident. A bird in a cage—that would have been just like Magus Rex. And the pantomime had told him exactly how he was going to end up in that cage.

No, the great wizard had acted throughout with his legendary equitableness. He had merely given him enough rope and had it not been for Zenobia's warning, he would certainly have hanged himself.

The key word in Zenobia's verse, the word whose significance had become clear to him only at the last possible instant, was the word "transports." Had he been sealed in by thousands of tons of falling rock, he would have had to dematerialize, sending the molecules of his body filtering through those of "solid" rock like the stars in colliding galaxies. This was not difficult—even some of the most ancient magicians had been able to do it. But what had Magus Rex said? "It might be fun to see what you rematerialize as." No, the tropical-bird costume was no accident.

A short barrage of fire-balls was enough to drive the white apes and centaurs howling from the captured landau. Valorius left one fire-ball scintillating overhead. The horse bucked and stamped nervously. There was only one of them now.

*"Ma jument! Ma jument!"* moaned the mustachioed little driver.

The centaurs had apparently run off with his prize mare. But they were out of sight by now, and there was nothing Valorius could do about it. Besides, one horse was enough to get the landau back to Paris.

But there was a delay in reexchanging costumes with the young actor. In the normal course of events, French pantomimists were not subject to being terrorized by white apes and centaurs. Certain stains and effluvia had to be dispelled before Valorius could again don his shimmering blue cape and tunic.

The mustachioed little driver had stood up to the ordeal much better. As a cab driver in Paris, he had probably seen even stranger things. A few horses' worth of shiny new gold coins restored him completely. He turned his (one) horse back toward the kaleidoscope of light and color glittering at the very bottom of the weird, silt-choked depression. The young actor sat in the back seat like the statue of a tropical bird.

A white ape snarled and pounded its massive chest, grimacing hideously. Valorius shot a green fire-ball at it, and it yelped and ducked behind a boulder. From the top of a hill he saw the palace of Magus Rex glowing luminescently in the distance.

# CHAPTER IV:
## ZENOBIA

"Ah, look, my darling daughter," said Magus Rex. "It's Valorius, come to visit us. How nice of him to just drop in on us like this."

The great wizard sat Indian-fashion on a musnud of overstuffed violet cushions. His long voluptuous robe was of violet silk; his glossy black hair and beard looked freshly trimmed; his long violet fingernails were impeccably manicured. But though he appeared as urbane as ever, there was something in the tone of his voice, an indefinable glitter behind his heavy-lidded eyes, that made Valorius tremble. Magus Rex was angry.

The musnud sat in the very center of a carved ivory dais, in one corner of a large, excessively decorated reception hall, like the throne room of some royal voluptuary with no worlds left to conquer. The fact that Valorius had to cross the entire hall under the gaze of those heavy-lidded eyes did nothing to bolster his confidence. Nor did the empty birdcage at the back of the dais. Only the sight of Zenobia, standing

calmly beside her father's musnud, gave him the courage to go on.

If her surroundings were overdecorated in Byzantine
splendor, Zenobia herself was splendidly underdecor-
ated. Her harem costume was mostly bangles and
gauze, accentuating rather than hiding her full breasts
and hips, her slender waist. She was somewhat above
medium height; her auburn tresses fell like spun silk
about her bare shoulders; her complexion was flawless,
glowing with youth and health. At first glance a
beholder might have been torn between calling her
beautiful or gorgeous. But there was intelligence in
her dark almond-shaped eyes, and a determined look
about her chin. She looked like a belly dancer with
strong character.

And she wasted no time showing that character.
Without hesitation she stepped down from the ivory
dais and stood beside Valorius. Hand in hand they
faced the musnud of Magus Rex.

"Well, well," he sneered. "What have we here? It
looks like a romance. Hands and hearts entwined, and
all that. Bah!"

"Magus Rex, my lord—" began Valorius.

But he was immediately interrupted. "Be warned,
you overreaching oaf! I've nearly come to the end
of my patience with you. You've ruffled my serenity,
and I don't like it one bit. I'm accustomed to having
things my own way, and I fully intend to go right on
doing so. And I most certainly will not tolerate any
half-baked boundary-hopping boobies tomcatting on
my nome."

"Oh, Father," said Zenobia, "why must you always
insult Valorius? You know he has a brilliant record at
the Academy. He'll be a Master Wizard soon, qualified
to establish his own nome."

"You know nothing about it, my darling daughter. I
insult Valorius because I choose to. What's the point
of being all-powerful if you can't insult people and
have them take it? His father was a pudding—"

"But a capable personal secretary," Zenobia reminded

him. "You always said so yourself. And the post is still vacant."

Magus Rex studied his long violet fingernails. There was a look of begrudging appreciation on his face. "So that was to be the scenario, was it? Lusty young secretary demonstrates abilities to ogrish father and at last gains consent for nuptials with beautiful daughter. Well, it won't work! I know all about Valorius' abilities," he sneered.

"You underrate Valorius, Father." She glanced significantly toward the empty birdcage.

Magus Rex's eyes narrowed and he looked suspiciously from one to the other. "There's some skulduggery going on here. Last night's affair was far too subtle for Valorius' thick wits to have solved unaided. Somehow he was warned."

"You're not being fair, Father," said Zenobia. "You, whose equitableness has become legendary. Valorius has studied long and hard. He's a fully qualified wizard, and you know it."

"While I revel in your flattery," said Magus Rex, "and appreciate your misplaced loyalty to this booby you are temporarily infatuated with, I must say once more, my darling daughter, that you know nothing about it. Yes, yes," he stopped her from interrupting with an impatient wave of his long violet fingernails, "I know he's read some of the old books and has learned to perform a few tricks. In fact, if I ever find myself desperately in need of somebody to pull a rabbit out of a hat, Valorius is just the fellow I'll call on. But the sum total of his abilities qualifies him for nothing but my contempt. And as for my legendary equitableness being questioned, I'll let this yawping yahoo himself be my witness. Can you honestly accuse me of any dirty tricks, Valorius?"

"No, my lord," he sighed, glancing at the birdcage. "It was all there for me to see."

Magus Rex chuckled. "You may well stare at the bars of the cage, Valorius. You would have been staring at them from the other side for a good long while had you not somehow been warned. There's even a little horn attached—see it there?—just like the one on your bicycle last night. You could have learned to squeeze the bulb with your beak whenever you wanted Zenobia to come and fill your seed bowl or clean the bottom of the cage."

"That's horrible, Father!" she cried, stamping her foot. "To change Valorius into a tropical bird and then make me clean his cage. I can't think of anything more insidious."

"I can," said Magus Rex. "Quite easily, in fact. But I'd benevolently decided on teaching him a lesson, rather than annihilating him. A few decades of cage cleaning, my darling daughter, would have transformed your outlook entirely."

"Never! My love for Valorius would have withstood any test."

There was an ironic twinkle in Magus Rex's eye. "You say that now. But I assure you, it is a hard thing to love a toucan."

Valorius, cautioned by a light squeeze of his hand, had remained silent. He knew now why Zenobia had summoned him. It had been a gamble, and it had apparently failed. But he had no intention of slinking away like a whipped dog. There had to be some way, no matter how dangerous or desperate, of getting into the good graces of Magus Rex.

The great wizard seemed to read his thoughts. "I hope you're not thinking of any kind of storybook challenge, Valorius." His voice was low and insinuating, hinting of mockery. "A contest for the hand of your ladylove?"

Valorius threw back his shoulders. "I am ready for any test, my lord. Set me a task, no matter how arduous, and I will not hesitate—though I die in the attempt." He knew he sounded foolish, but Zenobia squeezed his hand.

Magus Rex merely shrugged. "There's no point in prolonging this," he said. "It's time I gave you my adamantine decision in this matter. But first let's dismiss any puerile fantasies of tasks or contests which may still be rattling loose about your cranial void. Is there any contest, sport, game, or competition of any kind whatsoever out of the entire two-million year history of mankind at which you could even hope to defeat me?"

After several moments' reflection, Valorius had to admit: "No, my lord, there's none." He felt his shoulders begin to droop.

"That's a bit more like it," said Magus Rex, grinning derisively. "I'm happy to see that your mooncalfery has not deprived you of your sense of self-preservation. And you might just as well chase any thought of heroic tasks or derring-do out of your ill-dowered mentality. There's nothing you could possibly achieve, at no matter what cost in danger to yourself, that I can't achieve with a mere deft wave of the hand. Then, too, if I were to set you some storybook task to perform, I'd feel compelled to give you at least a reasonable chance of success. Which," he glanced at his daughter, "brings us back to my legendary equitableness."

Zenobia looked soft and angelic; her eyes looked into her father's with touching candor. But Valorius felt her little hand tremble.

"Now there's no doubt that Valorius could never have kept out of the birdcage without help," said Magus Rex. "But I find it hard to believe that my strict injunctions against communicating with him have been disobeyed. You haven't disobeyed me, have you, Zenobia?"

"I swear to you, Father, that I've strictly adhered to the letter of your every command."

"Hmmmmm. That sounds tricky. But you do love your jolly old father, don't you?"

"Yes, Father."

"And you wouldn't lie to him?"

"No, Father. Not unless I thought I could get away with it."

"That's my darling daughter! For you know very well that you can't."

The air suddenly crackled with energy, and Valorius felt Zenobia's hand stiffen as her father gazed searchingly into her eyes. Then the tension subsided.

"So you are telling the truth," said Magus Rex. "That's rather puzzling."

"I have obeyed your injunction—" Zenobia began.

"Yes, yes," he interrupted her. "You're up to something of course. But I don't mind that. An exceedingly long life has taught me that there is nothing quite so unbearable as a sincere woman. I'll get to the bottom of this in good time. The fact remains that this young lout is still on the wrong side of the bars. My little contrivance of last night was foolproof—I use the word advisedly—but somehow it didn't work. All contingencies were provided for—except failure. But somehow it failed."

"Oh, Father," pleaded Zenobia. "Please don't be angry with Valorius. Give him a chance to prove himself. He was so brave to come here, and so clever—"

"That's exactly the point, my darling daughter. I have a reputation for legendary equitableness, and now I'm stuck with it. After last night's fiasco—no matter how the pair of you brought it off—I can't treat him as he deserves without being considered a poor sport. A year or two chained to the bottom of a troglodyte cess-pit would be a wonderful opportunity for him to meditate upon his insolence. Be that as it may, I have decided in this matter, as in all others, to act equitably."

"I knew you would, Father," cried Zenobia.

"I don't doubt that. But perhaps the direction of my equitableness will not quite be that of your calculations." He said this in a calm voice, carelessly inspecting his long violet fingernails. But both Valorius and Zenobia stood tensely before him, like prisoners before the bar; for they knew that their fate was about to be pronounced.

"For many centuries," said Magus Rex in a low, ominous voice, "it was my good pleasure to travel in time. No age of mankind was beyond my reach, and I was sometimes gone for decades at a time. Most of time is hardly worth seeing, especially the last few hundred thousand years, since the collision with Balbek's Comet. But there are a few ages worth a leisurely sojourn—those ages styled by the callow as *decadent*. It is only then that the art of living reaches its nearest approach to human perfection. The very transience of such ages lends them a kind of autumnal charm. It is very pleasant to be alive then—assuming of course that one belongs to the opulent classes."

"But, Father," Zenobia protested, "you never travel. You've never left me alone since I was a child."

"Nor have I any intention of leaving you now. But you forget how brief is your mere century of life compared to mine. And while it's true that I've never so much as crossed the boundaries of my own nome since returning here with you, my darling daughter, you must realize that many, many centuries of travel and exploration preceded that time."

"Oh, no," gasped Zenobia. "Please, Father, you're not going to—"

"Take you away? Yes, as a matter of fact, that's exactly what I've decided to do. You've led a sheltered life, Zenobia. This is as good a time as any to broaden your education through travel. In short, we are going on a little vacation."

"For how long, Father?"

"For as long as necessary. I know that you've been happy here. My magnificent gardens and libraries have always been open to you, and I've provided you with some very interesting companions." He glanced sardonically at Valorius. "There have been many lavish entertainments, and you've never wanted for my own delightful company. Why you should now want the ineffectual moping blandly at your side is beyond me."

"But Father, Valorius is real, and I love him with all my heart."

"All your interesting companions have been real enough. And I know that they've given you great pleasure ." Again he glanced sardonically at Valorius. This time Zenobia blushed. "You know I'm a perfectionist."

"Yes, Father, but—I don't know how to explain it—it's just not the same thing."

Magus Rex was silent for several moments. A far-away look crept into his eyes, as if he were recalling some old event.

"There's something in what you say," he conceded at last. "In a mawkish moment one may desire companionship not of one's own creation. Fortunately, for the wise, such moments are rare and fleeting."

"But other wizards have provided their daughters with real companions," said Zenobia.

"I know the case you mean. But the poor girl was a dwarf, and her father only one of our lesser wizards. There's no comparison. And it was a rather stupid thing for him to have done in the first place."

"He was only trying to make his daughter happy, Father."

"And look what happened. Raising a troglodyte boy as a companion for his daughter! Even if she was a dwarf, that's no excuse. What did he expect?"

"Then it didn't turn out well?"

"There was a scandal of some kind, I believe. The troglodyte grew up into just the ugly, vicious young scamp one would have expected. Then he just disappeared, leaving the little dwarf heartbroken."

"Poor thing," murmured Zenobia.

"So you see, Zenobia, I realize that your passing infatuation with Valorius, while sadly misplaced, is at least not unique. The difference here is that you're the one who's going to disappear."

"Where are we going, Father?" Her voice was calm; her eyes wide with innocence.

"What a delightful creature you are, Zenobia," he said fondly. "So like your mother in so many ways." Again the strange faraway look flickered across his eyes. "Suffice it to say, we are going where your obnoxious suitor can't reach us."

At last Valorius spoke up. He had been silently

pondering the matter, and he now thought he knew what Magus Rex planned to do. He addressed Zenobia:

"You will be taken, I believe, somewhere into the ancient world. Probably into one of its more decadent ages."

"But why the ancient world?" asked Zenobia. "There are so many nicer ages we could visit."

"He wants to make sure you're out of reach."

"That's fairly clever of you, Valorius," said Magus Rex. "Not bad at all."

"But why is it out of reach, Father?"

"You're already looking for some means of subverting my plans, aren't you, my darling daughter?"

"Yes, Father."

"That's charming of you. And we are indeed returning to the ancient world. But that piece of gratuitous information will do neither you nor your objectionable swain the least bit of good."

"I don't understand." Zenobia looked from one to the other.

"Why don't you explain it to her, Valorius," Magus Rex sneered at him. "You've been blatting about your schoolboy qualifications since you first trespassed onto my nome. Let's hear some of the useless information you've been soaking up for the last few decades."

"The principle is really quite simple," Valorius began.

"But the practice is quite another matter," Magus Rex added complacently.

"Yes, my lord. It would be foolish to pretend that such wizardry as I have acquired—"

"But why can't you reach the ancient world?" cried Zenobia. "You do know how to travel through time, don't you?"

"Yes, of course. That's rather elementary—although I've never actually done so. The problem is not so much getting to the ancient world—"

"It's getting back again." Magus Rex surveyed his long violet fingernails. "It's something like jumping off a cliff. There's plenty of energy to carry you down. But jumping back up again is rather more difficult.

Only the greatest wizards have ever tried it. It's always been considered something of a feat. But no one has ever dared go as far back in time as I have."

"Then it's just a matter of energy?" asked Zenobia. "Psychic energy?"

"Very good," said Magus Rex. "You haven't been wasting your time in the little library I gave you. Finish your schoolboy twaddle, Valorius."

"Well, even in ancient times," he continued, "the laws of the conservation of energy were known. At least, in rudimentary form. What they didn't know was that psychic energy also obeyed these laws. There were tentative theories but these were usually recorded in the annals of charlatanism."

"Tell her about the aging, Valorius." Magus Rex shifted into a more comfortable position on his musnud. "That should especially interest her."

"There's that, too," Valorius sighed.

"Aging?" Zenobia looked interested indeed.

"The principles of controlling one's physiological processes were also known in rudimentary form in the ancient world. Fakirs, for instance, could slow their heartbeat or even to a certain extent control the temperature of certain parts of their bodies. We now can control virtually all our own physiological processes. Including, of course, the process of aging."

"But can't you do it in the ancient world too?" Zenobia asked, looking somewhat alarmed.

"Have no fears, my darling daughter," said Magus Rex. "I can control anything anywhere. Your matchless beauty is in no danger."

"But Valorius—"

"Will be stuck if he tries to follow us. Unable to return back through time, and subject to the normal processes of aging. In fact, now that I think of it, why don't you try and follow us, Valorius? It would give you a chance to show off your schoolboy qualifications."

"Is it really as bad as that?" Zenobia turned toward Valorius.

He nodded his head despondently.

"Oh, he wouldn't be completely helpless," said Magus Rex, thoroughly enjoying himself. "He would have some powers, I suppose. To return to my analogy of jumping off a cliff, it would be something like one jumping into space flapping one's arms. That would give him at least some control over his destiny." He grinned at Valorius.

For the next several minutes there was silence in the Byzantine throne room. Magus Rex gloated over his triumph, while Valorius had no choice but to suffer it as bravely as he could. Zenobia alone was not yet resigned.

# CHAPTER V
# THE SKALD'S DAUGHTER

"Where exactly in the ancient world are we going, Father?" asked Zenobia at last.

"To a place where your present infatuation will quickly dissolve amidst scenes of wonder and delight."

"And you won't be more specific than that?" Zenobia said thoughtfully. "Well, at least you can tell me when we're going."

"As soon as I've thoroughly gloated over Valorius' abject despondency. Now you may perhaps think me selfish and tyrannical in all this, Valorius. Not to mention overbearing."

"Well. . . ."

"But that's merely one more symptom of your callowness. You apparently have no conception of the prerogatives of greatness. This will someday be known as the Golden Age of Wizardry, and I, Magus Rex, all-powerful and yet of legendary equitableness, its crowning jewel. I will not have my daughter's affections alienated. Don't talk to me of love. You know nothing about it. In my own good time I shall choose a proper consort for Zenobia, a powerful wizard not unworthy of even my esteem. Not the impudent off-spring of a skald's daughter."

"I never knew my mother, my lord," said Valorius quietly.

"Now see what you've made me do!" cried Magus Rex, rising from his musnud. "I've made an unworthy remark." Then he checked himself and resumed his seat. "But let us act with our accustomed equitableness. I sincerely regret the tone in which I just referred to your mother, Valorius. She may well have been a woman worthy of even my regard. But, you see, I never knew her either."

Zenobia had been deep in thought for several moments. "You said a skald's daughter, Father. I thought the skalds lived millions of years ago. Viking bards or minstrels, or something like that."

"Ah, so your study of poetry is not just another passing fancy, like your mosaics of a few decades ago. You haven't been wasting your time if you can correctly identify the skalds with the Viking Age."

"But just a minute ago you said that you were the only wizard powerful enough to return from so far back in time."

"And so I am. Wizards generally select their con-sorts from the time of the Brazilian Hegemony."

"But that was only, let me see, sometime between the last Ice Age and the collision with Balbek's Comet, wasn't it?"

"Exactly. Oh, I know that even the most reputable wizards will say that the Brazilian Hegemony was mankind's zenith, the women the most desirable, and so forth. To my more exacting taste it was a rather humdrum age, marred by an almost universal social benevolence. No, the real reason why wizards have always considered it the world's great age is simply because that's as far as their powers reached. Even Valorius' father could have returned from the Brazilian Hegemony."

"But not from the Viking Age?"

"He was way out of his depth. He was a capable enough secretary, under my benevolent supervision. And I suppose he was competent in the more elementary arts of wizardry. But not the Viking Age. Not by a million years."

"But why did he do it, Father?" A fleeting look of hope began to appear in her eye.

"Who knows? He never talked about it. Perhaps I called him a pudding once too often. Perhaps he himself determined that his offspring should not be afflicted with his own spinal pliancy. For you see, my darling daughter, the Vikings, although revolting in many ways, were a truly valiant people."

"And so is Valorius." She gave him another encouraging squeeze of the hand.

"There is a difference between valor and mere stiff-necked impudence," said Magus Rex. "And who but a pudding would name his son *Valorius*?"

"But, Father," Zenobia protested, "didn't Valorius show great moral courage in coming here? And you have to admit that he showed great ability as a wizard in staying out of the cage you prepared for him. You chuckled all last night over—"

"I admit no such thing. He was warned—I don't know how yet—but he was most certainly warned. Left to his own devices, he would have ended up a toucan. And as for his so-called moral courage, I'm not at all impressed. In fact, I find moral courage admirable only in the abstract. For everyday service, give me a sleek groveler every time. Valorius' father, for instance."

"You haven't finished the story about the skald's daughter, Father," she reminded him. Valorius felt her hand tremble with excitement.

"Ah, yes." Magus Rex fluffed up the cushions of his musnud. "I had given Valorius' father permission to absent himself, thinking he would merely use it for a few-decades' holiday in the Brazilian Hegemony. Time being what it is, he was supposed to have returned here three days after he left. Which is, of course, the standard margin in calculating time travel. Imagine my shock when, instead of Valorius' father obsequiously awaiting me in the library, I found a message from him screaming for help in big gaudy red letters, telling me he'd gotten himself trapped in the time of the Vikings."

"I don't understand, Father," Zenobia frowned.

"It's the same principle as the messages I've recently taught you to send here in the palace. Except, of course, that it requires greater energy resources and concentration. You've become quite adept at it, my darling daughter, and it's a great convenience in a palace of this size. Forming letters across a gap in time is not much harder than forming them across a gap in space, so that—"

"No, no, Father. I understand about the message. But I'm still not clear how a qualified wizard could be trapped in time."

"Perhaps because you have your mind on other things, dear." He looked affectionately down at her. "In any case, I'll explain further. Now you understand that matter is really a form of energy, not unlike thought?"

Zenobia nodded.

"All right, then. For millions of years, countless billions of human beings have been converting the worldstuff of matter into the mindstuff of thought. That is, changing one form of energy into another. Sometimes whole patterns of psychic energy survive physical death and discorporation. Even among ancient peoples this energy was sometimes detected by rare individuals called 'mediums' or 'sensitives.' Rarer still were those able to manipulate this energy, even at the crudest level. Many ancient wizards were not without skill. But they were severely handicapped by a dearth of psychic energy with which to work and the scientific superstition that matter cannot travel in time."

"I see." Zenobia slowly nodded her head. "Then Valorius' father could never have gotten back from the

Viking Age without your help? There wouldn't have been enough available psychic energy to harness?"

"Well, in theory he might have managed it. But both he and his offspring would have been very old men indeed when they finally got here. Less loveable than even a toucan."

Valorius began to suspect that he was being subtly challenged. What surer way of disposing of an undesirable suitor than by luring him into some cul-de-sac of time?

"But it's possible to return immediately from any point in time, isn't it?" asked Zenobia. "You've done it yourself, Father. And you must have brought Valorius and his father back the same way. Won't you explain that part too? I don't understand."

"Hmmmmm." Magus Rex looked searchingly at her. "Are you trying to keep me talking in hopes of somehow outwitting me, Zenobia?"

"Yes, Father."

"But you saw how easily I squelched your transparent little scheme of smuggling Valorius in here as my personal secretary, and how certainly he would have ended up in a birdcage but for some skulduggery. And still you hope to prevail against me?"

"Yes, Father."

"Then, my darling daughter, I think it's time we left. You'll soon see that there's a vast difference between my powers and those of any other wizard who's ever lived, let alone this half-baked hankie-snatcher. I thought the ploy of letting him find your handkerchief last night was rather good, by the way. Now go to your room in the East Tower. I want to execrate Valorius some more before we leave."

Zenobia stifled a sob. Kissing Valorius on the cheek, she started disconsolately across the throne room. But then she stopped and turned back toward her father's musnud. Her gorgeous femininity and the look of child-like appeal in her eyes made her irresistible.

"Please, Father." She wiped a tear from her eye. "If I must leave, let the last thing I see be my own little library—not the East Tower. You know it's my favorite room. Let me wait there for you. I'd gladly wait there for weeks if I had to."

"Yes, yes, by all means go to your little library." He dismissed her with an impatient wave of his long violet fingernails.

Valorius now stood alone before the carved ivory dais. He steeled himself for the deluge of execration. But it never came. Magus Rex had apparently changed his mind.

"Go back to the Academy, Valorius," he said in a soft insinuating voice. "I'm used to getting my own way, and I'll get it now. You may think yourself clever about last night, and I'll admit I'm not at all pleased at seeing a perfectly constructed plan go awry. For your father's sake, I was going to treat you generously —a good lesson, rather than condign punishment. Don't say a word!" He held up a warning hand. "I must now endure some inconvenience because of you. But it won't take much more to make me forget my reputation for legendary equitableness. This won't be forgotten, Valorius. Oh, no. This won't be forgotten."

Then without warning the great bronze doors of the throne room clanged shut. Startled, Valorius whirled around. A rush of wind hit him full in the chest, driving him backward. He could feel the crackle of energy to the very roots of his hair. When he turned back the ivory dais was empty. Magus Rex had vanished.

But it suited the great wizard's sardonic humor to have left a memento of what might have been. In the middle of an overstuffed violet cushion, slowly opening and closing its absurd beak, sat a toucan.

# CHAPTER VI
# ON THE BRINK

It was late afternoon, weeks later, when Valorius first saw the red haze. Rubbing his eyes, he thought at first that it was just some kind of optical revolt against weeks of concentrated study. But the haze was still there, struggling to grow darker and redder. Then all at once it began to tremble like the arms of a weight-lifter trying to lift a weight beyond his strength. And then it was gone.

Valorius sighed with relief. Not because the red haze had vanished before it could condense into legible letters, but because now all doubt was removed.

During the last few weeks he had grown increasingly worried that he had misunderstood Zenobia's signal—asking Magus Rex if she could wait in her little library until they left. He had guessed that she meant for him to wait there as well. Now he knew that he had been right. Zenobia was trying to contact him across millions of years of time. She had failed the first time. But he was sure that sooner or later she

would succeed. He was now ready to wait here for
years if necessary.

Only now did he become aware of his surroundings.
He had found Zenobia's library a neat, clean, feminine
gallery of marble and glass. It was now a mess.
Ancient scrolls and books lay scattered all about;
coded tapes, convertor-discs, memory-cassettes, and
telecon-plaques were piled haphazardly amidst a poor
housekeeper's accumulated clutter of several weeks of
living. He had been too busy studying to tidy up.

The great library of Magus Rex covered several
acres. Valorius had studied everything he could find
about time travel. He had learned a great deal—of
theory. He felt like one who has learned an entire shelf
of archery manuals by heart, but has never actually
touched a bow. But at least he now understood why
even the greatest wizards seldom ventured backward
in time beyond the Brazilian Hegemony. It was largely
the matter of aging.

Most wizards capable of any degree of time travel
were very old men. In the ancient world they could
only be effective in the midst of large concentrations
of psychic energy—a battle, a riot, an orgiastic religious festival, a large witch coven, and so forth. Such
concentrations were short lived. An old wizard might
age to death while searching for a war or revolution.

There was probably a point in time beyond which
even Magus Rex dare not go. Although it was dangerous
ever to underestimate his powers. In any case, Valorius
was ready to follow whenever his beloved called.

For the next few days he hardly slept. Twice more
the faint red haze appeared; twice more it faded away.
He managed to capture its image on the visilux; but
even a microscopic examination was inconclusive. It
was just a faint red haze struggling to condense.

In fact, it never did become legible to the naked eye.
Only by evoking the visilux each time the red haze
appeared was he at last able to decipher the message.
Like the warning that had kept him out of Magus
Rex's birdcage, it was in verse:

> Beneath a gibbous moon I roam,
> Through volumes of despair;
> For though the giant's not at home,
> I cannot leave his lair.

And that was all. Just those four cryptic lines. But they had cost him many weeks of watching and the intense microscopic scrutiny of hundreds of visilux images to capture with certainty. He could not risk being wrong about a single letter.

Why Zenobia had chosen this strange means of communication was itself still a mystery. She had sworn that she had not disobeyed her father's injunction against any form of communication between them. Magus Rex could sense even the faintest physiological changes as acutely as an ancient lie-detector. It was virtually impossible to lie to him. Somehow she had communicated with Valorius without disobeying her father.

Although the verse might be considered ambiguous, it was not at all obscure. He saw at a glance where she had been taken—to ancient Rome, nearly two million years into the past. She had had trouble condensing the letters, but she had very cleverly condensed the message.

There had been many great empires in the long history of man, but that of the Romans was one of the earliest and most famous. If he remembered correctly, it had lasted over a thousand years. One of the few literary works to survive virtually intact from ancient times was Gibbon's DECLINE AND FALL OF THE ROMAN EMPIRE. That explained both "gibbous" and "volumes" in the verse. But who on earth was the "giant"?

He knew at least the general outlines of Roman history. An acolyte's first two decades of study at the Academy were aimed primarily at giving him an historical perspective. He could recall several of the "giants" of Rome's decline—Septimius Severus, Diocletian, Constantine, Theodosius, Theodoric the Ostrogoth.

All of them had had periods when they were "not at home." In fact, some of the later Roman emperors had hardly ever set foot in Rome.

But somehow he did not feel that these towering, firm-handed rulers would be to Magus Rex's taste. Besides, they had all had fairly long reigns. The exact times of their absences from Rome were a matter of conjecture, even to Gibbon himself.

Of all man's various means of storing knowledge, books were probably the least efficient for the quick retrieval of data. Magus Rex, of course, had instantaneous retrieval systems all over his acres of library. But only Magus Rex knew how to operate them. Impatiently, he carried the three fat volumes by Gibbon back to Zenobia's little library.

Fighting the temptation to skip pages, he plowed his way through centuries of monumental prose. He was just beginning to glance uneasily at the other two fat volumes, wondering if perhaps the "giant" were not some Byzantine ruler, when he turned to the reign of Maximin. He read:

> The stature of Maximin exceeded the measure of eight feet, and circumstances almost incredible are related of his matchless strength and appetite. Had he lived in a less enlightened age, tradition and poetry might well have described him as one of those monstrous giants, whose supernatural power was constantly exerted for the destruction of mankind.

There were listed testimonies that this barbarian giant, who had somehow become the emperor of Rome, could drink seven gallons of wine and eat forty pounds of meat in a day, break a horse's leg with his fist, uproot small trees, and so forth. More to the point were the facts that his reign was short—less than three years—and that he was almost never "at home," being continually engaged in distant warfare. Also, his brief reign was in the middle of the third century,

Ancient Reckoning, a period of license and demoralization. What could be more to the decadent tastes of Magus Rex?

With a sense of relief he hauled the monumental tomes back to their place on the shelf. He now knew where Zenobia had been taken. He also now knew that his greatest enemy would be his own impatience. There were veritable oceans of psychic energy upon which to draw, but to rematerialize in precisely the right time and place would take some careful calculation. Unlike Magus Rex, he could not afford the slightest error.

The faint red haze still appeared from time to time, but without ever becoming legible to the naked eye. Nonetheless it was reassuring. For the next several days he reviewed everything he had learned about time travel during the long weeks of waiting for Zenobia to contact him. Returning through time, even from ancient Rome, was perhaps not quite so impossible as Magus Rex suggested. At least, not for a relatively young wizard. Difficult and dangerous, yes. But not impossible.

Nor would Zenobia have risked calling him unless she knew of some way for him to get back if anything went wrong—even though his powers of wizardry would be reduced to a dangerous minimum in the ancient world. Magus Rex had not exaggerated that part.

He decided at last that he was ready. He had used every conceivable means to check and recheck his calculations. It was all still theoretical of course, but he had nothing more to do now but take the plunge. He recalled Magus Rex's analogy. Like a man poised at the brink of a mile-high cliff, jumping down would be a lot easier than jumping back up again. He just hoped he would land in the right place.

Toward evening, eleven days after he had first deciphered Zenobia's cryptic verse, Valorius left the palace. Magus Rex had created a small army of gardeners—mostly ancient Japanese—to tend the miles

of gardens surrounding his vast Byzantine pile. They
were just beginning to gather up their tools for the
night. They smiled and bowed politely as he passed.

Gardening reaches its highest development in decadent ages. The gardens of Magus Rex represented
virtually every major age of decadence in earth's history.
Valorius wandered by chance into an opulent garden
which probably belonged to one of the last dynasties
of the California Islands, one of the most luscious
periods in the history of man.

It was almost sunset. In the deepening twilight the
naked marble nymphs of a nearby fountain seemed to
glow with a radiance of their own. The California
Islands. How much they had contributed in so short a
time! How great their glory, and how tragic their end!
His thoughts turned idly to that amazing purple splash
upon the record of humanity. The California Islands
had flourished for only a few centuries after the
geological separation from the old North American
continent. But their wealth and luxury were proverbial;
self-indulgence was developed into an art form; the
arts themselves reached unsurpassed heights of skill
and craftsmanship.

In fact, now that he thought of it, he was surprised
that Magus Rex had not taken Zenobia to one of the
last dynasties of the California Islands instead of
Rome. But perhaps that was too close in time—just
prior to the last Ice Age. The psychic-energy level was
fairly high even then. Many times higher than that of
Maximin's Rome.

His thoughts continued to drift idly. How wonderful it would have been to have lived there. But the last
dynasty of the California Islands had been a horror
story. The onset of the Ice Age lowered sea level to
the point where the mutant hordes of the mainland
could reach the islands, and nothing could stop them.
But during those charming, luscious centuries that
preceded. . . .

Suddenly Valorius jumped to his feet. He would do
it—now! He stood on the brink of a two-million year

plunge, with the bottom nowhere in sight. His heart beat too fast; his loins felt weak and hollow. Like an actor with stagefright, he seemed to have forgotten everything he had ever learned. Never had it been so hard to concentrate. But slowly, with a great effort of will, he began to unify all parts of his mind, as he had been trained to do through decades of intensive study. At last he could feel his thoughts reaching out, becoming one with the ocean of psychic energy lapping all about him; unifying it, concentrating it, controlling it.

Then he was gone. The naked marble nymphs continued to pour forth their endless fountains of crystalline water. Night came to the gardens of Magus Rex.

# CHAPTER VII
# WHEN THE GIANT'S NOT AT HOME

Valorius found himself between the pillars of a classic marble portico. It was late afternoon of a cloudless summer day. The narrow streets were lined with sprawling four- and five-story apartment buildings, which sheltered everything below from the direct heat of the declining sun. It was warm, but not oppressive.

The huge apartment buildings, sometimes a whole block square, were ingeniously constructed of brick and stone, with facings of tasteful, cleverly arranged patterns of wood and rubble. Picturesque loggias and balconies relieved the storys; the pillars and railings were enlivened everywhere with masses of green vines and climbing plants; numerous windows, nearly all with a delightful miniature garden of flowers in row upon row of gaudily-colored pots, opened onto the street. It seemed to Valorius more like a teeming oriental city than anything he had ever imagined of ancient Rome.

Especially the people. For the narrow, well-paved street was a noisy seething hurly-burly of humanity.

Nearly every opening in the porticos at the base of the
apartment buildings housed some shop or stall or
booth; many of these extended well out into the street
itself. The bawl of hucksters competed with the hoarse,
wheedling cries of beggars. The din from the taverns
and open-air cookshops rose and fell like the waves of
the sea. Barbers set up their stools anywhere, shaving,
clipping, and perfuming their customers in the middle
of the street with a grisly array of iron and bronze
implements. But there were no wagons or vehicles of
any kind, and the colorful mob jostled about their
business without care or opposition.

It took Valorius several moments to recover from
the shock of transition. His first clear thought was to
be inconspicuous, but he quickly found himself the
center of attention. The Roman mob was always happy
to discover some fresh novelty. They all gathered around
him, bubbling with questions, comments, and laughter like so many spoiled children. Every race on earth
seemed represented, and it was neither his golden
hair nor his shimmering blue cape and tunic that
stirred their idle curiosity. It was his height.

The men were only a few inches over five feet tall.
There were surprisingly few women in the crowd, and
not one that he could see was even as tall as five
feet—the average being about four feet nine inches.
Valorius, standing well over six feet high, towered
above them all.

He was of course familiar with Latin, since nearly
all the ancient wizards had written in that language.
But try as he might, he could not make out a single
word of the hubbub assailing him from all sides.

Both men and women wore tunics much like his
own garment. He saw only two crusty-looking old
men wearing togas. The women's tunic was longer
and more gaily colored than the men's, but all these
garments—including the old men's togas—were im-
maculate. The very beggars looked well-scrubbed. Nor
did any of these sleek little people look like they had
missed many meals lately.

Valorius was now completely surrounded. He could
only smile and shrug helplessly at the barrage of
questions and comments coming at him from all sides
at once. When he tried to pronounce a few words in
Latin he only provoked a burst of laughter; an effeminate young man with pomaded hair mimicked his
accent to the further delight of the crowd.

There was a kind of nervous excitement about these
people. They never seemed to stand still, like revelers
whose wild party was just loud enough to drown out
the bill-collector pounding at the door. And Valorius
knew that there was indeed a bill-collector pounding
at the door, somewhere beyond the Rhine frontier.
That was why the giant was not at home. Assuming
of course that his calculations had been correct and he
was indeed in the Rome of Maximin.

He was just about to try and pronounce the emperor's
name when the shrill of a nearby flute caught the
crowd's attention. They turned instantly away from
him and jostled across the narrow street as if he had
never existed. He saw that the flute was being played
by a small girl in orange-and-black tights: a troup of
streetcorner jugglers were about to begin their act.
Under the arch of a nearby portico he saw a snake
charmer awaiting his turn to perform.

The entire city seemed to be in the streets. These
were the lords of the earth, and they seemed to
thoroughly enjoy the role. He could hardly guess how
many hundreds—or thousands—of people might be
housed in each of the incredible apartment buildings.
But like the "giant," the residents were not at home,
preferring the continual excitement of the streets to
the dullness of their sweltering apartments.

There was no apparent plan to the city. The narrow
streets wound this way and that. Lavish palaces stood
next to crumbling hovels; wealthy merchants had barbers and bricklayers for neighbors; even powerful sena-
tors were sometimes found dwelling spectacularly in
the midst of squalid tenements and bazaars.

In this strange egalitarian welter, where all races

and classes mingled indiscriminately, the most striking differences were between men and women. It was
only late in the afternoon that many of the latter
appeared in the streets and marketplaces of Rome.

As he wandered through the streets Valorius saw
only a scattering of shop women and female slaves, a
few female entertainers and white-robed priestesses;
for the most part the public life of Rome was a man's
world. Only when the shops began to close did the
women appear in numbers.

Like little painted dolls they moved through the
shadowed streets, drawing in their wake a rich train
of serving women and escorts. Few seemed engaged
in anything more urgent than visiting other painted
dolls. It must have taken them a good part of the day
to have attained their present splendor. So heavily
were they painted that their ages were impossible to
guess. Nor did their hair offer any clue, since they all
wore elaborate wigs of either the blond or red hair of
northern barbarian women or the glossy, jet-black
hair of Egyptian women.

Some wore the soft, brilliantly colored cottons of
distant India. Others were lavishly attired in irides-
cent silks, brought by caravan all the way from China,
and more valuable per pound than gold itself.

Their brows and arms whitened with chalk powder,
their cheeks and lips colored with red ochre, their eyes
accented with antimony, their hair elaborately curled,
pomaded and piled in tower-like coiffures high above
their heads, these women were mincing little descend-
ants of a once hardy peasantry nearly vanished from
sight. If some of them were old it did not show in their
well-cared-for figures.

A few of the painted dolls were carried in litters,
but most seemed to prefer walking in the open. After
all, they had not spent their entire day adorning themselves not to be noticed. Three times within the space
of an hour Valorius was approached by serving women
carrying notes from their mistresses. The notes merely
mentioned a time and place. He could only shake his

head dumbly at the incomprehensible babble of the serving women and move on.

None of the women seemed unduly disappointed. In fact, he suspected that the notes had been written before they had left home.

In an open forum, still lighted by the slanting rays of the sun, he came upon a veritable garden of these gaudy little creatures. No sooner had he stepped into the open than he saw three of them turn toward their maids with instructions. He got a close look at one who was less than ten feet away.

She was somewhat above average height, being nearly five feet tall. But her scaffolding of false blond hair made her nearly as tall as Valorius himself. She wore a long tunic of scarlet silk, dazzlingly embroidered in gold. Her complexion had been heightened to harmonize with the color of her dress. She carried a fan of peacock feathers in one hand; in the other she held a bright green parasol. Jeweled diadems, earrings, collars, brooches, pendants, bracelets, anklets, rings, armlets, jeweled buttons, a hairnet of spun gold, pearl-encrusted hairpins, and various trinkets set with precious stones bespangled her literally from head to foot. Even her little painted toenails had been pasted with flashing gems!

She looked him up and down with bold, appraising eyes, judging his points as if he were a prize stallion for sale. Apparently she approved, for she turned toward one of her maids. Valorius also turned—and fled.

He followed the narrowest, dingiest, most noisome street he could find, moving more or less downhill. Across an empty lot where a building had recently collapsed he saw the yellow waters of the Tiber. He was definitely in Rome. But was this the right Rome?

At last he came upon a placard bearing the name Maximin. With a sense of relief he read it from beginning to end. It was an announcement of tomorrow's program at the Circus Maximus, freshly inked onto Egyptian papyrus. But it was already marred by obscene graffiti. The "Blues" were this, the "Greens" were that. There was a scurrilous couplet to the effect that the size of certain of Maximin's body parts was not proportional to his stature.

Valorius was now certain that his calculations had been correct. He was indeed in the Rome of the giant Maximin, who was now probably off somewhere fighting the barbarians. But where was Zenobia? And Magus Rex?

It was now almost sunset, and the streets were emptying fast. Doors were shut and barred, shutters closed and bolted. Everything moveable, down to the last flowerpot, was secured. Fierce dogs were chained outside doorways, or turned loose in ferocious packs inside the walled courtyards of the wealthy. Night approached Rome like a marauding army. He stared anxiously into the gathering darkness.

He made the test in the shadows of a deserted portico. In his own world, with its oceans of psychic energy, it would have been easy. But here, concentrate as he might, he could hardly do a thing. He felt like a skilled archer without a string to his bow.

Not since boyhood had he felt so helpless. He could not speak the language. Soon he would need food and lodgings, and he was without so much as a clipped denarius. It had been child's play to create a silver franc at the carnival in Paris. Any money he got here would have to be earned. Or stolen. . . .

Then he recalled passing a goldsmith's shop in his wanderings through the city. It had been well guarded by armed slaves during the day, and was sure to be at least as well guarded at night. But how sound were its defenses?

He no longer had the power to create gold coins. But perhaps he still had power enough to steal them.

# CHAPTER VIII
## THIEVES IN THE NIGHT

When the sun set on Rome, it was the end of all light. There was not a single streetlamp in all the vast, sprawling metropolis. Every window and door was shuttered, locked, and curtained. If a single candle burned anywhere in the entire city, Valorius was not aware of it.

He had crossed untold centuries in search of his beloved, and had ended up a thief in the night. Nor, he soon realized, was he the only member of that eternal profession now on the prowl.

After all, so practical a people as the Romans would hardly have mounted such elaborate defenses without good reason. Darkness ruled the city, and thieves and cutthroats glided like shadows through the black streets.

The moon had not yet risen; unfamiliar constellations cast a cold and distant glow. From time to time some wealthy senator or merchant, surrounded by a retinue of armed slaves, litter-bearers, and old men and boys carrying torches and lanterns, would pass on his way to dinner. But these processions, like shoot-

ing stars that flash across the night sky, only seemed
to leave the streets darker than ever after their passage.

Valorius was not certain that he could even find the
goldsmith's shop again. He knew that Roman goldsmith shops also functioned like the banks of a later
period, lending money at interest and receiving de-
posits of money and precious goods for safe keeping.
Thus he was really a bank robber. Or would be if he
succeeded. At the moment, however, he could not even
find the bank, let alone rob it.

The miscreants slinking past him in the darkness
had no such grand ambitions. Like jackals they merely
prowled about the fringes of civilization, snatching at
what they could until they were caught. There were no
jails in Rome: the amphitheater was the fate of the
convicted criminal. With nothing to lose, even jackals
are dangerous. Valorius knew that he would have to be
careful.

Two-million years hence he had strode boldly across
the nome of Magus Rex, pacifying giant lizards, in-
timidating white apes and centaurs. Now he might be
hard pressed to defend himself against a common
cutthroat. He still had his size and strength, and
decades of rigorous physical conditioning at the Academy had given him uncommon speed and agility. But
his greatest defense was his eyes. He enlarged their
pupils until no cat in Rome could see half so well in
the dark.

It was close to midnight before he found the goldsmith's shop. The narrow brick street wound upward
toward a cluster of large apartment buildings crowning the top of a low hill. The character of the street
changed as he climbed. So did his thoughts about the
obstacles facing an ancient bank robber.

Dogs were everywhere. The goldsmith's shop stood
toward the middle of a long brick-and-rubble arcade.
Before he could get within fifty yards of it the night
erupted into a canine pandemonium of yelps, howls
and savage barking. It was like an open kennel.
Fortunately, the dogs seemed to be chained.

The opposite side of the street was lined with a walled enclosure of some kind—apparently the palace grounds of a Roman magnate. There was also a second, smaller arcade. Some of the howling and barking came from inside the walled enclosure. Valorius tried to keep within its shadows until he drew abreast of the goldsmith's shop.

He had hardly come abreast of the arcade when a heavy, powerfully-built watchman stepped into the street. He carried a lantern in one hand and a stout cudgel in the other. There was a grisly scar along the right side of his face, and part of one ear had been hacked away. He was probably an ex-soldier or ex-gladiator. He eyed Valorius suspiciously, but did not approach any closer than the middle of the street. He seemed ready for anything.

He held the lantern aloft, squeezing his cudgel with a grip that showed he knew how to use it. Step by step, never approaching closer than the middle of the street, he followed Valorius along the wall. The dogs continued to bark.

There was an oaken gate in the wall. The moment Valorius passed it, the watchman closed in. Evidently the gate was the only entrance on the entire street where a night visitor might have legitimate business. There was no place Valorius could have concealed a weapon in his tunic. But the veteran watchman took no chances. He faced him with legs spread slightly apart, weight evenly distributed in a slight crouch, and cudgel held ready. He was only a few inches over five feet tall, but built along the lines of an orangutan, all arms and chest. Valorius decided to halt.

The watchman growled something in a hoarse voice.

Valorius did not understand the words, but their meaning was clear: "Just where the hell do you think you're going?" Even with pen and papyrus he could not have replied, for it was unlikely that the watchman could read. Slowly he pronounced in Latin, "I go to visit a friend." He was not sure the watchman would understand him.

The watchman understood all too well. He spat contemptuously, sneering at the lame alibi. Then he pointed with his cudgel in the direction Valorius had come, and growled the Latin equivalent of "Beat it!"

Valorius hesitated. This was a public street. But the watchman hesitated not at all. Taking two quick steps backward, keeping his eyes riveted on Valorius, he knelt and rapped a sharp tattoo on the paving bricks with his cudgel.

Instantly five more watchmen appeared from under the arcades on either side of the street. All were of the same ex-soldier, ex-gladiator type, all wielded stout cudgels, and all seemed to know how to use them. They began closing in from all sides. An old man appeared out of a shadowy portico down the street. He held the leashes of what may have been the three biggest, meanest, ugliest wolfhounds in the entire Roman Empire. Then from right in front of the goldsmith's shop itself appeared another old man. He only had one animal on a leash, but it looked more like a bear than a dog.

Valorius opted for discretion. A stream of abuse followed his hasty departure back down the street. Gutteral laughter echoed through the night as he disappeared from sight. Roman burglars had their work cut out for them.

He could just picture Magus Rex gloating in triumph, his heavy-lidded eyes watching him with feline complacency. But what was he to do now? Making a dishonest living in Rome looked mighty tough. And he would starve to death before he could earn any money. Wages were probably not very high anyway. He knew from his studies that there was a public dole; but he was not a citizen. Hit somebody on the head, or try to snatch a purse? But nobody with any money ever ventured into the streets without an armed retinue. In any case, he did not like the idea of hitting or snatching.

He was in a residential-mercantile district of some kind, about half way up the slopes of a low hill. Public streets here were evidently public only by day. Ferocious dogs and gangs of sturdy watchmen took over at night. And now, approaching from a nearby street, he heard the rhythmic stomp of hob-nail boots: an armed patrol. They would certainly be alerted by the watchmen who had just chased him off that there was a prowler in the neighborhood.

Valorius had no intention of being picked up and held for "trial" in some reeking cell beneath the amphitheater. The patrol would be looking for him, so his hiding place would have to be a good one.

But the whole city was sealed as tight as an amphora. The houses were all built flush with the street and each other, without a single window on the ground floor. Balconies or bays overhung the street from above, so even climbing the houses was impossible. And there were dogs. And watchmen. And armed porters. And the rhythmic stomp of hob-nail boots was getting closer every second.

Only where a building had collapsed — apparently no uncommon occurrence in Rome — was there a break in the solid walls of masonry flanking the streets. Valorius picked his way through the rubble of the vacant lot as silently as possible. A sudden frantic scurrying startled him and he leapt aside. Several sleek cats bounded past him out of a hole. He did not like to think about what lay at the bottom of that hole, trapped beneath tons of falling debris.

The moon picked the worst possible time to rise. He had seen a glowing patch of red on the far side of the Tiber — fires were apparently no uncommon occurrence either — and there were the torch processions of the wealthy and powerful. But otherwise the Seven Hills of Rome had been as dark as when Romulus had first camped here, a thousand years before. Now there was moonlight. Even those unable to adjust their eyes would be able to see. Valorius crept behind a rubble heap at the back of the lot.

He heard the disciplined tramp of hob-nail boots turn onto his street at the uphill corner. He held his breath as they approached. Suddenly the patrol stopped.

Why? There were some barked commands, followed
by a staccato clatter of hob-nails on paving bricks.
What was happening now?

Then he recalled passing another collapsed building just about where the patrol had halted. They were
searching the ruins! And the moonlight now made it
impossible for him to leave his hiding place unseen.

He crept to the top of the rubble heap and peeked
over the top. From here he could watch the street
below without being visible. But if they searched the
ruins here. . . . Silently he crept back down again and
began looking for some means of escape.

He was penned in on three sides. Flanking the
ruins were huge apartment buildings, and at the back
of the lot stretched some Roman magnate's garden
wall, over the top of which he could see four huge
dogs moving restlessly back and forth in the moonlight.
Then the hob-nail boots resumed, coming right for him.

The patrol halted beside the ruins where Valorius
took cover. Again there were some barked commands
followed by the staccato clatter of hob-nails on paving
bricks. But this time Valorius could also hear the soft
crunch of booted feet moving through the rubble toward him. He retreated silently into the farthest corner of the ruins. He crouched in the shadows behind a
mound of crumbled brick and plaster.

Closer and closer came the helmeted and cuirassed
soldiers, poking and peering into every shadow with
swords drawn. They were short and stockily-built like
the watchmen, and they too knew exactly what they
were doing. There was no escape.

For a moment Valorius was tempted to stand up
and surrender. He was sure to be discovered in a
matter of minutes. To try and fight against so many
armed soldiers meant certain death. But surrender
probably meant the amphitheater. The thought of Magus Rex gloating down at him from the imperial
podium, as lions and tigers discouraged himself and
his fellow criminals from further wrongdoing, was
unbearable. And Zenobia,. would she be forced to

watch too? No, he had to put up at least some kind of fight, with whatever powers of wizardry he still possessed.

A squat, powerfully-built soldier, using his short-sword to thrust into the shadows as he advanced, was now only a few yards away. Valorius concentrated, unifying his mind, reaching out with his thoughts, becoming one with whatever energy there was around him. The soldier hesitated, swaying drunkenly back and forth where he stood. Then slowly his sword arm dropped to his side. He stared with unseeing eyes at the garden wall.

Two more soldiers approached; one carried a lantern. They spoke to their comrade, but there was no answer. Then all three of them were staring at the garden wall like a row of hypnotized chickens. Several minutes passed.

At last their captain barked recall. The trio turned and shuffled stupidly back into ranks. The captain growled at them, but like good soldiers they did not talk back. The tramp of hob-nail boots grew fainter and fainter as the patrol marched into the night.

Valorius rose from the shadows. Perhaps he was not completely helpless after all. His creative and kinetic abilities were severely limited here, but at least he could still control the minds of Roman soldiers. And watchmen? And dogs? He reascended the street toward the goldsmith's shop.

As Valorius proceeded up the street, one by one the watchmen stopped watching; one by one the dogs stopped barking. Never had the brick-and-rubble arcade been so peaceful.

A little old man sat on a stool beside the door of the goldsmith's shop. Beside him sat his bear-like dog (or dog-like bear?). Neither paid any attention to Valorius as he brazenly examined the padlock on the door. It seemed to be a primitive cylinder lock. He borrowed the watchman's lantern, and peered into the keyhole. He could see a bolt with several holes in it, into which a series of metal pins dropped from above.

On that far-off night when he had nearly ended up
a toucan, he had moved a monolith several feet thick.
His psychokinetic powers were now so reduced that it
would take a great effort even to move a pebble. But
surely he could manipulate a few tiny metal pins.

He succeeded. But it took more concentration than
he would have liked. It also took more time—several
minutes in fact. That could prove dangerous should he
ever find himself in a position where some enemy,
man or beast, had to be pacified instantly. With such
feeble powers he could never have succeeded against
Magus Rex's giant lizards, white apes and centaurs.
Nor would the lions and tigers in the amphitheater
wait patiently while he concentrated on them. But at
least he had been able to open the door.

A thick red candle guttered before the icons of some
exotic god. A wooden ladder rose along the far wall to
a mezzanine. The benches of the workmen, each with
the array of fine tools necessary to the goldsmith's art,
were scattered randomly about the shop. The confined air was warm and stuffy.

There was not so much as a loose flake of gold on
any of the benches. But behind a screen, painted
gaudily with the flowers and vines of some dream
garden, he discovered an iron safe. Standing nearly as
high as himself, the huge safe was firmly embedded
in the concrete floor. There were three keyholes in its
door, each requiring a different key. These locks were
far more complex than the one on the front door.

Suddenly he became aware of the soft padding of
bare feet on the mezzanine floor above. A guard who
slept locked in for the night? If this goldsmith had a
fault, it was not carelessness.

It only took a moment's concentration to halt the
barefoot guard in his tracks. He was even bigger and
meaner-looking than the watchmen outside. His big
hairy belly and chest swelled above a linen loincloth;
in his ham-like paw he carried the ubiquitous cudgel.
Rome was evidently a buyer's market for ex-soldier,
ex-gladiator types. Valorius left him staring into space

at the top of the ladder and returned to the problem of
the safe.

He soon realized that the heavier bolts and pins of
the safe's three locks were beyond his present psychokinetic powers. He needed more energy.

The streets were deserted. This was fortunate, for
the ensuing scene could not have failed to have aroused
the suspicions of a passerby. A tall youth in a shimmering blue cape and tunic would have been seen
moving unchallenged up and down the street. One by
one a whole troop of burly watchmen followed him
docilely into the open door at the middle of the arcade.
More suspicious still, the dogs were silent.

Valorius soon had seven watchmen and four aged
dog-handlers crowded about the iron safe. He needed
more psychic energy; their minds would provide it.
This was the first time he had ever tried this technique.
He had learned it while awaiting Zenobia's call in the
palace of Magus Rex. It would take far more psychic
energy than a handful of hairy watchmen could provide
to get him out of this time-trap. But it was all he needed
to throw the bolts and pins of the safe's three locks.

One glance inside revealed the reason for all the
soldiers, watchmen, ferocious dogs, locks and bolts. It
was a treasure trove! The workmen's projects — mostly
jewelry and gold tableware — were arranged in neat
compartments, ready for tomorrow's work. Trays of
precious stones, gold bars, gold wire, and even large
ingots of pure gold — the raw materials of the goldsmith's art — filled half the shelves of the large safe.
Because of their hardness the precious stones —
diamonds, emeralds, even the rubies and sapphires of
the East — were only very crudely cut and polished.
The most precious gem of all, the one used in the
goldsmith's finest work, was the pearl. Valorius could
have picked them out of the trays like a handful of
peanuts.

There were several sacks of gold coins on the two
bottom shelves; he poured generous handfuls into his
pockets. But he had no intention of plundering the

goldsmith. Besides, it would have taken him the rest of the night just to carry away the swag. He was merely an amateur cracksman, driven by desperation to take a "midnight loan" from this banker of antiquity. He fully intended to repay the goldsmith—later.

In spite of his great efforts of concentration he was still fresh as he left the shop. After all, wizardry was his chosen profession. But the watchmen and dog-handlers were not in such good shape. They would probably be exhausted for the next few days. He was not sure when they would come out of their trance— possibly in a few hours—but they had not been in-jured in any way. At least, not by him. What the goldsmith might do when he walked in tomorrow morning and found the whole gang of them staring at his open safe was another matter.

The next problem was to make good his escape. He had been lucky in his first encounter with a patrol, but it was only a matter of time until he was picked up. Even if he could speak the language he doubted that he could explain away all the gold coins in his pockets.

The waterfront was probably his best bet. It would not be so heavily policed, and he should be able to find lodgings for the night. He considered taking one of the watchmen's cudgels. The waterfront has been a notoriously rough district in all times and places. But he decided to rely on his still uncertain powers of wizardry, especially those sharpening his eyes. He widened his pupils until he could see as well as in broad daylight.

The Tiber gleamed like a silver ribbon in the moon-light. He clamped his arms to his sides to keep the swag from jingling in his pockets. There were more and more slinkers and scavengers as he approached the river, but he saw them long before they could see him. There were no patrols, however, and few watch-men. The principal duty of the nightporters—the building attendants here—seemed to consist in staying out of sight.

The residential-mercantile districts, sprawling up the slopes behind him, were the city of day. The waterfront was the city of night. There was no evil known to man that could not be found here. Thugs, drunkards, and prostitutes of various sexes increased in number until it seemed that every shadow held some victim or promise of vice. Squalid, reeking lanes— some not even paved—wound through the crowded warrens. Only the street leading to the Tiber bridge was patrolled. Valorius avoided it.

He also avoided the bands of roisterers, apparently young aristocrats. So did even the most hardened thugs. They could have squashed these primped and perfumed lordlings like so many ripe grapes. Just as the lions and tigers of the amphitheater could have squashed them. The silhouette of the Colosseum rose in the distance.

Turning a corner, Valorius found himself in a small plaza. During the day it evidently held a bazaar and —even more evidently—a fish market. It was dark and boarded up now, but there was a tavern still open. Painted in gold letters on a red field above its door was the name TIGRIS. The Tiger was the least unwholesome-looking tavern he had seen thus far. He started across the plaza toward it.

Just then a burst of effeminate laughter, shrill and affected, echoed out of an adjacent street. A moment later a band of aristocratic roisterers tumbled into the plaza. There were five of them, all in their early twenties; they were dressed in silk tunics and capes of brilliant colors. Their hair was curled and their faces painted.

Valorius did not have time to retreat. But at first the roisterers did not see him. Spoiled and pampered beyond redemption, totally unconcerned about what anybody thought of their behavior, they ran madly along one side of the plaza, pounding on doors, tearing down signs, and giggling like silly schoolgirls.

Then one of them, a girlish youth in a scarlet silk tunic with a garland of flowers on his head, gave a

shriek of delight and darted into the shadows of a
small apartment building. He reappeared a moment
later, dragging an unfortunate night-porter who had
not gotten out of the way quickly enough.

Here was sport! The five painted youths formed a
circle around the poor old man; they buffeted him
back and forth, giggling drunkenly at his terror. One
of them stooped down behind him while another shoved
him from the front.

The little gray haired night-porter tumbled into a
heap, and two of the heroic lordlings began kicking
him viciously in the ribs. Then a youth in orchid silk
had an inspiration. To the delight of his drunken comrades he began urinating on the prostrate old man.

The other four thought this such a wonderful joke
that they did the same. They sang and danced up and
down while the beaten, humiliated night-porter crawled
abjectly back toward his lodge.

For several minutes the five young aristocrats romped
about like mad monkeys, giggling and grabbing playfully at each other's crotches. Then one of them noticed
Valorius.

Here was more sport! The youth in the red silk,
perhaps trying to repeat his triumph of capturing the
night-porter, ran right up to Valorius. He grimaced
impudently up at him, and said something at which
the others giggled. The other four ran up to join their
companion.

A poor night-porter living in the shadows of the
Colosseum did not dare resist. But Valorius was not a
night-porter, and he stood a head taller than any of
these pampered drones. Mingled with the smell of
expensive wines was the scent of exotic pomades,
unguents, and perfumes. The youth in the orchid silk
was the first to buffet him, making an impudent face
as he did. Valorius knocked him down.

Stunned, the other four gaped in astonishment.
How dare anyone interfere with their sport! They all
carried daggers, although their rank was their real
protection. Valorius cared for neither. He cuffed them

right and left, and then escorted them across the plaza with a few swift kicks. He could hear the perfumed and painted quintet bawling impotent threats as they scurried back where they came from.

A gang of thugs and cut-throats had been attracted by the commotion. They stood like a pack of jackals in the shadows on the far side of the plaza, watching intently for any chance to dart in and snatch a purse or a life.

One of them stood somewhat apart from the others. He was a dwarf. But his eyes glittered with intelligence of a high order. There was a look of intense calculation on his face as he watched Valorius stride through the door of the Tiger.

# CHAPTER IX
## THE WOMAN IN THE VEIL

Valorius was jolted awake by a sharp rapping at the door. There were no windows in the dismal little cubicle on the second floor above the tavern. He had no idea how long he had slept. The fat, greasy candle guttering in front of the icon at the foot of the bed looked a few inches shorter. But how fast did fat, greasy candles burn?

The rapping grew louder and more insistent. He smiled as he walked across the room to the stout bar across the door, recalling the cunning look on the tavern-keeper's face last night. Perhaps Valorius had shown him too much money, but the tavern-keeper had been a bit too insistent about his guest's safety, pointing out repeatedly how the door could be barred from the inside. The trick mechanism for lifting the bar from the outside of the door was simple and easily foiled. He was not sure whether he had actually heard the door rattle during the night, or only dreamed it.

But there was no doubt that the door was rattling now. He slid the bar aside and opened it. He had expected to find the fat, greasy tavern-keeper. Instead, he found a fat, greasy woman who turned out to be the tavern-keeper's wife. She had a sealed letter in her fat, greasy hand and a look of greedy cunning on her fat, greasy face. Her former profession was suggested by her bold eyes and brazen mannerisms.

Apparently she had been informed by her husband that their guest could not speak Latin. She took in Valorius' golden hair and blue eyes at a glance, and said something that may have been German spoken with a heavy Swedish accent. But he did not understand her. Besides, he was only interested in the letter in her hand. There was only one person in Rome who could possibly know that he was here. Zenobia must have been watching for him.

His impatience betrayed him. Carelessly thrusting some money at the tavern-keeper's wife, he snatched the letter out of her hand and broke the seal. He did not notice her eyes widen at the sight of the gold coin or the angry glance she shot at the trick mechanism on the door.

The letter was written with black ink on parchment. Its direction was in Latin: "Valorius, to be delivered before the 3rd hour." The brief message inside, however, was not in Latin:

At the Flavian Amphitheater. Gate XII (the one directly behind the statue of the sungod). The 5th hour.

As he started to reread it, he became aware of another pair of eyes trying to peek at the message. He literally had to shove the woman out the door to get her to leave.

The injunctions of Magus Rex were not to be ignored— even by his darling daughter. Zenobia's previous messages had been in cryptic verse, which for reasons unknown was apparently not covered by her father's injunction against communicating with him. But this was prose, a plain communication if there ever was one. It was all very puzzling. Shaking his head, he memorized the message and then burned it.

Descending to the bar, he was given a Roman breakfast by the tavern-keeper's wife: bread, a small saucer of olive oil to dip it in, and a cup of sourish wine. The tavern-keeper himself was either still sleeping or, more likely, off somewhere rounding up a gang of bravoes to jump him should he stay here another night. One more body floating down the Tiber would cause no great stir in Rome.

Fat sausages, rings of onions, and bronze pitchers hung from hooks on the wall. The bar itself was of polished oak, inset along its entire length with wine amphorae. A wine bowl with a wooden ladle, covered to protect it from flies, was set out near the door, apparently for the walk-in trade.

Valorius stood at the other end of the bar, making the best of his Roman breakfast. The bread was fresh, the olive oil tastily seasoned, and the sourish wine not too unpleasant on an empty stomach. He knew that the tavern-keeper's wife was watching him out of the corner of her eye, but he ignored her. Through the open door he looked upon a lively crowded bazaar; a light breeze told him that the fish market was open. It was too early yet for the sun to reach the interior of the tavern through the glassless window beside the door.

There were several seedy-looking patrons, some still here from last night, scattered about the gloomy tables and benches. They were not particularly interested in Valorius: they had seen blond barbarians before. One of them, however, plucked up his courage and approached the end of the bar.

He was a pale, balding little man in his middle thirties. He looked shy and awkward. He also looked like he did not eat regularly. Unlike the other patrons, he was wearing a toga. Not a very clean toga, but a toga nonetheless.

He nodded to Valorius and said something in polite Latin. Failing to get an answer, he too tried a few words in a language that may have been German

spoken with a heavy Swedish accent. Then he tried
what may have been Greek or Syrian, and even some
strange tongue that reminded Valorius of someone
trying to gargle with molasses. At last, in desperation,
he tried sign language.

Taking a sheaf of scribbled parchment out of the
folds of his toga, he pointed to it and then to Valorius'
half-finished breakfast. Apparently he was just a poor
poet offering to read one of his works in exchange for
breakfast. Valorius nodded. This was exactly what he
had been looking for. Not the poem, but the poet.

He signalled to the tavern-keeper's wife that he
would buy the poet's breakfast—and a second one for
himself—and that they would share it at a corner
table.

She smiled knowingly. In her world there was only
one way to construe such a gesture. But it didn't
matter, just as long as the blond barbarian with the
pocketful of gold coins stayed until her husband got
back. Valorius had guessed correctly that he was off
rounding up a gang but he was naive in believing that
they would not attack until after dark.

While the poor poet ate his breakfast—ravenously,
but with some show of refined table manners—Valorius
reviewed in his mind the proper technique for acquiring a foreign language. This had been dealt with only
cursorily at the Academy. The Brazilian Hegemony
was the only major foreign civilization in which a
wizard was ever likely to find himself, and everybody
knew Portuganza. But Valorius had learned everything the Academy had to teach. Despite Magus Rex's
scoffing, he really had the makings of a first class
wizard.

He had nearly two hours until his appointment
with Zenobia at the Flavian Amphitheater. He let the
starveling poet finish his breakfast, and even ordered
him a second.

At last the balding little man sat back on his bench,
sighing contentedly. It had been two days now since
his last full meal. But he let this contentment last only

a moment. Dutifully, he took out his sheaf of poems
again, ready to pay for his breakfast with a recital
(that this huge blond barbarian would not understand
a word was not his fault). He took a drink of wine and
cleared his throat.

But Valorius shook his head. Then the poet offered
to sing him a song. He had composed it himself, and
though his voice was rather weak it was well-trained.
In fact, he considered singing for his breakfast a quite
generous gratuity: a simple recital of some of his
latest verses should have been more than adequate.
But again Valorius shook his head. The poor poet now
began to look uncomfortable, as if he too began to
construe the gesture of buying breakfast in the same
light as the tavern-keeper's wife.

Valorius quietly set his mind at rest — literally. Unifying his own mind, then that of the poet, becoming
one with the energy patterns of the poet's mind, he
slowly and patiently acquired a mastery of spoken
Latin. The process took nearly an hour. It was a
strange sight, two men facing each other across a
table in the darkest corner of the tavern, neither so
much as blinking an eye.

The tavern-keeper's wife hardly blinked her eyes
either. In fact, the only time her greedy scrutiny left
Valorius was when somebody strolled in from the
bazaar outside to ladle himself a cup of wine out of
the common bowl. Had the patron filled his cup too
full, or left too small a coin in the dish, she might
possibly have had a word or two to say about it. The
regular patrons of the Tiger knew better than to try
any such tricks on her.

She busily washed cups in a big wooden tub whose
water was changed unfailingly every week or two,
tended the bar and tables, and, in general, kept a very
sharp eye on everything. Especially on Valorius.

The instant he rose from the corner table she was
after him. Her blandishments were shameless. She
even offered him a free room where he could be alone
with his friend. Valorius politely rebuffed her. But his

courtesy was wasted. She had seen the color of his
money and was determined to get an even closer look.
Although somewhat hampered by being forced to use
sign language, she wheedled like a true professional.

She was also somewhat hampered by Valorius' size.
In the long history of mankind there have been many
societies in which men did not ordinarily strike women.
This was not one of them. Experience told her that it
might be a painful error to push a man this size too
far. Her most devastating weapon was her tongue—
and he didn't speak the language! She followed him
into the street, wheedling and tugging at his cape.

Not far from the door she reached a kind of merce-
nary watershed. The thought of such a prize slipping
through her fingers was maddening. On the other
hand, to stray any farther from the unguarded tavern
would mean certain pilferage. Gnashing her teeth in
impotent rage, she turned on her heel and stormed
back into the Tiger. Her veteran patrons were all carefully looking the other way. The tavern cat, a sly old
mouser with a bitten-off tail, scuttled for cover. She
began preparing the tirade she would launch against
her lout of a husband when he finally did get back.

Meanwhile, Valorius pushed through the crowded
bazaar, with the starveling poet tagging along at his
heels. The women gossiping around the fountain made
some remarks as they passed. The poet blushed, much
to the delight of the women. In fact, the remarks
might have made a centurion blush. Valorius kept
walking. The fifth hour, the hour of his appointment
with Zenobia, was fast approaching.

He knew the general location of the Flavian Amphitheater or "Colosseum," as it would be called in later
centuries. But he soon discovered that the streets of
the real Rome were far more tortuous than those on
maps and reconstructions. Two turns past the street
leading to the Tiber bridge and he was lost.

The balding little poet was having trouble keeping
up with Valorius' long strides. The toga was not designed for fast walking. He had no idea where the

huge blond barbarian was going, but he seemed to be generous with his money. That was as good a reason as any to tag along.

"Do you know the way to the Flavian Amphitheater?" the barbarian suddenly asked in flawless Latin.

The little man gaped in astonishment. "Why, yes, of course," he stammered. "In fact, I was going there myself. It's a game day, and I had planned to hold a reading near the Colossus. But you speak—"

"That's not important now. I have an appointment near Gate Twelve, at the fifth hour. Direct me there and I'll make it worth your while."

The poet listened raptly, his head cocked to one side. "That's marvelous!" he cried. "Who was your teacher? You look like a, uh, like one of the northern peoples, and yet you speak like a brilliantly educated Roman. I've never heard Latin pronounced so perfectly!"

Valorius repressed a smile. "Let's just say that I learned from a very good teacher. And now . . . I'm afraid I don't even know your name."

"Titus Lengo." He looked expectantly up at him, but there was no sign of recognition. "Oh, well," he sighed, "I'm still relatively young. Someday they'll know my name!"

"Titus Lengo, my name is Valorius." The two exchanged formal bows. "But, as I said, I have an appointment—"

"At Gate Twelve. Yes, I remember. It would be a pleasure to act as your guide," he said, formally assuming the role of cicerone. "Please to follow me, Valorius."

Despite his shy, awkward appearance, Titus Lengo knew his way around. As they approached the Flavian Amphitheater togas became more and more common. Everybody seemed to be moving in the same direction.

"I'm afraid you won't see much of the animal show," said Titus Lengo, deftly guiding Valorius past a knot of people gathered around a snake-charmer. "It'll be nearly over by the time we get there. Unless, of course, you're interested in seeing some miserable criminals slaughtered. I think it's disgusting myself, but some people like that sort of thing. The mob screeches with laughter whenever Hannibal tears some terrified wretch to pieces. But give them anything requiring real skill, and they lose interest. People of culture are just not appreciated in Rome these days. But if you're really interested in animal acts—and some of them are rather splendid—you should come back this afternoon. The morning show is mere butchery."

"No doubt. But who, or what, is Hannibal?"

Titus Lengo looked surprised. "You mean you've never heard of Hannibal? I mean no rudeness by this, Valorius, but you're quite a mysterious fellow. Your name and appearance are those of a, uh, of a northern person. And yet you have none of the uncouthness one generally associates with such people. You don't seem to know your way around Rome, and yet you speak the most flawless Latin I've ever heard." He shook his head in wonder. "But in answer to your question, Hannibal is an elephant. The biggest elephant in the world, and also the meanest. He's rather a mystery too."

"Oh, in what way?" asked Valorius. By keeping Titus Lengo talking, he would keep him from pulling out his sheaf of poems and reciting. Besides, he was not quite so pressed for time as he had thought. They had passed through a forum in which a huge sun-dial stood. It was only a quarter past IV.

"Nobody has ever seen an elephant like Hannibal before," said Titus Lengo. "In fact, nobody even knows where he came from. Some say he's an African elephant, but he's twice the size of an African elephant. He's even bigger than Bucyrus!"

"Bucyrus?"

"Oh, I'm sorry. If you don't know about Hannibal, then you would hardly have heard of Bucyrus. Now there's a real elephant! He's the favorite of the best people in Rome. There's not a trick he doesn't know, and all very dignified. None of your cheap circus tricks for Bucyrus! He even writes in Greek. Last

month he ended his act by kneeling in front of the
imperial podium and writing the emperor's name in
the sand with a gold wand. In Greek no less! Of
course," he glanced cautiously over his shoulder,
"Maximin can barely speak Latin, let alone Greek. I
understand he's at the northern frontier now, so word
probably hasn't reached him yet. But it's sure to make
Bucyrus' owner a rich man, as soon as he does hear
about it. He's performing this afternoon. I mean, of
course, Bucyrus. Not," he chuckled, but again glanced
cautiously over his shoulder, "the emperor."

"And not this morning?" Valorius asked quickly,
seeing Titus Lengo absentmindedly reaching into the
folds of his toga for his sheaf of poems.

"This morning!" he cried, looking shocked. "I should
say not! Bucyrus is an artist, not a butcher. Oh, but
you don't know, do you? You see, the morning spectacle is mostly animal exhibitions. It's all rather brutal,
but the rabble demand it. None of the best people
attend. They're at the theaters now, and simply wouldn't
dream of going to the amphitheater until the gladiatorial games this afternoon. It's just too vile!" he sniffed.
"As for myself, if I don't attend the theater in the
morning, I generally hold a reading." His hand again
strayed into the folds of his toga.

"How far are we now?" Valorius asked quickly. "I
don't see any familiar landmarks."

"Landmarks? You mean temples and palaces? But I
thought you wanted to go directly to the Flavian
Amphitheater. That's why I've stayed away from the
imperial roads. It's less crowded this way. But if I'd
known that you wanted to do some sightseeing—"

"No, no," Valorius assured him. "I have no time for
that now. Are we getting close?"

Titus Lengo led him to the opposite side of the
street.

"See that golden head just over the top of the
bakery there? That's the Colossus. It stands in the
square next to the Flavian Amphitheater, and it's
nearly as high. It's a statue of Apollo, or, as some

people think, of Mithras. But it's some sun god or
other. Do you see the rays extending from its crown?
It's supposed to have been erected by one of the old
emperors, centuries ago. Nero, I believe. In fact," he
chuckled, "I've even heard that it was once a statue of
Nero himself, and that the head was cut off and
replaced by that of the sun god you see now. I don't
know if it's true, but it makes a good story. Careful
now," he warned. "We're getting close. Keep your
hands on your money."

Valorius quickly saw that this was sound advice—
although, strictly speaking, it was not really *his* money
he was keeping his hands on. They had hardly stepped
out of the shadows of the narrow backstreet when
they were engulfed by a raucous, jostling mob of
thousands: mountebanks and jugglers, snake-charmers,
peddlers, puppeteers, and professional story-tellers,
each surrounded by an eager, gawking crowd. Beggars
and cripples were everywhere with their hands out,
bawling for alms. There was also a ragamuffin ferret-
eyed horde of men whose profession was not hard to
guess, shuttling back and forth through the press.
Valorius clamped his arms tightly to his sides.

"This way," cried Titus Lengo, taking him in tow.
"Gate Twelve is right behind the Colossus. You can't
see it from here."

There was scaffolding at the base of the Colossus,
where some kind of maintenance work was in progress.
But there was nobody working now. An elderly man in
a ragged tunic lay face down in the sun at the bottom
of the scaffolding. He may have been sick, or even
dead, but the crowd ignored him. As they passed,
Valorius saw one of the ferret-eyed ragamuffins kneel
beside the man, skillfully run his hands up and down
the body; then, having apparently been beaten to the
loot, rise and weasel his way back into the mob.

"Don't bother," said Titus Lengo, seeing Valorius
staring at the body. "The patrol will throw him into
the river before he starts to stink. There's Gate Twelve,
where the woman in the veil is standing." He smiled.

"Is that who you have the appointment with, Valorius?"

At first he thought it might be. The woman in the veil was looking in his direction, as if she was expecting him. But she was several inches shorter than Zenobia. Roman ladies contacted men in public by sending one of their maids. Perhaps she was a messenger. For all he knew, Zenobia may have been living here in Rome with her father for years now, and was simply doing as the Romans did.

Valorius halted about sixty feet from the entrance to Gate XII, in the shadow of the Colossus. The woman in the veil never turned her eyes from him although her view was continually interrupted by the flow of the crowd.

"This is where I wanted to go," he said. "You've been a most instructive guide, Titus Lengo. Many thanks."

"The pleasure was mine, Valorius." He bowed formally. "Any time I can be of service. . . ." But he did not move off at once, and looked somewhat embarrassed. "You said, uh, I believe, something about. . . ."

Valorius had forgotten the promised gratuity in his curiosity over the woman in the veil. Distracted, he reached into his pocket and handed the balding little poet a gold coin. The gesture was met only with silence. He then handed him another coin, thinking the first had not been enough.

But it had been. In fact, about fifty times too much. Titus Lengo's silence had been one of shock, not scorn. The second coin nearly floored him. He stared and stammered as if he had lost his reason.

"Oh, Valorius, I never expected anything like this!" he cried. He seemed torn between his poverty and the guilt of cheating a stranger who had been kind to him. "This is far, far beyond anything my poor services might be worth. No, I just can't do it. You're a stranger in Rome, and I don't want to take advantage of you. I mean, you bought me breakfast, and, well. . . ."

"Keep the money, Titus Lengo," said Valorius. "I'm indeed a stranger in Rome, and perhaps I'll need your services again. Where can I find you? At the Tiger?"

"Certainly not!" he sniffed. "I happened to be in
that squalid den last night merely by accident. I have
a room of my own. But, uh, the quarter's rent was due
two weeks ago, and the landlord. . . . Well, he said I
should sleep elsewhere until. . . ." He shrugged. "But
now. . . ." Again he seemed torn between conflicting
emotions.

"But now," Valorius finished for him, "you'll be
able to pay some of the rent."

"Some!" he cried, staring at the two coins. "Valorius,
have you any idea how much money you've given me?"

"We'll discuss it later," he said. "I must leave you
now. How can I find your room — in case I need your
help again?"

Titus Lengo gave him detailed instructions for finding the apartment house. "You don't mind climbing a
few stairs, do you? You see, my room is on the fifth
floor, just under the roof. It's not very big I'm afraid.
But I'm only there at night. During the day I'm usually at the Quill, which is in the next street. Unless, of
course, I'm holding a reading."

"You said you were going to hold a reading today,"
Valorius suggested, trying to get away.

"Not now. There's no point in working when I have
money. But really, Valorius," he frowned, still in two
minds about the coins, "this is a great deal of money
for so little —"

"I'll let you earn it later," he promised. "And now,
Titus Lengo, if you'll excuse me. . . ."

"Oh, a thousand pardons! Of course, you have your
appointment. You know where to find me, and I hope
to see you again soon. Perhaps then you'll tell me how
you, a stranger in Rome, ever learned to speak Latin
so beautifully." He bowed once more, turned, and was
swallowed by the crowd.

Valorius started to walk toward Gate XII and the
woman in the veil. The crowd seemed to be moving in
that direction now as well, and several times he heard
the name "Hannibal" spoken. Apparently it was al-

most time for the monster's performance, and the
mob was hurrying to get to their seats. The woman in
the veil continued to watch him as he approached.

There was a muffled roar from inside the amphitheater. The crowd outside hurried even faster toward
the gate, jostling him rudely out of the way. Anybody
who fell in such a press would probably never get up
again. The name "Hannibal" was shouted eagerly back
and forth. Especially by the women, who made up a
good third of the crowd. The scream of an angry bull
elephant rose above the hubbub.

The woman in the veil had moved to safety at one
side of the gate so she could avoid being trampled to
death. Romans did not live by bread alone—they also
needed circuses. Valorius had never seen such looks of
avid craving on human faces before. Woe to anyone—
even an emperor over eight feet tall—who deprived
these people of their brutal amusements.

A smaller man would have been carried helplessly
into the amphitheater like a cork on a raging flood.
Valorius was able to fight his way out of the mob just
before he reached the gate. The instant he broke free,
the woman in the veil motioned for him to follow. She
quickly led the way around the base of the wall. There
was another roar from the crowd; another angry scream
of a bull elephant.

The woman motioned for him to hurry; she was
almost running now, leading him toward an unmarked
gate just ahead. It stood exactly at one end of the long
axis of the oval structure. Strangely, there was no
crowd here. The woman wore a tunic of homespun
linen which fell to her ankles. Her veil was the same
brilliant violet that Magus Rex painted his fingernails.

The woman led him through the gate, but instead
of climbing the stairs to the arena she turned to her
left down a short passageway. There was a barred
door at its end. Two grisly-looking gladiators stood
guard. He hesitated.

The woman in the veil turned toward him. She was
young and shapely, but her bold eyes reminded him of

the tavern-keeper's wife at the Tiger.

She whispered a single word: "Zenobia."

He hesitated no longer. This was a strange trysting place, but perhaps it was the only one she could find where they would not be discovered by her father's watchful eyes. Such crude and brutal amusements would hardly appeal to the refined tastes of Magus Rex.

He followed the woman through the door, ignoring the insolent stares of the two gladiators. But instead of finding Zenobia waiting for him, he found—an avalanche. Exactly how many men pounced on him from all sides he never found out. It could not have been less than twenty.

Trussed up like a sacrificial lamb, he was bundled through a dark maze of corridors, past endless congeries of animal cages and pits. Growls, snarls and hisses met him from all sides. From somewhere far above he heard the sound of the crowd, rumbling like distant thunder. The woman in the veil had disappeared.

At last he found himself outside a row of cells. There was more light here, and he saw that the cells were crowded with wretched, terrified human beings of all ages and sexes: hundreds of them. The stench was abominable. A broad ramp led upward to what he guessed was a door into the arena itself.

It had all happened so fast that he hardly had time to think. He was trussed about the arms and chest with stout cords; a score of burly gladiators held him fast on all sides. He could not even turn his head. But he was not completely helpless: he could still concentrate—or so he thought.

He began to unify his mind, to reach out with his thoughts. But suddenly a bronze gong wanged metallically just behind his head. He started, his concentration broken. He tried again. This time a shrill whistle sounded in his ear. The gladiators laughed. He heard the cell doors being opened behind him. A whip cracked.

Now he was really helpless. Physically immobilized, it was impossible now even to concentrate. Every few seconds some new noise—clangs, whistles, yells, howls—sounded a few inches away from his ear. These ignorant, thug-like gladiators could not possibly know why they were making the noises. They were merely obeying orders. Only another wizard would try to interrupt his powers of concentration.

It looked like Magus Rex's trap had worked this time. Zenobia had never sent the message. The violet veil worn by the woman who met him at the gate should have warned him. The great wizard was usually more subtle than this; but apparently even his legendary equitableness had its limits. A scarred and crippled old man hobbled up the ramp and unbolted the door to the arena.

A scream sounded next to Valorius' ear, breaking his last chance to concentrate. The gladiators pinioning his arms laughed brutally. Then he was shoved forward up the ramp.

The old cripple opened the door. Just as he reached it his bonds were cut and he was flung headlong out onto the cruel, blood-drenched sands of the arena. The sunlight blinded him. The roar of the crowd deafened him.

# CHAPTER X
# THE BESTIARIUS

The first thing that met Valorius' eyes was a leg, the bloody stump of a human leg. It lay on the sand not five feet away. He leapt to his feet, adjusting his eyes to the strong sunlight. Bodies and parts of bodies were strewn all across the arena. Towering above the carnage stood the monstrous bull elephant, Hannibal.

No wonder Titus Lengo had called the creature a mystery! Indian elephants stood nine or ten feet at the shoulder; but the difficulties and expense of transporting them made them mere curiosities to the Romans. The relatively small African forest elephant —no more than seven or eight feet high—was the beast used in processions and spectacles. It had also been the war elephant of Rome's greatest enemy, Hannibal of Carthage. But that great captain's namesake was an African bush elephant. Twelve feet high at the shoulder, with ten-foot tusks curved like scimitars, the brute could not have weighed less than eight tons. How such a monster could have been transported all the way from East Africa was a mystery indeed.

Forty thousand blood-thirsty voices screamed for more carnage. They were not interested in mysteries. They wanted blood and slaughter.

There was still one man left on his feet from the first batch of condemned criminals: a swarthy, bearded miscreant with only one good eye, probably a captured bandit or footpad. Cunningly he had stayed out of sight directly behind the monster. The mob howled insanely and pelted Hannibal with debris, trying to get him to turn around.

Hannibal swayed back and forth, his great tusks sweeping before him each time he moved his head. He seemed to sense that something was not as it should be. The bearded wretch with one good eye continued to hide directly behind him. But Hannibal was an old hand at this sport, and this dodge had been tried on him before.

Without warning he suddenly wheeled around. The man was caught by surprise. Frantically he tried to leap behind him again, but it was too late—he had been seen. Hannibal's angry scream cut through the howls of the mob like a knife through suet. Dodge and dart as he might, the bearded wretch could not long elude the great bull elephant. He was caught from behind and flung twenty feet in the air. Stunned and broken, he tried to crawl away. Hannibal ambled over to where he had fallen and knelt on him, crushing him to a pulp. Forty thousand Romans roared their delight.

The arena wall was about fifteen feet high; its face was protected with metal rollers and its top surmounted by a bronze balustrade to prevent wild animals from climbing into the crowd. The imperial podium, where sat the wealthy senatorial families, was further protected by a moat. The arena itself was about fifty yards by eighty. Valorius stood with thirty others along the wall just to one side of the long axis. They were hard-looking men and women, condemned for various offenses to die in the arena.

The only exception was a fat, oily little man dressed in an embroidered tunic. He was haggard and unkempt,

but obviously used to good living. All at once he broke
away from the others and ran to the imperial podium.
He knelt in front of the moat and raised his pudgy,
manicured hands beseechingly to those above him. He
was evidently some wealthy merchant or speculator
who had offended someone in power—perhaps Maximin himself. These were his former friends and associates, but now they only laughed. A woman of inde-
terminate age, gaudily dressed and painted, cynically
tossed him a rose. The gesture caused great merriment among those seated about her.

The fat, oily little man stared dumbly at the rose.
Mechanically he started to pick it up. Just as his
fingers touched the petals a flourish of trumpets
sounded from an arcade nearby. He dropped the rose
as if he had been stung. His quondam friends and
associates found this highly amusing. Perhaps they
suspected that those who did not laugh loud enough
would be brought to the emperor's attention. Looking
down from the imperial podium was much preferred
to looking up at it.

All this time Hannibal had been moving aimlessly
about among the slaughtered, stomping and mutilat-
ing their bodies. He carried the stump of a human leg
in his trunk. The flourish of trumpets called his attention toward the imperial podium. At last his weak
little eyes perceived the fresh batch of victims. He
dropped the bloody stump and trumpeted savagely.
Opening his huge fan-shaped ears, he began to shuffle
swiftly across the sand, throwing his huge legs outward and forward as he charged. The fat, oily little
man was too stricken with terror to move as the
monster bore down upon him.

Trident-wielding bestiarii began to drive the condemned away from the wall. Valorius did not wait to
be jabbed in the back. There was energy here, the
concentrated psychic energy of fear and sadistic excitement. The bearded wretch with one good eye had given
him an idea. He raced across the sand, circling behind
the charging bull elephant.

Few noticed him. The eyes of the mob were on Hannibal's next victim. At the very last moment the fat, oily little man threw out his hands and screamed in terror. Hannibal snatched him up in his trunk and smashed him down onto the sand. Placing a huge forefoot on his chest, he began ripping his arms and legs from their sockets and throwing them into the crowd. An arm landed in the imperial podium. There was some good-humored skipping out of the way and the exchange of aristocratic witticisms.

Valorius stood directly behind the monster. Concentration was extremely difficult. Only by bringing to bear all the acquired discipline of decades of study could he accomplish anything. Last night he had controlled the minds of a gang of burly watchmen and their dogs. With so much energy concentrated here, surely he could control the mind of a single bull elephant.

The monster shook its great head from side to side, seeming to exult in its butchery. The brutalized mob shrieked its approval, already looking forward to more and even bloodier scenes of carnage. The condemned men and women were urged farther out into the sunlight by the tridents of the bestiarii. At last Hannibal noticed them, and his cruel, ten-foot tusks lowered ominously. Forty thousand tongues screamed for blood. The condemned cringed helplessly. The trident-wielding bestiarii prudently retreated toward the safety of the barricades. Then—nothing happened.

At first there were some angry shouts from the stands nearby, and some debris rained down on Hannibal. Then an awareness that something unusual was happening began to subdue the crowd. If there was anything they loved more than blood it was novelty. Eighty-thousand eyes suddenly became aware of a tall, slender, golden-haired youth in a shimmering blue cape and tunic. They watched him walk fearlessly around to the front of the monstrous elephant. Again—nothing happened.

Why didn't Hannibal tear him to pieces? Never

within living memory had the Flavian Amphitheater
been so silent. Several minutes passed. Still nothing
happened. Murmurs of discontent began to ripple
through the crowd. If there was not going to be any
more blood, then there had better be some kind of
novelty. There were some shouts of impatience.

Valorius wondered what to do next. He could not
just walk away and leave the eight-ton monster just
standing there. Then he had an inspiration. Titus
Lengo had mentioned an Indian elephant named
Bucyrus that wrote things in the sand. He strode to
the edge of the moat and called into the imperial
podium above.

Those sitting in the upper tiers of the four-story
structure could not hear what he said. They only saw
a pomaded dandy dressed in red silk trousers step
hesitantly to the bronze balustrade and toss his walking-
stick across the moat. What happened next was the
subject of conversation for weeks to come.

Hannibal shuffled docilely forward. To the wonder
of all he bowed to the imperial podium, then lowered
himself gingerly onto his knees. Taking the walking-
stick in his trunk he began scratching at the sand in
front of him. When he had finished he rose, bowed
again, and stepped back.

Only those sitting in and around the imperial podium could actually see what he had written. But no
Olympic sprinter could have outrun the news as it
raced from neighbor to neighbor around the vast oval.
The ferocious Hannibal, the largest and most powerful creature ever seen in Rome, had written in the
arena sand VIVAT MAXIMIN. The applause was
tremendous.

The dandy in the red silk trousers was bouncing up
and down like a flea on a griddle: his walking-stick
would make his fortune. There was no great enthusiasm elsewhere in the imperial podium. They had all
prudently applauded the emperor's name. But it had
been written in mere Latin, not Greek. Just what one
might expect from a vulgar brute like Hannibal!

There was an air of snobbish disdain about the whole coterie of exquisites in the imperial podium. Few of them would have been here at all except for the fact that a member of their intimate set happened to be the editor of this morning's animal exhibitions. Like all the best people in Rome they preferred the more refined afternoon spectacle.

Valorius had no trouble spotting the editor. He was a pale, nervous young man who looked as if he wished he were in one of the theaters, baths, or brothels where he normally spent his mornings. Next to him sat a plump little woman, dressed and painted like a precious doll; she held a green parasol over her head, possibly to keep her face from melting in the sun. Her dictatorial manner toward the editor indicated that she was probably his mother. Today's spectacle had certainly been her idea, arranged and paid for in hopes of getting him elected to some ornamental public office. He listened nervously to her lecture on how to deal with this unexpected event. She shoved a purse at him and nodded peremptorily toward Valorius.

But Valorius had other ideas. Now that Magus Rex knew he was in Rome, he would need all the help he could get. It would not come from the aristocracy. The proletariat had little money and less initiative; but they comprised ninety-five percent of the population. Even the most despotic of emperors — Maximin, for instance — deferred to their centuries-old demands for bread and circuses. Rome ruled the world, and the mob ruled Rome. Valorius turned his back on the imperial podium.

It was a triumphal procession. Flowers and coins rained down on him from above. Both he and the eight-ton monster shuffling tamely behind him were loudly praised. There were even some derogatory remarks made against Bucyrus, but these came from less reputable elements. The majority of the crowd had yet to be won over by Hannibal.

Valorius halted before the low-price seats at the far side of the arena. Both he and Hannibal bowed to the

rabble as formally as they had bowed to the imperial
podium. This democratic gesture was cheered lustily
by the mob. The more prudent, however, moved further up into the stands. There were no rollers or
bronze railings on the wall here, and it was not unknown for wild animals—especially the big cats—to
climb into the crowd and cause some degree of inconvenience. Also, as Valorius learned later, Hannibal
sometimes succeeded in snatching spectators from
the top of the wall. In fact, getting country people
visiting Rome for the first time to move to the front as
Hannibal passed beneath was a favorite practical joke
with the mob. A fifteen-foot wall was no insurmount-
able barrier to a twelve-foot elephant with a long
trunk.

But that long trunk now held only a dainty walking-
stick. There would be no snatching of unsuspecting
provincials from the top of the wall today. Valorius felt
more and more confident about functioning with low
energy resources. He was the real performer in this
bizarre spectacle. The mob looked on in wonder as
ferocious Hannibal knelt docilely in the sand and
scratched out another message in large block capitals.

The roar was deafening. Tens of thousands of screaming Romans leapt to their feet, yelling themselves
hoarse, as the news swept around the oval arena.
What was Bucyrus to this! No more would that pompous pachyderm intimidate them with his aristocratic
airs, his writings in Greek for the educated upper
classes! From now on the mob would have an elephant of their own, a great gray hope to throw in the
tusks of the stuck-up Bucyrus. And that elephant's
name was—Hannibal!

Grown men wept for joy, embracing complete
strangers; several women became hysterical; ragged
urchins scurried up and down the stairs and benches
like mad squirrels. For there in the sand before them,
in three-foot letters (and much neater than any
letters ever drawn by Bucyrus), were the words VIVAT
ROMA. And not in your effete Greek either. But in

manly Latin. The mob was delirious with joy.

A veritable hailstorm of coins fell from the stands as Valorius continued his triumphant circuit of the arena. Following the normal practice of the amphitheater, these were duly collected by attendants and a high percentage honorably turned over to him afterward. Twice more he halted and had Hannibal write popular slogans in the sand. Once he even had him solve a simple problem in arithmetic. It turned out to be a higher sum than Bucyrus had ever even attempted. The mob was now on the verge of mass hysteria.

Fistfights broke out in the stands. The rival Bucyrian and Hannibalian factions, which were to ravage the streets of Rome for weeks to come, were already forming. The red, blue, green and white factions of the chariot races had long thrown Roman society into a fanatical turmoil, but these color lines were now down. The new elephant factions were definitely class oriented. And Hannibal was the elephant of the people!

By the time Valorius had completed his circuit of the arena, and once more stood before the imperial podium, he had pretty well decided on his course of action. Thanks to the goldsmith last night and the amphitheater mob today, he had plenty of money. But for reasons unknown Magus Rex had apparently forgotten his legendary equitableness. Being temporarily turned into a toucan was one thing; being permanently dissected by a raging bull elephant was quite another. The great wizard had discovered him on the very day of his arrival in Rome, which indicated a spy network of some kind. He could combat this only with spies of his own.

His greatest fear, of course, was that Magus Rex had already taken Zenobia away, leaving him stranded in time. He might eventually work his way back to his own age, although his theoretical knowledge of time-travel was still untested. But what then? Wait in Zenobia's library for another verse to appear? In any case, he would first have to find out whether or not Zenobia was still here. And if so, where. That meant

that he needed spies, spies who knew their way around
Rome.

There were a few cried of "Mitte! Mitte!" Let him
go!

Valorius no longer had any worries about being
executed. A huge sadistic brute like Maximin was
capable of anything. For instance, he might even think
that he was being mocked by having a huge sadistic
brute like Hannibal write his name in the sand. But it
would take weeks to find out his opinion. In the
meantime Valorius knew that he was safe.

Not so with the other condemned criminals. The
trident-wielding bestiarii had reappeared. If Hannibal
would not execute them, there were plenty of lions,
tigers, hyenas, crocodiles, wolves, and bears slavering
in the pens below the arena who would.

The dandy in the red silk trousers had retrieved his
walking-stick, he was elated that it had been his imple-
ment used to write the emperor's name in the sand.
With any luck at all that would be worth at least a
month of banquet invitations.

Others were not so happy. The editor of the games
looked paler and more nervous than ever. At his
mother's urging, he stood at the bronze balustrade
above, brandishing a purse for the benefit of the crowd
before he tossed it to Valorius (although he looked as
if he would rather have thrown something heavier at
him). The purse landed near the limbless torso of the
fat, oily speculator. The gesture was applauded without enthusiasm.

The mob was becoming bored. Hannibal had given
them something to throw in the face of the aristocracy,
but at the moment he was just a gray eminence.
Nobody had been slaughtered in over half an hour.
They wanted spectacle, continuous spectacle.

Valorius decided to give them a show. Scooping up
the purse, he flourished it over his head for all to see.
Then he tossed it back up to the editor. A hush fell
over the mob. What was he doing? Was he being
insolent? Valorius allowed the tension to mount. All at

once he pointed toward the line of condemned criminals and, gesturing theatrically, held up his left arm, the gladiator's traditional appeal for mercy.

The gesture appealed to the debased sentimentalism of the mob. They roared their approval. The blond barbarian was passing up wealth to plead for clemency for his comrades. Thousands of thumbs were turned up; thousands of handkerchiefs were waved all over the amphitheater.

Valorius now brought Hannibal into the act. He stood directly in front of the monster as if appealing to him. The mob saw him again gesture theatrically toward the condemned criminals. Hannibal turned his head toward them; then back again. He raised his left foreleg as if he too were appealing for mercy. Tens of thousands of thumbs were turned up; tens of thousands of handkerchiefs were waved all over the amphitheater.

The pale, nervous young editor glared down at Valorius. He had never wanted to sponsor these wretched games in the first place. Now what was he to do? He doubted if he had any authority to release condemned criminals. He hated making decisions; so did all his friends. Oh, why had he ever let his mother talk him into this? She had threatened to cut off his allowance, but she had threatened that before, many times. And now what was he to do? If he released the criminals and the emperor didn't like it, he himself might end up on the other side of the arena wall. But if he didn't release them, the mob might storm the podium. That they would also tear his mother to pieces would be small consolation for his own sufferings.

His mother, however, had not been just standing there, grinning weakly at the uproar of the mob; she had been moving among her senatorial friends, getting their legal opinions. Rushing back to the railing, she whispered something in his ear. He sighed with sheer relief, and for several moments almost did not hate her. She had discovered a precedent, one which absolved him of all responsibility.

Raising his hands for silence, he motioned the

condemned criminals toward the podium. They seemed reluctant to come any closer to Hannibal—ten years of savage mayhem were not erased by ten minutes of docility—but they were tridently encouraged forward. The men tried to jostle the women to the front, where they would be slaughtered first should Hannibal change his mind.

This was the first chance Valorius had to scrutinize them. He had never seen such deep-dyed viciousness in human faces; if anything, the women were even harder-looking than the men. No order existed for those condemned to the arena; it was merely a haphazard lot of thirty-odd murderers, footpads, procuresses, poisoners, stranglers, necrophiliacs, incindiaries, and even one tall emaciated man reputed to be a vampire. They were just what he was looking for.

The young editor made a sweeping gesture of imperial largesse which he had seen recently in the theater, and dramatically turned his thumb up, granting clemency in the name of the emperor to the whole deplorable lot of caitiffs and hellhounds in the arena below. The mob roared its approval. So magnificent had been his gesture that for several moments his mother almost did not despise him. His election to the meaningless public office for which she had him campaigning was now assured.

A brigade of attendants moved hurriedly about the arena with rakes and wheelbarrows and fresh sand, collecting scattered limbs and torsos, and preparing for the next spectacle. The Master of the Games took charge. With the arena sense of over thirty years in the business, he knew that after what had just happened the next event had better be something strong. He had a large feather-bed wheeled out. Its appearance was greeted with loud applause.

A woman who had poisoned several of her in-laws at a banquet was to be raped by a trained zebra and then eaten alive by leopards. This number was an old favorite with the mob, and always warmly received.

Meanwhile Valorius was arranging a later meeting

with his gang of caitiffs and hellhounds. The reputed vampire seemed somewhat dazed by the strong sunlight; all the others watched him suspiciously.

Nobody they knew would ever throw away a fat purse just to save thirty lives. Valorius did not depend on their gratitude but on the solid chink of coin. Several of them laughed sardonically when he mentioned the Tiger, as if they knew the place all too well. Those that did not slink out the exits went up into the stands to watch the rest of the show.

A gang of sweating slaves toiled at the windlasses, lowering the elevator carrying Hannibal into the pits below. The Master of the Games took personal charge of this operation too. It turned out that he was Hannibal's owner. He had been making good money out of him for nearly ten years. Now he hoped to make a fortune.

Valorius at last agreed — verbally — to his terms, but refused to sign anything until he had a lawyer read it first. The Flavian Amphitheater was a reservoir of psychic energy; ready access to it might be important.

He lingered for a few minutes in the arcade at the east end of the arena. His shimmering blue cape and tunic made him conspicuous, but the mob had already forgotten him.

The multiple-poisoner of her in-laws was being exhibited naked to all and sundry. No sooner was she tied spread-eagle to the feather-bed at the center of the arena than a frisky-looking zebra pranced into the open. There was a great deal of good-natured ribaldry as he trotted lustily toward the feather-bed. All eyes were on the ensuing scene.

Perhaps not quite all. One set were fixed angrily on Valorius. They glittered with intelligence of a high order. As they watched him depart down the ramp, they narrowed with intense calculation.

# CHAPTER XI
## INVITATION TO A MYSTERY

Valorius was soon the toast of Rome, the most celebrated bestiarius in a century. Every palace, apartment building, shop, tavern, bath, and brothel in the
city and surrounding suburbs rang with his name. In
ever widening circles the news spread outward to the
provinces. There was no threat from Maximin, which
was about as close as he ever came to a compliment.
The lucrative contract Valorius signed with Volpinius
Rufus, Master of the Games, provided him with the
wherewithal to continue his search for Zenobia. There
he had no luck at all.

The waterfront district was known, appropriately
enough, as the "Wolf's Den." Over half the caitiffs and
hellhounds he had saved from execution actually
showed up at the Tiger. Night after night he sent them
prowling through every quarter of the city in search of
some clue as to the whereabouts of Magus Rex and
Zenobia. The only thing they ever discovered was how
to get more money out of him.

The fat, greasy tavern-keeper's wife showed him

more respect now, since most of his hired miscreants were old accomplices. Her husband was an ex-gladiator who knew how to bide his time until he found an opening. In fact, Valorius had the uneasy feeling that he was in the midst of a pack of ravening wolves just waiting for a chance to pounce. There were ominous signs of impatience at the speed with which they were getting his money out of him. And still no sign of Zenobia.

He was getting plenty of messages, all the wrong kind. The stars of the arena seldom lasted long. But while they lived there was nothing that the idle, dissolute populace of Rome did not offer them. Love, in every conceivable shape and hue, came panting after them from every conceivable direction.

Most notes came from rich women, whose panders and servitors flocked the performers' exit at the amphitheater from morning till night on game days. There were less creditable notes, such as those from effeminate young editors that he and Hannibal had helped elect to some worthless public office. They nearly all wanted to "thank him personally" for his services. Nonetheless he had to read every note. One of them might be from Zenobia.

Only once did he follow up on a note. The results of that interview altered his whole strategy. Millions of years hence it was to give him an insight into the career of Magus Rex that even the great wizard himself lacked. It was a strange interview indeed.

As the number-one box-office attraction in Rome, the notes descended on him like the flakes of a winter snowstorm. He learned to keep the note-bearers at bay by avoiding the performers' exit at the amphitheater and the open plazas where the little painted dolls held their afternoon promenades. He stayed close to the small flat he had taken as a sleeping room. The rest of his time, when not actually performing in the arena, he spent at the Tiger, directing his fruitless search for Zenobia.

Returning to his room one evening, after another

wasted session in the "Wolf's Den," he was surprised
to find someone waiting for him. He had never seen
the sleek little man before, but he was familiar by now
with the type. Professional panders had hounded him
since his first triumph in the arena. But this was the
first one enterprising enough to have traced him to his
flat.

He wore an elaborately curled wig; his face glowed
with a thick layer of cosmetics; his insinuating smile
was just too pearly to be believed, in more ways than
one. In the shadowy hallway it was impossible to
guess his age. Forty? Sixty? Coaxing, wheedling,
tantalizing, he promised delights that Venus herself
would have been hard put to deliver. Then he pro-
duced the inevitable sealed note.

Valorius sighed. It had been a long day. A morning
performance at the amphitheater; a long, grueling,
frustrating afternoon at the Tiger. Now another invitation to a tryst. But he did not dare pass up any
attempt to communicate with him. Zenobia would
hardly have employed such an emissary. On the other
hand, perhaps employing a man who had spent a
lifetime discreetly arranging secret trysts was the only
way she could avoid her father's vigilance. He broke
the seal on the note.

It was just the usual invitation. Wearily, he started
to hand it back to the meretricious little man. Then
something caught his eye. Carrying the note to the
lantern at the end of the hallway, he examined it
closely under the light. He could hardly believe his
eyes. But there was no doubt about it. The note had
been printed with movable type!

Valorius was thoroughly bewildered. He saw varia-
tions of this same note about eleven times a day on
the average. But movable type! Could it be Zenobia?
Was this some means of evading her father's injunctions against communicating with him, like the occult
verses that appeared out of thin air? It had to be
investigated.

The night-porter leered knowingly as they passed

his cage at the entrance. A curtained chair and eight stout bearers stood waiting in the street. The little pander drew aside the silk curtain, grinning up at him like a happy crocodile. Valorius hesitated. It was possible that Zenobia had arranged all this; it was equally possible that it had been arranged by Magus Rex. He had not forgotten the trap that had nearly cost him his life in the amphitheater. He decided to walk.

With link-boys running on ahead, the chair and its bearers wended their way up a hill rising out of the heart of the city. It was a hill of palaces. Valorius' knowledge of the topography of Rome was still rudimentary, but this could only be the Palatine. He walked at a safe distance behind the chair. The little pander had taken his place inside.

Near the top of the hill they halted before the gates of a palace. These opened like magic. The pander scrambled out of the chair and led the way through a series of fantastic gardens inside the walls. Valorius was now on his guard. These gardens were too much like those that surrounded the palace of Magus Rex to be an accident.

The interior decor was also suspiciously similar to the taste of Magus Rex. It resembled a dark museum. Rare paintings covered the walls; every niche and corner was filled with pagan statuary; the floors were a carnival of lovely mozaics. The bas-reliefs may have been Assyrian; the delicate faience-ware was definitely Egyptian. Grecian urns expressed flowery tales; huge marble eidolons alternated with fragile cameos, carved ivories, jades and porcelains. Hall after hall was crammed with the art treasures of the ancient world. The palace seemed endless. There was everything here but light.

Valorius widened the pupils of his eyes, or he would have had to grope in the darkness. The sleek little pander was so familiar with the palace that he did not need light to find his way. He had evidently been through here many times before.

An unseen censer filled the air with a musky, faintly

erotic perfume. It grew muskier and more erotic as
they proceeded through the dark, museum-like halls.

At last the pander halted before a curtain of onyx
beads. He coughed discreetly. A muffled voice said
something that Valorius did not quite catch. But the
pander understood.

"Please to enter, Valorius." He held the curtain aside
with oily politeness. "My mistress expects you."

Valorius stepped warily into the room. It was hardly
lighter than the halls behind him. A small taper fluttered
in a sconce of red crystal on the wall beside him; a
golden thurible, hanging from the ceiling, glowed with
a thousand tiny, watchful eyes. It filled the air with a
narcotic incense. He heard the clitter of onyx beads
behind him, and the discreet whisper of sandals as
the pander tiptoed away.

Widening the pupils of his eyes still further, he
became aware of an old woman reclining on a couch
in a dark corner. A wine ampulla and jeweled goblets
stood ready on a porcelain table beside her. She was
dressed and painted like a very young woman, although she was probably closer to eighty than seventy.
Had she known that he could see her in the dark, she
certainly would not have screwed up her face like that,
squinting at him through a large gem or piece of
quartz the way a weak-eyed old woman might have
squinted through a lorgnette centuries hence. She
seemed to like what she saw.

Valorius sighed. It had been a trap all right, but not
of Magus Rex's making. The fact that the old woman's
billet-doux had been printed with movable type was
probably just some inexplicable historical anachronism.
He decided to end the interview as politely as possible.

"Good evening, madam," he said, bowing formally.
"You have been good enough to honor me with your
attentions. How may I be of service to you?" He hoped
the question would not be taken literally.

The old woman was startled. She had probably
expected some barbarous accent, rather than the polished Latin of a well-educated poet. Her gardens, her

art treasures, the large rack crammed with scrolls just behind her couch, all revealed that she was a woman of taste and culture. Her morals were merely those of her time. It would be vulgar to let her continue to believe that he could not see her.

"That is an extremely attractive cestus you're wearing, madam," he observed. "Such delicate carving in so hard a stone as jade shows rare workmanship."

The woman gasped. The gem-stone she used as a lorgnette slipped from her hand and fell clattering to the tile floor. Instinctively she composed her heavily-painted face into an expression resembling that of a seductive mummy.

"Permit me, madam." He strode across the room and returned her gem-stone.

She seemed disconcerted that he could see her so well. Sharp eyes were not in her best interest. But she thanked him with elaborate courtesy, trying hard not to sound too much like a raven with asthma. Her claw-like fingers brushed the back of his hand invitingly.

"Won't you take some wine, Valorius?" She reached for the long-necked ampulla at her side. "I should dearly like to know how you can face that great brute of an elephant day after day. The mere thought of it simply terrifies me." And she gave a girlish little shudder of fright which she had been using with great success for the better part of a century.

"No thanks, mother," he said gently. "I'll take no wine from that bottle."

He was afraid that she would be angry. But she merely sighed, replacing the ampulla on the porcelain table beside her. For a moment she looked sad, seeming to recall a time when she had no need of drugged wines, narcotic incenses, or darkened rooms. Then she shrugged, and an impish grin wrinkled her face.

"At least you didn't call me grandmother. That's some consolation." She reached for a bellcord hanging behind the couch. "You are obviously more than just another beautiful barbarian, Valorius. I am curious."

A servant slipped into the room through the onyx

curtain. The old woman ordered candles and refreshments.

"This wine you will enjoy," she assured him. "It is a vintage Falernian, and I shall drink from the same bottle. Since you are evidently not inclined toward anything more intimate than conversation," she added impishly, "you might at least grant that solace to a lonely old woman. Please be seated."

Put in such a way, it would have shown a barbarous lack of courtesy to just walk out. A polite goblet or two could do him no harm. Besides, there was always the chance that he might hear something that would eventually lead him to Zenobia. This was a woman of great wealth and refinement. If Magus Rex was still in Rome, he would not be living in the slums.

The tale she told him was one of the most incredible he had ever heard. The dry bones of civilization that peek distortedly out from the chronicles and histories of past ages give but a poor hint of what the vibrant living society was like. If Rome was the history of war and empire, splendor, expansion, madness, and decline, it was also a lost kaleidoscope of millions and millions of human lives, picturesquely living out their own forgotten histories of birth, death, love, family, triumph, despair, hatred, cruelty, adventure, kindness and mystery. Valorius now heard one such history, a history no one had bothered to record.

When the wine and candles were brought, and he had readjusted the pupils of his eyes, he realized how really beautiful the woman must once have been. She seemed shy at first, as if afraid of his contempt for the mummified ruin she knew herself to be. But he showed no sign of contempt or loathing (which she had experienced more often than she cared to remember in recent years); only a kind of patient curiosity that encouraged her to talk about herself. Also, there was something in his shimmering blue eyes that belied his youthful countenance, a breadth of forehead that seemed strangely inharmonious with his athletic build and position in the arena. It reminded her of someone she had known long, long ago.

She had been a temple acolyte on one of the Greek Isles. Pirates had captured her during a raid and sold her in the slave market on Delos. A Roman merchant had bought her, a girl of fourteen, as a speculation. He sent her to the best dancing school in Rome. She had beauty, a good mind and disposition, and had been well educated. He hoped to turn a fat profit when he resold her. She also had a sense of humor, and her pranks kept his household in continual turmoil. Despite this, he received a number of substantial bids for her. But he did not sell her. He was a sharp dealer, and he knew that her market value was increasing every day.

He was also a gambler, one of the most successful in Rome. He played for high stakes and usually won. One night, however, he lost over half his vast fortune to a man named Mirarius. The merchant was in despair; never had he had such an incredible streak of bad luck. Then Mirarius made him an unheard-of proposition: he would bet everything he had won thus far against just her, on one cast of the dice. Needless to say, the merchant jumped at the chance: he could have bought her a hundred times over for what he had already lost. The dice were cast. Again Mirarius won.

Overnight she became the talk of Rome; and for the next decade she reigned as the most admired courtesan of her day. Mirarius acquired a huge fortune, gambling and investing; his horses always won, his ships always came home. He took her traveling throughout the world. Mirarius was a great scholar, and spent years of study in the libraries of Rome, Athens, Pergamum and Alexandria. His collections of art treasures were those that now filled her palace.

It had lasted ten years, a decade-long saturnalia of love and study and adventure. Then one day he told her that he had to leave. He transferred to her his entire vast fortune. No one, not even she, knew where he had come from; she did not know to this day where he had gone. He just selected a few choice pieces of art, then — disappeared.

"And though I found it prudent to marry into the nobility — my last husband died long before you were born, Valorius — I've lived here ever since." She filled his goblet with the last of the Falernian. "Thanks to my early schooling, and the years of study with Mirarius, I acquired a taste for reading. My library, as you may guess from this small portion of it, is large and comprehensive. The fortune he left me is so vast and cunningly diversified that not even the exactions of several emperors have hurt it. Many years have passed — I won't tell you how many, Valorius, or you really will start calling me grandmother — but I have wanted for nothing. Except, perhaps, eternal youth. It is a pity," she added, more to herself than him, "that the body dies so much faster than the mind or desires."

She squinted at him for a moment, hesitated, then with a little shrug like a tiny bird ruffling its feathers, she held the gem-stone to her eye. In the candle light, he could see that is was a piece of quartz naturally warped in such a way that it provided some degree of magnification. She squinted at him through it for several moments.

When at last she lowered her "lorgnette" there was a strange, almost frightened, look on her face. She drank from her goblet with an unsteady hand, blinking rapidly.

"You have listened patiently to an old woman's tale, Valorius," she said in a whisper. "Perhaps I am in my dotage, or I have had more wine than is good for me, but you remind me strangely of him."

"Him?"

"Mirarius. Not in appearance, but in something about the eyes. I'll never forget that look, not if I live to be a hundred. Which," she sighed, "I very nearly have. One would think that a woman my age would know better." She grinned impishly at him. "But it seems that I don't. Would you like some more wine? I don't think I'd better have any more myself."

"Thank you, no," he said. His patience in listening to her tale had not been completely disinterested. She was sure to be well informed on affairs in Rome—as a matter of self-preservation, if for no other reason. She could open many doors; perhaps one of them would lead to Zenobia. But he was still wary. The last door that had been opened for him led straight to the blood-drenched sands of the amphitheater. "You've given me a very entertaining evening." He rose to depart.

"It's been most entertaining for me as well, Valorius. Although," she grinning more impishly than ever, "not quite the kind of entertainment I had hoped for."

They both laughed at this, now completely relaxed in each other's company. Whoever this strange Mirarius had been, he certainly had had a fine taste in women. What a treasure she must have been in her youth! But there was still something he was curious about. He took the printed billet-doux from his belt.

"How was this done?" he asked. "It was surely printed with movable type."

All this time she had been reclining in Roman fashion on her couch. But now she sat bolt upright, staring speechlessly at him. For a moment he was afraid that he had frightened her into some kind of fit.

When he finally got her to relax, the truth came out. It was this strange Mirarius again. While imprecating on a shoddily copied text in the library at Antioch, he had dropped a careless remark about the advantages of movable type. She never forgot anything he said. Years after he had disappeared she had had a Greek artificer carve a set of type out of lead. The Greek died shortly afterward (she did not say how), and she had kept the invention secret ever since.

"And it has been extremely useful, Valorius," she nodded sagely. "I can print love letters by the score, without them ever coming under the eyes of untrustworthy servants. The saving in time, the vastly increased size of my audience, and the neat, error-free nature of the compositions have given me a decisive advantage over all my rivals. You won't let the secret get out, Valorius, will you? Handwriting is very difficult for me now."

He assured her that her secret was safe—for another thousand years to come. This was the second greatest irony of time he had discovered here tonight: that an aging courtesan should use the invention of printing merely to give herself an advantage over her rivals. The secret would die with her. The greatest irony was the fact that he was actually older than she was. If he remained in Rome long enough he would eventually look older—although his present occupation did not threaten him with any kind of longevity.

She had no idea where Mirarius had learned about movable type. He had spoken of many marvels during their years together.

"He was the most wonderful man I've ever met," she added. (Which, Valorius guessed, was probably saying a lot.) "That's why I get so angry when I hear this charlatan, Arcanius, being compared to him." Her fists clenched like the talons of an angry sparrow.

"Arcanius?"

"The so-called *Second Mirarius*," she said contemptuously. "At least that's what the clowns and Goths of society have taken to calling him. Just because he affects long violet fingernails! How absurd!"

Valorius was stunned. "You mean the original Mirarius had long violet fingernails too?"

There was soon no doubt about the identity of the Second Mirarius, a successful gambler with a beautiful daughter who was unusually tall by Roman standards. But what about the first Mirarius? Had Magus Rex traveled through millions of years of time to live with this woman when she was young, probably during the reign of Marcus Aurelius? It seemed that the ironies of time were endless. He left the palace with his head spinning over the possibilities.

The only thing he now knew for certain was that his gang of caitiffs and hellhounds were bilking him. Magus Rex and Zenobia were in Rome, or had been until the last week or two. This should have been easily discovered. But were they still in Rome? He made his own discovery the very next morning.

It was another game day. The Flavian Amphitheater was packed as usual; but now the crowd contained thousands of the idle rich, who came early to see this new wonder of the rabble. Bucyrus was still their champion; their applause for Hannibal was skimpy and condescending. Valorius was put on his mettle to give them a good show.

It was the woman with the violet hair that attracted his attention. She was seated in the imperial podium, wearing a temple treasury of gold and precious gems. Great piles of brilliantly violet hair shimmered like spun silk above her enameled face. It was the same color as Magus Rex's fingernails; it was also the same color as the veil worn by the woman who had almost lured him to his death on his first morning in Rome. He found it difficult to concentrate on Hannibal.

As he appeared before the imperial podium at the close of his act he got a closer look at the woman. She was already the center of a great deal of attention. He suddenly became aware of the young woman seated at her side. She was dressed modestly in a tunic of Indian cotton; her head was covered with a simple linen shawl, her face with a veil of Sidon gauze. As the violet-haired painted doll at her side turned to exchange compliments with some aristocratic friends, she lowered her veil. It was Zenobia!

His concentration was now completely broken. A portal stood open at the far end of the moat. He could be at her side in an instant. But she shook her head and quickly replaced her veil. The message was clear: do not try to approach me now, it is too dangerous.

At that moment the little painted doll turned back. She thought that Valorius was staring at her. She simpered and twirled her green silk parasol coquettishly. Even the renowned Valorius was smitten with her! This was one of the best days she had ever had.

Then he became aware of titters breaking out all over the imperial podium. Neighbor nudged neighbor, nodding toward Hannibal. As the news spread through the stands there were shouts of laughter. The effeminate young man who was the editor of this morning's spectacle seemed embarrassed about something. His mother, seated at his side, glared daggers at Valorius.

All this time Hannibal had been kneeling nearby, writing in the sand. But Valorius had been too distracted by the sight of Zenobia to give him his full attention. The editor had paid handsomely to have the epithet PATRON OF THE ARTS written in two-foot letters next to his name. Hannibal had made a grammatical error: he had written "patrona" instead of "patronus." PATRONESS OF THE ARTS.

"You can't fool Hannibal!" shouted the crowd.

It was a dangerous situation. To offend a wealthy Roman matron could result in lions and tigers. They were mistresses of their own fortunes, and ruled their husbands with rods of iron. Some rich women married so often that they were said to reckon time not by the names of the consuls but by the names of their husbands. The woman glaring down at Valorius had not paid to have her effeminate son mocked.

He acted quickly. First he had Hannibal correct his grammatical error, rewriting "patronus" in the sand. Then he led him on an impromptu circuit of the arena. Everywhere they stopped he had him write, HANNIBAL PRO Q. SULPICIUS (the name of the effeminate young editor). This won great popularity for Q. Sulpicius, and later won him election to a meaningless public office over two equally worthless rivals. His mother seemed pleased.

She no longer glared daggers at Valorius when he once more stood before the imperial podium. Her look was much more inviting. So was her son's. But Zenobia and the woman with the violet hair were gone.

# CHAPTER XII
## MAY THE BETTER ELEPHANT WIN!

Valorius sat on the edge of his bed, gazing down into the teeming street below. It was not a game day. The afternoon sunlight mingled with the sounds and sights and smells of a doomed imperial city. Ordinarily he would have been at the Tiger by now, but he was getting discouraged by the lack of information gathered by his troup of spies. If they knew where to find the gambler Arcanius and his beautiful daughter, he realized they were certainly not going to tell him if it meant the end of their funding.

He toyed with the note in his hand: another obscene invitation. Then he rose and tossed it into the hamper in the corner. But the hamper was already filled to overflowing with such invitations, and the note fell on the floor. He ignored it. For the next hour he paced restlessly back and forth.

To make matters worse, the Master of the Games, Volpinius Rufus, was insisting that he change his act. The mob demanded novelty. The spectacle of Hannibal traipsing obediently around the arena like the family

pooch was beginning to pall. Valorius had never given
much thought to his act; to him it merely provided the
wherewithal to continue his search for Zenobia, and
kept him close to the major reservoir of psychic energy
in Rome. Now he had to improve it and he was not
sure he knew how.

He stopped pacing and headed for the door. His
whole situation was deteriorating rapidly. He needed
help. There was only one person since his arrival in
Rome who had acted toward him in good faith.

The patrons of the Quill were all more or less poets.
Small legacies, public readings, and the sporadic
patronage of the rich maintained them in cultured idle-
ness. Military service had long since been lifted from
their flimsy shoulders. On the frontier, a thousand
miles away, barbarians in the service of Rome were
fighting barbarians not in the service of Rome. But
here at the Quill, all was serene.

"Why, Valorius!" cried Titus Lengo, shaking his
hand. "You've become quite famous. Your name is
bruited everywhere these days. I haven't actually had
a chance to see you perform yet myself." He smiled
apologetically. "But I'm sure your act is, uh, well
worth seeing."

He introduced several of his feckless colleagues.
None of them had seen the act either, although they
were all polite and good-natured about it. Valorius
quickly realized that they were Bucyrians to the last
poetaster.

"Gentleman," he said in an accent that surprised
them with its purity, "if you don't mind the company
of a poor bestiarius from the amphitheater, I'd like to
buy you a drink. Tavernkeeper, drinks all around!"

There is no authenticated account, in any land or
time, of a poet ever turning down a free drink. The
tavernkeeper's ladle bobbed in and out of his amphorae like a hungry duck over a pan of grubs. This gave
Valorius a chance to draw Titus Lengo aside. An agreement was quickly reached.

The timid, balding poet still felt obligated toward

him for his generosity the first time they met. Like
many feckless, good-natured people he was only effec-
tual on behalf of others. With Titus Lengo acting as
his agent, Valorius' fortunes improved overnight.

The crew at the Tiger grumbled and threatened, but
their efficiency improved wonderfully. Titus Lengo
offered a reward for information, and cut off all other
subsidies.

It was the reputed vampire who claimed the reward.
He discovered that the gambler Arcanius lived with
his daughter in a palace in the suburbs. Unlike those
on the Palatine Hill, the palace of Arcanius was
inaccessible. Surrounded by high walls, it was constantly patrolled by a small army of watchmen and
watchdogs. If Arcanius was indeed Magus Rex, Valorius
knew that these would be the least of his defenses.

The reputed vampire, as always somewhat dazed,
claimed to have actually seen Zenobia seated with the
woman with the violet hair in the peristyle garden at
the center of the palace. How he had gotten past the
walls, dogs, and watchmen he did not say. But his
information seemed accurate, and Valorius paid him
the reward. He wandered off into the night still looking
somewhat dazed.

Valorius was in as much of a quandary as ever.
What had Magus Rex been up to all this time? After
the first attempt to have him slaughtered by Hannibal,
the great wizard had made no further move against
him. Even that trap had been crude and uncharacteristic; so crude and uncharacteristic in fact that Valorius
could almost have believed that somebody else had
been responsible—had that been possible. Perhaps it
had just been a fit of wizardly pique, later regretted.
But even that was uncharacteristic. Magus Rex was a
millennarian rake. Everything he did was coldly logical.
Even his sometimes rather occult pleasures were cal-
culated and self-aware.

Nor had he any more idea now of what Zenobia
was trying to do than when he first left the forests of
Antarctica. Did she think she could somehow soften

her father toward him? If that was her plan, it did not seem to be working. Having him torn to pieces by a raging bull elephant showed that the softening process had a long way to go. There were many questions he would like to ask but, although he now knew where to find Zenobia, he had no opportunity to ask them.

Titus Lengo had renegotiated his contract with Volpinius Rufus. By researching the accounts of the great bestiarii of the past, especially the great Carpophorus of whom the poet Martial had written so elegantly, he had also helped Valorius prepare a new act.

The Flavian Amphitheater was packed from morning until night. Valorius now had to perform for both the bloodthirsty rabble in the morning and the more refined sadists and degenerates in the afternoon. Ticket prices were raised. There was of course a riot over this; the experienced Volpinius Rufus suppressed it so adroitly that scarcely a hundred people had to be killed. Valorius' renown soon surpassed even that of the most famous gladiators and charioteers.

His first appearance at an afternoon spectacle was treated with cold disdain. These well-washed aristocrats prided themselves on their enlightened attitude toward the arena. Needless to say, they were all Bucyrians. Hannibal was considered a contemptible brute, and Valorius himself merely a low barbarian. The animal acts at the afternoon spectacle were usually feats of skill, not orgies of bloodshed. The bestiarii, especially Bucyrus' trainer, were respected professionals. Nearly all fallen gladiators who had put up a good scrap saw the crowd turn thumbs up.

Even bloodshed was handled with restraint. For instance, from time to time a naked girl was sent into the arena to be swallowed alive by a giant python. It was a specialty act, and never overdone. Many aristocrats were quite snobbish about it. Whereas the mob would only have howled for stronger stuff, they alone appreciated the finer points. For in these degenerate times there was only one giant python in all of Rome, and it took the snake over a month to digest a single naked girl. This lent the spectacle an ephemeral charm only appreciated by nobler natures.

Valorius knew that he could never hope to win the applause of such an audience with his morning act. Hannibal would have been hooted out of the arena. But thanks to the researches of Titus Lengo, he was a success. The aristocrats came to jeer, but they stayed to cheer. Not even the legendary Carpophorus ever created such a sensation.

While Valorius waited on the ramp, eight stentorian-voiced men with megaphones spaced themselves along the walls all around the arena. These were the announcers. When they announced his name, it was greeted with only contemptuous silence. Then the orchestra of flutes, drums, trumpets, horns, and an enormous hydraulic organ played the overture. The scarred and crippled old man opened the arena door for him.

He entered driving a silver chariot drawn by four huge Hyrcanian tigers. Given time to concentrate, he had learned how to control several animals at once, even though the psychic energy resources were lower at the afternoon spectacle. Like a skilled charioteer he made a triumphal circuit of the walls. There was some begrudging applause as he drove to the center of the arena and unleashed the tigers.

First he had them dance on their hind legs and perform some complex acrobatic feats. Slowly he was winning the crowd over. Then he had an attendant release a hare, a piglet, a duck, and a goose, sending the four Hyrcanians coursing in pursuit. Each brought back its respective prey unharmed, held gingerly in its savage jaws. The hare, the piglet, and the duck were scared senseless. But the goose was still full of fight, ready to take on all four tigers at once. This provided some unexpected comic relief, and won Valorius great applause. By the end of the performance even the most aristocratic of the audience had moderated their sneers.

With Titus Lengo's help, he was able to vary his act so that nearly every performance saw some fresh novelty. Three centuries of bloody spectacles, on which half the revenues of a vast empire were expended, had exterminated much of the wildlife on three adjacent continents. Antiquarians might sigh for the good old days, but there was still enough material for a good show. Wolves and bears were still plentiful; it was still possible to find ample numbers of auroches, ostriches, hyenas, leopards, lions and tigers. There was even an old polar bear and a pair of three-hundred pound orangutans. But not a single rhinoceros could be found for the arena, and the hippos and man-eating crocodiles were now reserved for the naumachia across the river. Condemned criminals and various political and social offenders made ample compensation, however.

These unfortunates were largely reserved for the morning show. Neither Titus Lengo nor Volpinius Rufus saw anything untoward in having a batch of criminals slaughtered by Hannibal. The vicious, bloodthirsty mob demanded a vicious, bloodthirsty spectacle—or watch out! Valorius had no choice but to give the crowd what it wanted. His act was simply a variation of his initial performance. Hannibal was first allowed to rage among the condemned, pulping and dissecting in his old manner. Then Valorius "tamed" him, and had him write democratic slogans in the sand in vulgar Latin. But at the advice of Volpinius Rufus he no longer had Hannibal solve arithmetic problems. The mob tended to resent having an elephant work sums they could not work themselves.

Bucyrians still attended the morning show in small numbers. They sniffed their perfumed handkerchiefs disdainfully as Hannibal rampaged through the arena below. With an exaggerated politeness that should have warned them, the mob always encouraged them to take the best seats in the house. In fact, it was an inside joke to get aristocrats who had never attended a morning show before to move as close as possible to the arena wall. Hardly a performance went by without one or two perfumed Bucyrians being snatched from the top of the wall by Hannibal. Volpinius Rufus did not go out of his way to warn them. The spectacle of an aristocrat being tossed thirty feet into the air and then pulped or dissected was a great crowd-pleaser, and nobody could blame the Master of the Games. Many said that the look of surprise on their faces alone was worth the price of admission.

Valorius' greatest danger came not in the arena itself, but below it. It was not to be expected that his rival bestiarii would take his sudden rise to stardom lying down. Especially the star he had eclipsed: Bucyrus' trainer, a wily little Greek. Cages were left open, shutes left unlocked; the animals in his act were secretly goaded and tormented before being sent into the arena. He was constantly on guard, but it was through Hannibal that his enemies finally got to him.

Despite his wealth and fame, he had kept his small flat. He had just started to set his defenses up before going to bed one night when he heard an anxious knock at the door. It was Titus Lengo.

"Oh, it's terrible!" the poet wrung his hands. "Hannibal. You've got to come. . . . In all honesty, I've never really. . . . But this is terrible!"

Valorius hurried with him to the amphitheater. The Colossus loomed above them in the moonlight like a lost Titan. The pits below the arena were a bedlam of growls and snorts and hisses. Torches cast a feverish glow about Hannibal's enclosure.

"He's been poisoned," said Volpinius Rufus.

The great brute lay on his side, scarcely breathing. One of his attendants was missing. The other two looked hardly more alive than Hannibal, trembling with fear that they might be held responsible. It was too late for any kind of antidote.

Instead of calling for medicines, Valorius called for a stool. Only by keeping the huge heart beating until the poison was eliminated by natural metabolic processes could Hannibal be saved. Valorius sat beside him all through the night, rapt in concentration.

Meanwhile Volpinius Rufus tried mightily to suppress the news, sending messengers flying in all direc-

tions to say that Hannibal was merely sick. But
apparently somebody had acted before him. By morning all Rome knew that Hannibal had been poisoned.

Bucyrus wrote in Greek; his trainer was a Greek.
Who else could have been the poisoner? The mob
forthwith stormed the Greek quarter, raping, looting,
and burning. The Jewish quarter was also pillaged.
What the Jews had to do with it was never explained —
except perhaps that they were generally more clever
and enterprising than the Romans. Besides, they had
women to rape, shops to loot, and houses to burn.
What better excuse than the poisoning of an elephant?

The raping and burning were quickly surpressed by
the Praetorian Guard, and the looting returned to
more official channels. But the lines between the
Hannibalian and Bucyrian factions were now irre-
vocably drawn. Rome hovered on the brink of civil
war.

A decision had to be made quickly, but Maximin
was a good two weeks away by imperial relays. Although Rome was topheavy with officials, no decision
of any importance was ever handed down before the
emperor's opinion was known. The wages of initiative
were a rendezvous with lions and tigers in the arena.
But civil war could result in the same thing. The
spineless ineffectuals holding the once-mighty offices
of consul, praetor, quaestor, aedile, and tribune put
their curled and pomaded heads together. Their solu-
tion was rather clever.

It was obvious that both elephants should temporarily be sent into exile. But that might not be the way
Maximin looked at it. So they found an elderly senator
who was on his deathbed, and who had no living
relatives subject to reprisals. They elected him Dictator.
Then every consul, praetor, quaestor, aedile, and tribune in Rome immediately left to worship the Genius
of the Divine Maximin at distant shrines. The new
Dictator would order the necessary exiles in their
absence.

The moribund senator had other ideas. Since he

was already dying, he had nothing to fear from either
the emperor or his spineless officials. He decided to
go out big. Cackling with senile delight, he handed
down his own decision.

Rome was stunned. It was beyond the wildest
dreams of the mob. Aristocrats wrung their hands in
despair; then bet every denarius they could lay those
very hands on. It was to be a fight to the death,
Hannibal versus Bucyrus! May the better elephant win!

Unlike the moribund Dictator, Volpinius Rufus had
living relatives. The command came while he was
filling out his "card" of gladiatorial and animal spectacles that would precede the main event. He sighed and
threw down his quill. He had been half expecting it
for some time now. But it would have to come today of
all days!

But Volpinius Rufus, old hand that he was, recovered
quickly and acted to maximize profits and absolve
himself from any and all responsibility. He got his
orders to hold the bout put in writing. Then he raised
ticket prices exorbitantly. The protests over this were
hardly noticed amidst the continual battles between
rival Hannibalian and Bucyrian gangs that wracked
the city. Carpenters were set to work day and night,
erecting temporary stands and barricades. A full cohort of Praetorian Guards was assigned to guard each
contestant in the bout.

The moribund old senator had decreed that the
rival trainers would ride their respective elephants
into battle. Fortunes changed hands hourly in the
feverish betting that followed. Despite the fact that
the city was now under martial law, Hannibalian and
Bucyrian gangs made the streets unsafe. Armed guards
sealed off the floor of Valorius' apartment from the
throng of touts, tipsters, thrill-seekers, and would-be
assassins besieging the building. Nobody but the Master of the Games himself was permitted inside.

"I have a message for you, Valorius," said Volpinius
Rufus, looking rather embarrassed. "It's from my sister."

Valorius broke the seal on the note. It was just

another invitation to a banquet tonight, the eve of the big contest. He could have papered his wall with the invitations he had already received. It seemed that Rome would be one continual banquet tonight.

"I'm afraid I don't know your sister, Volpinius Rufus," he started to refuse as politely as possible. "The note is unsigned, and I—"

"Oh, it's from Volpina all right. You mean you've never heard of Volpina?" He looked at him in disbelief. "I thought everybody knew Volpina. In fact, I'm surprised she hasn't contacted you by now. Especially after the way you stared at her the day Hannibal made the mistake writing in the sand."

"Does your sister have violet hair?" cried Valorius.

"Yes, that's her latest color," he sighed. "Used to be red. But in spite of all the notoriety," he hastened to his sister's defense, "she's still way above all her rivals. She's as rich or richer than any of them, but while they're almost all vicious or depraved, she's never slipped below cultured decadence. At least, not often. It's the times, not Volpina."

Valorius looked doubtfully at the note again. The address was different from that of the gambler Arcanius and his beautiful daughter.

"Oh, yes," said Volpinius Rufus. "I was told to mention the name of a city when I gave you that."

"A city?"

"It's in the east. Sometimes I get leopards and hyenas shipped from there. It's called Palmyra."

Valorius quickly wrote a note of acceptance. He could not remember exactly when Zenobia, the fabled Queen of the East, had reigned in Palmyra. Perhaps she was just a child now, playing her little girl's games and completely unaware of the destiny that would one day lead her to defy the entire Roman Empire, almost bringing it to its knees. His own Zenobia was defying an even greater power, Magus Rex. Having a friend mention the name of a city was not, strictly speaking, communicating with him. But it was skating awfully close to the letter of her father's injunction.

Bathed and groomed like a Roman dandy, he left his flat just after sunset. He refused the armed escort provided by Volpinius Rufus. His famous shimmering blue cape and tunic made him conspicuous, but the wretches prowling the dark, deserted streets were Hannibalians to the last cutthroat. They were sure to have bets on him. He needed no other protection.

There were relays of link-boys waiting for him at the corner of Volpina's street. But they did not escort him to the front gate. A Greek butler met him at the garden door and led him to a side entrance. An elegant Syrian took him from there, leading him through a maze of dim corridors to a private antechamber. Valorius was still on guard against possible treachery. The Syrian asked him to wait in a lisping voice and discreetly retired.

# CHAPTER XIII
## VOLPINA'S BANQUET

The gorgeous trappings reminded him of the apartment of the old courtesan. But there were no books here. Candles burned in cressets of rose crystal, spreading a seductive warmth through the antechamber. A golden thurible perfumed the air with exotic musk. An embroidered silk curtain was drawn across the entrance to the main apartment beyond.

Suddenly the curtain was drawn aside. In the rose-colored light her hair was more lavender than violet. Of all the little painted dolls he had seen in Rome she was easily the most splendid. She stood a good inch or two over five feet; her figure was voluptuous and well-proportioned. A lavender tunic of Sidon gauze fell in pleats to her exquisite little ankles, leaving just enough to the imagination to be more alluring than nakedness.

There was a light placed strategically in the chamber behind her against which she silhouetted herself. The effect was ravishing. With a graceful flick of the wrists she closed the curtain behind her, and glided toward him with mincing little steps.

"Welcome to my house, Valorius," she said in a voice of husky seductiveness that had been achieved by screaming in the vaults under the palace.

Valorius bowed and stammered clumsily. She seemed to enjoy his confusion. It was a scene made to order for a veteran temptress.

Her smile was warm, inviting; her dark eyes alluring, submissive. She looked about thirty, which meant that she was probably a good ten or twenty years older. Her face was expertly painted, perfectly complementing the color of her hair and tunic. Earrings, brooches, armlets, anklets, rings, bracelets, and pendants were distributed lavishly about her person. She held a fan of peacock feathers over the nakedness beneath her gauze tunic in such a way that his eyes were unconsciously drawn to every voluptuous curve of her body. For a moment he forgot all about Zenobia.

So rapt was his gaze that he scarcely noticed the discreet cough that sounded in the darkness outside the antechamber. But its effect on Volpina was electric. She gasped in fright. Her practiced coquetry vanished in an instant. She grabbed his arm like a fishwife grabbing an eel, and pulled him into the chamber behind her. He was too startled to resist; there was a look of genuine terror in her eyes. Yet she seemed to be enjoying herself too. With a frantic gesture she cautioned him to silence and closed the curtain, leaving him alone in the room.

He listened intently, but there was not a sound. Was this another trap? There were some rather interesting devices of padded leather on the marble table, but nothing he could use to defend himself. He tiptoed back to the curtain and listened.

The antechamber beyond suddenly erupted with a babble of voices, mostly Volpina's. She wheedled and pleaded excitedly with someone. His voice was muffled by the curtain, but Valorius thought he recognized it. The curtain was suddenly jerked aside and he found himself standing face to face with Magus Rex.

He was dressed in an impeccable white toga. His
hair was pomaded and combed forward in the Roman
manner; his black silky beard was elegantly barbered.
He was quite possibly the most distinguished-looking
man in Rome. But Valorius had never seen him taken
so completely unawares. It was as if he were genuinely surprised to see him here in Rome.

"I'm not really happy to see you here, Valorius," he
said at last, regaining his composure. "How on earth
you ever managed it—"

"You're not angry with your Volpina, are you,
beloved?" she cried. "Can you really believe that I
would deceive you?"

"Yes, to both questions," said Magus Rex.

She wailed and postured and waved her peacock
fan wildly about, the very picture of theatrical despair.
Then she fell histrionically to her knees and threw up
her arms in supplication.

"You're not going to beat me!" she cried hopefully.

The blush on Magus Rex's face may only have been
the effect of the rose-colored lights. He looked down at
her for a moment. She continued to wail and wring
her hands in terror.

"Restrain yourself, Volpina!" He lifted her to her
feet. "Your guests are beginning to arrive. Go see to
their comforts, and send my daughter to me."

Volpina did not argue. Whether she was anxious to
carry out his commands or to relate what had just
happened to her friends (and rivals), she left without
another word.

Nor did Magus Rex say anything until Zenobia
appeared. She was dressed in barbaric finery that
made even Volpina look dowdy by comparison. She
had curled her auburn tresses just enough so as not to
look conspicuous among the fantastic hair styles affected by Roman women. But her face was her own.
Her dark almond-shaped eyes shone warmly as she
glided across the antechamber and took Valorius by
the hand.

Magus Rex remained deep in thought for several

minutes. Only when the young couple's propinquity threatened to go beyond the hand-holding stage did he rouse himself.

"That will be enough of that!" He motioned Zenobia away. "Now pay attention to me, the pair of you. There's some skulduggery afoot, and I mean to get to the bottom of it."

"But, Father—"

"Not a word! Now, first of all, my darling daughter, have you disobeyed my injunctions against communicating with Valorius?" He hovered over her like a thunderhead ready to explode with all the force of nature. The candles dimmed. The air crackled with energy.

"No, Father," she answered without batting an eye. "I have obeyed your injunctions to the last letter."

The storm subsided. Magus Rex seemed more puzzled than displeased.

"Now there's no way Valorius could have traced us here without your help." He slowly stroked his black silky beard, a look of begrudging appreciation in his eye. "And yet you're not lying to me."

"The entertainment awaits your signal, Arcanius." Volpina had appeared at the door. "The dice-players are already at the gaming table. It should be a profitable evening for you." Before Magus Rex could say a word she swept across the room and took Valorius by the arm. "In the meantime, I shall present our famous bestiarius to my guests. All Rome awaits the outcome of tomorrow's contest, Valorius."

Magus Rex had little choice but to bring up the rear with Zenobia. His heavy-lidded eyes narrowed vindictively. This boded ill for the players awaiting him at the gaming table.

This was the first full-fledged banquet Valorius had ever attended, despite the hamperful of invitations. From the way Volpina flaunted him before her guests, and the cold looks he got from some of her rivals, it was not unlikely that some of the senders of those invitations were here tonight. All the guests were wear-

ing garlands of roses, which were believed to delay the
onset of drunkenness.

Volpina placed a similar garland around his neck
as they entered the banquet hall. A velvety haze composed of the fumes of cooking, lamps, wines, the
perfumes and pomades of the other guests, the roses
around his neck and the garden of blossoms scattered
on the floor and tables engulfed him. The effect was
almost overpowering.

The Romans dined in reclining positions. Three
sloping couches were set around each marble table,
the fourth side of which was left open for service.
Each couch held three guests, men and women reclining indiscriminately side by side, thus each table held
a comfortably intimate dinner party of nine. While
Volpina gloated over her coup in getting the famed
Valorius for her banquet, Zenobia made some subtle
reclining arrangements.

The dice-players looked relieved when Volpina at
last called them to the couch for dinner. The man
known as Arcanius had wasted no time in bankrupting
a Spanish speculator. While the other gamesters filed
into the banquet hall, the ruined Spaniard hurriedly
left the palace—presumably to rush home and open
his veins.

That left thirty-five guests reclining about the four
marble tables, but there was enough food to have fed
a Pannonian Legion. The banquet was presided over
by a professional carver, called the "dancer." The name
was apt. Wielding an incredible assortment of razor-
sharp knives and cleavers, he whirled and leaped and
postured amidst a battery of sideboards, each groan-
ing beneath a bewildering menagerie of cooked animals.
Valorius identified a roasted boar nearly the size of a
pony, some roasted ducks and peafowl, and what was
probably a boiled calf. He was not so sure about the
other cooked animals.

He found himself on a couch between Volpina and
her arch rival, a fiftyish little harpy named Lucilla.
While course followed course and goblet followed goblet,

the two rivals made much of him. They plied him with lobster, spiced peahen eggs, pomegranate seeds, dainty little sausages, and dormice dipped in honey and poppy seeds. The professional carver danced continually up to their table with joints and tidbits of every known edible fish, flesh, or fowl. Such fare would have broken the constitution of a centurion. Valorius noticed that from a whole course the banqueters would take only a few bites. The rest they threw on the floor.

Sandals were removed at table. While the two women plied him with goodies at one end, they played footsies with him at the other. Magnus Rex reclined on the couch of honor across from them. Even through the din and the merriment there could be heard from time to time the faint, ominous tattoo of long violet fingernails on the marble tabletop. Zenobia, reclining at his side, seemed much happier about the general course of events.

Valorius was embarrassed by the blandishments of the Roman belles. Nor did the huge quantities of strange food and drink he had to consume add to his comfort. As the courses and goblets progressed, so too did the cattiness of the women reclining on either side of him. Volpina was the cleverer of the two, and usually got the best of the exchanges.

Lucilla got a gobbet of goose down the wrong pipe and coughed violently.

"Take a deep breath and drink some wine, dearie," said Volpina. "You have to be careful, you know. Remember that time you coughed so hard at the theater and your poor husband spent the next act on his hands and knees searching for your teeth? Now just take a deep breath. That's right. And nobody's ever had to coax you to drink more wine, have they?"

When Lucilla finally stopped coughing she made a snide remark about violet-colored hair.

"Tell us, Lucilla dear," Volpina asked innocently. "Is the rumor true that you and your face are no longer sleeping together?"

Lucilla did much better in the matter of husbands.

She had recently married her eleventh, while Volpina was known to be unsuccessful as yet in her campaign to marry her tenth—the gambler Arcanius. Only when they were both required by nature to withdraw from the banquet hall did they call a truce. They agreed to retire together since neither would leave the other alone with Valorius. With a sense of relief he watched them depart, smiling amiably and displaying their veteran charms to best effect.

When he turned back he found Magus Rex glaring at him across the table, his heavy-lidded eyes mere slits.

"Even my sublime patience has its limits, you tom-catting nuisance. But," he shrugged, "once again I find my legendary equitableness on the line. My only con-solation, Valorius, is the thought that soon you will be an old Roman."

"It's really a shame the way Volpina is acting tonight," said Zenobia at his side.

"Yes, there's that too," Magus Rex sighed. "Volpina's carryings-on certainly haven't made my position any easier."

"In all fairness, Father, you have to admit that Valorius has shown great skill and enterprise in follow-ing us here. How can you fail to give him credit for his courage? And it's not his fault that Volpina is attracted to him."

"Tell me, my darling daughter, are you trying to use my sense of fair play as a weapon against me?"

"Oh, Father. I love Valorius, and—"

"All's fair in matters of the heart. Yes, yes, I won't argue with that—despite your egregious taste."

Valorius remained silent. He knew that nothing he could say or do would favorably impress Magus Rex. And Zenobia seemed to know what she was doing. He nibbled at a paté of nightingale livers.

"We've been happy in Rome, Father," said Zenobia. "This last year has been the most exciting of my life. There's so much more to see and do than I ever could have hoped from reading that dull old history book."

"The one by Gibbon? But you asked to bring it with you."

"Because I didn't know anything about ancient Rome. And there's still so much we haven't seen yet—"

"It won't work, Zenobia."

"I don't know what you're talking about, Father."

"But did you perhaps know all this time that the famous bestiarius Valorius was the same lout now so uncouthly sprawled before us upon yond triclinium?"

"Yes, Father."

"And you never told me—even when I teased you about the similarity in names."

"I would have if you had asked me."

"You remind me more of your mother every day, Zenobia." A strange faraway look flickered across his eyes.

"But we are going to stay in Rome for a while, aren't we, Father?"

"I think you know me better than that. I'm tempted to just return home and let Valorius find his way back the best he can." He held up his hand as Zenobia started to interrupt. "Yes, yes, I know I promised to show you the ancient world. And I fully intend to keep that promise. Rome has pleased me more than I had expected, although we are perhaps a generation or two past its vintage ripeness. That can't be helped now. But there are other ages ripe with decadence. They contain full as many attractions as Rome. More important, they do not contain Valorius."

"That's not really fair. Look what Valorius has done for my sake. He's crossed two million years of time, he's become the star of the Flavian Amphitheater, he's even dared—"

"To defy me, Magus Rex. That I grant you took a bit of daring. But as to his other accomplishments—Bah! And a circus is just where he belongs."

"How can you say that, Father?" Zenobia wheedled sweetly. "After all, you've never even seen Valorius perform."

Magus Rex chuckled in appreciation. "Now you've maneuvered me into a position where seeing the oaf's tricks would be the equitable thing to do, haven't you?"

"Yes, Father."

"What a treasure you are, my darling daughter. I see little danger of your ever becoming that most insufferable of all creatures, a sincere woman."

"But we will see the big bout tomorrow, won't we, Father?"

"Oh, all right," he said, quaffing from the golden goblet at his side. "We'll see the tuskers tussle, if you really want to. Who knows, we may have the pleasant surprise of seeing Valorius gored or stomped. But be prepared to depart at a moment's notice. Saying good-bye to Volpina is a treat I think I can bring myself to forego. In short, I don't want anybody to know we're leaving."

"Izelta will know," Zenobia nodded thoughtfully. "She always knows about such things."

Valorius stopped nibbling his paté of nightingale livers and listened attentively.

"She'll know no such thing," Magus Rex said impatiently. "Your Izelta has some knowledge of herbology, but she's nothing more than a common witch who makes her living as a professional poisoner. You vastly overrate her powers. I've let you visit her and her hideous cronies because all occult knowledge is useful. Besides, you seemed to have lost interest in your poetry. Do you still compose poetry, Zenobia?"

"Sometimes." She was careful not to look at Valorius.

"Well you'll have plenty of time for composition where we're going. But unless your Izelta is actually seated beside you at tomorrow's barbarous spectacle she won't know a thing."

"She never leaves her hovel beside the river," Zenobia said. "But she'll know just the same."

"You're up to something, aren't you?"

"Yes, Father. But I wouldn't dream of disobeying you."

"Dream all you want," he said ominously. "Just
don't do it."

The two rival belles returned to the couch. Or rather
Lucilla did. She seemed put out about something.
Volpina had taken the opportunity to change into an
even more revealing tunic. She was encouraging her
guests to greater efforts of gluttony. Some of them had
already made their first trip to the vomitorium, and
looked ready for another twenty courses. As Volpina
finally returned in her new tunic, which was hardly
more concealing than a fishnet, Valorius could not help
noticing that her violet-colored hair was not confined
to her head. Like Magus Rex, she was a perfectionist.

Lucilla soon drifted away. Rather than halving
Valorius' problems, it doubled them since Volpina
now had a clear field. It is never bad strategy for a
woman to provoke a man who seems a bit slow in
proposing marriage into a fit of jealousy. Once more
Valorius heard the tattoo of long violet fingernails on
the marble tabletop. Zenobia's eyes twinkled with
merriment.

At last Magus Rex gave up and returned to the
gaming table. His equitableness apparently did not
extend to his fellow gamblers. Or perhaps it did.
They were a sleazy-looking assortment of merchants
and speculators, mostly Greeks and Spaniards. And
it took a lot of denarii to maintain the palace of
Arcanius.

Volpina's blandishments subsided into little more
than a mild flirtation. That was enough to make her
rivals at the banquet envious, and she knew better
than to push Arcanius too far. But Valorius had no
chance to talk with Zenobia. Every time he started to
say something relevant, she quickly shook her head
and nodded toward the gaming table. Magus Rex's
injunctions were evidently still in effect.

The guests represented the full sexual spectrum.
There was not an eye that Valorius caught that did not
hold some lewd message. It was difficult to get notes
past Volpina, but the Romans were an ingenious people.

Zenobia seemed to be enjoying his embarrassment.
Magus Rex ignored them.

None of the sleazy-looking merchants and speculators he was fleecing had acquired their fortunes by
equitable means. Now they were losing them like magic.

At last Valorius left his couch and drifted toward
the gaming table. Zenobia was not allowed to talk to
him; Volpina's flirtations and the lewd winks and
invitations of her guests were getting on his nerves.
Besides, he needed a few minutes of intense concentration to put his digestive tract in order. The vicinity of
the gaming table seemed to be his only possible
sanctuary.

He stood a few feet away. Magus Rex still ignored
him. Nor did he seem to notice what was going on
among his fellow gamblers. Something was up. The
way they looked at each other and then at Magus Rex
indicated that some silent agreement had been reached.
They waited until he turned from the table to have his
goblet refilled.

The movement was so quick that Valorius himself
hardly noticed. Only from the size of the betting on
the next throw did he guess what had happened. A
pair of loaded dice had been slipped into the game.
Magus Rex took the cup from an oily African speculator.
He did not seem surprised by the size of the bets,
although every player had literally bet a fortune. He
covered them and cast the dice.

They rattled across the table and came to a stop,
quivering like jumping beans. Several players gasped.
It was the "throw of Venus," the highest possible
combination. Valorius marveled at the great wizard's
psychokinetic powers. There was hardly room on his
side of the table to stack his winnings. A wave of
desolation swept over the rest of the table.

Valorius decided it was time to go. The game could
not last much longer, and with it would go his sanctuary.
He started to cross the banquet hall when he suddenly felt himself being watched. He turned and found
himself looking right into the eyes of Magus Rex. One

look told him that he had better not say anything to
Zenobia. She smiled encouragingly as he bowed to her
from across the room.

Volpina quickly came to his rescue. It would be
unwise to taunt Arcanius any further, but if she couldn't
have the celebrated Valorius herself she didn't want
any of her guests to score the triumph. She led him
straight out of the banquet hall.

Valorius picked his way through the food littering
the floor. This was not easy because the mozaic design
represented a floor covered with scattered food. The
guests were misbehaving themselves in various ways.
Nearly all of them were drunk, roses or no roses. It
would have been difficult to leave without Volpina's
help.

She handed him over to the elegant Syrian who in
turn handed him over to the Greek butler. Roman
enterprise amazed him. There were actually two professional panders waiting for him in the street with
notes from two of the guests he had just left. They
were smooth and insinuating, but he had no trouble
outrunning them. Soon he had left even the link-boys
far behind.

Tomorrow would determine his fate. But there was
still work to be done tonight. He would need Titus
Lengo's help to find the witch Izelta and her hovel by
the river. He had no idea what Zenobia was up to, but
it might be his only chance of escape. He did not want
to end up an old Roman. Then, too, there were financial arrangements to be made.

It looked like the dice were stacked against him; like
Magus Rex he would need the highest possible combination to win. He turned the next corner and wended
his way downhill toward the waterfront. Someone at
the Tiger was sure to have heard of a professional
poisoner named Izelta.

# CHAPTER XIV
# THE THROW OF VENUS

Valorius knew that he should be concentrating on the ordeal before him, but his mind wandered back to last night's banquet. If he had loved Zenobia before, how could he describe his feelings for her now? Where in all the two million year history of mankind could he hope to find another like her? Let Magus Rex sneer at his "mooncalfery." Let him take Zenobia to the ends of time and space. Somehow he would follow. And perhaps someday—

"Valorius!" cried a distraught voice behind him. "There you are! Is everything ready?"

Valorius smiled. This was the seventh or eighth time that Volpinius Rufus had come running to him for reassurance. Being Master of the Games at the Flavian Amphitheater was a lucrative position—provided everything went well. He had been up half the night, checking and rechecking everything even remotely connected with today's program. Caged animals were positioned at the shutes and elevators. Veteran gladiators of every school stood dressed and

ready. Beautiful girls of every hue stood undressed
and ready. The band was well-rehearsed. A Greek had
just finished tuning the hydraulic organ. Every available sailor had been brought up from the fleet at
Micenum to position the colossal multi-colored awning that shaded the stands from the summer sun. Hot
chickpea vendors were already circulating through the
crowd. Everything that could be done had been done.
But the Roman mob was unpredictable, and there
was always the chance that the show would be a flop.
In which case the Master of the Games might find
himself enlivening the next performance. It had happened before.

"Do you think Hannibal will put up a good fight?"
he asked anxiously. "He still looks a little weak from
the poisoning. But he ate a whole bushel of melons
this morning. If he doesn't put on a good show—"

"Relax, Volpinius." Valorius patted him on the
shoulder. "Everything's just fine."

"Do you think we should start early?" he muttered,
more to himself than Valorius. "The place is already
packed. They might start tearing up the seats. . . . But
what if somebody important isn't here yet?" He rolled
his eyes distractedly. "But nobody's more important
than the mob. Not even the emperor. Yes, I think we'd
better start right now." He scuttled up a nearby ramp
still muttering to himself.

The fanfare reverberated from above. Muffled applause rumbled through the underground labyrinth
like distant thunder. Valorius hurried up the ramp to
take his place in the opening procession.

The Hannibalian mob shrieked like crazed savages
the moment he appeared. The Bucyrian aristocrats
sneered with cultured derision, applauding instead
for the wiry little Greek who was Bucyrus' mahout.
Waves of red and gold and amber billowed across the
sands of the arena as a light breeze ruffled the great
multi-colored awning. Seating capacity had been raised
to nearly eighty thousand, and it would not take an
especially agile lion or tiger to bound over the make-

shift barricades into the crowd. There was not an empty seat anywhere.

The colossal arena seethed like some nightmare bedlam of humanity. There was plenty of psychic energy here. Valorius knew that he might need every last vibration.

Like Volpinius Rufus, he too had been up half the night. His old gang of caitiffs and hellhounds were of course all Hannibalians, and all had money riding on him. He found several of them at the Tiger in various states of drunkenness. They were overjoyed to see his money again, but he had learned his lesson from Titus Lengo. Not a single denarius changed hands until he had actually gotten the information. Izelta's hovel was on the waterfront, not far from the Flavian Amphitheater. Politely but firmly removing the fingernails of the fat, greasy tavernkeeper's wife from his tunic, he bought a last round of drinks and departed. He hoped forever.

He had no trouble finding Titus Lengo. But the lawyers were not happy at being summoned in the middle of the night. The size of their fees, however, quickly reconciled them to late hours. He used the bulk of the fortune he had accumulated as a star bestiarius to buy annuities for Titus Lengo and his fellow poetasters at the Quill. The rest of the money was to be deposited in the safe of a certain goldsmith "until called for." He kept only two purses for himself. No matter where Magus Rex took Zenobia, a few gold coins might come in handy. There would also be expenses for his escape.

It was almost dawn before all his arrangements had been made. It was unlikely that Magus Rex would go backward in time—there were too many decadent ages in the millennia to come—but Valorius nonetheless made calculations for every possible contingency. Years might pass before another such concentration of psychic energy was available and then it would be too late. He was now ready for a quick departure from Rome.

The insane cheering of the mob drowned out even the eerie bellowing of the hydraulic organ. The colorful procession of gladiators, bestiarii, acrobats, and semi-naked girls slowly circled the arena. They halted at last before the imperial podium.

The moribund old senator was closer to ninety than eighty; he sat bundled to his ears despite the summer heat. But he had been elected Dictator, and his word was law. He leered down at them like a mad mummy.

Then he slowly raised his scrawny, arthritic hand. Silence fell upon the crowd. They did not know what to expect. A harangue? A donative of some kind? Perhaps even a last senile defiance of the emperor? But the withered old mummy just leered impudently around the arena. A hundred and sixty thousand eyes were on him, and he was evidently enjoying every moment of it. He was going out big, and he knew it. Never in his life had he received so much attention. The rug covering the pathetic little bundle of skin and bones that was his body trembled violently. At first it was thought that the excitement had been too much for him. Then those seated nearby realized that the old man was silently cackling with glee. Only when the mob showed signs of restlessness did he make a second feeble gesture. A roar shook the arena. The spectacle had begun.

The huge awning that gangs of sailors had hoisted up on the masts ringing the outer wall shaded all but the center of the arena. Into this patch of sunlight stepped six pairs of gladiators, brandishing their swords, bucklers, spears, nets, and tridents in life-and-death combat. Meanwhile, Valorius and the other performers filed back down the ramps leading to the underground labyrinth. Titus Lengo stood waiting.

"Here's the deposit voucher, Valorius," he said. "The goldsmith was overjoyed. It seems he's had some kind of bad luck lately."

Valorius carelessly slipped the voucher into his tunic. He was surprised at the guilty look on the little poet's face. But it was hard to believe that he had embezzled any of the money. Titus Lengo looked this way and that, disconsolate. At last he confessed.

"Please don't be angry with me." He could not look Valorius in the eye. "You've been so grand about the annuities and everything. Poets were appreciated in the days of the great Ennius, but it's so hard to make a living these days. I mean, and not lower your artistic standards or cater to the mob. And now. . . . Oh, I feel like such a traitor!"

"Tell me about it, Titus Lengo," Valorius said calmly.

"It was just a gesture. Please believe that it was nothing personal. But, well, I felt that I really had to take a stand. There's just too much irresponsibility these days, Valorius. People are afraid to stand up for what they believe. And even if it was only a gesture, I just had to do it." His voice dropped to a whisper. "I bet on Bucyrus."

Valorius patted him on the shoulder, just as he had the distraught Master of the Games. These were the scions of one of the world's first great empires. Their ancestors had no doubt sometimes been anxious and distraught, but the issues involved had been of a somewhat different magnitude. Those old Romans, on the other hand, had probably been too stern and serious to have been much fun at a party—if they had parties at all.

"I have a job for you, Titus Lengo."

"Anything, Valorius." He was as happy as a puppy that his benefactor had not condemned him for his betrayal. I'd like you to look through the crowd for a woman with violet hair."

"Violet hair?"

"She'll probably be seated in or near the imperial podium. Will you do it for me? I have to prepare the animals for my entrance."

"Yes, of course, Valorius. Anything." He bustled up the closest ramp, just as a bloodthirsty roar shook the amphitheater.

The orangutans gave Valorius the most trouble. They were the most intelligent beasts in the entire

underground menagerie, and their minds the hardest to
control. The polar bear was cunning and treacherous,
but not really very bright. The Hyrcanian tigers had
been a regular part of his act almost since the first
day. But there was not much he could do about
Hannibal. A fight was a fight. A full cohort of Praetorian Guards still protected the great bull elephant
from any possible Bucyrian skulduggery. He stood
chained in their midst, and seemed calm enough. But
his beady little eyes watched slyly for any Praetorian
careless enough to stray within reach of his trunk.

"I'm so sorry, Valorius," Titus Lengo apologized as
he joined him at the top of the ramp. "I've looked
everywhere, but I can't find a single woman with
violet hair. Maybe she's changed the color of her wig,"
he suggested.

"Maybe she's not here yet." He scanned the imperial podium.

Magus Rex had promised to witness the great bout.
But perhaps he had timed his arrival so that he would
not have to sit through the preliminary atrocities.
Arena attendants had fixed hooks into the performers
of the last exhibition, and were dragging their bodies
toward the ramps. Other attendants raked fresh sand
over the pools of blood.

The next exhibition was an obscene parody of gladiatorial combats, an old favorite with the mob. It pitted
beautiful young women against dwarfs. But since
beautiful young women were a lot cheaper to buy than
dwarfs, the combats were always heavily weighted in
favor of the latter. The girls had only daggers, while
the dwarfs were fully armed with swords and bucklers.
It was supposed to be a re-enactment of the legendary
war between the Dwarfs and the Amazons.

The "Amazons" wore only skimpy loin-cloths. The
armored dwarfs sported huge leather phalluses, and
their movements were so comically grotesque that
the mob laughed uproariously to watch them hacking
and slashing at the bare-breasted girls. Several girls
already lay dead or dying on the arena sand. Then

suddenly the whole spectacle went sour.

A strapping Goth wench, nearly six feet tall with long flame-colored hair, fought with the fury of despair. Somehow she had managed to stab two of the dwarfs. The others scuttled out of her way. There were hoots and catcalls from the crowd, but the dwarfs refused to fight.

Then out of nowhere appeared the most fantastic dwarf Valorius had ever seen. He had been sadistically despatching the wounded girls on the other side of the arena. But now he rushed into the fray. He was as grotesque as the others, but there was nothing clumsy or ungainly about him. He was as agile as a cricket.

The desperate woman fought courageously, but the dwarf, leaping and dancing back and forth, methodically cut her to pieces.

Even as she lay helpless and bleeding upon the sand, the girl was too proud to beg for mercy. The mob would probably have spared her life, but this show of barbarian pride offended them. They turned thumbs down, and with a demonic flourish the dwarf mercilessly cut her throat.

The girl's flame-colored hair would bring a nice price from the wig-maker. That was some compensation for Volpinius Rufus. But two of his high-priced dwarfs had been wounded, perhaps fatally. And the mob was offended. He raised his hand, and troops of acrobats came running and tumbling into the center of the arena: the last act before the great bout. Then he noticed Valorius standing at the top of a nearby ramp, and signaled for him to get ready for his grand entrance.

Valorius nodded. He gave one last glance at the crowd for a woman with violet hair, then turned and descended the ramp.

On the far side of the arena the troop of dwarfs had remained above ground to watch the great bout; their ungainly little bodies were huddled together at the top of an unused ramp. But one stood somewhat apart from the others; it was the strange demonic dwarf who had so sadistically butchered the Goth woman. The other dwarfs watched the acrobats. He watched Valorius, eyes narrowed in calculation.

The arena attendants scurried for cover as Valorius threw open the animal cages. The unearthly hideousness of the orangutans made them more terrifying even than the polar bear or the Hyrcanian tigers. Two years ago their cage had been left open. The sequel had been rather gruesome. Even faithful Titus Lengo looked nervous.

"Perhaps I'd, that is to say, be, well," he stammered, glancing apprehensively at the orangutans squatting grotesquely not ten feet away. "I mean, perhaps I'd be more useful, that is to say, looking for the, uh, woman. . . . Does she really have violet hair? I mean, of course she has, if you—"

"That's a good idea," said Valorius. "Go look for the woman with violet hair. If you find her for me, I'll be eternally grateful." He smiled down at the timid, balding little poet. "I mean that almost literally." He shook his soft little hand for what he knew was the last time.

"Yes, Valorius, I'll look for her." Titus Lengo could not tear his eyes away from the orangutans. He nearly stumbled over the polar bear as he backed away. "I'm glad to help, any way I can. And please believe that I wish you nothing but good fortune. It was only a gesture. But that brute Hannibal! He's so much bigger than Bucyrus." He stepped gingerly around the Hyrcanian tigers. "I'll look for the woman with the violet hair. And those tusks! I mean, on Hannibal of course. Not on the. . . ." He grinned weakly, then turned and fled up the ramp.

"Farewell, Titus Lengo," Valorius called after him.

The chariots stood freshly painted and ready behind the entrance portal. But there were limits to the services that even the most cringing of arena attendants would perform. Valorius had to harness the polar bear and the Hyrcanian tigers himself. The costumes for the orangutans stood ready at hand, but he himself had to dress them. Nor could he allow his attention to wander too far. His control of the bear and the tigers was complete, but the orangutans were a constant menace. Perhaps it was just as well that he had not been able to find Zenobia in the crowd. He could not afford to think of other things with two apes ready to burst loose on a rampage the moment his concentration faltered.

Finally he was ready. If he had had any pride in his profession he would have been ashamed of himself. It was all cheap and theatrical. Titus Lengo could justly have accused him of catering to the mob. But he did not want some disgruntled Hannibalian interfering with him during the ensuing events. A moment's delay might be fatal. The mob took their circuses very seriously, and he could not afford to let Bucyrus' mahout humiliate him. The wiry little Greek had recently devised a stunt that he could not match. He had been forced to fall back on cheap theatrics to neutralize its effect.

Valorius peeked through the bronze grate in the portal. The Greek handled his collection of lions, tigers, bears, and giant dogs with a skill that was almost genius. Needless to say, he was saving his masterpiece for last. Valorius knew that he himself was still putting on the most elegant wild-animal show ever seen in Rome. But the Greek could do something that he could not do. That was all that mattered to the mob.

A pack of starving hyenas was now turned loose in the arena. The applause came mainly from the best seats, those at either end of the arena's shorter axis. This aroused some nasty shouting and catcalling from the Hannibalian majority. But it was nothing to the probable reaction if their man, Valorius, should allow himself to be bested. And it was indeed a skillful and courageous feat he had to top.

Lions, tigers, bears, and even wolves had to be specially trained to attack human beings in the arena. Not hyenas. A hungry hyena is all business, and there is nothing it won't do for a meal.

The wiry little Greek walked on stilts from one side of the arena to the other, with scores of huge hyenas leaping up at him from all sides. Their powerful jaws snapped shut only inches below his feet; their weight crashing against the stilts threatened to bring him down at every step. It took an expert to maintain his balance.

Valorius had to admit that the Greek had him beat. Despite all his wizardry, he doubted that he could ever learn to walk on stilts that well. And there were too many hyenas to control effectively. If they ever brought him down he would stay down.

The Greek reached the far side of the arena to tremendous cheering from the Bucyrian sections. The Hannibalian mob shouted defiance, but it was obvious that they thought their champion had been topped. Many would consider themselves personally affronted if Valorius did not come up with something spectacular. Some might even seek revenge on him. Cheap theatrics or not, he had to keep their knives in their tunics long enough to escape Rome.

The hyenas were driven from the arena. The band broke out in a raucous fanfare; the hydraulic organ whooped and squawled. Valorius leaped into his chariot just as the bronze portal slid open. The mob cheered lustily, more in defiance of the aristocrats than with any real enthusiasm. They were surprised to see two chariots enter the arena.

The first, pulled by a team of four Hyrcanian tigers, with Valorius holding the reins, sped swiftly and gracefully across the sand. The second chariot was a ludicrous sight: two grotesque orangutans held the reins of a big clumsy polar bear which lumbered clumsily into the open.

Then the mob got the point. Howls of laughter rose from the upper tiers. People leaped from their seats, cheering, slapping each other on the back, thumbing their noses at the imperial podium. The aristocratic Bucyrians looked on in silent outrage.

"Valorius! Valorius!" screamed the mob. "Hannibal! Hannibal!"

The recent elephant factions had transcended the color lines of the chariot racing teams, but the old circus loyalties had not been forgotten. Since the days of Caracalla, the "Blue" faction, supporters of the team of charioteers that wore that color in the circus, had always been associated with the common people. The "Reds" were also popular with the mob. "White" and especially "Green" were the colors of the aristocracy.

Valorius wore his shimmering blue cape and tunic as he wheeled his bright red chariot into the sunlight. The green chariot lumbering behind him was pulled by a "White" bear; the two orangutans inside were wearing "Green" tunics cut in the latest fashion of the aristocracy. The mob howled with delight.

No bestiarius in the history of the arena had ever put on such a show. The Hyrcanian tigers danced and capered; the polar bear walked tightropes, balancing a green parasol on its nose; the orangutans scratched obscene verses in the sand, satirizing the foibles of the upper crust. Then Valorius had the animals perform a parody of the aristocracy's current favorite at the theater, *The Wrath of Ajax*. The polar bear was a big hit as a buffoon Ajax. In a way it was just a puppet show. But the mob loved it.

So too did the moribund old Dictator. He leered gleefully down from the imperial podium as Valorius pulled his tigers to a halt. There was now certain to be a major riot at the end of the day. This was much better than dying alone and forgotten, mourned by no one.

A flash of violet caught Valorius' eye. Magus Rex and Zenobia had just arrived, slipping into seats near the top of the imperial podium. Volpina fluttered like a butterfly in the shadows of the great awning; she was dressed as usual in the gaudiest of pagan finery, favoring various shades of violet. Magus Rex and Zenobia, however, wore flowing robes, probably over the costumes of some past or future decadent society. Beside them stood a large trunk.

Zenobia smiled down at him. She turned to whis-

per something in his praise to her father. But Magus
Rex only sneered and shrugged.

It was now time for the elephants. By the time
Valorius got his animals out of the arena, Hannibal
was already being positioned on the elevator. The
brute looked even surlier than usual, as if sensing the
excitement in the amphitheater above. But Valorius
hurried past him. The two guards at the end of the
passageway jumped to attention.

"There might be trouble upstairs," he warned them.
"But you must keep this door clear for me. I shouldn't
be gone more than a quarter of an hour." He slapped
the heavy purse hanging from his belt. "I'll pay my
way back in."

The two guards assured him of their loyalty. Both
were devout Hannibalians, but the promise of even
more money strengthened their faith.

Valorius had to keep this entrance open at all costs.
It was rarely used. But no matter which elephant
won, there was sure to be a riot. He had to be able to
get in and out of the amphitheater without delay the
instant Magus Rex and Zenobia disappeared. The
guards, of course, had bet heavily on the bout. They
wished him luck.

The arena attendants looked relieved when Valorius
appeared. They were still terrified of Hannibal, despite his good behavior in recent weeks. They used
long prods to position him in the elevator, but looked
ready to run for their lives the instant he lifted his
trunk. Some of them even helped the slaves with the
windlasses that hoisted the elevator platform and its
eight-ton cargo to arena level.

Bucyrus was already in the arena. His eyes were
rather weak, but there was nothing wrong with his
nose. He knew that there was another bull elephant
somewhere in the arena, and immediately took up a
defensive position. The wiry little Greek had trouble
controlling him.

Valorius, using a completely different system of
control, had no trouble at all with Hannibal. He led

the brute straight to the imperial podium.

First he had Hannibal scratch with a cane in three-foot letters the slogan VIVAT SEXTUS ASINIUS. This was the name of the moribund old Dictator, who cackled with glee. The fact that his name had been written before that of the emperor would alone have condemned him to death. He leered delightedly down at Valorius. The mob understood and approved, as they did any kind of insolence toward the rich and powerful.

Then Hannibal scratched in the sand in four-foot letters the name ZENOBIA. Valorius knew that it was schoolboyish. But Zenobia smiled warmly down at him, touched by the simple gesture. Magus Rex shook his head, as if he thought Valorius had outdone himself in bumpkinish idiocy. Volpina looked miffed.

It was now Bucyrus' turn to be presented to the imperial podium. Valorius led Hannibal to the other side of the arena, where he had him scratch the usual popular slogans in the sand. These always pleased the mob. They were more pleased that Valorius had humiliated the Greek—the hyena stunt was not really all that impressive. And they were delighted that Bucyrus was giving trouble to his trainer.

The aristocrats were disappointed, but they could understand Bucyrus' apprehension. After all, he was giving away a ton in weight and a four-foot reach in tusk. And being the brighter of the two elephants, he seemed to realize why he was here. Despite all the Greek could do, Bucyrus could barely scratch his own name in the sand. Any arithmetic he had ever learned had gone right out of his head. The mob was pleased to see that under pressure he was no smarter than they were.

At last the Dictator raised his arthritic old hand. Trumpets blared. Betting came to a frenzied halt. The hot chick-pea vendors made their last sales. Eighty thousand decadent Romans sat on the edge of their seats. The great bout had begun!

Valorius had to get his own ladder. Not until he was

mounted on Hannibal and moving away did an arena attendant venture out to retrieve it. Valorius felt sharp bristles stinging his legs as he tried to settle himself comfortably on Hannibal's neck. Bucyrus shuffled warily toward him from the far side of the arena.

A hush swept through the crowd as the two elephants approached each other. The first shock of the combat would be the most violent. Bucyrus was not afraid of his larger opponent, but seemed somewhat confused over his odd behavior. Hannibal strode complacently toward him, head up and ears back. One bull elephant did not approach another in that manner. Even the wiry little Greek seemed perplexed.

When the two elephants were within twenty yards of each other, Valorius released his control. Hannibal awoke as if from a dream. He suddenly found himself standing in the center of a packed arena, facing a bull elephant nearly his own size. But his primitive instincts took over immediately. His huge ears spread like the sails of a ship; he trumpeted angrily through his upraised trunk; shifting his great bulk from side to side, he lowered his head and began swinging his ten-foot tusks back and forth. Any moment he would charge.

Bucyrus was going through similar motions. But he was also using his brain. He charged at the precise moment that Hannibal's duller mind had finally made its decision to attack, catching him in mid stride. The shock of the colliding behemoths almost knocked their mahouts sprawling. Both Valorius and the Greek clutched frantically at the necks of their mounts. The two elephants grabbed each other by the trunk and began ramming with their foreheads.

They were evenly matched. Hannibal was the stronger of the two, but the smarter Bucyrus had more forehead area. The howling and shrieking of the mob drowned out even the tremendous crashing of the two brutes, as again and again they rammed each other, their trunks entwined. There would be some new spectacle tomorrow. There had better be! But this was today's spectacle, and the mob threw their blood-thirsty hearts into it. The psychic energy level rose like a tidal wave.

Valorius dared not lift his eyes from the combat. One slip and he might find himself beneath eight tons of trampling elephant. Nor was the wily little Greek past hurling a knife at him the moment he turned his eyes away.

Nonetheless he knew the instant Magus Rex and Zenobia were gone. A crackle of energy swept through the amphitheater, and for a moment the crowd was strangely drained of enthusiasm. There could be only one explanation. For some reason the great wizard had decided not to wait until the end of the bout. Valorius could not wait either. He did not care what the mob might think of his sudden defection.

He slid from Hannibal's back, regaining his balance the instant he hit the sand; then he raced for the nearest ramp. But he had not taken ten steps before he knew why Magus Rex had left so soon. The awning had collapsed. Heavy strips of colored sail-cloth were falling on the crowd below. And it was obviously no accident. Everybody knew that there would be a major riot after today's spectacle. Had one of the elephant factions tried to get the jump on the other, the way Bucyrus had gotten the jump on Hannibal? No wonder Magus Rex had not waited.

Valorius kept running. Just as he reached the ramp a huge brown bear appeared from below. He leaped aside, avoiding the swipe of the bear's claws by inches. From behind the barricade he saw hundreds of wild beasts — lions, tigers, wolves, bears, hyenas, leopards, even his two orangutans — pouring into the arena from every ramp. It was pandemonium. Who could have planned all this? Was it a parting shot by Magus Rex? He could not see how anyone but a great wizard could have wielded such power.

He glanced toward the imperial podium. The aristo-crats had abandoned their dignity and were trampling each other in trying to reach the exit. Volpina sat half

buried in red sail-cloth, tearing her violet hair and
staring distractedly at the two empty seats beside her.
The moribund old Dictator threw back his head with
maniacal laughter, holding up a golden goblet in a last
toast to Rome. He had never dreamed of such an exit.

Several leopards had clawed their way over the
barricades and were savaging the crowd. Another huge
brown bear lumbered past Valorius. But the ramp was
now clear — for the moment. He vaulted the barricade
and plunged into the darkness of the underground
labyrinth.

The two guards threw open the door the instant he
appeared. He raced past them without a word. The
carnage outside the amphitheater was nearly as great
as that inside. Panic-stricken people raced about madly,
the strong trampling the weak underfoot. The air crackled with psychic energy.

He dodged through the shadows of the Colossus
and sped down a reeking backstreet that dipped toward the waterfront. It took him only minutes to
reach the hovel. The miasma of unwashed humanity
mingled with the pungencies of exotic herbs. Izelta
might have been the twin sister of the moribund old
Dictator. She was pouring powdered pumice on a
freshly inked scrap of papyrus as he burst through the
door. A faint red haze still lingered in the gloom. But
the letters were now illegible.

The whole transaction took less than a minute. The
crone cackled toothlessly as he crossed her palm with
gold coins. But there were two sheets of papyrus, not
just the one he had expected. The second had been
written some time ago. He recognized Zenobia's handwriting. It was an essay outlining the principles of
time-travel under low energy conditions.

Valorius already knew — at least in theory — how
that was done. The verse which the crone had just
copied out was hardly dry. It seemed to point to some
time in the future. That was all he had to know at the
moment. He stuffed both pieces of papyrus into his
tunic and shot out the door like a bolt.

The two guards were still faithful to their word. He tossed them the bag of gold as he plunged once more into the underground labyrinth. Most of the exits were now blocked with crushed and trampled bodies. But some of the ramps were clear. The scene that met his eyes was an opium-eater's vision of Hell.

A whole new dimension had been added to Roman entertainment—audience participation. Lions, tigers, and leopards clawed their way through the temporary grandstands. The two orangutans had climbed into the imperial podium and were mauling the aristocrats. He did not see Volpina; evidently she had escaped.

The arena floor was a living exhibition of the survival of the fittest. The wolves fought in packs, as did the lions. The bears and tigers were rugged individualists, fighting single combats until they were brought down. The hyenas were savage only when cornered. And in the middle of it all, Hannibal and Bucyrus, their trunks still entwined, continued to ram their foreheads together. Both elephants were dazed, but neither would surrender the field. The hyraulic organist, valiantly sticking to his post, played the national anthem.

Valorius needed several minutes of total concentration somewhere in the midst of this storm of psychic energy. But concentration was impossible so long as he was in constant danger of being dragged down from behind by a wild animal. Then he spotted the polar bear not fifty feet away. It stood ready to fight, but not even the most ferocious lion or tiger dared challenge it. Valorius could not hope for a better sentinel to stand guard while he concentrated.

Dodging through a pack of wolves, he raced across the sand. The wolves started in pursuit, but skidded to a halt at a safe distance from the polar bear. Valorius had already conditioned the creature's brain; it took only a moment to regain control. The other animals continued to hang back.

It was the most difficult thing he had ever done. He had studied diligently for the better part of a century, but no course at the Academy had prepared him for total concentration in an environment like this. First he unified his own mind. Then slowly, patiently, he began reaching out—

Suddenly he sensed danger. He whirled around just in time to duck a heavy javelin hurled at him from the grandstand nearby. Two more javelins followed, one barely missing his right leg.

A group of armed gladiators charged through the crowd above, scattering beasts and men right and left. In command was the strange, demonic dwarf. He danced back and forth on top of the wall, frenziedly trying to get his men to charge into the arena. But the pack of snarling wolves milling about below tended to discourage them. The dwarf screamed insanely, threatening them with his miniature sword. They would not budge.

Valorius did not wait for them to bring up more javelins. The polar bear cut through the sea of wild beasts like the prow of a ship. Soon he was out of javelin range. But it was harder than ever to concentrate. Once more he unified all parts of his mind. Then he reached out into the field of psychic energy seething all about him; unifying it, concentrating it, and at last controlling it.

The polar bear blinked its eyes. It stood alone in the midst of a pandemonium of beasts and men at the very center of the arena. It looked bewilderedly about, as if just awakening from some ursine dream. Then it took up a defensive position. But no animal attacked.

# CHAPTER XV
# THE SABBATS

The Black Death raged unchecked throughout Europe. Two rival popes spread doubt and uncertainty among the faithful from two rival papal seats, Rome and Avignon. The breakdown of civil authority poisoned the land with rapine and cruelty. Robber barons and robber bishops looted merchant and peasant alike, and famine stalked from village to village. The Jacquerie was only a few years away. But more and more people were turning for consolation to the Old Religion, stinting themselves by day that they might come alive, if only for a few hours, amidst the forbidden practices of night. Unspeakable tortures awaited those who were caught. Still, the reign of Satan waxed great in the hearts of the people, for only Satan seemed to offer them hope.

Months of wandering through medieval France had given Valorius some new insights into wizardry, especially its darker side. Tomorrow night was the night of the full moon. The Black Mass would be celebrated on the heath four miles outside the walls of Lacerre.

What he needed now was a girl.

The gates of Lacerre were closed for the night. Just outside its walls, on the northern highroad, stood a little thatched inn. Around its stone fireplace a motley gathering of waggoners, soldiers, wandering monks and scholars, thieves, vagabonds, and strolling players ate, drank, laughed, and sang with the abandon of the hopeless.

At this time of night the inn was pretty much a law unto itself, and Valorius had made himself conspicuous by having a new candle placed upon his table. Such an extravagance betokened a full purse.

He sat in a screened alcove apart from the others. The fact that he was dressed in the black robes of a Dominican friar would not protect him from attack, since these days even holy men were fair game. Some of the most formidable swordsmen in Europe were monks.

Valorius adjusted his candle and continued working at his occult calculations. Several sheets of parchment (another interesting extravagance) lay on the table before him. To one side lay two scraps of ancient papyrus. These had been identified by one of the wandering scholars. It was the superstitious dread of sorcery more than anything that had thus far preserved Valorius from attack. The servants of Satan were more respected these days than the servants of God.

There was nothing startling about a Dominican friar pondering over occult calculations. Monks and priests, even bishops, were turning in increasing numbers to satanic practices. Those discovered were punished severely by the Church. The Sorcerer Bishop of Cahors had recently been skinned alive and roasted over a slow fire until he began to suspect the error of his ways. Valorius would probably not be the only one in ecclesiastical garb at the Black Mass tomorrow night. But he would not be admitted without a girl.

He shook his head. The Roman amphitheater had provided a tremendous springboard of psychic energy. His calculations showed that there would not be quite enough energy at tomorrow night's Sabbat to transport him the full distance. He would fall about two generations short. That is, if he had correctly interpreted Zenobia's verse.

How these cryptic verses evaded Magus Rex's injunction against any form of communication he did not know. This one had almost eluded him. For three whole days after he had first rematerialized in an onion field in medieval France he had pored over the quatrain. He had even begun to suspect that the witch Izelta had made some kind of clerical error. But witches were always careful to get their spells and incantations letter perfect. He had read and reread the four lines until he could have recited them in his sleep:

> With time's vagaries love must ever reckon,
> The hours that mark, the centuries that score.
> The moment comes when we must loose or
>    beckon,
> Assume the end, embrace the years before.

The instant he had grabbed the scrap of papyrus from the witch's hand he had understood the phrase "centuries that score": the twentieth century, Ancient Reckoning. But when and where in the twentieth century?

What had really confused him was the word "beckon." Zenobia had used the same word in the verse that had saved him from being turned into a toucan:

> Our only love has beckoned,
> And instantly we start;
> Forgetting in that second
> That transports of the heart
> Prepare a cage apart.

"Beckon" in that verse had meant exactly what it said, a sign or signal. The word had an entirely different meaning in this last verse. At dusk of his third day in the onion field the answer had finally come to him.

"Beckon" did not refer to any kind of sign or signal; it referred to a name: Luther Beck. The "end" in line four could only mean Beck's coup in the year 1999, A.R. — the end of the twentieth century and the beginning of the Black Ages. The moment he understood that, everything else fell into place. It was obvious that Magus Rex would have chosen one of the "years before" Beck's coup. The years after were a nightmare of concentration camps and mass executions. But how much before? The use of the word "embrace" had been rather subtle.

Zenobia had been taken by her father to the year 1997, A.R.; two years before Luther Beck and his Blackshirts took over ancient New York. The Black Ages that followed lasted nearly a thousand years. But the frenetic sensuality of the years just before rivaled that of ancient Rome. The ancient New Yorkers had perhaps lacked the decadent refinement of the ancient Romans, but their decline and fall had been much swifter. They too had sensed the end of their world, and like the Romans before them had thrown themselves body and soul into luxurious debauchery. It was indeed an age that would appeal to the decadent tastes of Magus Rex.

"Brother Valorius," said a timid voice.

He raised his head. The girl was pale and thin, no more than eighteen years old. She limped slightly as she stepped into the light of the candle. A childhood accident had left one of her legs shorter than the other. She was pretty by the standards of the times; she had washed her face within the last couple of days and she still had most of her teeth. Strangely, she seemed reassured by the occult calculations on the table. A dabbler in the black arts was more to be trusted than an ordinary monk.

"I have talked with the others," she whispered, glancing over the top of the screen. She had already made sure that the motley gathering about the fireplace was too far away to hear what she said, but one did not take chances in matters such as this. "The sheep and hogshead of wine have been accepted. But, well, you are a stranger, and—"

"I'm not a spy, Griselda," said Valorius. "I have my own reasons for attending the Sabbat, and will give them whatever assurances are necessary. Please sit down. I have another matter to discuss with you."

The girl sat timidly on the edge of a stool.

"Now you know that I must be accompanied to the Sabbat by a woman," he continued.

She nodded, her eyes wide with fright.

"Then why shouldn't it be you as well as another? If my first offer was not enough, I'm willing to increase it." He pushed a large gold coin across the table. "Take that for now, Griselda. It's for the work you've done already."

She wrung her hands, looking everywhere but at Valorius. That she was outside the city gates after dark was dangerous in itself. But though the danger was great so was the temptation. She stared down at the gold coin as tears began to run down her cheeks. It would have taken her ten years of drudgery to have earned that much money.

Valorius laid his purse of Roman coins on the table. The girl blinked in wonder. Not even the baron had that much money.

"Accompany me tomorrow night," he said, "and you shall have enough money for an enterprising young man to buy a mill of his own."

The girl looked wistfully at the purse. She was already eighteen, well past the age when most girls marry. Being lame and without a dowry, she had little hope of ever being anything more than a childless scullery drudge for the rest of her life. All that would ever be hers was the pallet on which she slept in a corner of the merchant's kitchen. The miller's son sometimes joked with her when he delivered flour from his father's mill. She knew that he wanted to set up on his own; she also knew that there was a mill for sale in the neighborhood. It was out of the question for a miller's son to marry a lame scullery wench without a dowry. But if she had one, enough to purchase the mill. . . .

"You won't have to remain for the ceremony, Griselda," said Valorius. "But I can't get past the sentinels without a woman. The moment I'm admitted to the Sabbat, you may return home."

Wiping the tears from her eyes, the girl picked up the coin with trembling fingers. Torn between the terror of being tortured to death in the baron's dungeon and the dream of becoming a miller's wife, she fell to temptation. She looked like she had just sold her soul to the Devil.

And indeed Valorius had a satanic appearance when she met him the next night at the edge of the forest. The full moon had just risen, and before her was a tall, slender figure dressed in the black robes and cowl of a Dominican friar. But she did not turn back. Though he were Satan himself she would keep her part of the infernal bargain. She may have sold her chance of salvation for a miller's son. But what could be worse than living the rest of her life as a childless scullery drudge? She led Valorius into the forest.

They met the others in a ruined cemetery about two miles outside the walls of Lacerre. Valorius pulled down his cowl so that they could see his face. His fair hair reassured them. They may have been ready to worship Satan himself—but not quite yet. The sheep and hogshead of wine he had contributed to tonight's dark carnival had already been sent ahead.

They soon joined the long files of men and women winding through the forest. Beneath the twisted limbs of huge black oak trees, in and out of moonlit clearings, through the ruins of an ancient fane, the files slipped noiselessly through the night. Security was tight. Dark sentinels appeared from nowhere, looked them over, then disappeared again into the trees.

The oaks suddenly opened onto a bare and blasted heath. Eldritch desolation stretched for miles beneath the sickly pallor of the full moon. Not far from the edge of the forest a knoll swelled above the heath like a cancerous growth. An ancient dolmen rose at its top like the talons of a monstrous obscenity thrusting upward out of the deepest regions of the earth. Silhouetted against the moon stood a creature larger than a man; it was black and shaggy, and from the top of its head curved the horns of a goat. It stood as motionless as an idol to one side of the ancient dolmen. Bonfires ringed the base of the knoll, and Valorius could not make out exactly what the creature was through the swirling smoke.

The dark ceremony was already in progress. The bodies of scores of naked women glistened with "flying ointments" brewed with hemlock and belladonna; they cavorted in drugged frenzy on greased broomsticks. The music of flutes, drums, and tambourines accompanied the dance. Weird incantations rolled down the knoll in a deep muffled voice. Hundreds of robed cultists reeled drunkenly in and out of the swirling smoke. A procession of masked celebrants approached across the heath; their torches burned with sulphurous green flames.

Valorius was about to send the girl home, when suddenly they found themselves in the middle of a wild Witch's Round. He could not afford to attract attention, so he took the girl's hand and together they leaped and whirled with the celebrants in their frenzied dance.

The girl was not so terrified as he had thought she would be. The mood of dark revelry was infectious. Her eyes were glassy; a bacchanalian smile slowly parted her lips. She was lost.

All at once hundreds of celebrants rushed ecstatically toward the knoll. The weird music rose in a crescendo, its diabolical attraction drawing the satanists through the smoke of the bonfires like an infernal magnet. The girl started to follow, but Valorius grabbed her arm.

"Here, Griselda." He gave her enough money to dower a miller's son twice over. "Now leave while you can. You have committed no sin as yet."

The girl tried to pull away but, entranced by the spell of Satan, she also wished to rush headlong into the smoke with the other blasphemous children of darkness. The bacchanalian smile on her face became the snarl of a caged animal. She tried to bite his hand.

He shook her and slapped her face. At last she snapped out of it. She looked about her like someone who has just awakened from a nightmare. Then all at once she understood where she was. A look of terror came into her eyes. Clutching the gold coins as if she were clutching the miller's son himself, she turned and fled into the night. None but Valorius saw her go.

All attention was centered on the top of the knoll. Pulling his black cowl over his head, he began working his way upward through the crowd. They welcomed him into their midst as if he were Satan himself. Their minds reeled with mystical fervor and the weird music; most were heated by wine or drugged by the "flying ointments." All were in a state of hysteria. Psychic energy swirled about the knoll, as thick as the smoke of the bonfires.

Valorius stood in the shadows of the ancient dolmen. The witches, male and female, young and old, danced round and round the top of the knoll in the light of the torches. Through the haze the full moon looked pale and diseased. But its light illuminated clearly the sinister figure he had seen from the base of the knoll.

It was an eidolon of greased black wood. Its shaggy, evil-looking face was goat-like; goat horns were carved above, and a huge erect phallus was carved below. In past ages this same eidolon had been called Bacchus or Pan or Priapus. Tonight it was called Satan. The names changed, but the Old Religion lived on. A black goat was tethered to its side.

On the other side of the eidolon stood the priestess. Her long black hair was tangled about her beautiful face like the snakes of a Medusa. She was dressed in a parody of a nun's habit. Like an evil Madonna her beauty was unspeakably cruel and depraved. All about her, bewitched by the flutes and drums and tam-

bourines, her flock danced obscenely. The air was
thick with the smoke of hazelwood and musk, the
pungency of hemlock and belladonna, the reek of
human flesh. Scores of naked bodies glistened in the
moonlight.

The music ceased. The witches stopped dancing in
mid-step and gathered about the black eidolon. With a
gesture of defiance the priestess flung aside her nun's
habit. Her figure was full and mature; her breasts
heavy and sagging. The scars of whips, pincers and
the rack could be seen in the eerie greenish light,
disfiguring her naked flesh. She was Satan's bride.
She turned and mounted the eidolon of greased black
wood.

The witches chanted blasphemously, encouraging
the obscene consummation between the priestess and
Satan. Valorius slipped out of the shadows of the
prehistoric dolmen. The psychic energy level was rising toward its peak, and he began to prepare his mind.
Slowly he began to unify all parts of his consciousness.

The priestess climbed down from the eidolon. Her
beautiful face was so contorted with the ecstatic
abandonment to evil that she hardly looked human.
Her flock shrieked obscenities. A fallen stone, resembling the altar at Stonehenge, lay nearby. She was
Satan's bride; her naked body was the altar upon
which the Black Mass would be celebrated. Shamelessly
she lay supine upon the cold stone.

An unfrocked priest began reciting the Lord's Prayer
backward, making obscene gestures with his left hand
over the naked body of the priestess. It was a mockery
of the sacrament of absolution. In fact, the entire
Black Mass was merely an obscene parody of Church
ritual. A witch wearing a devil-mask held up an inverted
cross. It was a fervently religious age, and the blas-
phemy of all that was held sacred goaded the as-
sembly into an hysterical frenzy. They tore at their
hair and flesh, howling obscenities.

Valorius began to reach out with his thoughts into
the vortex of psychic energy swirling all about him;

concentrating it, controlling it. Then he was gone.

In the days to come it would be whispered that Satan himself had attended the Sabbat. Many saw the tall figure in black standing in the shadows. None saw him leave. It was noticed that the frenzy of the rites abated somewhat at the precise moment that Satan disappeared.

It was late in summer as Valorius strode through the darkening streets of the city. Its quaint medieval structures reminded him of the walled town of Lacerre, where centuries ago a crippled scullery drudge named Griselda had married the miller's son and (he hoped) lived happily ever after. But this city had a strident efficiency about it, an almost sterile cleanliness, unknown in medieval France. The streets were brightly lit; but in spite of the banners and placards hanging everywhere, the atmosphere was not that of a carnival. It was more like the deadly calm that proceeds a ghastly, terrifying storm.

The rally had been going on now, night and day, for nearly a week. The parades and speeches were replete with pagan symbols and pagan pageantry, but nothing of pagan freedom and joyful celebration. Only vengeance and hatred, cloaked behind a deadly efficiency. The Leader himself was scheduled to speak at the city's huge concrete stadium, casting defiance into the face of a confused world. The air already crackled with psychic energy.

Valorius had no trouble getting through the gates, but he seemed to be the only one there with blond hair and blue eyes not in uniform. The huge stadium was jammed. Flags and banners were draped everywhere; pagan symbols in red, black, and white blazoned from every arm; a massive band, made up almost entirely of brass and percussion instruments, thundered one barbarous march after another. Martial songs were sung, and everyone seemed to know the words. Valorius, seated directly behind the podium at the east end of the stadium, had to fake it.

Tonight was the climax of the past week of efficiently organized parades and demonstrations. Tens of thousands of tense, expectant human beings sat rigidly amidst the inhuman efflorescence of banners and symbols: an impressive spectacle in its own macabre way. The Leader had an uncanny flair for the dramatic. He would not appear on the dais until expectancy had risen to a fever pitch, which was the moment Valorius was waiting for.

He reviewed his calculations. Assuming that he had correctly interpreted Zenobia's verse, he should have no trouble at all. If he could not successfully transport himself a mere two generations, then he deserved every epithet ever heaped on him by Magus Rex. There was at least as much available psychic energy seething through the concrete stadium as there had been in the Roman amphitheater; far more than at the Black Mass.

The last few weeks had been simplicity itself. If all time travel were this easy, there was no place he could not follow Zenobia. A single Roman coin had brought him a small fortune. And never had he experienced such deference for blond hair and blue eyes. It was almost mystical. The movement's initiates themselves were largely the gutter sweepings of northern Europe but somehow they had been disciplined into a robotic efficiency.

The Leader was generally classified in the history books as a kind of crude precursor of Luther Beck, although his Reich did not last anywhere near a thousand years. Valorius had seen pictures of him but he was completely unprepared for the absurd figure that now strutted out onto the dais, especially the broad hips. He advanced to the microphone with ladylike steps, as tens of thousands of right arms went up in Roman salutes. Tens of thousands of throats hailed him; tens of thousands of pagan flags and symbols were waved. The band blared and thundered.

The Leader launched at once into a venomous tirade. His voice elicited a kind of macabre fascination, and

tens of thousands of fanatics were rendered almost
delirious with malice toward the targets of his diatribe.
In Magus Rex's recreation of ancient Paris, one of the
mimes at the pantomime theater might have bur-
lesqued a Roman emperor in much this fashion.

Valorius did not speak the language, but he heard
the word "Juden" pronounced over and over again,
each time with more hatred than the last. The Leader
was literally gnashing his teeth. The Jews were a
people with a disproportionately high number of
scholars and artists; their merchants were disproportionately successful. What better focus for hatred
than the successful nonconformist? The hysteria rose
in a violent crescendo. Valorius had no trouble unifying
his mind with the psychic energy clustered about him.

The Leader never noticed the empty seat directly
behind the podium. What he did notice was a sudden
diminution of enthusiasm. Where he had expected
insane cheering after a particularly rousing statement,
he got only polite applause. This was no way to conquer the world! He decided to bolster party morale by
having a few people shot in the basement of the local
police station.

One whiff told Valorius that his calculations had
been correct. Acrid industrial fumes hung in the air
like the hazelwood smoke at the medieval Sabbat.
This was ancient New York all right, in the last years
of the twentieth century. While he had transported
himself across only a couple of generations, not even
Magus Rex could have faulted his calculations. He
had been accurate to within a few hours.

It was a midsummer night, shortly after midnight.
He found himself in a large park at the very heart of
the city. Most of the park's lights had been broken and
never replaced, and darkness stretched for a mile in
either direction. Surrounding the park were luxurious
apartment buildings, many stories high and brightly
lighted despite the late hour. Electrified fences separated
the buildings from the park.

The park itself was a camp of marauding barbarians. Valorius widened the pupils of his eyes. He sensed his danger.

Numerous campfires glowed in the darkness. Tents and hovels were scattered irregularly about the hundreds of acres of park. There were also a number of black patches; he might be able to slip through these unseen. He wore a plain dark business suit of two generations ago but it would be conspicuous among the rag-tag costumes of the park's denizens. Those that he could see appeared to be in advanced states of drugged or drunken mindlessness. Sanitary conditions were evidently quite primitive.

If Magus Rex and Zenobia were anywhere in ancient New York, it would not be here. He moved cautiously through the park toward the lights of the luxury apartments. He soon realized that there were others prowling through the darkness, as alert as hungry jackals. His eyes gave him an advantage. He saw them long before they saw him.

He read English, just as he read a number of other dead languages, but what he needed was some contemporary Titus Lengo to teach him how to speak it. The timid little poet who had befriended him thousands of years ago would not have lasted long amidst such viciousness and squalor. He himself would have to be careful.

A low crumbling wall marked the old boundary of the park. Down the center of a broad avenue ran a high metal fence topped with strands of barbed wire; electric cables were attached to the fence at regular intervals. Banks of armored floodlights made the avenue as bright as day. Uniformed guards in steel helmets patrolled the other side of the fence. They all carried machine-guns.

These were flimsy defenses against a Master Wizard but there was not much more available psychic energy here than there had been in ancient Rome. The primitive machine gun was sufficiently lethal. Valorius stood silhouetted against the floodlights pondering his next move, leaving himself exposed.

He was accosted immediately. Three young thugs stepped out of the bushes behind him. They were dressed in the odds and ends of military uniforms; tangles of greasy hair hung to their shoulders; their faces were sallow and pimply; their drug-crazed eyes glittered feverishly. All three had knives.

They taunted him with words he could not understand, japing and giggling. Cowardly and sadistic, they apparently had some morbid need to humiliate their victim before they attacked. But their "victim" in this case happened to be the most renowned bestiarius in the history of the Roman amphitheater. Valorius braced himself for their attack. There was no time to concentrate.

Although they were armed and he was not, they still did not attack from the front. Jackal-like, they tried to slip behind him so they could stab him in the back, all the while giggling playfully. He sent two of them tumbling down the incline into the darkness below. The third slinked out of reach before Valorius could get his hands on him, genuinely stunned that anyone would dare fight back. Like the roistering aristocrats in ancient Rome, he screamed impotent threats as he scurried back into the safety of the bushes. Valorius left the park and headed west.

Garbage collection seemed to be rather sporadic; some of the streets were hardly less noisome than those of medieval France. Ancient Rome had been remarkably egalitarian; but here, luxurious enclaves were rigidly segregated from the sea of viciousness and squalor lapping all about them. There was no evidence of law enforcement outside the enclaves.

He needed a safe place to sleep; soon he would need food. Disposing of the Roman and medieval coins in his pocket would probably be a more delicate matter than it had been in the Nuremburg of two generations ago. There seemed to be no particular veneration here for blond hair and blue eyes, either.

But the major problem was that he could not speak the language.

Many of the streetlights had been broken, and he stayed in the shadows as much as possible. Turning a corner he came upon a barricade of old furniture, crates, abandoned automobiles, and assorted junk stretched from one side of the street to the other. But the barricade was deserted. It had probably been thrown up during a recent riot or uprising of some kind, and nobody had bothered to tear it down again. A small opening had been excavated to one side. He passed through it without opposition.

He glanced at the street sign, which hung slightly askew from a rusty lamppost. It read "42nd St." Toward the middle of the block he saw a group of people loitering about the entrance of a tavern. Adjusting the pupils of his eyes, he approached them.

# CHAPTER XVI
## 42ND ST.

Shabby tenements stretched for miles. The shops were boarded up for the night; the doors and windows were barred and shuttered. Skeleton automobiles, stripped of every valuable part, stood abandoned along the curb or in empty lots. Only three streetlamps on the entire block still burned; a rusting lamppost lay across the sidewalk. There were no vehicles of any kind in the streets. The gutters were choked with the litter of paper food containers, soaked again and again by summer rains and trodden into a noxious papier mâché. The stench of uncollected garbage mingled with the acrid fumes of industry.

Everywhere Valorius turned the same face stared down at him. Luther Beck. Some of the posters were new; some torn and weathered. There were announcements of rallies and demonstrations, demands for the release of imprisoned party loyalists, and various proclamations. Every poster was surmounted by the same face. Luther Beck.

It was not the face of a conqueror or religious

fanatic. Middle-aged, pudgy, with little pig eyes looking
out from behind frameless spectacles. It was the face
of a bureaucrat, evil only in its merciless banality.
Valorius could picture such a man routinely dissemi-
nating death and terror with a rubber stamp. Perhaps
that was the worst kind of evil.

He found a barber shop whose window was protected only with a metal grate. The clock inside showed
that it was still three or four hours before dawn. A
dead cat lay rotting in the gutter nearby.

The group outside the tavern did not notice his
approach. A bespectacled little man was surrounded
by a gang dressed in uniform black shirts. The men
were all rather nondescript; the women rather dumpy
and unattractive. But their black shirts seemed to give
them an overweening sense of self-importance. The
argument was getting noisy.

The bespectacled little man spoke with the patience
of a scholar trying to explain the obvious to a class of
backward children. Valorius could not understand what
he was saying, but it seemed to make his audience
angry. They tried to shout him down but he would not
be silenced. He kept talking in his patient scholarly
voice, although it was obvious that he was afraid of
them.

A dumpy young woman with a bad complexion
began screaming obscenities at him. He was still not
intimidated. Then she began slapping and kicking
him. Suddenly he was being cuffed from all sides. His
spectacles were knocked off and blood flowed from his
nose. It looked like he was in for a good beating,
perhaps a fatal one. Without his spectacles he could
not even see to fight back.

Then one of the attackers noticed Valorius. He
shouted something to the others, and despite their
anger they obeyed with military alacrity. They stopped
pommeling the little man and turned in a body to face
Valorius. Yet they did not attack. They began talking
heatedly among themselves, as if arguing about which
party mandate covered the situation. Perhaps the one

about beating up people in front of witnesses. In any case, the whole gang turned and started down the street. By the time they reached the first empty lot they were marching in step.

Some people had come out of the tavern to watch the beating. Disappointed, they straggled back inside. The little man leaned against a railing, holding a handkerchief to his bloody nose. He looked dazed. Valorius bent down and picked up his spectacles. Only one of the lenses had been cracked.

They stood alone in the deserted street. The city was strangely quiet. It took the little man several minutes to recover from the shock of the attack. Blood still trickled from his nose, his right cheek was cut, and there was a deep scratch on his neck. But he did not seem to be badly hurt. The first thing he noticed was the way Valorius was dressed.

He said something, apparently a question of some kind. But it was unintelligible. He looked puzzled. Valorius had acquired a speaking knowledge of classical Latin, medieval French, and contemporary German. He had no idea how English was pronounced. The little man had the look of a scholar, but his access to foreign languages was evidently restricted to a reading knowledge. He shrugged helplessly.

Valorius looked at him. He looked at Valorius. Neither so much as blinked an eye for the next forty minutes. The banal, evil face of Luther Beck looked down on them from a hundred posters, but the black-shirted group did not return. A muffled outburst rose from the tavern nearby; two sharp explosions sounded in the distance, perhaps gun shots. The industrial fumes hovering above the city blotted out all but the brightest stars.

The man suddenly found himself standing face to face with a tall stranger wearing a business suit two generations out of fashion. He blinked and adjusted his cracked spectacles.

"Let me introduce myself," said Valorius with a New York accent. "My name's Val. I just got into town."

"Dave Brusman," said the man, taking his hand. He still looked bewildered. "Nice to meet you, Val. And I mean that. If you hadn't come along when you did those lousy Blackshirts would have kicked my ribs in." He shook his head. "I don't know why I do it. It's like trying to argue with a parrot. They make the same sounds over and over again. Their minds are like something out of Pirandello: 'Six Clichés in Search of a Slogan.' And they don't have to look very far for their slogans these days. Not any farther than good old Luther Beck."

The name Pirandello meant nothing to Valorius, but Luther Beck was everywhere.

"Do you think the Blackshirts will be back?" he asked.

"Who knows? It's still just a game to most of them. They just like dressing up in their black shirts and having all the answers to everything. Say, speaking of dressing, where in—please don't be offended—but where in the world did you get that suit? You don't watch old movies, do you?"

"No, I'm afraid I don't know—"

"It's like something Cary Grant might have worn." He looked Valorius up and down. "Although you look more like a young Randolph Scott, or maybe Gary Cooper. But don't mind me, Val. I'm just a nut on old movies. Not many people care for that sort of thing any more. It's all this jazz-porn stuff nowadays. You've heard the slogan: 'It's JP, babsie, or it's nothing.'" He shook his head disgustedly.

"No, I'm afraid I've never—"

"Don't mind me, Val." He dabbed at his nose with his handkerchief. "I'm just nervous. You'd think it would be the other way around. But the more frightened I am the faster I talk. I just can't seem to pass one of these lousy Blackshirts without giving a speech."

Valorius decided that the best way to get him calmed down was to let him talk himself out.

"It's mostly the Dollies, of course," he continued.

"But I hear even the PW's are starting to go in for it now. Jazz-porn, I mean. That is, the ones that don't watch football games twelve months a year. Now who with any brains could watch a hundred football games a year? It's an interesting sociological phenomenon. I'm a sociologist, by the way. Not that it matters any more. Nothing does." He touched the scratch on his neck and winced. Suddenly he looked suspicious.

"Say, you're not a D.I. man, are you?" he asked warily. "If you are you're wasting your time, Val—or whatever your name really is. I've been in the D.I. files for years. Check under 'Harmless Crank.' The most subversive thing I've ever done is go to old movies and read a lot of unpopular books. If you people had any guts you'd be cracking down on Luther Beck."

"I'm afraid nothing will stop Luther Beck now," said Valorius. "Not for a thousand years. But I don't even know what a D.I. man is, or Dollies or PW's, or any of those names you just mentioned. I'm telling you the truth, Dave. I just got into town."

"All right, so I'm a born mark. But somehow I believe you, Val. You look too bright to have anything to do with the Department of Investigation—unless you design their computers. And if you're a con man, you're the smoothest I've ever met. In New York, that's saying something. It's just that you sound exactly like you've lived here all your life, just as I have." He shrugged. "I can't figure it out. Maybe the Black-shirts hit me once too often."

"I need your help, Dave," Valorius said simply. "Come over by this streetlamp, I want to show you something." He fished a coin out of his pocket and held it under the light.

Brusman whistled. "Severus Alexander," he read the inscription. "Third century, if I remember correctly."

"That's right. I have a number of coins from that period, and some from a few centuries later. They're all gold coins, and should—"

"Hold on a second, Val." He took a closer look at the

coin. "This is a Roman aureus—I know that much about numismatics—but it looks brand new."

"It's not a forgery." Valorius read his thoughts. "In fact, I'd like to turn the coins over to an expert. They're all the money I've got."

Brusman looked quizzically at him. "You know, I'm beginning to think I really did get hit once too often by those lousy Blackshirts." He reached in his pocket and handed him two paper bills and some debased coins of silver-plated copper. "Here, Val, it's all the money I have. That's all right, take it. I have a friend who's a retired coin dealer. He was also curator of a museum."

"Do you think he'd be interested in buying the coin?"

"I doubt it. The only collectors with the kind of money to buy a coin like this all live on the other side of the fence. But they'd consult a professional before they bought it."

"I assure you it's genuine," said Valorius.

"I'll take your word for it." He smiled. "If it isn't, I'll just tell my friends that I bought a genuine Roman gold coin at three o'clock in the morning from a guy in a Cary Grant suit. It wouldn't be the first time I've been had."

"If your friend knows coins, he'll know that this one is genuine." He hoped he would not have to rob another bank. Security here looked even tighter than in ancient Rome.

"Oh, don't worry about that. He's an old man now, and still lives on this side of the fence. But he knows his coins. I'll show him this one."

"When will you see him?"

"First thing in the morning. Where do you live?"

"Nowhere yet. As I said, I just got into town."

"I get it." Brusman nodded. "But I'd better warn you. If these coins are hot, my friend won't have anything to do with them. Your best bet would be somebody on the other side of the fence. It's mostly Dollies and PW's around here. And Blackshirts," he added distastefully. "By the way, my friend will probably know if these coins are missing from some-body's collection."

"They're not. But now I have to look for a place to stay, so you'll have someplace to contact me tomorrow. I don't know how much the money you gave me is worth—"

"Intrinsically, it's almost worthless. But it should keep you going for a couple of days anyway. It's legal tender. And if you're really looking for a place to stay, there's always a couple of furnished rooms vacant at the dump I live in. It's cheap, and better than sleeping in the street." He shrugged. "I really can't say much more for it."

"Sounds fine. But won't your night-porter, that is, your landlord or building manager be asleep by now?"

"Not old Fika." He laughed. "His bedtime is usually about noon. Him and his pals are probably still watching JP on the tube. It's on twenty-four hours a day now, and Fika's got a new TV-3. The dump is only a couple blocks away. We turn here. It's best to walk down the middle of the street at this time of night. There are too many dark gangways and burned-out buildings."

Only two streetlights were unbroken on this block. The barricade looked months old, and the center of it had been opened to traffic. Empty lots and aban-doned buildings flanked the street; the walls and fences were now only used to support posters of Luther Beck.

"Oh, by the way," said Brusman, glancing warily from one side of the street to the other. "It's best not to repeat what I said about Dollies and PW's, especially to Fika and his pals. They're all Dollies—even Fika, who's got a regular income from his building. That's why they have so much time for pill-popping and booze and jazz-porn." Suddenly he tensed. "Over on the right," he whispered. "I can't quite make out how many of them there are. Let's hope they're too far gone at this time of night to outrun us."

Valorius, his pupils widened, had seen them the

moment he turned the corner. He counted eleven of
them moping in the area of a burned-out tenement;
they were hardly more than children. They did indeed
look too drunk or drugged to give chase. He was only
worried about weapons.

"Don't worry about guns," Brusman reassured him.
"The only people with weapons any more are the
Blackshirts. It's best just to keep walking. If you say
anything back, it only encourages them."

A young girl drunkenly shrieked obscenities at them
as they passed. She was no more than thirteen. The
rest of the gang encouraged her, and her shrill jabber
followed them to the end of the block.

The rooming-house was a dingy four-story brick
building near the corner. Weird sounds were muffled
by the hum of a new airconditioner. Colored lights
flashed and whirled on the slats of the steel shutters
covering a ground floor window.

"Told you they'd still be at it," said Brusman. "Maybe
you'd better let me handle this, Val. Frankly, you're
just a little bit odd. Fika might get suspicious. All he
cares about is the money, but he doesn't want his
building wrecked. You'd better give me back some of
the money. . . . No, that's enough. You'll need the rest.
Just let him get a look at you, and I'll do the talking."

It took five minutes of knocking to get an answer.
The miasma of beer, tobacco, marijuana, and stale
sweat swirled into the hallway as Fika opened the
door. He was a bloated man in his late fifties; his eyes
looked like they had been boiled. He glanced drunkenly
at Valorius as Brusman explained. Nodding, he shuffled back inside to get the key.

His four pals were of much the same type. They
were all drinking canned beer and smoking cigarets of
various kinds. Glancing at Brusman and Valorius,
they winked at each other and exchanged some rather
broad innuendoes. But they could not keep their eyes
off the video screen for long. It covered several square
feet with vivid three-dimensional color; it was the
only light in the room. Its effect was mind-boggling.

Scene followed scene with no connection, each last-
ing no more than a minute or two: armies marching,
landscapes being devastated by floods or hurricanes,
animals being slaughtered, primitive dancing, weird
geometric patterns, and special effects. Every second
or third sequence was sexual, presenting every conceivable combination of men, women, children, and
animals in lewd sex acts. The colors were unnatural,
varying continually through the entire spectrum.

The sound had no connection with the picture. A
cacophony of strange voices spoke, sang, chanted,
whistled, and shrieked; there were machine and
animal noises, the throb of primitive music. To Valorius
it made no sense at all. But perhaps that was its
attraction.

"It's JP, babsie, or it's nothing," said Fika, returning
with the key.

His pals sniggered. On the screen an old satyr
much like themselves was in a hayloft with two naked
boys. The colors had been reversed.

"I hope your friend likes his room, Mr. Brusman,"
Fika said knowingly, winking at his pals.

They exploded with laughter. Brusman's jaw muscles tightened as he took the key, but he said nothing.
Valorius followed him up two flights of stairs and
down a dim corridor.

"It's pretty clean," said Brusman, turning on the
light. "I mean, no bugs or rats. Here's the key. There
are some real weirdos in the building, so you'd better
bolt your door. Anything else you need, Val?"

"A lot of information. But that can wait. What time
do you think you'll be able to see your friend?"

"Crack of dawn." He grinned. "I'm dying to know if
this is all real. Not only the coin, but you too, Val.
Don't get me wrong," he added quickly. "You saved my
neck. If it weren't for you I'd probably be sprawled in
the gutter now—courtesy of Luther Beck and company.
But let's face it. You don't run into a guy in a Cary
Grant suit with a brand-new gold coin that's really
two thousand years old every night of the week. If you

want to tell me about it, fine. If not, not. It's your business. See you tomorrow. Remember to bolt your door."

Valorius did more than bolt his door; he barricaded it with everything but the bed. The underhanded tricks of Magus Rex in ancient Rome had left him bewildered, they were so unlike his legendary equitableness. Not that a barricaded door would stop Magus Rex—nothing would. But it might stall any agents he employed. The great wizard had somehow discovered him the very day he had materialized in ancient Rome—although he seemed surprised to see him at Volpina's banquet. Perhaps he already knew of his presence here in ancient New York.

A bare lightbulb was the room's only light. Wallpaper peeled from the walls; the woodwork was cracked and greasy. The bed was probably not much more comfortable than the floor. Stout bars and shutters cut off any ventilation from the single window. It was like an oven. During the day the heat would probably be unbearable.

As he undressed he thought wistfully of the luxury in which Magus Rex had certainly ensconced himself and Zenobia by now. Probably inside the most decadent enclave in New York. On "the other side of the fence," as the expression went.

# CHAPTER XVII
# THE COLLECTOR

Valorius sprang out of bed and bundled on his clothes. The pounding at the door grew louder. It was a cloudless summer morning but only a mid-winter gloom filtered through the grimy window. He hurriedly dismantled his barricade.

"Val? Are you all right?" Brusman's muffled voice came through the door.

"Sorry to keep you waiting," he said, pushing the wardrobe aside and unbolting the door.

"We were worried when you didn't answer right away." Brusman burst into the room. "Are you all right?"

"I'm fine. I guess I must have overslept." He glanced suspiciously into the corridor.

Two burly men stared expressionlessly over Brusman's shoulder. They looked like Blackshirts out of uniform. The midwinter gloom was even deeper in the dingy corridor.

"Don't worry," said Brusman. "They're with us."

"Did you get a chance to see your friend yet?"

"I did more than see him, I brought him. And he's more than a friend, he's my uncle—great-uncle, really. Uncle Mel, come on in. Val, meet my uncle, Mel Silverstein. He's my grandmother's younger brother," he explained.

The old man shook hands with a surprisingly firm grip.

"Val," he smiled amiably. "It must be convenient, having only one name. But at my age it's nice being introduced as younger anything. May I please sit down? It's been an exciting morning for me."

"Yes, here." Valorius quickly brought a chair. "I was using it to barricade the door."

"And a good idea too." The old man mopped his brow with a large red handkerchief. "Whew! That climb! You couldn't get a room on the first floor, maybe? And it looks like another scorcher. It's eighty already, and not yet ten o'clock."

Valorius glanced uncertainly toward the two big men who had remained in the corridor.

"David," said the old man, "close the door. That's better. They're just hired help, Val. Bodyguards. Believe me, even a retired coin dealer needs bodyguards these days. I donated my collection to the museum years ago, but just a rumor is enough to get me killed. I went through all this as a boy." He shook his head sadly. "And now it's started again. Only this time nobody seems to be fighting back. But that's another story." He smiled amiably up at Valorius. "Today we're talking about coins. And let me tell you that this is the most perfect specimen of a Severus Alexander aureus I've ever seen."

"How soon could it be converted into cash?" asked Valorius.

The old man looked curiously at him.

"Let me be frank with you, Val," he said. "If I know anything in this world, it's coins. But to me this coin is a mystery. Now I know I'm an old man and maybe my memory isn't what it used to be. So I checked the catalogs, even though I myself wrote most of them. I even made phone calls." He raised his eyebrows. "This is a perfect specimen, and I would stake my reputation that it's genuine. Yet there's no record of it anywhere." He looked at Valorius for an explanation.

"I came by the coin honestly, Mr. Silverstein," said Valorius. "I'm afraid that's all I can tell you."

The old man shrugged. "All right, so be a mystery man. And I must confess—and you shouldn't be offended—that my first thought was that the coin had been stolen. But no private collector reports such a loss, and no museum ever had such a coin in the first place." He lowered his voice to a whisper. "David tells me you have more coins."

Valorius laid the leather purse on the table. The old man opened it with trembling fingers. He put a jeweler's glass to his eye and examined one of the coins.

"I can't believe it!" he gasped. "A Julia Mammea aureus, and it looks like it's fresh from the mint. And these others!"

"Take it easy, Uncle Mel," said Brusman. "Remember your heart."

The old man was literally panting for breath.

"Thank you, David," he said, mopping his brow with his red handkerchief. "I'm fine. But you're right I shouldn't get excited. Not that there's all that much to live for these days. It's just that, well. . . . Let me be frank. Forty years a coin dealer, twenty years curator of a museum, and this is the finest collection I've ever seen assembled in one place. Even this leather purse looks a thousand years old."

Valorius suddenly had an idea. "Mr. Silverstein, would you consent to act as my agent? At the usual commission, of course. But the coins must be converted into cash as soon as possible. You see, I'm presently without funds—"

"Yes, David told me," said the old man, looking quizzically at him. "You know, the older I get the less certain I am about life. There are many strange things in this world." He shrugged. "But as to acting as your agent, Mr. Man-With-One-Name, my answer is yes—with conditions."

"Such as?"

"At my age money means nothing. My wants are few, and I have enough to live comfortably until I die. Or until Luther Beck's thugs drag me out in the middle of the night."

"Uncle Mel—" Brusman began.

"Please, David. You have the makings of a brilliant scholar, but you're too young to understand these things. But that's another story. As I was saying, I will act as your agent on condition that you donate my commission, in coins, to the museum. They don't dare open the doors to the public any more, but we have to go on pretending that civilization still exists. Is that agreed? Fine. I'll have the contract drawn up at once. Needless to say, the only collectors with this kind of money live on the other side of the fence. But I know them personally, and arrangements will be made as soon as possible."

"For tonight?"

The old man shrugged. "If you like, yes. But if it's cash you need, take this as an advance on the sale." He handed Valorius a sealed envelope. "Believe me, Val, you're not the first person forced to sell a fine collection I've ever dealt with. Or the fortieth, for that matter." He rose from his chair. "Since you're in a hurry, I'll start making phone calls at once. May I take this Julia Mammea aureus with me? I've never seen one so fine."

"Yes, of course. Keep it as an advance on your commission."

"I was hoping you'd say that," he grinned. "It's a museum piece if ever I've seen one. I'd hate to see it wasted on those. . . . Well, to each his own. And if you'll take an old man's advice, get yourself some new clothes. We'll be meeting the collectors at a party—"

"A party?"

The old man smiled wryly. "It's always party-time on the other side of the fence these days. David will help you pick something out. Your suit is charming,

Val. I myself had one just like it when I was a young man. Continental cut and everything. It brings back memories. But such things aren't worn on the other side of the fence. They don't wear suits any more, they wear costumes. And some of the women hardly even do that. I'll contact you probably late this afternoon. But for God's sake, be careful," he added in a whisper.

"And you be careful too, Uncle Mel," said Brusman. "You know how concerned I am, and how many times I've warned you—"

"I know, I know." The old man waved it away. "But I've lived all my life a free man, and it's too late to change. If I have to start living like a rat in a trap, maybe living isn't such a good idea after all. Besides," he nodded toward the corridor, "I've got my good friends Gog and Magog to watch out for me."

"They're big enough," Brusman said doubtfully. "But I don't trust them."

"So who trusts anybody these days?" The old man shrugged. "In any case, if I'm not mugged or murdered, I'll contact you probably late this afternoon. David, take care of our mysterious friend." He disappeared down the corridor with his two huge bodyguards trailing sullenly behind him.

Brusman quickly locked the door.

"I wish he wouldn't take so many chances, a man his age." He shook his head. "His shop isn't even a shop any more, just a place where he and his cronies get together and talk about the old days. But he averages about five robbery attempts a month anyway. And there's no use calling in the police. They can't do anything. But, like Uncle Mel says, that's another story. The problem now is to get you dressed up so you can make your debut at the ball tonight. And from what I hear about the goings on on the other side of the fence, it really will be a ball."

The stores had taken down their metal screens and shutters, but armed guards were always at hand where anything valuable was sold. Even the clothing store had an armed guard patrolling the racks of gaudy finery. Valorius was surprised to see so many unoccupied people during working hours. Brusman explained when they were safely back in the furnished room.

"They're Dollies or PW's, most of them. But you said last night that you'd never heard of either, didn't you? Well, it's best not to use the terms too freely in public. Some people are sensitive about such things, and the terms are not exactly complimentary."

"Does PW stand for 'prisoner of war?'" Valorius recalled the term from his readings in ancient history.

"Say, that does go back a few years, doesn't it? And I suppose they are prisoners of a kind of war. But, actually, the terms Dolly and PW come from a very important book of a few years ago: STRUCTURE AND PATTERN IN MODERN SOCIETY by Colbridge and Eddy. Luther Beck has made it a rare book, but it was extremely influential when it first came out."

"That's right," Valorius recalled. "Luther Beck did a lot of book burning, didn't he?"

Brusman look curiously at him.

"But then what does the term mean?" Valorius asked quickly. He would have to be more careful about what he said. These ancient New Yorkers seemed to be a lot shrewder than the Romans had been.

"PW?" said Brusman. "It's the initials of 'pyramid worker.'"

"Pyramid worker?" Valorius wondered for a moment if he had possibly gotten his ancient history mixed up.

"They don't actually build pyramids, of course," Brusman explained. "It's just that Colbridge and Eddy compared them to the people of ancient Egypt, endlessly building useless structures. The PW's today work on big public works projects trumped up for them by the government. Mostly historical monuments and things like that. You can't help feeling sorry for the PW's. At least they make an effort."

"And the Dollies don't?" Valorius finished opening the boxes and began laying out his new clothes on the bed. "Is that term from ancient Egypt too?"

"No, that goes back to ancient Rome. You see, Colbridge and Eddy were really trying to put modern society into an historical framework. 'Dollies' comes from dole. That is, people who live their entire lives on government subsidies. But I suppose it's not really their fault either." He shrugged. "The trend started a couple of generations ago, about the time they made that suit you're wearing. Computerized farming was the last straw—overnight almost everybody had to become urban. But the new automated factories were also eliminating jobs. The problem is simply that ninety percent of the human race is now economically superfluous."

Valorius was interested. The history he knew was mostly about major personalities, not economic trends. To him this was simply the age of the infamous Luther Beck. Evidently there were more factors involved.

"That's what I was trying to explain last night," Brusman continued. "The Blackshirts didn't know what the hell I was talking about."

"Is that why they jumped you?" He crushed the empty clothing boxes and stuffed them into the garbage pail.

"Not exactly." Brusman touched his swollen cheek; there was a small bandage on his neck. "Only about three percent of the population now have any real economic function. Even adding their jackals and camp-followers, you still get no more than ten percent. I was trying to explain last night that all Luther Beck and his henchmen really want to do is replace the ruling three percent with themselves. The Blackshirts would then just be the new jackals and camp-followers. That's when I got slugged." He shook his head. "I should know better by now. You can teach parrots new words, but you can't get them to think. How does it fit?"

Valorius had begun trying on his new clothes. It was a strange costume, although he had been assured that it would be considered distinctly conservative inside the fence. The shirt was of scarlet silk, with puffed sleeves and a collar that opened halfway down his chest; it was belted at the waist, but hung outside the trousers to mid thigh. The trousers themselves were skin tight, of some black elastic material with the sheen of fine satin. A black cape lined with scarlet silk hung from two golden rings on his shoulders. Black leather boots and a scarlet Robin Hood cap finished off the costume. It was almost a parody of the peasant dress he had seen in medieval France. He had worn stranger costumes.

"Oh, by the way," Brusman warned him. "Don't say anything about Dollies or PW's or Luther Beck inside the fence. In fact, don't talk seriously about anything at all. It's considered bad form. The latest fad is a kind of affected baby-talk called *babsie-rapsie*. I'm never invited inside the fence any more because I'm too serious. My articles are read by about three hundred other scholars who can't do anything about anything even if they wanted to. Sometimes I think we're just like Uncle Mel and his cronies, uselessly talking about the old days." He turned to answer the knock at the door. "That must be from Uncle Mel now."

But it was only a sullen, flashy-looking youth with a large paper bag. It was the lunch they had ordered from the fast-food stall down the street hours ago. He delivered it to Brusman as if he were doing him a favor.

"Probably cold by now," he said, relocking the door. "Lucky we only ordered cheeseburgers."

Before they had finished the cold cheeseburgers there was another knock at the door. This time the message was from Uncle Mel. One of his bodyguards sullenly handed them a sealed envelope. Evidently he had been instructed to wait.

Brusman chuckled as he read the attached note. "Leave it to Uncle Mel! Here's the contract, a list of interested collectors he's already contacted, and a full itinerary for tonight. He would have been a tycoon in the business world."

Valorius signed the contract without reading it. Brusman witnessed it; the huge bodyguard also added his signature in the clumsy, rounded hand of the functional illiterate. Then he left—as silent and sullen as he had come.

"Your first stop," said Brusman with a grin, "is the museum, to deposit Uncle Mel's commission. Then it's party time. He'll be here in a cab at nine. That means you've still got a few hours to wait. My advice is to take a nap. That's what I'm going to do. Anything else you need before I go?"

"Just more information," said Valorius. "Where inside the fence would a wealthy, highly-cultured voluptuary most likely be found?"

"Well," Brusman said thoughtfully, "they're all more or less wealthy inside the fence, or they couldn't live there. And most of them are skilled at some complex profession. But highly cultured? I'm not sure I know what you mean."

"For instance, an exquisite connoisseur whose taste runs to decadence."

"Hmmmmm. There's only one place that I know of where such a person might be found. But when you say *wealthy*—"

"He would have access to virtually unlimited wealth."

"Then he would almost certainly be found at Club Sybaris. But if you're thinking about getting in there, forget it. Try Fort Knox. It's easier."

"Where is this Club Sybaris?"

'Club Sybaris is in the enclave just off Central Park. Exactly where inside, I don't know. But I hear that if you get within a mile of the place you're lucky."

Valorius thought he could get somewhat closer than that. He did not take a nap after Brusman left. His thoughts were mostly of Zenobia. Somehow he had to contact her before Magus Rex knew that he was here in ancient New York. Assuming of course that he did not know already. Since the great wizard had made no move against him, as he had in ancient Rome, this was at least a reasonable assumption. How he might react when he did find out was not pleasant to contemplate.

The unventilated room was hot and stuffy. Valorius had to make certain adjustments in his body temperature. He sat beside the open window looking into the street below. Some ingenious Blackshirt had pasted a huge poster of Luther Beck on top of the flat roof of a garage, so not even those in the buildings above could escape that banal and evil face. Again and again he tried to foresee all possible contingencies. And with Magus Rex virtually all contingencies were indeed possible. But he made little headway. It was all too confusing. At last he decided just to trust Zenobia; perhaps she could succeed in somehow persuading her father of his worthiness as a suitor. He had no choice but to persevere, confident that she would not ask him to follow without good reason. Nor would she willfully endanger his life.

Brusman reappeared punctually at a quarter to nine. They waited in the dim hallway just inside the front door. All cabs operating outside the fence were armored, but it was not wise to dawdle between the front door and the cab—that was where passengers were most vulnerable. The sounds and smells emanating from Fika's room indicated that he and his pals were at it again. Or still.

Valorius had brought only half the coins with him. The rest he had hidden in his room. He waited until the cab had actually appeared before he handed Brusman the sealed envelope containing the location of the hidden coins. A few mountain sanctuaries would survive for the first few decades of the Black Ages, and the coins might enable the bespectacled little scholar to reach one of them.

"Open that if I don't get back," he said, shaking Brusman's hand.

Then he hurried down the front steps. The cab was armor-plated; the windows and tires bullet-proof. Mr. Silverstein was alone in the back seat. The instant the door closed the driver pulled away from the curb— and just in time.

A gang of toughs came tumbling out of a gangway

on the opposite side of the street, but the cab was already out of reach. The last to arrive was a dwarf; his short legs had prevented him from keeping up with the others. He barely had time to read the license plate before the back lights of the cab disappeared around a corner.

# CHAPTER XVIII
# CLUB SYBARIS

The museum was an imitation-Greek structure, begrimed with decades of soot. It stood outside the enclaves, so it had to have guards and an electrified barbed-wire fence of its own. The public had once been admitted daily; now a special permit was needed to get inside. But Silverstein was a former curator, known by sight to all the guards. Even so, the armored cab was not allowed to park inside the fence. Valorius was photographed at the entrance.

"I must apologize for all this crazy rigmarole," said Silverstein, leading the way though the darkened halls. Many of the display cases were boarded up. "And such a shame that the public must lose all this! But what are you going to do? Theft, I could understand. But it was all this crazy vandalism. Better a troop of baboons than what we used to get in here! Would you believe that they actually used to come with hammers hidden under their coats! It was a game for them—to see how much they could wreck. And now it's lost to everybody!" Shaking his head, he led the way up a dark flight of stairs.

The steel door looked out of place in the marble doorway. It was evidently a new security measure. Silverstein pushed a button. A moment later a peephole slid open. At last the steel door itself was opened, and they entered a corridor which ended in a second steel door. A miniature television camera followed their every step.

Walnut wainscoting gave the office a sense of solid comfort, but the thin elderly man who rose to meet them looked anything but comfortable. His desk was strewn with old catalogs.

"Mel, I just can't believe it's true," he cried. "You weren't kidding me on the phone, were you?"

"Let the coins themselves be my witness," said Silverstein. "But I must tell you, Bob, that I myself can hardly believe it. Here's the mystery man himself." He introduced him to Valorius, who turned over the leather purse. The two old men trotted at once to the desk.

For the next half hour they were in a kind of numismatic ecstasy. Jeweler's glasses flashed; the pages of musty catalogs were riffled feverishly; gasps and expletives broke forth every few minutes. They would probably have remained hunched over the coins half the night if Valorius had not hurried them along. He almost had to drag Silverstein out of the office.

"So how can I be sure we've made the right choice?" he moaned. "Maybe we should have kept a second Severus aureus and let the Maximin denarius go. These decisions take time."

Valorius opened the cab door for him. "You'll have all the time you want, Mr. Silverstein. I may not need the coins after tonight."

"Things don't move that fast, Val. Every collector on the list I showed you will jump at the chance. But a sale such as this takes time. And if you're in such a hurry, why do you want to start with the fourth person on the list?"

"He lives in the enclave just off Central Park, doesn't he?

His eyes narrowed. "So what's so important about
the neighborhood just off Central Park?"

"There's someone there I'm expecting to meet. In
fact, I may have to leave you for a while once we're
inside the fence."

The old man looked suspiciously at him. "Val, tell
me the truth. You're not up to something, are you? I'm
acting in this matter in good faith. And I shouldn't
want—"

"I'm afraid I can't explain, Mr. Silverstein. But I
assure you that I'm in no way jeopardizing your good
name or trying to take advantage of you. Let me show
my own good faith in this matter." He handed him the
leather purse.

"Who are you really, Val?" He looked oddly at him.
"So I'm an old man, and sometimes old men get crazy
ideas. But I have this strange feeling. . . . " Then he
shook his head. "That's ridiculous! Don't pay any
attention to me. I don't know what I'm talking about.
But, to get back to business, I do know coins. Mystery
or no mystery, I'll make for you the best deal—"

The driver slammed on his brakes. The cab screeched
to a halt just after turning the corner. They were
instantly engulfed by a mob of brawling young men
and women. It was a riot. The driver had no chance to
back the cab out of the street.

"Blackshirts again!" grumbled Silverstein. "Are all
the doors locked? Then we should be safe. We just sit
tight until the police get here. Not that they'll do
anything," he shrugged.

The floodlights from the enclave three blocks ahead
were the street's only illumination. Two rival gangs
fought viciously back and forth, silhouetted against
the distant light. The Blackshirts were outnumbered.
But they were better disciplined and more ruthless.
They had no qualms about stomping a fallen opponent,
male or female, and they seemed to be better armed.
Both sides took swipes at the cab with clubs or chains.
The armor and bullet-proof glass defied them.

The cab driver turned around and rapped at the

glass partition, then pointed down the street.

"The police van," said Silverstein. "I think he wants us to close the vents. See that handle in the middle of the door? That's right. Turn it as far as it will go. I'll get the other side. I hope this guy has his emergency air tank filled. I'm in no mood for a whiff of F.I.X."

"Fix?"

"They're initials, F—I—X. Exactly what chemicals they stand for I couldn't say. It's a stun gas."

The armored police van plunged right into the midst of the rioters, knocking several of them down. A greenish fog rose all about the van. The riot stopped within seconds. Scores of young men and women were turned by the gas into glassy-eyed automatons. All their movements were in slow motion.

"Night after night." Silverstein shook his head disgustedly. "The police are getting good at rounding them up. Not that it makes any difference. Luther Beck will have his goons out of jail before morning."

With the bored efficiency of the overworked, the police began leading the now zombie-like rioters back to the van. One by one they were neatly packed inside like so many slabs of meat. Nor had those beyond the reach of the stun gas gotten very far. Hardly had the van stopped when policemen in helmets and gas-masks tumbled out of every door like giant beetles. Their pistols fired darts trailing long wires connected to the van by insulated cables. Like tiny harpoons the darts imbedded themselves in the skin of those trying to flee. They froze in their tracks until they were reeled in like fish.

"Just look at that, will you?" muttered Silverstein. "A normal kid would at least struggle. But these kids are so experienced in going to jail that they know every trick. One move too many and they get knocked out with fifty thousand volts from the wire. So not a twitch. Once upon a time young people like this learned other things, like law, or medicine. Ach, what's the use!" He shook his head wearily. "They'll all be out of jail before morning anyway."

The last of the rioters were soon packed into the police van and the anti-riot equipment recovered. It was all very efficient. Valorius noticed, however, that the policemen never turned their backs on the crowd that had gathered.

"We can open the vents now," said Silverstein. "F.I.X. is only effective for a few minutes."

There was a sharp rap at the cab window. Two young Blackshirts who had not been involved in the riot stood at the door. Their pamphlets had different titles, but the banal, evil face of Luther Beck was printed on every cover.

Silverstein waved them away, shaking his head distastefully. The two Blackshirts looked at him with eyes that seemed to say, "Someday you won't refuse us anything." Then they turned and began distributing their pamphlets among the crowd.

A double-gate system was used at the entrance to the enclave. The armored cab entered a giant cage of chain-link fencing; the outer gate was relocked the moment they were inside. Straddling the fence was a guardhouse built of reinforced concrete and shatter-proof glass. The cab was searched while everyone, including the driver, entered the building. A uniformed technician sat behind a pane of bullet-proof glass. The cab driver had been through it all before. He did not have to be told to put his hands, palms down, on the identity plate. A moment later his picture and complete dossier appeared on a video screen. A green light flashed. The technician nodded to the guard.

Meanwhile another guard had dialed the number Silverstein had given him. On a small video screen appeared the refined, intelligent face of a middle-aged man who was evidently trying to look young. He wore a kind of court jester costume, and looked slightly intoxicated. There seemed to be some kind of party going on behind him.

"Good evening, Mr. Poynter," said Silverstein. "I've brought the young man I told you about this afternoon."

"Silvy-babsie!" The man on the screen clapped his hands like a happy baby. "You come see ickle me. Goo-goo! Pease tell nize man I'se hap-hap see you. Upsy-daisy! Goo-bye, babsie." And the video screen went dark.

Silverstein sighed and turned away as he explained. "Everybody talks like a baby. And thinks that way, if you ask me. But nobody asks me anything," he muttered. "I'm just an old man. Let's go, Val."

They entered another world. The buildings inside the fence were older than those on the outside, and hence better designed and constructed. They had all been lovingly cleaned and renovated. Well-tended lawns and gardens filled every open patch of earth; the streets were clean, and all the streetlamps were lighted. Even the parks were open at night. The people were healthy and intelligent-looking. They seemed carefree, almost abandoned, in their continual round of amusements. It reminded Valorius of a colossal farewell party. He alone inside the enclave, save Magus Rex and Zenobia, knew to what it was they were saying farewell.

"No, no, I insist," he said as the cab pulled up in front of an old-fashioned luxury hotel. "You go on ahead, Mr. Silverstein. I'll pay the fare."

"So be a big spender! You won't get an argument from me. I'll meet you in the lobby, from where I must phone upstairs. And from where," he smiled, "I can't overhear any questions you are asking the driver."

Valorius watched the old man trot across the sidewalk and enter the revolving door. These ancient New Yorkers were indeed a lot shrewder than the ancient Romans had been.

"Club Sybaris?" The cab driver pondered his question. "Sure I know where it is. But I never took nobody there. If you can afford to get into Club Sybaris you can afford a private chauffeur. Look, pal, if you're thinking of crashing the joint, forget it. It would take an army to get you inside."

Valorius paid the fare, including a generous tip.

He held a ten dollar bill in his hand.

"I just want to know where it is," he said.

"Sure, pal," said the driver, glancing at the ten, "anything you say." His directions were concise and easy to follow. "But like I say," he added, "it would take an army to get you inside. The cops can't even get in the joint. Which proves what I always said—if you got money you can get away with anything."

Silverstein was standing in front of a video screen just to the right of the revolving door. An armed guard stood at his side.

"Val, over here!" he called.

The same refined, middle-aged face smiled babyishly from the video screen.

As Valorius approached it burbled, "There nize ickle boysie. Goo-goo! Upsy-daisy, babsies. Whoopsie." Then the screen went dark.

"And would you believe, he's a world famous architect?" Silverstein muttered. "But that's the fad, so what are you going to do? I hope you like parties, Val. This one covers the entire sixth floor."

"There's been a change in plans, Mr. Silverstein," said Valorius hurriedly. "I have to see someone right away. You have the coins, so you really don't need me. I'll meet you here later."

The old man looked at him for a moment. "Val, I wish I knew who you really are. So then I'll see you later. And if I don't, I don't." He walked across the lobby toward the elevator.

It was sad to realize that Luther Beck and his Blackshirts would soon doom the very existence of such men. Valorius felt less sympathy for the others he had seen inside the enclave. They had abandoned their social responsibility for a merry-go-round of self-indulgence. But not all the armed guards or electric fences in the world would hold out the Black Ages. He pushed through the revolving door and out into the balmy summer night.

It took some doing to reach even the club's security system. Like the walls of a medieval castle the outer buildings of four city blocks, elegant three- and four-story structures of the previous century, had been run together; all the alleys and gangways had been walled off. There was only a single passage through this outer wall, a kind of porte-cochère with fortified gates at each end. In addition, each building in the outer wall had its own security system. Only on the inside of this wall did the real defenses of Club Sybaris begin.

Every building in the outer wall was occupied; the tenants had apparently all been carefully screened. Several of them awoke hours later as if from a trance. The last thing they remembered seeing was a tall man in a scarlet silk blouse and skin-tight black trousers. But nothing seemed to be wrong. The matter was never reported.

The structures right behind the outer wall had all been cleared away. A cluster of elegant brownstones stood at the very heart of an open park: this was Club Sybaris. The park rivaled the gardens of Magus Rex in its opulent floriculture. Golden light globes gave everything the unearthly lusciousness of a Chinese screen; the myriad perfumes of exotic blossoms overpowered even the fumes of industry. How many hidden television cameras and electric-eyes the garden also contained, Valorius could not even guess. He would not get far on foot.

A single road wound through the park. Members of Club Sybaris passed through the double gates of the porte-cochère, left their chauffeur in the guard-building, and were driven by a special guard through the park. There was no other way in. What further defenses might surround the cluster of brownstones at the center of the park could not be seen through the golden light.

Valorius stepped out of the shadows. He was careful not to stray too near the park itself as he approached the guard-building.

The inner gate was armor-plated; its stanchions were of reinforced concrete. There were no gate crashers

at Club Sybaris. Both guards carried machine-guns;
they started to raise them as Valorius approached. But
then they relaxed. A few minutes later a black limousine entered the tunnel between the two gates. The
passengers were identified and their chauffeur replaced
with the special driver who wore a scarlet silk blouse
and skin-tight black trousers.

Valorius' driving would not have won any prizes,
but he managed to keep the limousine out of the
flower beds. There were two passengers. The limousine's
owner was a sleek, ruddy old gentleman with glossy
white hair and mustache. His companion was no
more than twenty, with long blond hair and the complexion of a fresh peach; a silk gown clung like a
second skin. The limousine's owner was evidently
generous with diamonds; the heavy-lidded sensuality
of his companion hinted at another kind of generosity.
They were half way to Club Sybaris before Valorius
realized that the companion was not a woman.

As the limousine approached the center of the park,
Valorius could see that the cluster of brownstones
actually formed a single structure. He parked the
limousine the best he could. His two passengers docilely escorted him past the guards hovering at the
entrance.

It was fortunate that he was dressed conservatively.
Great voluptuaries tend to be conservative, if not
reactionary. A whole gamut of servants, minions,
panders, procurers, lackeys, scullions, puppets, and
flatterers is vital to the more elegant forms of vice, and
liberalism invariably creates a servant problem.

Evidently it took a long time to acquire enough
wealth to afford a place like this: club members were
middle-aged to elderly, with only a scattering of spoiled
sons and nephews. The service personnel outnumbered
members about twenty to one. The conservative dress
code did not apply to them. They were dressed or
undressed according to the taste of the members they
served. Valorius was accepted as a prodigal son or
nephew.

The cluster of brownstones had been unified only spatially. A kaleidoscope of sensuality ranged through the labyrinthine rooms and passageways, from the most refined to the utterly bestial. No taste was ungratified. Club members were the elite of ancient New York's wealthiest and most powerful. They seemed to know that their time had come—the feast before the deluge. If Magus Rex was anywhere in New York it would be here.

The structure was four storys high, but there were basements and even sub-basements. There was no pattern to the corridors that wandered through the structure; the carpets were plush and inches thick. Most of the rooms were private. Even the open saloons were rather intimate, and all the members seemed to know each other. It would not be a good idea just to stroll about asking questions.

He came upon a saloon that was more like an extended boudoir, all satin and lace. The lights were dim, the music soft and mellow. The club members here tended to be more elderly than middle-aged; some were actually decrepit. But the hostesses were barely pubescent; except for some leaves and feathers in their boyishly-cut hair, they were stark naked. In spite of the satin and lace the scene had a classical air: dryads being ogled by lecherous old satyrs. One old man just inside the doorway was actually drooling, whether from lust or senility was hard to tell in the dim light.

One dryad stood by herself in an alcove. She looked a year or two older than the others, perhaps sixteen. She was apparently on her break. She sipped a green drink of some kind from a tall glass filled with ice cubes. Her cigaret was violet colored with a gold filter. She was not at all abashed by her nakedness.

"Lookin' fer somethin', honey?" She smiled brazenly.

"My uncle," said Valorius.

"Oh," she sounded disappointed. "What's his name?"

"Well perhaps I'd better describe him to you. A man of about fifty—"

"Sounds too young to be down here." She took a long drag on her violet-colored cigaret.

"He's extremely distinguished looking. Silky black beard and hair, slightly gray around the temples."

"Say, wait a sec!" She suddenly looked very interested. "He doesn't maybe have, like, long violet fingernails, does he?"

"Yes," said Valorius with a sigh of relief. "That's exactly the man I'm looking for."

"You mean Rex Maguson is your uncle!" she cried. Then she caught herself; afraid she was making too much noise, she peeked warily out of the alcove. "So what am I worried about?" She shrugged her naked shoulders. "These old goats can't hear any more — among other things. But is he really your uncle? I mean, Rex Maguson? Oh, wow! But what are you looking down here for? Like you'd ever catch Rex Maguson with these old billygoats!"

"I was supposed to meet him here, but he didn't say where."

"Say, you're new here, aren't you? Yeah, I thought so. Well, he's probably upstairs playing cards. Most likely bridge, 'cause it's still early. And," she added with a sniff, "your cousin's there too."

"You don't like her?" He needed an emissary to Zenobia, but one he could trust.

"Oh, she's all right, I guess. Everybody thinks she's such a big glamour-puss. But anybody'd look good if they had the money to spend on clothes she does."

"You don't get much to spend on clothes, do you?" He laughed, relaxed and happy as he neared the end of his long quest.

She giggled like a schoolgirl, blushing with pleasure rather than embarrassment. "I will pretty soon, though. Only three more days and then I go upstairs. Started breaking in last week. I'm getting too old for down here." She took a deep breath, swelling out her burgeoning young breasts. "These old grandpas only like kids, and I'll be sixteen next month. Say, I got an idea! I could show you where your uncle is myself.

Sure, why not? Here, gimme, say a hundred, make it two fifties if you got. . . . That should do it. Be right back." She glided away like a dryad through a satin forest.

When she returned she was wearing a kind a gold silk chlamys, with Grecian fretwork in chocolate brown all along the border. It was held by a golden clasp over her right shoulder, exposing that side of her body. It was even more alluring than her nakedness had been. She wore little golden sandals on her feet.

"Well, I tried." She grinned. "I told Madame Otero— that's my boss down here—some new member wants I should show him around. But she said 'No' like she always does—the old cow! Then I said you gave me a fifty, and I give it to her. But then she saw I had something else in my hand. That's the trouble down here—no place to keep your tips. So I had to fork over the other fifty too." She shrugged. "Only three more days. Then I go to work for Madame Merode. She's nice. And I get to wear some nice clothes. At least more than down here." She giggled. "This way. Finding the right elevator's sometimes tricky. By the way, what's your name?"

"Val, uh, Maguson," he said.

"My name's Pixie. At least it is down here. I haven't picked out my name for upstairs yet. Madame Merode suggested Lenore. But I don't know." She frowned. "That sounds kind of spooky, don't it? My real name is Barbara, Barbara Blocker. But they don't like names like that around here. I'm taking dancing lessons. Then maybe I can get in one of the shows. That's where you make the most money. Except if you want to work in the basement," she added distastefully. "Some girls actually like that kind of stuff. You know, getting beat up and that. But I'd rather be a dancer. I can do the hoochie-koochie already and I've got my name already picked out—Yasmin. Don't you think that's pretty?" She chattered merrily away until they reached the elevator and entered it.

Valorius was no longer listening. The confrontation

awaiting him just two floors above was, perhaps literally, a matter of life and death. He concentrated, trying to still the pounding of his heart.

The girl pushed a button and the elevator rose silently; seconds later the doors slid silently open. "Here we are. See that big velvet curtain, the maroon one at the end? That's it. None of the big shows start for an hour yet, so he's sure to be in there playing cards. From what I hear, he's real good too."

The brassy music of a carnival came from somewhere nearby. Down the corridor from the velvet curtain were the doors of an auditorium. The music was muffled and would not be heard in the card room.

"Oh, that's just the variety show," said the girl. "Comedians and acrobats and stuff like that. Some of the old-timers like it. But you just about have to be a circus star to get a job there. And there's not really that much money in it anyway."

"Could you deliver a message for me?" asked Valorius.

"Not on this floor. I'm not even supposed to leave the elevator. That's why we walked so far to get this one, so's I could point out the place you wanted without actually going onto the floor. Which is against the rules. At least for three more days. Then I'll be working steady up here. If you like you could drop in some night. I mean, if you got nothing else to do. It's way around on the other side of the Club. But anybody could tell you the way to Madame Merode's. I don't know if my name'll be Lenore or not, but you could just ask for the new girl. They'll know who you mean."

"Here," said Valorius, handing her a hundred dollar bill. He would just have to find another emissary to Zenobia. "And thanks for everything. You won't have to tell Madame Otero about that, will you?"

"Fat chance!" She laughed. "With clothes at least you got somewheres to hide your tips. Remember, Madame Merode's. I mean, if you got nothing else to do." She smiled mischievously at him as the elevator doors slid shut.

# CHAPTER XIX
## THE MOOT

The corridor was decorated in maroon and gold. Just to his right were the ormolu doors of the music hall; at the end of the corridor to his left were the maroon curtains of the gaming room, in front of which a transverse corridor opened in either direction. Where that might lead remained to be seen. The ceiling varied in height; the corridors varied in width, their levels broken here and there by ramps. The variety-show music could barely be heard. The corridor was deserted.

He had no idea if Zenobia had made any progress in convincing her father of his eligibility as a suitor. The first thing he had to tell her was exactly where he might receive another message verse—just in case. He still had to find some way of contacting her before Magus Rex knew he was here.

He started to part the velvet curtains, but then hesitated. What if Magus Rex was playing cards just on the other side? He should have asked the girl how this particular gaming room was laid out. Should he try and find someone to take a card or message in to Zenobia? But Magus Rex might be on the lookout for just such a thing. If he took Zenobia away from ancient New York—

Suddenly he realized that he was being watched. In the shadows at the end of the transverse corridor to his right stood a group of strange-looking people. Most of them were smoking cigarets. Through the doorway behind them he could see stagehands moving props and sets. He realized that they were merely the performers for the variety show. A cadaverous-looking man in a tuxedo stood with a scantily-clad young woman: the magician and his assistant. The juggler stood in the doorway with an armload of plates, ready to go on. A troup of dwarfs dressed grotesquely in satin tights began some warming-up exercises. They were probably part of a tumbling act. None of them was looking at him now. But one had been.

The last thing he wanted was to arouse suspicion. It was now too late to retreat. He parted the maroon velvet curtains and stepped into the gaming room.

He found himself in a dim foyer. Individual lights illuminated the gaming tables, but the spaces between were unlighted. It was as good a chance as he could have hoped for. He could look about the gaming room unobserved.

It took him less than two minutes to locate Zenobia. She was wearing a diaphanous gown with a striking decolletage; her long auburn tresses fell seductively to her bare shoulders. She wore little makeup and only a few simple pieces of jewelry. But even in a room filled with beautiful women she was stunning. Her dark almond-shaped eyes were intent on the game before her.

She was playing backgammon with a florid-faced man who was also intent upon the game. There were many of his type seated about the gaming tables; tycoons who looked like they enjoyed playing for high stakes, but who played to win. They were the last tycoons the world would see for a thousand years. Valorius saw no sign of Magus Rex.

There was no way he could get Zenobia's attention from where he stood. It was not unlikely that any message he sent her would first be delivered to Magus Rex. He tried to stay out of the light of the gaming tables as he crossed the room toward her. He was at her side before she saw him.

Her eyes widened in surprise; she seemed happy to see him. She rose to her feet, smiling warmly. But before either of them could say a word, a distinguished-looking figure stepped between them.

"Damn your impudence!" cried Magus Rex. "Did you really think the pair of you could bilk me twice with the same ploy?"

He stood with arms akimbo directly between them so that they could not communicate by so much as a wink. All play in the gaming room had stopped; scores of eyes were on them. His voice had apparently been so loud that it had carried into the corridor outside. The dwarf tumblers crept in through the velvet curtains and stood watching from the foyer.

"Now am I correct in assuming that this is the first time you two have contacted each other here in New York?" Magus Rex continued in a loud voice.

"Yes, my lord." Valorius knew better than to try and lie. "But you see—"

"Then I've got you, you blundering punkie. None of your circus tricks will get you out of this one."

"Please, Mr. Maguson." The dapper little floor manager came hurrying across the room. "You're disturbing—"

He never finished. One glance from Magus Rex sent him scurrying back to his station. But the tycoon Zenobia had been playing backgammon with was used to giving orders, not taking them. Not only had he lost six straight games, but a popular magazine had just listed him as the tenth richest man in the world (his own calculations put him at least as high as seventh). He was in no mood for interruptions. He swelled up like an angry bullfrog.

"Now see here, Maguson," he cried. "You know the rules of the house. I won't have—"

"Shut up, Gittings!" said Magus Rex.

And to the wonder of all, Gittings did shut up.

"Father, if you'd only listen for just—"

"Not a peep, Zenobia." He turned toward her. "You've been playing tricks on your father, trying to get your own way. Not that I mind that. It proves that you have a fine womanly spirit."

"Oh, but, Father, Valorius has been—"

"Not another word!"

Zenobia dropped her eyes. She knew that there was a point beyond which it was not safe to go.

"I know what you're going to say," he continued. "That Valorius' skill and persistence do him credit, and wouldn't he make a wonderful personal secretary? Bah! He's just too dumb to know when to quit."

"But, my lord, if I have acted in any underhanded way—"

"I'd have squashed you like a beetle, you blathering nuisance. And I will if I ever see you again. Equitableness be damned! You've caused me all the inconvenience you're going to, Valorius. If you follow us again, even life in a cage as a toucan will seem pleasant. Not that you will ever be able to. By whatever means my darling daughter is evading my injunctions, she can't communicate with you if she doesn't know where you are. Somehow the witch Izelta was used as an agent in Rome. Don't interrupt, Zenobia! Exactly how, I don't know. But I'm sure that your evasions—however you're working them—need agents or direct contact. Zenobia has no possible agent here in New York. I've seen to that."

"Father!" she cried, outraged. "I'm surprised that you'd ever stoop to such a thing. You, with your legendary equitableness."

"You're trying to put me in the wrong in order to gain a moral advantage, aren't you, my darling daughter?"

"Yes, Father."

"How like your mother you are in so many ways."

He smiled indulgently. "But as I was saying, you have no agents. Nor have you made any real contact until now. So I have Valorius just where I want him. If by any chance he were ever to come looking for us again. . . ." He flicked his long violet fingernails. "But that's impossible. If you really want to look for something, Valorius, I suggest you look for the Fountain of Youth. You're going to need it sooner than you think." He laughed sardonically.

The lights dimmed. A wind rushed through the room. A maelstrom of cards, gaming boards, and poker chips swirled upward. Women screamed; men barked with astonishment. Tiny blue sparks of static electricity scintillated through the darkness. When the lights came on again, Magus Rex and Zenobia were gone.

A woman laughed hysterically. Several men demanded that "Somebody do something about it."

Valorius could only stare hopelessly at Zenobia's empty chair. He was wizard enough to have sensed the concentration of psychic energy in the room. But he knew that it would have taken a far greater wizard than he was to have read the vibration patterns and determined exactly where in time and space Magus Rex had taken Zenobia. He sighed. How could he ever have been so foolish as to think he could challenge the great Magus Rex?

Then he realized that people were staring at him, scores of them. Angry, indignant voices began to demand that he be apprehended. It was time to leave.

He turned and strode resolutely toward the door. Nobody tried to stop him. The dwarf acrobats had crept back through the velvet curtain. He found them huddled together in the corridor outside. One of them was sitting on the floor, somewhat apart from the others, making rapid calculations with pad and pencil. He glanced up at Valorius as he hurried past; there was intelligence of a high order in his eyes; a nasty grin twisted his mouth.

Anybody could walk *out* of Club Sybaris; leaving

an enclave was a lot easier than getting in again. It was well after midnight by the time he reached his room. For hours he lay fully dressed on the bed, staring at the cracked and grimy ceiling. From the teeming streets outside his window he could hear the barbarous last gasps of a dying civilization. There seemed no way out of the dilemma. Magus Rex had triumphed.

He knew that he could find concentrations of psychic energy. Perhaps a rally of Luther Beck and his Blackshirts. If the rally was big enough, and the hatred insane enough, he might launch himself across as much as two thousand years of time. But what was two thousand to two million? He would need a great deal of luck to get back to his own time at all, and even with luck he would be at least middle-aged when he got there. And Zenobia. . . . He sighed. Zenobia would still be as young and beautiful as ever.

Hours passed. He became increasingly conscious of the lumps in the mattress. An eerie gray light began to filter through the industrial smog that had settled on the city during the night, but still he could not sleep. No cage prepared by Magus Rex could have been as effective as this one. He could not stay here: the Black Ages were barely two years away. There was no way Zenobia could contact him. Perhaps he should just go back to being the star bestiarius of the Roman amphitheater. A short life, but a merry one. And no matter where he remained in the ancient world his life would indeed be a short one. He turned off the light bulb and lay back down on the bed.

A reddish tint began to fill the room. He did not bother to look out the grimy window. Not even the most brilliant of sunrises interested him at the moment. Never had he felt so utterly lost. The bedsprings squeaked as he tossed and turned, trying to find a comfortable position. The reddish glow in the room was more vivid than ever. Perhaps the industrial fumes had a filtering effect on the upper bands of the spectrum. He glanced out the window, surprised to see only a gloomy overcast sky.

All at once he realized that the reddish haze was coming from the room itself. He sprang out of bed. Was it possible? How could Zenobia have discovered that he was here? He recalled the first message she had sent through time to her little library in the palace of Magus Rex. It had taken many sleepless nights and hundreds of visilux images to decipher it. This time there was no waiting. Bright red letters solidified with the intensity of a neon sign:

> Valorius, my love, I am telling you true,
> My father has taken me to the time of Empress
>     Wu.
> About three years before the Reign
> Of Terror and so much death and pain.
> From Changan, which is the capital city,
> Please rescue me through your love and pity.

He snatched a pad and pencil from the top of the dresser and copied it down. Zenobia's ability to send such messages had improved tremendously; he was not sure that he could create such vivid letters himself. But the quality of her poetry had certainly suffered.

Nonetheless she had contacted him. Perhaps she had not had any time for literary composition. Doggerel or not, she had once again saved him from ending up in a cage. And the fact that she had contacted him at all proved that somehow she had gotten her father to relent. The threat in the gaming room at Club Sybaris could no longer endanger Valorius. Zenobia would never have lured him to certain destruction. He began preparing to leave ancient New York.

The Tang Dynasty had been a golden age of sorcery. That was one age in which Magus Rex would not have to assume the role of a professional gambler. Sorcerers were the most esteemed members of Chinese society. They had made many important discoveries in the art of telekinesis, and he had studied their writings at the Academy. He knew that the Empress Wu was generally considered to have been the most cruel and dissolute woman ever to flourish in the ancient world. But he could not recall exactly when in the Tang Dynasty she had reigned. Before he completed his calculations he would need more accurate information.

Brusman must have been a sound sleeper. It took Valorius five minutes of hard pounding to get him to the door. He fumbled with his thick spectacles, looking sleepy and disheveled. For a moment he did not recognize Valorius.

"Huh? What happened? Oh, Val! It's you. What the hell time is it? Come on in. I'll make some coffee. Just got to sleep an hour ago. Ran into a couple of grad students I know. Talk, talk, talk," he laughed sleepily. "Oh, yeah. How did it go last night? Uncle Mel left me a note saying I should call him in the morning. It was under the door."

"Listen, Dave, something's come up. Do you have a book on Chinese history, one on the Tang Dynasty?"

Brusman rubbed his eyes and blinked several times. "You woke me up at dawn to ask if I have a book on Chinese history? You haven't been. . . . No, no, you're not the type. Too straight." He took a deep breath. "Well, let's see. I know I've got. . . . Tang Dynasty?" Two whole walls were covered with floor-to-ceiling bookshelves stuffed with books and periodicals. "I've been meaning to get all this organized. Here's an outline history of China. I know I've got another book. Tang Dynasty, you say? I don't think I've got—"

"This should do." Valorius, checking the index, began reading at top speed.

"Say, you're pretty fast. Take one of those speed reading courses?"

"Something like that," mumbled Valorius, scanning the pages as fast as he could turn them. "Have you a pencil and paper? Thanks." He jotted down some figures.

Brusman found two more general works on oriental history, and Valorius checked these as well. The story of the Empress Wu was not a pretty one. But he now had the exact dates of her reign, and a pretty good idea why Magus Rex had chosen that particular period of time. The Tang nobility of the late seventh century, A.R., had watched helplessly as the ruthless, dissolute Empress Wu consolidated her power. They knew what was coming and devoted their days—any one of which might be their last—to a cultured epicureanism beyond the dreams of even Epicurus himself. Magus Rex would feel right at home.

"Empress Wu?" Brusman glanced over his shoulder. "That's not the one. . . . Yeah, now I remember. That's the Chinese empress who used to take hundreds of kids down to the river and have their heads cut off. She had a mad monk who was supposed to have the biggest. . . . Well," he chuckled. "If I remember correctly, she was a kind of female Elagabalus—all promotions were anatomically based. And she was still going strong in her seventies. Is that the one?"

"That's her." Valorius handed him back the books. "Never mind the coffee, Dave. Thanks, but I need some sleep. What time are you going to see your uncle?"

"Oh, about noon, I guess. He just asked me to drop by."

"Will you stop by my room first?"

"Sure." He looked at him for a moment. "Please don't be offended, Val, but you're kind of a strange guy. Nice, but a little strange."

Valorius smiled. "See you in a few hours. Sorry to wake you, but it was important."

"How could the Empress Wu. . . . At this time of. . . . Never mind. I'll knock on your door about eleven."

That interview and the ones that followed were of little help. Valorius was anxious to be gone, but nearly a week passed before he was ready. Brusman did some research work for him at what was no longer the public library. Calculations were checked and rechecked. But these alone would get him no place without a springboard of psychic energy. And Luther Beck was out of town.

The barbarian horde squatting in Central Park provided fairly high energy levels, especially at night, but nothing of the magnitude he needed. What would some day be the California Islands were still part of the mainland and a big Blackshirt rally was being organized in the doomed city of Los Angeles. But at the moment there was no means of getting there. Railroad and airline strikes had paralyzed transportation; striking truckers had barricaded the major highways. The very provisioning of the city was in jeopardy. Nor could he transport himself. It would take nearly as much energy to reach Los Angeles through space as to reach the Tang Dynasty through time.

"What about the JP moot?" suggested Brusman, as they sat in Valorius' room one afternoon. "I gave up trying to figure out what you're up to days ago, Val. And I think Uncle Mel's a bit scared of you. By the way, that was very generous, letting the museum get all the coins. They'll pay you what they can for them—when they get the money. But, frankly, I wouldn't expect too much. It seems that the only free money around these days goes for jazz-porn. 'If it's not JP, babsie, it's nothing,' " he quoted bitterly.

"But what about this JP moot?" asked Valorius.

"It's going on right now, out on Fire Island. It was all fenced off till a few months ago, but the mob kicked down the fences. But the big JP stars don't come until tomorrow night—Purvis, Kabumpa Konzert, Oomgowah Chops, Vintage Pork, and I don't know who else is supposed to be there. If you want concentrations of people, that's the place. Should be a couple hundred thousand anyway, mostly kids. All drunk or drugged, and all howling like crazy animals. Funny thing is, though, almost all of them are from inside the fence. But it's been sold out for weeks, and they're none too gentle with gate-crashers from what I hear. Dozens, maybe hundreds have been killed in the last few years. When Kabumpa Konzert played just last year nearly thirty young kids, some only twelve or thirteen—"

"Dave, I don't suppose I could talk you into taking me there?"

"No chance. I'm sorry, Val, but you couldn't get me to a JP moot for love nor money. Anything but that."

Valorius nodded. "Then how about some information?"

"Information I've got." Brusman grinned. "And it's about all I've got these days. Not that it matters any more."

"Just tell me how to get there."

"Fire Island is only about forty miles away, but getting there for a JP moot is kind of a problem. Not even the armored cabs will take you, and until they settle the transit strike you'll need some kind of private transportation. I'll ask around. Maybe I can get you a lift."

Valorius spent the following day preparing for his journey. There was nothing ambiguous about the doggerel verse Zenobia had sent him this time. After rechecking his calculations he went shopping. Clothing stores in this New York were mostly costume stores, and the most popular costumes were parodies of the dress worn by the peasantry and working classes of past ages. He had no trouble finding the pajama-like garments worn during the Tang Dynasty; he even found a straw hat that would have been right at home along the banks of the Yellow River. He used his last money to buy a coil of gold wire from a dental supply house. By the time he got back to his flat that afternoon Brusman had found him transportation.

"These kids agreed to take you," he explained. "But keep the windows open. It's fashionable to stink these days. And watch yourself! Maybe you should take a club or—"

"I'll be all right," said Valorius. "Have you still got that sealed envelope I gave you?"

"Sure." Brusman grinned. "And I'm proud to say that it's still sealed."

"If I'm not back by the end of the week, open it. And here, you'd better hang on to my room key.

The rent's paid for a couple of weeks yet."

The bespectacled little scholar nodded. "My guess is that you don't expect to be back by the end of the week—or ever. You're a strange person, Val. Nice, but a little strange." He shook hands as if he knew that this was farewell. "But be careful. There's a lot of nasty critters prowling around these JP moots."

The first nasty critters he had to contend with were the young people who drove him to the moot. There were five of them—three boys and two girls, all under twenty. They were harmless enough—silly, feckless and self-indulgent, they swilled cheap wine and smoked cannabis the whole time. They never stopped talking, although it was seldom anything but slogans and babsie-rapsie. Their nastiness was mostly olfactory. Valorius kept his window open.

The continual construction strikes had left the road in poor repair. But the new vehicle handled the cracks and potholes without any apparent damage, not that its young driver cared how much damage was done. They reached Fire Island shortly after sunset.

The speculators running the JP moot had at least partly repaired the old fences; guards were stationed at the most surmountable points. The moot had been sold out for weeks, and nobody in the car actually had a ticket. The five young people planned to join the thousands and thousands of others mobbed outside the fence. Valorius left them to see if he could get a little closer.

Weird shrieks, howls, and a cacophony of primitive music droned and throbbed and shrilled through the summer night. The volume was mind-boggling; sound waves thundered out of batteries of gigantic loud-speakers, hitting him like a physical force. He walked along the fence until he found a stretch where the repairs had not yet been completed. Three hairy louts armed with machetes stood guard. They glared menacingly at him as he approached. Then they just glared at nothing at all.

Inside the fence, hundreds of thousands of young

people sprawled uncouthly around an elevated stage.
There were no seats; no sanitary facilities. The big
show was scheduled to begin in forty minutes, but
many of these young people, some hardly more than
children, had been here for days. They barely noticed
the primitive howling and leaping of the troupe of
young men and women performing on stage.

Vicious young thugs moved jackal-like through the
mob; nobody resisted them, though a friend might be
mugged not ten feet away. Valorius had to step carefully as he moved toward the stage. His pajama-like
costume and straw hat were hardly noticed.

There were enough people here to fill a large city,
crowded unmercifully inside a guarded fence like a
flock of sheep waiting to be shorn. Within the next
few years many of them would be crowded inside
fences of another kind, and Luther Beck and his
Blackshirts would be even less merciful than the speculators that had organized this JP moot. A group of
naked women, their bodies decorated with lumines-
cent paint, now danced and sang with semi-hysterical
frenzy on the lighted platform above. This was the
last act before the start of the big show.

Valorius worked his way into the thickest knot of
humanity he could find, as close to the stage as possible.
He stood literally shoulder to shoulder with the surrounding people. Many of those around him, especially those with poor figures, had stripped off all
their clothes. The paraphernalia of the opening number in the big show was now being assembled under
the stage. He read the name KABUMPA KONZERT on
several pieces of equipment. Somebody shoved a spittle-
flecked gallon-jug of cheap wine under his nose. He
pretended to drink and passed it on. The stench was
abominable.

A smattering of applause followed the luminescently
painted women off the stage. Then an incredible array
of gadgets, props, and odd-looking musical instruments took their place. The sight of them acted like a
detonator. Hundreds of thousands of young people

exploded with wild cheers. Kabumpa Konzert! Men
and women of all colors and sizes, dressed in weird
costumes or no costumes at all, began to file on stage.
Grotesque human freaks scuttled and capered onto
the stage after them, leading a nightmare troup of
animals. The musicians were as fantastic as the
performers. Hundreds of thousands of voices chanted,
"Kabumpa! Kabumpa! Kabumpa!"

Then onto the stage bounded a four-hundred-pound
Negro. He was dressed in a skin-tight costume covered with silver sequins; his hair rose from his head in
a fuzzy ball the size of a bushel-basket. His song was
the biggest hit of the day. It consisted of only three
words—"Tiger hoodoo now"—shrieked over and over
again in a harsh and grating voice.

All around him leapt and whirled men and women;
animals howled and barked and grunted; the human
freaks postured obscenely; the musicians kept up a
racket that fell somewhere between a cat fight and an
automobile collision. The amplifiers expanded every
vibration until the audience felt like it was in the
midst of a tidal wave of sound, battered and crushed.
They responded with emotional frenzy.

Valorius decided to start unifying his mind while he
still had a mind left. Slowly he became a part of the
tidal wave of energy rising upward all around him.

The next thing he knew he was standing by a
lacquered teak bridge which spanned a small canal. It
was an hour before sunset.

# CHAPTER XX
# THE DANCE OF SLASHING THE ENEMY

A range of hills rose above the city walls to the northwest; their peaks were clad in broad-leafed forests, glistening like caps of emerald in the declining sun. Just beyond the north wall rose the towers of the New Palace, looking down upon the inhabitants of Changan like hungry birds of prey. Nobody knew when or where the agents of the Empress Wu would pounce. And yet the people went about their daily round of existence grasping at any scrap of pleasure that came their way. It was the hedonism of despair.

It took Valorius only a few minutes to orient himself. He could not help recalling his original fears over plunging into the currents of time. Now he was a seasoned time traveller. So long as he stayed in his own depth he felt himself equal to any challenge — even here amidst the low energy levels of ancient times. The problem was that his depth was rather shallow compared to that of Magus Rex.

Unlike in Rome or New York, there would be no problem discovering the great wizard here in Changan.

Magus Rex was not Chinese, and his long violet fingernails were not exactly inconspicuous. Nor would
Zenobia go unnoticed. How she had been able to
contact him this time was a wonder in itself. She may
have been living here in Changan for months, or even
years now. Perhaps a greater wonder was how she
had gotten her father to relent; Magus Rex had not
been joking when he threatened him with annihilation
if he dared to follow them again. Not only had he
dared, but he had succeeded.

There was a gasp behind him. He may have become
seasoned to disappearing and reappearing at will, but
others had not become seasoned in witnessing it. A
Chinese woman and her little boy were staring at him.
The moon-faced little boy held a stick with a candy
monkey at the end; he was too young to realize that
people do not ordinarily just pop out of thin air. His
mother knew better. She made the universal sign against
the evil eye, and quickly exposed the amulets that
both she and her little boy wore on silver chains
around their necks.

Valorius hesitated. The woman smiled knowingly:
her amulets were too powerful for the foreign sorcerer,
and he could not prevail against them. She began to
chatter happily, evidently quite pleased with herself
for buying the right kind of amulets. A crowd began to
gather. They too made the sign against the evil eye and
exposed various charms and amulets. Some of them
began shouting and pointing. He did not have to
speak the language to know that they were telling him
to go back where he came from.

He knew that there was a sorcerers' quarter somewhere in Changan. The crowd seemed to be pointing
toward the north wall. Just to the east of the New
Palace he could see a low hillside crowded with exquisite walled mansions and tea gardens. The sorcerers
here seemed to do all right for themselves.

He crossed the lacquered teak bridge. On the far
side of the canal he glanced back at the crowd; they
instantly waved their charms and amulets at him. The

little Chinese boy merely stared at him with his button
eyes, nibbling at his candy monkey. Valorius bowed.

The gesture was well received. People grinned and
nodded to each other, sucking in their breath as a sign
of contentment. The foreign sorcerer was acknowledg-
ing his defeat in the face of their charms and amulets.
They politely returned his bow.

Valorius strolled contentedly through the narrow
winding streets of the capital. His costume was not
too different from the clothing worn by ordinary people.
He pulled his straw hat down over his eyes; but there
was nothing he could do about his height. He got
some uneasy glances. A few people made the sign
against the evil eye as he passed.

He reached the sorcerers' quarter just after sunset.
The streets were nearly deserted, and delicious smells
of Chinese cooking mingled with the fragrances from
the walled gardens. He decided he would not have to
spend time acquiring the spoken language. The lilacs
were in full bloom and he plucked a sprig about the
same shade of violet as Magus Rex's fingernails. Gold
wire was a universal currency in ancient China. A
sprig of lilac and a snippet of gold wire was all the
language he needed to find Magus Rex.

The first teahouse he came to was as exquisite as
the painting on a silk screen. Strings of rose-golden
lanterns hung above a garden so ethereal that it seemed
unreal. Elfin bridges spanned tiny brooks; miniature
trees in curious enameled urns surrounded the little
teahouse at the center of the garden; privacy was
maintained by a wall of lacquered bamboo.

Beside the bamboo gate stood two porters. There
was nothing delicate or ethereal about either of them.
They folded their brawny arms and watched him
approach out of the corners of their eyes.

Valorius strode right up to the larger of the two and
bowed. Startled, the man unfolded his arms; he glanced
anxiously across the stone path toward his fellow
porter. There was no help there. Working in the
sorcerers' quarter was lucrative, but you always had

to be careful—especially with foreign sorcerers. Valorius was obviously not Chinese.

He reassured them by flashing his coil of gold wire. They bowed low, smiling ingratiatingly. It seemed that he spoke their language after all.

First he unwound an inch of wire. Then he held up the sprig of lilac and pointed to his fingernails. The larger porter only frowned. But there was a sharp intake of breath by the smaller, and he scuttled across the path. He bowed low, grinning and bobbing his head. He explained something in rapid Chinese to his fellow.

Then the bargaining began. First the porters bit the gold wire. It was quality dental gold and easily passed the test for purity. They smiled and bobbed, but Valorius had to walk away twice before an agreement was reached. One of them would lead him to the sorcerer with the long violet fingernails for two inches of gold wire. He suspected that he was being fleeced—in fact, the porters seemed disappointed that he had capitulated so soon. But he wanted to see Zenobia as soon as possible. Perhaps she had even brought her father around to accepting him as his personal secretary.

The sorcerer with the long violet fingernails was certain to be dining at this hour in the most exclusive teahouse in Changan. The two porters raised their eyes in celestial awe at the mere mention of its name. The smaller of them guided Valorius right to the gate. It sat on the crest of a low hill not far from the eastern bridge to the New Palace.

There were six stout porters at this gate. The gardens and teahouse were proportionately more ethereal; a whole fairy forest of miniature trees surrounded the goldfish pond. A mere half inch of gold wire got Valorius a personal escort to the teahouse door. He had never seen a garden so exquisite, other than that surrounding the nome of Magus Rex.

A wizened old man dressed in brocaded red silk met him at the door. They exchanged formal bows. The spicy aromas of Chinese cuisine enveloped them.

Valorius' costume was simple and unprepossessing, but his coil of gold wire was greeted with transcendent politeness. He exchanged his shoes for a pair of dainty silk slippers.

Behind a beaded curtain sang the sweetest voice he had ever heard; she was accompanied by a stringed instrument of some kind.

Painted screens discreetly maintained the privacy of the dining alcoves without muffling the lovely song. Mats of bamboo-fiber covered the floor; rose-colored lanterns made everything seem warm and cheerful.

Valorius had kept his sprig of lilac. But the wizened little man looked very doubtful about disturbing the dinner of the foreign sorcerer and his daughter. An inch and a half of gold wire removed his doubt. Valorius followed him toward a secluded alcove.

Zenobia gasped in astonishment. She gaped at him as if he were the last thing in the world she ever expected to see in Changan. She actually looked frightened. Magus Rex rose to his feet like a thundercloud.

"I warned you, you infernal nuisance!" he cried.

Valorius was too stunned even to move, helpless before his impending doom. This was not the reception he had expected. He was a Master Wizard, but trying to resist Magus Rex would be like trying to fight a tiger with a hatpin. He could feel the waves of psychic energy gathering about him. He looked at Zenobia for the last time. She could only shake her head in utter astonishment.

But the energy storm suddenly subsided. Magus Rex looked from one to the other, and he slowly smiled.

"What have we here, a mix-up of some kind? You seem startled at the appearance of your ineligible swain, my darling daughter. Could it be that the pair of you have gotten your signals crossed? Come, come! Is that all you two can do—stare at each other?" A sardonic twinkle crept into his heavy-lidded eyes. "This just may turn out to be more amusing than returning Valorius to his constituent elements. Pest that he is! Let us all be seated and have a nice cup of tea."

The teahouse had fallen silent during this exchange. The wizened little man in brocaded red silk stood as silent and inscrutable as a jade statue. He had not reached his present venerable age by interfering with sorcerers. Magus Rex said something to him in Chinese. He grinned and bobbed his head. Then he turned and clapped three times.

The singing girl returned to her lovely song. Lackeys scuttled toward them from all directions, as the wizened little man led the way to a private room. He held the beaded curtain aside as they entered. The lackeys covered the low table with fruit, wine, tea, nuts, and dainty spice cakes. A boy circled the room swinging a golden censer, leaving clouds of incense in his wake. Magus Rex nodded. Instantly they were alone.

"Oh, Father," said Zenobia, regaining her composure. "Wasn't Valorius splendid in finding us here? And I never even. . . . That is to say, hasn't he shown just the kind of skill and initiative you'd want in a personal secretary?"

Magus Rex selected a plump roasted chestnut from the porcelain dish in front of him.

"Well, he may not be quite the pudding his father was. The fact that he's the offspring of a skald's daughter probably accounts for his bovine persistence. Please don't interrupt yet, Zenobia. You were only going to talk away from the subject in hopes of putting me on the defensive by making me feel guilty about something or other. Weren't you?"

"Yes, Father."

"You grow more charming every day, my darling daughter."

"It's really not fair." She pouted. "How can a woman get around you when you know all the tricks?"

"Perhaps she might start by telling me I'm too clever to be gotten around. But here's Valorius mooning at you like an infatuated schoolboy."

Zenobia had her hair piled high and lacquered in the Chinese fashion. Her silk gown brought out all the exuberant femininity of her gorgeous young body. She looked so beautiful that it literally took his breath away.

"Magus Rex, my lord—" he began.

"None of your yammer, you puling mooncalf! You just came within a split second of rejoining the elements. Be satisfied with that."

"You never would have forgiven yourself, Father," said Zenobia.

"Oh, I think I would have gotten over it in time. But it seems that I, even I, Magus Rex, almost acted with undue haste. I have decided instead to act in so judicious a manner that none may gainsay my legendary equitableness. You've been after me for millions of years to appoint Valorius my personal secretary, Zenobia." He waved his long violet fingernails magnanimously. "The job is his."

"Oh, Father!" cried Zenobia, blushing with happiness. "I just knew you'd do the equitable thing. Will we be going home to the palace soon?"

"That depends on what you mean by we." He popped a dainty little spice cake into his mouth and refilled his porcelain cup with wine.

"I don't understand, Father," said Zenobia. "Aren't you going to give Valorius the job when we get back to the palace? You're not going to go back on your promise, are you?"

"A promise is a promise, my darling daughter. Valorius shall have the job the moment *he* gets back to the palace."

She gasped. "But that's millions of years! I thought that you would. . . . I mean, that as soon as we. . . . That is—"

"That as soon as you'd gotten around your jolly old father that he'd take the pair of you back with him and you'd live happily ever after? Well, I won't. Valorius has been crowing about his qualifications and all he's learned at the Academy—the Academy which I founded, by the way—so now we'll see what he's really made of. What could be fairer than that?"

"But you went back in time to rescue Valorius and his father," Zenobia protested.

"Which only proves that even my judgment is not infallible."

"Besides, you never finished telling us the story of Valorius' father and the skald's daughter."

"I'll tell you when we get home—if you're still interested. And now I suppose you're going to tell me there's not enough psychic energy for him to get back, so that I'm not really being fair?"

"It isn't fair," she cried. "You know that if Valorius ever does get back. . . . Well, he'll be—"

"Rather elderly and decrepit? Perhaps. It all depends on him. I've offered him the job, and it's his whenever he shows up to claim it. There's equitableness for you!"

"Father, sometimes you're so, so . . . insidious."

"But you do love your jolly old father?" He bit into a dainty spice cake with the lazy contentment of a spoiled cat.

"Yes, Father. But just now you're being horrible."

Magus Rex grinned sardonically. "You know, Valorius, perhaps you'd have been better off as a toucan. Even if you do manage to get back, I'm afraid you'll look rather grisly. I'll reserve a bench for you in my garden where you can doze in the afternoon, dreaming your senile dreams and mumbling of the things you've seen in your long, long travels. Zenobia can come out every few hours and wipe your chin." He smacked his lips over the sparkling pungency of his rice wine. "Really exquisite! I'll miss it. Now if you had the puissance of a truly great wizard, Valorius—me, for instance—you could return in the twinkling of an eye. I hope you don't think I'm taunting you."

Zenobia lowered her eyes. Whether in thought or to avoid witnessing his humiliation, Valorius could not tell. He wondered if she would still love him if he looked, say, only about sixty. Though he knew that he would probably look a lot older than that, if he ever got back at all.

"By the way, Valorius," said Magus Rex. "You will be careful, won't you? The empress—charming creature that she is—has her own inimitable way of entertaining people she doesn't like. I hope she doesn't take it into her head to round up foreign sorcerers."

"Oh, be careful, Valorius," cried Zenobia. "She's a living devil. People are dragged off to the palace every day to be killed or tortured."

"That's just what adds so much zest to the times," said Magus Rex. "The wealthy and cultured throw themselves into their debauchery with delightful abandon, as if there were no tomorrow. Which, for many of them, there isn't."

"Will there be a tomorrow here for us, Father?" said Zenobia. "I mean, we're not just going to flee from Changan the way we did from New York?"

"I do not *flee* from anywhere." Magus Rex raised his left eyebrow. "We left New York without ceremony to preclude any further skulduggery—"

"There's been no skulduggery, Father. I swear to you, I haven't the faintest idea how Valorius ever managed to follow us here."

"I believe you, Zenobia. In fact, it was your unfeigned astonishment that preserved Valorius' cellular cohesion. Although you may be somewhat less uncertain about how he was able to follow us to Rome and New York." He sampled a kumquat. "This reminds me of a charming story the Greeks used to tell about a young popinjay named Icarus. Like Valorius here he impudently soared too high and got his wings singed. His discovery that falling was a lot easier than climbing was a salutary lesson for him. Although I'm afraid he didn't have long to appreciate it."

"Wasn't that the story where Icarus' father had to flee from some island?" Zenobia asked innocently. "Without any kind of ceremony?"

"You are really a treasure, my darling daughter. The great wizard who gets you for his consort will be fortunate indeed. Whoever he may be." He sneered at Valorius. "But now I couldn't leave at once without risking the imputation that I fled, could I?"

"No, Father. Besides, isn't there someone you'd like to say farewell to?"

"Dear little Plum Blossom," said Magus Rex. "But I had no intention to depart abruptly. Too many lovely things would suffer. Just listen to her sing! A Chinese nightingale."

"But how could an abrupt departure hurt Plum Blossom?" asked Zenobia.

"He has to draw the psychic energy from some-where," Valorius spoke up at last. "That's why he probably brought you here in the first place."

"Ah, very good, Valorius," said Magus Rex. "So even your obtuseness has sensed the exceptionally low level of psychic energy. Nor does the charming Wu permit gatherings of any kind. Except, of course, for her regular mass executions. But even then there's too much oriental resignation to be of much use to the novice. That is indeed why I brought you here, Zenobia."

"I know, Father. That's why I never . . . I mean, why I've tried so hard to make you appreciate Valorius' true worth."

"A waste of time, my dear. Not all the sophistry in the world could make a silk purse out of Valorius. His true worth indeed! Bah!"

"My lord," said Valorius. "Others must judge of my qualifications. Although, as you know, my record at the Academy stands unsurpassed by any other wizard now in residence. I can only say that I love your daughter with all my heart. Not only her grace and beauty, which everyone who sees her must admire, but the charm with which—"

"Enough of your mooncalfery, Valorius. Even your impudence is preferable to that."

"Oh, Father," Zenobia pouted. "You could have at least let Valorius finish what he was saying."

"Let him finish tomorrow. I have magnanimously decided to grant the pair of you a full day together." He popped the last of the spice cakes into his mouth, smiling with feline contentment.

"A full day!" cried Zenobia. "How wonderful of you, Father."

"Yes, my dear. Since I intend to spend the afternoon saying farewell to Plum Blossom and completing arrangements for her future well-being, you have my permission to spend the whole time with Valorius. And you may complete whatever arrangements of your own that you wish. Perhaps you've been thinking of peeking into my library when we get back home in hopes of conveying to him the lore of instant transport?"

Zenobia frowned, but said nothing.

"I'm afraid it doesn't work that way, my darling daughter. You see, Valorius already knows how to transport himself. He's just not very good at it. Not all the lore in my palace could help him get back one second sooner."

"What time will we be leaving tomorrow, Father?"

"Don't worry, my dear. You'll have the full day I promised you. Make your farewell scene just as mawkish as you please. We won't be leaving until tomorrow night, and I sincerely hope that Valorius clings to your side to the very last moment. Although I'm afraid he won't be able to accompany us to the festival."

"The festival?" cried Zenobia.

"You've always wanted to attend a court festival. Now you shall. The divine Wu shows her celestial moderation by holding no more than three lavish festivals a week at the New Palace, consoling herself on the off days with modest orgies. Tomorrow night there will be a real gala, the celebrated Dance of Slashing the Enemy. The courtyard will be filled with singers, dancers, musicians, and executioners. I understand that her patrols have been working overtime for weeks now, rounding up enemies to be slashed."

"Be very careful, Valorius," said Zenobia. "She has spies everywhere. Don't trust anybody, and watch out for the patrols."

"If they pick you up," added Magus Rex, "you'll regret to your dying day—which won't be long coming—that you muffed your chance to become a toucan. The cage in my palace is still empty, but I'm told that the charming Wu has cages of her own. Scores of them. And if you don't fit, her corps of surgeons will be glad to make the necessary adjustments. But she does have a sense of humor."

"Please don't tell those horrible stories, Father. You know you're only doing it to tease Valorius."

"There's some justice in that remark, my dear. But really I'm only trying to enliven our little party. Valorius has been even more of a wet blanket than usual. Perhaps he's still stupefied by having nearly been redistributed among the elements."

"My lord," said Valorius firmly. "It is neither fear nor any lack—"

"Oh, don't start again!" Magus Rex silenced him with an impatient flick of his long violet fingernails. "Even your lumpish stupefaction is preferable to that. But I'll content myself with a single anecdote, illustrative of the empress' celestial sense of humor. It's really a play on words. You see, the Chinese have a charming euphemism for the transports of love—'The bones and marrow melt in drunken ecstacy.' In a puckish mood, Wu had all her court rivals, including the dowager empress, rounded up. She said she was going to turn her court into a Court of Love. So she had all their hands and feet cut off, then had them thrown alive into huge wine vats to pickle. Now whenever a stranger asks after the dowager empress or the imperial courtesans, Wu tells him waggishly that 'Their bones and marrow melt in drunken ecstacy.' I understand that it's become a kind of running gag up at the New Palace. Wu's courtiers laugh uproariously every time she springs it."

Zenobia made a wry face. "You're going to invite Valorius to stay with us tonight, aren't you, Father?"

"Ah, I'm so sorry, Valorius. But the mansion happens to be full at the moment. No vacancies. So it looks like you'll just have to take your chances in the streets." He clapped his hands three times.

The wizened little man in the brocaded red silk

slipped discreetly into the room, smiling and bobbing with mannered politeness. Magus Rex tossed him a gold coin and said something in Chinese. The man smiled more broadly and bobbed almost in half; then he whispered to a lackey hovering just outside the bamboo curtain. A few moments later a doll-like young girl slipped shyly into the room.

Magus Rex did her the honor of rising to his feet and bowing. The purse he handed her caused her to gasp. Then he made an elaborate speech, praising her voice and artistry. Belying her name, Plum Blossom blushed like a ripe peach; she was more moved by the compliments than the purse. Magus Rex bowed again. She left, trembling with happiness.

"You know, Father," said Zenobia. "You can be really charming when you want to be."

"It's not a matter of charm as much as equitableness. That which is venerable I venerate; that which is execrable," he glanced at Valorius, "I execrate. Now give Valorius directions for your tryst tomorrow. But keep them simple, or he'll spend the whole day wandering about the city with a frown on his face."

Valorius in fact spent a good part of the night wandering about Changan. The midnight streets clattered with armed patrols, but his eyes gave him all the advantage he needed to avoid them. What he needed now was a safe place in which to think. Magus Rex was certainly up to something, and the sorcerers' quarter was best avoided. He still had his coil of gold wire, but nobody in the city would take him in. At last he found lodgings for the night in a caravanserai for merchants in the silk trade, outside the western wall of the city. All the races on earth followed the Silk Route, even Vikings. Nobody here made the sign against the evil eye when they saw him.

He got little sleep. Magus Rex had been just too generous in allowing him to meet Zenobia tomorrow. What was he up to? The great wizard cherished his daughter's love and would not want to impair it by destroying him outright, unless severely provoked. Last night had been a close call. Perhaps Zenobia had sent her verse prematurely, misunderstanding the degree to which her father had relented. On the other hand, perhaps Magus Rex really was being generous, a last display of his legendary equitableness before returning home. After all, what did he have to lose? Valorius knew all too well that he could not follow them directly through time, no matter how many verses Zenobia sent him. He could only plod.

He adjusted the mosquito-net around his pallet. It would soon be dawn and he was still confused about his next move. Tang China was an energy vacuum. The great shaman cult-center of Tibet in the following century was the only significant springboard of psychic energy he could hope to reach. The totalitarian rallies and JP moots of the twentieth century might get him past the Black Ages. But what good would that do him? He would still have to hop, skip, and jump for a million years after that before the planet's general level of psychic energy was high enough for him to make any real progress. Not to mention controlling his aging processes.

Toward morning he finally fell asleep. Most of the silk merchants were already on their way by the time he got up. He breakfasted on bean curd and several cups of strong tea. Then he sent a lackey to buy him more fashionable garments. This might be the last time he would ever see Zenobia and he wanted to look his best.

Her palanquin arrived in the bazaar punctually at noon. She seemed apprehensive about something, and quickly led him through a maze of narrow, winding streets. Several times she glanced over her shoulder. At last they reached a kind of walled promenade along the riverfront. The palanquin bearers remained at a discreet distance.

"What's wrong?" asked Valorius. "Are you being followed?"

"I'm not sure." She glanced into the trees. "At first I thought he was just a beggar child looking for alms.

But the way he looked at me. . . . Yes, there he is!
Among the ginko trees. Now he's ducked out of sight."

"But who would use a child as a spy?"

"It's not a child," said Zenobia. "It's a dwarf."

"A dwarf!" He whirled around.

"He's gone now. The important thing—"

"But I keep running into dwarfs wherever I go. It's
the strangest thing, Zenobia. But in ancient Rome,
and even in New York—"

"It's not important now, beloved. We have so little
time together. Come, let's walk along the riverbank. I
have been thinking about what you should do next."

She still believed that someday she would bring her
father to relent. Her idea was simply that he should
return to ancient Rome and await further developments.
Strangely, she avoided direct reference to any kind
of communication between them. She merely recom-
mended the witch Izelta as being knowledgeable in
herb lore.

"You're famous in Rome," she added. "And at least
then I'll know where you are. I just wish I knew what
my father was up to." ·

"So you had that feeling too?"

"He was chuckling about something all morning.
But he didn't say anything. He just told me to spend
as much time with you as I like, and that I could even
stay with you until just before the festival—"

"That's it! The festival!" Valorius slowly shook his
head. "And I have to admit that once again he gave me
enough rope."

"You mean like the poor pierrot at the carnival in
Paris?"

"Even more obvious. This time it's a festival, the
Dance of Slashing the Enemy. And that in itself should
have told me something."

"Why? I thought Father was just going to use the
concentration of psychic energy—"

"That's just the point. Your father doesn't need
concentrations of energy. What he'll probably do tonight is just let the empress know in some way that

he, a foreign sorcerer, was responsible for it all."

"Responsible for what?"

"If he's going to take you across two million years of time, the energy will have to come from somewhere. Changan will be like a dead storage battery for days to come. The people won't be hurt, although they may stumble around for a while like they just got out of bed. But the empress' festival will be spoiled and—"

"She'll blame it on foreign sorcerers?"

"Exactly. That's what your father meant when he said something about rounding up foreign sorcerers. And the whole region will be so drained of psychic energy that I couldn't get away if I wanted to."

"So that's why Father wanted me to stay with you up to the last minute. Oh, Valorius," she cried. "You must leave right away."

He agreed. "I had planned to accompany a silk caravan at least as far as the Jade Gates. But none leaves for the next few days, and now I don't dare wait."

"Where were you going?"

"Lhasa, in Tibet. The Jade Gates are the major pass into China from the west, so there's bound to be an army defending them. In the next century Lhasa becomes a great shaman cult-center. An army should provide me with just the concentration of energy I'll need to get there."

"There's an army stationed downriver," said Zenobia. "This is a tributary of the Yellow River. The empress keeps a huge retinue at a city called Loyang, about two hundred miles from here. One of Father's drinking companions, a charming old scoundrel called Shyu, has mentioned it several times. If only he was telling the truth!"

"Is this Shyu a liar?"

"He's an historian. The official Court Historian for the whole dynasty. He owns several palaces. Nobles pay him fabulous sums of money to get distinguished places in history for their ancestors. A wealthy merchant recently gave him a whole village just to have

his grandfather win a famous battle. Shyu says that
the dead must serve the purposes of the living."

"Yes," said Valorius. "I ran into a similar problem
when I was reading the history books of the twentieth
century. In any case, the river merchants will know all
about Loyang. Just so I leave Changan ahead of the
empress' agents."

"Then you must leave at once. Don't even go back to
your lodgings. I wanted us to have at least one day
together, but it's more important that you get safely
back to ancient Rome. Then, if Father relents—and I
just know he will!—we'll be together and—"

"And our bones and marrow will melt in drunken
ecstasy." He smiled, drawing her into his arms.

She clung to him, trembling slightly. "Oh, don't
even say it! That was a terrible story. But you must
hurry. Empress Wu really does things like that. And
she does have cages where she keeps people." She
kissed him, reluctantly pushing herself away. "No,
don't follow me, beloved. You must escape while there's
still time."

She signaled to her palanquin-bearers, who stood
discreetly just out of earshot; they hurried forward to
meet her. With a last smile of encouragement she
slipped inside the silk curtain. The palanquin was
soon lost in the crowd.

Valorius hurriedly left the promenade, pressing
through the narrow, teeming streets until he reached
the docks. His arrangements were soon made; there
was indeed a garrison city called Loyang downriver,
and a salt merchant was leaving within the hour. A
few coils of gold wire got Valorius deck passage.

By nightfall the barge was well downriver. Fortified
by a delicious fish curry and several cups of excellent
tea, Valorius sat on deck making occult calculations
by lantern light. Neither the salt merchant nor any of
his crew approached him; they made the sign against
the evil eye whenever they thought he was not looking.
The hours drifted by like the current of the dark river.
The stars came out. The lanterns of the other barges

crowding the river glimmered in the night.

A wild commotion broke out on deck. There were shouts and cries of alarm all over the river; a fearful wailing arose from the barge nearby. Valorius looked up. Bands of light scintillated above Changan like the aurora borealis.

He threw down his pen and sighed. Magus Rex and Zenobia had left Changan, leaving him two million years behind. From the magnitude of the energy storm ripping into the palace of Empress Wu, it was probably lucky that he had left Changan when he did.

# CHAPTER XXI
# THE CITY OF THE SORCERERS

Stark winds rushed across the top of the world, scouring the barren mountainous plateau of Tibet. The landscape looked weird and unreal, as if it belonged to one of the outer planets and not to earth. The dismal half-light of dawn enhanced this strange unearthliness. Winter was almost over, but the rarefied air bit cruelly into the lungs; only its intense dryness made the cold bearable. In the distance the bleak granite walls of Lhasa, built no man knew when, beetled above the ground like the sepulcher of an entombed giant. Pitted, lichenous stones squatted among patches of stunted vegetation. There were no trees as far as the eye could see.

As the pallid sun crept over the volcanic peaks to the south, the winds began to abate. There was little snow on the ground and the land warmed rapidly. The mountainous plateau itself remained stark and dismal, but the roads leading to Lhasa were soon alive with color. Magic and religion were much the same thing in Tibet. Legions of monks and sorcerers prospered side

by side upon the labor of a superstitious populace.
There were more sorcerers than farmers; more monasteries than villages. Monks in sweeping red cloaks
converged from all sides upon Lhasa like armies of red
ants. Some rode donkeys, some even fine horses; most
were on foot. Veiled sorcerers filed along the sides of
the road.

Even larger streams of people moved in the opposite direction, away from the city. These were the
inhabitants of Lhasa, fleeing the promiscuous tumult
of the monks and sorcerers.

Nobody was safe from the brawls of the monks,
from the continual slashing and maiming as monastery fought monastery. The sorcerers were even more
dreaded. People disappeared and were never heard of
again; there were rumors of strange rites, of ritual
murder and human sacrifice.

Those fleeing the city let the monks and sorcerers
have the roads; they themselves picked their way among
the boulders of the plain toward the safety of outlying
villages. Only after the annual ceremonial was brought
to its blood-drenched climax would they return.

Valorius had had no trouble getting to Tibet. He
recalled from his readings that one of Empress Wu's
epithets was the "Warrior Empress." Her army at
Loyang had provided him with as strong a springboard as he could have desired. But if she had wanted
to round up all the sorcerers here, it would have taken
an army at least that size just to have guarded them.

He was still dressed in the peaked fur cap, leggings
and quilted jacket of a Chinese merchant, but the
guards at the city gate asked no questions. For all they
knew he was a powerful sorcerer.

Learning Tibetan would have been a lengthy process,
since he had no knowledge of the written language.
The ANALECTS OF MAGUS REX spoke scornfully
of Tibetan sorcery, and the whole era tended to be
ignored at the Academy. But he knew enough about
the evil practices of these monks and sorcerers to
realize that he needed a safe place in which to stay

until the great ceremonial, six days from now. He still had several coils of gold wire, and, with most of the population gone, there were plenty of vacancies. The problem was finding a dwelling he could barricade.

The Tibetans built their houses without doors. The outer walls had stout gates, but doorways inside the courtyard were merely curtained. Furniture was simple, and Valorius could see no way he might barricade a curtain. There was no pattern to the narrow streets; the people just built their houses wherever they would fit. He inspected several dwellings without taking one, wandering at random through the maze-like streets. He soon realized that he was a conspicuous figure.

The city was a bedlam of chanting and shrieking; savage brawling broke out whenever bands from rival monasteries ran into each other. Blood flowed freely and there was no quarter given to the fallen. The maze-like nature of the streets made these brawls hard to avoid, and any shadow might hold a sorcerer ready to pounce on the weak and defenseless.

Valorius had just rejected lodgings in a public hostelry, when he ran smack into two bands of monks flailing savagely at each other. He quickly retreated into the nearest street. Unpaved and noisome, he thought he had stepped into an open sewer. High walls blocked out the feeble winter sun, and there were no windows. The street was a dead end.

As he turned back he found two sorcerers blocking his exit. Evidently they had taken him for a merchant who did not know his way around the city. Their devil-masks were skillfully carved, painted and inlaid with ivory—probably several generations old. They brandished their insignia before them as they advanced, wailing eerily and making occult passes through the air. Merchants were fair game for every sorcerer in the city.

Despite Magus Rex's well-known scorn of Tibetan sorcerers, Valorius knew that they were perhaps the earliest practitioners of hypnotism. These two were adepts at the art, and worked as a team. One caught and held his eyes; the other rhythmically swung a shiny medallion back and forth in front of his face. The voice that spoke was muffled by the devil-mask, drowsy and far away. Valorius stared back.

When he finally emerged from the dead-end street he was wearing the flowing blue robes of a Tibetan sorcerer. A gold scapulary, inscribed with charms and incantations, hung to his knees; the miter he wore on his head was made from rows of carved ivory plaques and miniature skulls. He carried the leering devil-mask on a cord over his shoulder. He not only found himself less conspicuous in the streets but also saw that landlords now showed him more respect. He leased an entire house near the eastern gate.

The most ferocious watchdogs bred in the ancient world were bred right here in Tibet. The result of thousands of years of selective breeding, these super-dogs were not quite as large as the Great Danes later bred in Europe. But they were all muscle and bone. And teeth. The house itself was no more attractive than others he had inspected, but for some reason the owner was in a hurry to leave town and agreed to throw his dog into the bargain.

Valorius barred the outside gate and left the watchdog in the courtyard. He hardly bothered about the inside doors. A Siberian tiger might have gotten in, but it would have to have been a very determined animal. He got his first good night's sleep since leaving Tang China.

The next morning, he went to explore the grounds at the Machindranath Temple, where the great ceremonial would take place. At first he thought that a morning fog was oozing into the city, but as he approached the temple he realized that it was actually an immense cloud of incense.

Thousands of red-cloaked monks, shivering and stamping their feet in the early morning chill, had already gathered for their daily handouts of bread and soup. The voices of thousands more chanted inside the temple, whose open portals revealed a whole pantheon of idols, richly inlaid with gold, ivory, and precious stones. The colorful shops and bazaars surrounding the temple square were already doing a brisk business. It was a magnificent spectacle.

He visited the square every morning for the next few days. The rest of his time he worked at his calculations. He had left Rome amidst an uproar and it was important that he return at the proper time. Titus Lengo and the witch Izelta had been dead for centuries now, but they were still alive in the Rome of the giant emperor, Maximin. He would need their help while he waited for Zenobia to contact him. He hoped he would not end up waiting a lifetime.

Wealthy pilgrims, surrounded by their retinues, sometimes added to the morning spectacle at the Machindranath Temple. The most splendid visitor of all appeared the day before the great ceremonial. Sixteen bearers, flanked by an armed escort, bore a golden palanquin across the temple square, scattering monks right and left like the prow of a ship. At first Valorius thought that it was some potentate or his wife. Then he realized that the palanquin was also surrounded by a retinue of seven wizards. Even from where he stood he could sense their power.

This was surprising. But he was even more surprised when the curtains were drawn. It was only a child, evidently being taken to see the sights of Lhasa. Like the wizards, the child was clearly not Tibetan.

Then he noticed something strange about the child, a certain disproportion in its limbs, an awkwardness in its movements. He edged closer. Suddenly he realized that it was a dwarf child! It was perhaps eleven or twelve years old, but stood no higher than the average four-year-old. Valorius had the uneasy feeling that he had definitely been seeing too many dwarfs lately.

Why it was being guarded by seven powerful wizards and a large escort of armed servitors he could not even guess. This was certainly not the same dwarf that had tried to kill him in Rome, nor the one that had followed Zenobia in Changan. Puzzled, he finished his marketing for the day and returned home.

His coil of gold wire was almost gone. The food bill for his watchdog was three times his own, but out of prudence he kept it well fed. Looking at the monster he sometimes wondered if the colossal "dragons" carved in the temples were not really stylized images of these incredible dogs. In any case, he got a good night's sleep.

The temple square was almost deserted the next morning. The great ceremonial would begin at sunset and last until dawn. Perhaps the monks and sorcerers were resting up for the orgiastic rites that night. He filled his market basket, wondering if perhaps he should not get some rest himself.

His watchdog looked more like a carved dragon than ever as he entered the courtyard. The sky was gray and murky; the air dry and chill. But he could scarcely see the dog's breath. It sat on its haunches just inside the gate, its eyes staring at empty space. Was it sick? Had it been drugged or poisoned by some sorcerer? He hurried into the house with his market basket, intending to take a closer look.

"Come in here, you insufferable nuisance!" boomed a voice from the reception hall.

Magus Rex sat Indian-fashion on a pile of cushions beside the brazier. There was a look of controlled fury in his eye. He was alone.

"Where is Zenobia?" he said angrily.

"Zenobia?" Valorius dropped his market basket. "But, my lord, I don't understand. I thought Zenobia—"

"She's gone. I didn't think you'd have the temerity. But it had to be checked out."

"But how did you find me here?" Valorius cried in wonder.

"Where else would a pipsqueak like you get enough energy to go anywhere? I returned to Changan, and you were not among the foreign sorcerers rounded up by the empress. So you had to be here. I've visited thirty of these beastly ceremonials already, looking for you. And they call themselves sorcerers! Dabblers and mountebanks! Bah!"

"I regret that I had no other choice, my lord. Although I realize that in the ANALECTS you state that in the two million years of sorcery this is the last place—"

"Oh, stop!" He impatiently flicked his long violet fingernails. "My darling daughter is gone, and all you can do is recite your schoolboy lessons! And don't make any of the idiotic suggestions I sense rattling about your cranium. I have already considered every possible contingency, and have now checked them all out. Which means that there remains only one possible place Zenobia could have been taken. But right now we're going to leave this necromantic snake-pit." He rose to his feet.

"You mean you're going to take me with you?" he cried.

"I have been reduced even to that extremity, yes. You're going to help me get Zenobia back. And you may as well forget any fancies about this being a ruse on her part, hoping that I'd be forced to come back and get you. She has been abducted by a powerful wizard."

"A wizard? But what wizard—"

"No wizard who has ever lived would be powerful enough to take my darling daughter from me." His heavy-lidded eyes glittered with controlled fury.

"But I don't understand, my lord. How could—"

"Your understanding is the last thing I need, Valorius. Now just relax and do nothing."

"But, my lord," he protested. "I'm capable of at least—"

"Of at least shutting up and doing as you're told!"

"Yes, my lord."

Instantly he felt a surge of psychic energy converging around him like iron filings around a powerful magnet. A blue aura formed about the brazier. Something hit him like the sound wave from a tremendous clap of thunder. Then he was standing on the carved ivory dais, beside the musnud of Magus Rex.

For several minutes he could only stare stupidly about the Byzantine reception hall. Servants swarmed all around him, carrying golden trays heaped with savory viands, crystal decanters and goblets, and even a spare musnud for him to sit on. When the cobwebs finally left his brain he found himself seated before an exquisite feast. The servants were gone.

Magus Rex ate with epicurean relish, but the look of controlled fury never left his eyes. After weeks of rancid Tibetan food, Valorius' appetite temporarily overcame even his concern for Zenobia's safety. The food was so delicious that he could hardly keep himself from gobbling.

At last the servants returned with scented finger-bowls and towels; they cleared the table, leaving coffee and liqueurs. Only when they were gone did Magus Rex speak.

"Now let's get to the bottom of this, Valorius. First tell me how Zenobia was communicating with you. That, I believe, is the key to her abduction."

Valorius hesitated.

"Oh, come now!" Magus Rex said impatiently. "You couldn't possibly have followed us to Rome or New York or Changan unless Zenobia had contacted you in some way. Where's your sense of proportion? This is no time to worry about betraying confidences, or any such nonsense. Now how did she do it?"

Reluctantly, Valorius explained.

"She sent the messages in verse?" Magus Rex raised his eyebrows. "I see now why the minx asked me to teach her how to form letters at a distance. She said it would be a convenience in so large a palace. And yet she was telling the truth when she swore that she hadn't disobeyed me." He stroked his beard. "Do you remember any of the verses? The one that kept you out of the birdcage, for instance?"

"I remember them all, my lord. All the verses — well, the first two at least — required careful examination to be understood. I couldn't help memorizing them." He recited:

> Our only love has beckoned,
> And instantly we start;
> Forgetting in that second
> That transports of the heart
> Prepare a cage apart.

"It was only at the last moment that I finally—"

"Yes, I can just picture you biting your lip over that one," said Magus Rex. "But I think I understand now. That explains why she wheedled me into giving her permission to write poetry *anywhere*. And the verse is ambiguous enough so that she could even convince herself that it was not really a message. Bless her feminine heart!" He smiled in spite of himself. "Not even my powers could detect a lie."

Valorius explained the circumstances under which he had received the second verse. Magus Rex looked thoughtful.

"And you say that the witch Izelta copied down the verse?"

"She copied the letters, my lord. The language was meaningless to her."

"Nonetheless, this means that it was possible for somebody else to have gotten hold of the verse. Or at least to have discovered how Zenobia was contacting you. But she was genuinely surprised to see you pop up in Changan. What went wrong?"

"Nothing as far as I can see, my lord. I had given up all hope of ever seeing her again, when suddenly the verse telling me exactly where she had gone appeared in my flat in New York."

"What do you mean *exactly*?"

"There was nothing ambiguous about it. Not only were the directions the clearest but the letters themselves by far the most vivid of any message. . . . That is to say, of any verse she wrote."

"Recite it." He leaned forward on his musnud like

a cat getting ready to pounce.

The verse had been so explicit that Valorius had not had to study it. He had to think for a moment before the words came back to him:

> Valorius, my love, I am telling you true,
> My father has taken me to the time of Empress
>      Wu.
> About three years before the Reign
> Of Terror and so much death and pain.
> From Changan, which is the capital city,
> Please rescue me through your love and pity.

Magus Rex said, "That solves at least part of the mystery. But to have so much power and to be so utterly devoid of sensibility makes one wonder just what we're up against."

"Perhaps Zenobia didn't have time for literary effects."

"Zenobia never wrote that verse, you booby. Any more than you sent the message summoning her to the boundary of my nome."

"Message?"

"Yes. Apparently Zenobia received what she thought was a message from you. Her maid reports seeing a red haze begin to form in the air and then being sent from the room. That night, while I was amusing myself elsewhere, Zenobia drove to the boundary of my nome. Just outside stand the ruins of an ancient city, and some troglodytes report seeing her there. Then the trail ends."

Valorius wondered what Zenobia had expected to find waiting for her in the ruined city. A doddering old man who had just plodded across two million years of time? Perhaps not. He had surprised her by appearing in Changan. But if she hadn't sent the verse leading him there, who did?

"And there are no clues at all?" Valorius asked.

"None. She just disappears without a trace. I've scoured the planet; every wizard on earth has searched for her." He shrugged. "Nothing."

"What wizard would ever dare to challenge the power of Magus Rex?" This seemed to Valorius the most incredible thing of all.

"No wizard who has ever lived," said Magus Rex. "Which means that Zenobia's abductor has not lived yet."

"You mean she's been taken into the future?"

"There's no possible alternative. It is universally recognized that I am the most powerful wizard that has ever lived. But, improbable as it seems, it is a logical possiblity that an even more powerful wizard may arise sometime in the future. Or, at least, a wizard that may think himself powerful enough to challenge me."

"But why would he challenge you in such an iniquitous manner, my lord?"

"On that we can only speculate. His utter lack of poetic sensibility is one clue to his character. Another is the fact that he would take such great risks to get Zenobia for his consort."

Valorius frowned. "Then there must be some reason why so powerful a wizard would not simply ask your consent. You've told me rather often that you planned to give her—"

"To a wizard not unworthy of even my regard. Exactly. So there must be some reason, beyond the powers of wizardry, which might render him ineligible. With me or with Zenobia. So he had to abduct her."

"I'm afraid I still don't see how that is a clue to his character."

"For a certain type of person, Zenobia would have great prestige value. She would be a mighty attribute of his greatness. After all, she's the daughter of the most powerful wizard and the most beautiful woman who have ever lived."

"You've never spoken of Zenobia's mother, my lord." He hesitated. "Nor have you ever told me the story about how my father—"

"Your father was a pudding, Valorius. There's no two ways about that. But somehow he wooed and won the beautiful daughter of a Viking skald. They lived happily together on one of the small northern islands, and I suspect that your father had no intention of ever returning. He gained fame as a doctor. But he could not save the life of his young bride. She died shortly after you were born."

"Then my father could not have controlled his aging processes either."

"He chose glory over immortality, just like in the old Greek story. But he decided that he did not have the right to make that decision for his infant son. I had to go back and fetch the pair of you."

Valorius could understand his father's choice. The blood of the Vikings flowed in his own veins and he knew that there were more important things in life than mere longevity.

"It was that adventure which started me thinking," Magus Rex continued. "My powers were boundless, but I thought myself only a king of shadows. I searched through all of time for the most beautiful woman who had ever lived. She was a mountain princess in ancient Circassia, about to be sent to the harem of the King of Palmyra. I won her with only a very minimal use of wizardry. It was perhaps the noblest thing I've ever done. But I was punished for my arrogance. We lived at Alexandria, and it was there that Zenobia was born. By the merest chance her nurse had taken her from the palace that day. . . . But nothing can be done about it any more." His long violet fingernails closed like talons. "Those responsible died soon afterward. And now Zenobia too has been taken from me."

"Wasn't someone else taken away recently?" Valorius asked thoughtfully. "I believe you said something about the grandchild of a wizard—"

"Yes, one of our lesser wizards. His daughter had a child by a troglodyte boy he had foolishly raised as her companion. Then one day both father and child disappeared, leaving the poor little creature heartbroken. As a matter of fact, that's the first thing I investigated. But there's nothing to it. The father merely

returned to his people, and how a plump young child
would fare among the troglodytes is obvious."

"But didn't you say that the wizard's daughter was
a dwarf?" Valorius cried.

"Yes, but what does that have to do with Zenobia's
abduction?"

"Maybe everything." Step by step he recounted his
series of strange encounters with dwarfs, including
the mysterious dwarf child he had seen in Lhasa.

For the next twenty minutes Magus Rex sat on his
musnud like a carven idol. His heavy-lidded eyes
scarcely blinked. At last he began to smile.

"Yes, that's the enemy's weak point. How many
wizards were guarding the dwarf child?"

"Seven, my lord. And they seemed powerful wizards."

"Their punishment shall be swift and condign. But
first I may be able to get them to volunteer some
information. What a strange thing is time, that one's
own ancestor is the point at which he is most vulnerable! And where in all the two million years of mankind
would I be least likely to appear? Yes, Valorius, the
wizard that abducted Zenobia has read the ANALECTS."

"How may I be of service, my lord?"

"At the moment the best thing you can do is just
stay out of the way. I grant you the run of the palace. I
shall return in three days."

"Yes, my lord. The minimal margin of error for time
travel."

"It would not be wise to overlap oneself. That's
why I've never ventured into the future. But now it
seems that I, even I, Magus Rex, am not immortal.
For no wizard powerful enough to challenge me could
ever rise so long as I lived. Now stand back, Valorius."

The great bronze doors clanged shut. A wind rushed
through the hall, crackling with energy. Then the
musnud of Magus Rex stood empty.

# CHAPTER XXII
# THE FASCICLES

The three days of waiting had barely elapsed when Valorius received the summons. He followed the ancient Japanese gardener back to the palace. Twilight was fast fading into the blackness of night, and the other gardeners were beginning to gather up their tools. Magus Rex was pacing back and forth in front of his musnud.

"I need your help, Valorius," he said. "Now sit down and listen carefully."

Valorius was too stunned to say a word. Magus Rex needing his help! He drew a stool to the front of the ivory dais and sat down, expectantly.

"The dwarfish ancestor of the enemy has been removed to a less accessible realm," Magus Rex continued, "and the seven wizards that guarded him have been reestablished under a mountain in Antarctica. But first I drew the most timid of the seven aside and convinced him that there were far worse things than even a Tartarean sojourn. After a couple of free samples he became quite loquacious. I have a great deal to thank you for, Valorius."

"How so, my lord?"

"It seems that the enemy has been planning to abduct Zenobia for many years. Your uninvited appearance on my nome upset his entire operation. The last place he ever expected to see me was the ancient world. Your stumbling into Lhasa when you did was a marvelous display of dumb luck."

"Have you discovered where Zenobia has been taken?"

"Yes, and that's why I need your help."

"Anything, my lord. I am ready to face any challenge. No power is too awesome—"

"Yes, yes." Magus Rex waved him to silence. "I have no doubts about your courage. Frankly, Valorius, I've always thought that you'd be more at home sacking a city than studying at the Academy. But if you lack skill, you have shown at least some degree of resourcefulness. And that's exactly what I need. In fact, you must not use any wizardry at all unless your very life depends on it. The defenses of the enemy would be sure to detect you."

"But where has Zenobia been taken, my lord?"

"Greenland."

"Greenland?"

"Its great Central Depression makes it ideal for his purposes. As you know, Greenland was covered by a huge icecap until quite recently. The ice is gone, but the center of the island is still depressed hundreds of feet below sea level. The ideal place to concentrate psychic energy."

"But why would he—"

"I'll explain as I go along. Now just listen carefully."

"Yes, my lord."

"The wizard I interrogated gave me some rather puzzling and contradictory information. It seems that the enemy has created a kind of vast fairyland in the Central Depression, evidently to impress Zenobia with his powers. The conceited little wretch thinks he can make her come to him willingly. Don't interrupt! The magnitude and diversity of this fairyland are beyond even my great powers. That's what's so puzzling and contradictory. And you say the dwarf who tried to have you killed in Rome did not attack you himself?"

"No, my lord. He stayed on the arena wall trying to get his henchmen to attack me."

Magus Rex looked thoughtful. "If he can wield such vast powers, why does he always work through agents? For obvious reasons he wanted you out of the way, and yet he never attacked you himself. Why not? After all, you're relatively inept. A wizard as powerful as he is would have little trouble disposing of you. He completely dominates the planet, nine thousand years from now. And yet he even tried to use me as an agent, apparently expecting me to destroy you the moment you appeared in Changan. Perhaps he thought he could win Zenobia more easily if she had reason to hate me. Perhaps he was afraid of tipping his hand too soon." He shrugged. "In any case, he doesn't expect me to follow him. And he certainly doesn't expect me to use your help."

"My lord, I am ready to face—"

Magus Rex waved him to silence. "Now here are the calculations you'll use to get there. It's only nine thousand years, and you have plenty of energy to work with. But it's vital that you materialize at precisely the right time and place."

Valorius glanced at the inscribed tablet. The calculations were hardly flattering: they were rendered in the painfully obvious detail a great mathematician might use in laying out a problem in basic arithmetic for a backward schoolboy.

"You will materialize outside the enemy's fairyland, exactly three days after I arrive. By then I will have drawn him away from Greenland in single combat, wizard against wizard. The forces involved will rock the planet. But whatever happens you must somehow reach Zenobia and get her to safety."

"Yes, my lord. I swear that I will do everything in my power to rescue Zenobia."

Magus Rex sighed. "You're not listening, Valorius. I repeat, you must not use any kind of wizardry unless it's absolutely necessary. The enemy would be sure to detect your presence, and then nothing I could do would save Zenobia. And I doubt if you'll be able to rescue her. It's not quite that simple. We may have to make a deal."

"His ancestor for Zenobia?"

"Exactly. But we must be careful how we go about it. He'll certainly have some contingency plan for destroying Zenobia, even if I should—"

"Destroy Zenobia?" Valorius cried.

"Think for a moment. Now you're sure that the dwarf who tried to kill you in the arena was the same one who sadistically butchered the Goth wench?"

"Positive, my lord." Valorius began to feel uneasy.

"Doesn't that add up to a rather ominous picture? Sadistic, cruel, cowardly, emotionally insecure, and deluded with his own grandeur. He would be capable of destroying Zenobia out of sheer spite, rather than lose her."

"I understand, my lord."

"Exactly where in this paranoid fairyland he's stashed her, I don't know. The only information the wizard I interrogated could give me was that she's somewhere near the very center of the island. That means you may have thousands of square miles to cover, and only a few days in which to do it. The transportation will range from the most ancient to the most modern. Use it, and not your own powers of transportation. I'll try to keep him busy as long as possible—never victorious, never defeated. But always remember that his powers are immense. Perhaps even greater than my own. Although that remains to be seen. Just get Zenobia to some place of safety and defend her as long as you can. The people you meet will be real people, just as they are in the pleasure-domes I've created for my own amusement. You may even be able to rally some of them to your side. In any case, no wizardry!"

"No, my lord."

"I'm depending on you, Valorius." Magus Rex looked keenly at him. "If you were strong enough to transport Zenobia along with yourself, I'd just have you bring her back here. But you're not, so don't try it. The enemy would probably detect the appearance of a wizard that powerful anyway. Now are there any questions?"

"No, my lord."

"Remember, I'm depending on you."

The energy needed to transport Magus Rex a mere nine thousand years created hardly a riffle in the Byzantine reception hall. Valorius needed more time. He memorized the calculations so that there would be no possibility of error on his part. That Magus Rex could have made a mistake was unthinkable. Concentrating as he had never concentrated before, bringing to bear all the skills of wizardry he possessed, he became one with the forward-sweeping tide of psychic energy. . . .

It took only moments to reorient himself. He stood at dawn on a barren plain, pocked and gouged by the tremendous weight of ice it had carried until quite recently. It was an eerie place. The air was crisp and cool; gray mists oozed through patches of stunted vegetation. It reminded him of Tibet except that there were no mountain ranges here; only scattered monadnocks which had stood like islands above the sea of ice. For as far as he could see the land was a barren waste.

The plain sloped downward before him. At a juncture less than a mile away, it suddenly sloped upward at an identical angle. At first Valorius thought he had made some error, despite all his care and concentration. There was no sign of any human habitation, let alone a vast fairyland contrived to impress Zenobia. Then he realized what the juncture between the two slopes actually was.

The pleasure-domes of Magus Rex could be seen from a distance; there were no obstacles to entering them. The mirror-like barriers and the strange sense of discouragement felt by anyone approaching them were only perceived by those trying to get out. If indeed the dwarf wizard had recreated fascicles of various lands and times, he would need similar means to keep them isolated. He also seemed afraid of people getting in. Were there troglodytes in Greenland? A wizard so powerful could hardly have enemies.

As he moved down the slope toward the juncture, Valorius became aware of streamers of light flashing across the horizon. It was like the aurora borealis, except that it was to the south. Magus Rex had been here three days already, and the enemy had evidently gone forth to meet him. There was no time to waste.

He came to within a hundred yards of the juncture before he first sensed the urge to turn back; it became almost overpowering as he advanced. Then he saw a tall figure in a shimmering blue cape and tunic striding downhill toward him. He walked right through it.

He found himself at the outer edge of a broad ramp. The city was a beehive of activity; conveyers and electric autos carried people from level to level; pedestrians bustled about their affairs with brisk efficiency. Titanium and glass were the dominating materials; the functional structures rose with clean lines into the morning sky. The austerity and almost sterile cleanliness was rather oppressive. Zenobia was not likely to be impressed. Nor was she likely to be here.

He recognized where he was, of course. The delta-hawk insignia displayed everywhere would have told him that, even if he had not recognized the black-and-silver uniforms of the officials. The Delta Freestate had risen after the Battle of Fostoria had finally brought the Black Ages to a close. A military aristocracy dedicated itself to rebuilding a desolated earth. Materially, their ant-like discipline achieved an awesome grandeur.

Magus Rex had chosen his point of entry with care. The dialect spoken here would not be unintelligible to the dialect Valorius had learned to speak in ancient New York.

It was an awesome achievement of wizardry. And yet there was something strangely lifeless about it, a mechanical listlessness unlike the vivid recreations of Magus Rex. Everything was just too perfect, inhumanly perfect.

Valorius had picked up a few tricks at the Tiger in ancient Rome. Getting money and inconspicuous clothes was not difficult, even without the use of wizardry. The city covered hundreds of square miles, and he had no time to waste with policemen or officials. He began looking for some means of transportation.

The electrobus driver did not seem to notice his uncertainty about the size of the fare. Valorius handed him the largest coin he had stolen and got change. The vehicle was designed strictly for function, not beauty. The crowd of people inside did not seem much interested in the scenery; they glanced listlessly over the miles of neat parks and gardens as they passed. They were clean and healthy-looking, of various races. Several of them wore black-and-silver uniforms.

Valorius had materialized on the eastern side of the island. His major concern was making sure that the electrobus was moving toward the Central Depression, which lay somewhere to the northwest.

As they passed the center of the city a strange thing happened. The passengers simultaneously all turned the same way. Valorius also had the urge to do the same, although there was nothing of interest outside the window. They were cruising at the lowest level of the city, enclosed by walls of brick and metal. He forced himself to look the other way. A metal obelisk stood by itself in the middle of an open plaza. Nobody was looking at it. The plaza was mysteriously empty.

Stealing an electrocar was easier than he had thought. The delta-hawk glowering down at virtually every street corner tended to discourage non-conformity of any kind. Theft was a dying art, and precautions against it were seldom taken any more.

The auto was small and functional; it seemed sturdy enough for rough driving. He had no idea what he would find on the far side of the mirror-like barrier, but he was still much too far from the center of the island to expect these recreations to be contiguous. No wizard could be that powerful.

He loaded his stolen electrocar with food and drink. The fringe of the city was utterly deserted, and he plunged straight into the mirage.

It was as he had expected. Great distances lay between the dwarf's fascicles, which loomed like colossal soap bubbles upon the glacial wasteland as far as the eye could see. These were more like the pleasure-domes of Magus Rex; they could be seen from the outside, and there would be no trouble entering them. He hoped to enter as few as possible.

The power that could create and sustain so many brilliant recreations of past wonders was mind-boggling. Why hadn't the dwarf disposed of him? He had the uneasy feeling that perhaps there was some other power behind all this. Was the dwarf merely the agent of some even greater wizard?

The terrain sloped generally inward. Some kind of construction work had been going on lately; there were rough access roads and insulated cables running from fascicle to fascicle. Some kind of communication system? Did the dwarf—or whoever was the real power behind all this—maintain a network of spies? He would have to be careful.

He covered over a hundred miles before nightfall; dawn was only a few hours away at this northern latitude during summer. The fascicles were closer together now, and the power-supply of his electrocar nearly discharged. Tomorrow or the next day would bring him near the geographic center of the island. Then the real search would begin.

He did not have to use any wizardry to sense the "energy pole" of the island's center looming before him. It was somewhere amidst the concentrated fascicles there that he would find Zenobia. They were only a few miles apart now; soon they would be contiguous. Transmission cables lay on the ground like the web of a colossal spider, but there were no more roads. He abandoned his electrocar.

To his right, like a toy city imprisoned within a shimmering soap bubble hundreds of square miles around, he saw the endless villas of a magnificent dark-skinned people. He was not sure of the period of history. It was probably one of the African Successor States, or perhaps an early dynasty of the Papuan Empire. In either case there would be only one fate for a person with blond hair and blue eyes. Chains would seriously impede his progress.

The fascicle to his left was at first even more mysterious. It looked like nothing but an open steppe. As the moon rose he began to make out a few outlying structures; the closest was the terminal of some kind of hover-coach line. But where were the cities? He slipped through the barrier and approached the terminal.

There was no problem about fares: the line was government operated. The six other passengers for the night journey were all oriental, too polite to stare at him. He was certain that he had seen the ornate bronze scrollwork before; bubble windows and booths of quilted silk gave each passenger a certain degree of privacy inside the coach. Their destination was nowhere in sight. Barren steppe stretched endlessly in the moonlight.

If there were cities. . . . Of course. Now he realized where he was. The Andigan Republic was the apogee of centralized bureaucracy. It had flourished in Central Asia throughout the later Radiation Epoch, when much of the earth's surface was uninhabitable. The cities were underground.

Now he began to wonder if the dwarf wizard was not the real power behind this strange fairyland after all. Every fascicle he had seen represented some triumph of authoritarianism: absolute monarchies, military oligarchies, police states, monolithic bureaucracies. They all had achieved material grandeur; conversely, not one of them had even approached literary or artistic eminence. As Magus Rex had pointed out, the verse that had appeared in his flat in ancient New York was devoid of poetic sensibility. If these fascicles had been recreated to impress Zenobia, their creator apparently considered himself the measure of all things. Such a person might indeed destroy something beautiful rather than let others have it.

The hover-coach glided smoothly across the steppes on its cushion of air. As a mode of transport it was not very fast, but it did not require roads. The stations were mere blisters of glass screening the tops of elevator shafts. The passengers chatted or read or watched a ballet on a three-dimensional video screen. Two sleek elderly gentlemen in jade-green uniforms were playing three-dimensional chess. In the booth behind them a woman was teaching her nubile daughter how to knit. They both wore gaudy flounced skirts.

It was shortly after midnight that the atmospheric effects erupted in the southern sky. The passengers left their games and amusements to watch. Valorius remained in his booth on the opposite side of the hover-coach; one glance had told him that the streaming lights and colors were not natural effects. They were closer than at dawn.

After a while the passengers became bored and returned to their games and amusements. Only once more did they all look out their bubble windows at the same instant. Valorius had the strange urge to do the same, just as he had had in the center of the Deltan city. He forced himself to look the other way. The metal obelisk rose out of the steppe like a finger pointing to the stars. There was nothing around it.

The hover-coach route lay somewhat to the south of his true line of approach across the Central Depression. When it ended he was the only passenger still on board. The coach settled to the ground like an exhausted beetle, and he climbed down and strode away into the night. Not far away he met a familiar figure striding toward him.

All that night and the next day he followed a bewildering succession of monoclines, subterbuses, and hydrovans. Toward evening he thought for a moment that he had stepped back into ancient Rome. Roman eagles were displayed everywhere; people in uniform saluted each other like centurions. But it was all a sham, a pompous mockery of the worst elements of the Roman Empire. At least the trains ran on time.

The people in the railroad car were noisy and colorful, as if their authoritarian regime was unnatural to them. Many of them took the people in uniforms as a joke. The people in uniforms, however, took themselves very seriously. This was the only fascicle he passed through in which the arts seemed to flourish. But here, too, he came upon the same mysterious phenomenon: everybody looked out the windows on the same side at the same instant. Standing in the twilight on the opposite side was a metal obelisk. Valorius sensed that he was getting closer to the "energy pole."

The railroad terminal was plastered with posters of this civilization's leader, just as every vacant wall and billboard in ancient New York had been plastered with the face of Luther Beck. But this face was more amusing than sinister. The pose was that of a village panjandrum playing a Roman emperor at an annual pageant. Valorius ran the gauntlet of officials, spies, inspectors and bureaucrats, and slipped out of the terminal unseen. Soon he slipped out of that whole world of mock-Roman pageantry.

The central sea covered hundreds of square miles. Valorius walked along the strand at sunset, looking for some kind of human habitation. Were the cities here also underground? He mounted a low tor and looked around. There were some plowed fields further down the shore, but no sign of human dwellings. The agriculture looked rather primitive. The fields clustered about an inlet from the sea, a narrow fjord whose steep rock walls seemed to extend inland for several miles.

Then something flashed across the setting sun out at sea. At first the light blinded him; then the ship glided swiftly out of the sun, its dragon-prow pointed directly at the fjord down the coast. The square sail was striped red and gold, shimmering in the rose-golden light of the setting sun. Sixteen pairs of oars thrashed the sea into foam as the Viking ship sped homeward; the shields of the warriors hung from the bulwarks like emblems of victory. Valorius could feel the battle cry rising in his throat.

He had a motley assemblage of coins in his pocket. Silver and a famous name were the true gods of the Vikings, and they were ready to slaughter anybody who crossed their path. But they were hospitable to strangers — especially those with a pocketful of silver.

It was after dark by the time Valorius reached the edge of the fjord. The auroral storm was hundreds of miles closer than it had been last night. Below him the torches and lanterns of the Viking stockade shuttled back and forth in the dark.

It was a semi-circular embankment topped with wooden palisades; several Viking ships had been dragged onto the sand, and sharpened stakes driven into the water around them. The gates were closed, but silver was a magic key among the Vikings. He picked his way down the slope toward the stockade below.

# CHAPTER XXIII
## THE HALL OF ODINKAR

Asfrid was a young minx. With twinkling blue eyes she handed Valorius his trousers, grinning mischievously at his confusion. She was no more than seventeen, but mature for her years. Silver pins supported her golden tresses; a silver collar of tiny birds, fish, and runic symbols circled her neck; a silver amulet in the shape of the hammer of Thor lay between her heavy breasts. Her red woolen tunic did not quite reach the middle of her thighs, and her leather boots stopped well short of her knees; her bare legs were strong and shapely. She was the daughter of Odinkar the Good.

Valorius bundled on his baggy blue trousers and leather jerkin while the girl appraised his form and figure. Courage and the ability to drink great quantities of ale were Viking virtues; modesty was not. She seemed to approve of his slenderness. Most Vikings, even young ones, had pot bellies; they were heroic eaters as well as drinkers.

A single silver coin had gotten him everything he

needed, from a place to sleep to new clothes. He did not have to speak the language. The coin had been carefully weighed and tested, but nobody had been interested in its inscription. Silver was silver.

Finding boots and a jerkin to fit him had been easy—most of the Vikings were at least as tall as he was—but the trousers were baggier about the waist than he could have wished. The sturdy leather belt had to take up the slack.

The house of Odinkar the Good was a ramshackle affair, something like a barn to which spare rooms had been tacked on as needed. And in fact half the house was a barn; that was the first thing Valorius had noticed when he entered last night. The cows, pigs, and sheep were screened from the living quarters, but their presence was all too evident. The floor was of beaten earth, and it was not a good idea to go barefoot. Dogs were everywhere.

The alcoves off the entrance hall were filled with beds. The Vikings got up whenever they felt like it, and drunken snores joined the early morning clatter as the slaves prepared breakfast. There were no chimneys, and the smoke got out the best way it could. Valorius' eyes smarted.

He followed Asfrid into the central hall. Parallel rows of oaken pillars supported the roof; the walls were wainscoted with rough planks of oak, in front of which were ranged heavy oak benches. Several of these were occupied. Vikings were already (or still) playing a board game of some kind, sliding smooth pebbles and bits of amber back and forth with intense interest. Their flagons of ale were continually replenished by slaves. Nobody seemed to mind the smoke or stink or bawl of the animals. In fact, they would probably have missed it.

Odinkar the Good was a mountain of a man, with a walrus mustache. He stood before the hearth, yawning and scratching his great hairy belly. His morning toilet consisted of hawking and spitting into the fire. He watched with bleary eyes as slaves carried in tables covered with linen cloths; somebody handed him a tankard and he absent-mindedly tossed off a quart or so of ale. A sheep was turning on the spit.

The Viking women were also of robust proportions. Their morning toilet was more elaborate than that of the men, consisting for the most part of arranging their hair with combs of carved antler, although some of them also spat into the fire. They wore long woolen gowns of various colors fastened at the shoulders by silver brooches. Ermine cloaks were common, but many of these had been in the smoke so long that they looked more like mink.

The morning meal merged into the afternoon meal; for some of the hardier trenchermen it also became the evening meal. Board games, songs, heroic tales and an occasional dog fight enlivened the feasting. Robust Viking children played at various rough-and-tumble games, laughing and squabbling. Their education was furthered by sundry cuffs and backhanders. Nobody paid much attention to Valorius. Even Asfrid was careful not to show too much interest in the presence of her father.

At last Valorius had to push himself from the table. He could hardly stand. Even though he had managed to surround a good three pounds of mutton and a gallon of ale, Asfrid looked disappointed in him. The slaves were putting a fresh calf on the spit.

The Viking stockade was even more squalid by daylight. Most of the houses were like that of Odinkar the Good: ramshackle wattle-and-daub barns roofed with turf. There were no paved streets. The Vikings just built their houses wherever they felt like it.

Valorius slipped outside the stockade and climbed to the top of the hill overlooking the fjord. Nobody bothered him. The only time the Vikings ever seemed interested was when there was silver involved, in which case they were very shrewd indeed.

It was a cool, overcast day. If there were any atmospheric effects they were hidden by the clouds.

Ten miles out at sea the air wavered like the heat

waves rising from a tropical desert; an invisible wall cutting straight across the cold gray waters. This wavering effect was most intense toward the center, where something special was being protected. An island? A promontory? Shreds of fog lay here and there upon the waters. In the opposite direction, at the head of the fjord, he could just make out a metal obelisk. There was no time to examine it.

Zenobia was certainly not here. He wondered if the dwarf wizard had created all this just to taunt her. Perhaps the cowardly little wretch was fascinated with raw courage, just as he was fascinated with authoritarian regimes. The fog was beginning to creep inland as he followed the strand toward the south. Without recourse to wizardry the best he could do with the relentless presence of Viking mutton and ale in his stomach was to try and walk it off.

The strand was damp and slippery; the gray translucence of the fog made it harder and harder to pick his way, and he felt increasingly discouraged. Then he saw something move just ahead, something human. He was unarmed. Silently he picked up a flat rock and crept forward. Gradually he could make out through the fog the form of a tall figure creeping toward him with a flat rock in its hand. With a sigh he straightened up and tossed the rock away. He was glad the fog prevented anybody from seeing what a fool he was making of himself. He strode right through his own image.

The fog reached less than a hundred yards inland. He climbed a low hill and looked around. In the distance loomed the walls of a city. The central sea, or lake, was evidently not so large as he had thought: its shores were divided between only two fascicles. It took him less than two hours to reach the city.

The small harbor was filled with wooden galleys. The fog was pierced by electric lights; totemic statuary of stone and teak ringed the docks, where a tall, powerfully-built oriental people moved efficiently about their work. The walls of the city were covered with brilliant glazed tiles; dragon motifs predominated. And yet the gates were electrically operated.

Valorius was puzzled. Where in the ancient world had such a civilization existed? It took several minutes for the answer to come to him. The proximity of the Viking realm was misleading; this was not from the ancient world at all. Zenobia was even less likely to be here than in the Viking stockade, although this was also a realm that might endear itself to a cowardly little sadist like the dwarf wizard. The Kalamandran League had flourished for centuries on the islands between Australia and Asia, the first great civilization to emerge after Balbek's Comet. It had been utterly destroyed amidst the universal loathing of mankind. This might be a recreation of Kalamandra itself.

He could now see that the intense wavering at the center of the sea was definitely an island. He could expect nothing but refined cruelty from the Kalamandrans. If he were to get to the island at all, the Vikings would have to take him there. He wondered if he had enough silver. He headed back to the Viking fascicle.

The fog had lifted by nightfall, but the sky was still overcast. Valorius had no idea how close Magus Rex was to Greenland. "Never victorious, never defeated," he had said. But how long could a stalemate be maintained? Either alternative would bring the dwarf wizard flying to Zenobia, and Valorius had no illusions about his own ability to stand up to him.

It was after dark when Valorius got back. Asfrid led him to a seat at the very foot of the line of tables; but it was not done discourteously.

Every Viking settlement maintained a skald—what Valorius' own grandfather had been. Odinkar the Good's was seated at the foot of the line of tables that ran the length of the hall, reciting some plaintive tale of warriors dead and gone. Odinkar himself presided at the center of the line, where he could keep a bleary eye on the hearth.

The evening meal looked suspiciously identical to the morning meal; several Vikings were asleep at table, using platters of greasy mutton as pillows. Their hardier comrades were still eating and swilling heroically.

When the skald at last finished his heroic tale, Asfrid sat him next to Valorius. None of the Vikings seemed to notice that the song was over; although they probably would have noticed had the women failed to keep the platters and drinking-horns filled. Asfrid smiled and nodded toward the skald, then she hurried down the room to chase a dog that was trying to climb onto the table.

True to his profession, the skald had some knowledge of languages. He had no trouble understanding Valorius' Latin; although Valorius could hardly understand his. There was a complacent sleekness about the skald, like a cat long pampered by the fireside. But bards went to battle among the Vikings, and the man was unusually large and powerful for his profession. He would have dwarfed Titus Lengo.

The skald agreed to handle the whole transaction to arrange Valorius' transport to the island. There was a trading expedition planned for the next day. Valorius gave him his largest silver coin and the man approached the center of the hall. Odinkar was laboring at a roast loin of pork, refreshing himself from time to time from a stone tankard; his walrus mustache was greasy and sopping wet.

The effect of the silver coin was magical. No sooner did the skald lay it at Odinkar's elbow than he bellowed for the scales; there followed several minutes of weighing and testing. Then the clippers were called for. To the Vikings a silver coin was just so much silver, and Valorius' coin was cut to bits. Odinkar kept some, the skald kept some, and the rest were returned as "change." The ship left at dawn.

All the Vikings were more or less hung over when they first dipped their oars into the waters of the

fjord the next morning. But they bent their backs
with a will, and the dragon ship darted out into the
open sea.

Even paying passengers were expected to lend a
hand, at rowing as well as fighting. Valorius shared a
bench amidships. He had a steel sword and a stubby
spear with a leaf-shaped blade at his disposal; his
round wooden shield, painted with a red rooster, hung
from the bulwarks. His benchmate was a sandy-bearded
old villain, as grisly and battle-scarred as an old bear.
Last night's ale oozed from his pores.

The sky was still overcast, but there was no fog.
The big square sail was striped red and white; reefing
lines were held by members of the crew so that the
sail could be instantly lengthened or shortened for
quick changes of speed. It was full speed ahead this
morning, a good ten-knot clip straight for the center of
the sea. Odinkar the Good sat at the tiller like a
bleary-eyed walrus, barking commands. The rudder
was actually a kind of large steering oar fastened to
the right side of the ship, and it took a mighty grip to
control it.

Valorius could not see the water in front of the ship,
and had no need to. The moment he sensed the sandy-
bearded old villain to his left slacken his stroke, he
leaped to his feet. The mirage lay dead ahead.

The whole crew showed signs of discouragement,
of wanting to turn back.

Valorius gave Odinkar two more silver bits and
flashed a couple of silver coins, which he then slipped
back into his belt. His lessons in ancient Rome had
not been wasted; he wanted the ship to lay to until he
returned, and promise of payment to come would be
far more effective in achieving that end than payment
now.

His handling of the coracle raised some guffaws on
deck, but soon he got the hang of it. It was a round
skin boat and tended to rotate in the water unless
the paddle strokes were short and quick. His sense
of discouragement was greater than he had ever

known, but he kept the coracle moving forward.

The Vikings had had little curiosity about why he should want to paddle off in the middle of the sea. His silver had been reason enough. They raised their oars and broke out the drinking horns. Odinkar the Good broached a fresh cask of ale with his fist.

# CHAPTER XXIV
## THE CONCRETE PALACE

Valorius paddled right through the mirage. He had guessed many things last night, wondering what he would find on the mysterious island. The last thing he expected to find was the palace of Magus Rex. Or, at least, a shabby facsimile of the palace. Only weeds grew in its gardens.

He hid the coracle among the rocks, keeping out of sight. The island covered only a few square miles, most of which was barren rock. Miles of ice had once crushed the region hundreds of feet below sea level; it was only just beginning to rebound isostatically, and the small island had not long been above the surface of the waters. The waves had washed smooth the scars left by the glaciers. It would be hard to approach the palace unseen.

The only cover he could find was a long trench, at the bottom of which a transmission cable lay like a giant black worm. It ran from a corner of the palace directly into the sea. If the dwarf wizard maintained a communications network, it was certainly an elaborate one. Similar cables extended to all sides of the island.

The trench was barely waist deep, and Valorius had to walk bent over while straddling the cable. He had nearly a mile to cover, and his back soon began to ache; several times he had to rest, and even crawl. It took him an hour to reach the palace.

Only now did he realize that it was not built of marble, but of a low-grade concrete. It also displayed a low grade of architecture: the engineering seemed competent enough, but the proportions were all wrong. The windows were streaked and garbage littered the grounds.

Zenobia would hardly be impressed. This was not so much a facsimile of her father's palace as a nasty little parody. But if she was not in either the Viking or the Kalamandran fascicle, she had to be here. He could only hope that the dwarf wizard was not here too.

The masonry was also shoddy; metal pins had been left in the concrete, which was already beginning to crack and flake. The transmission cable entered the structure through the foundation. Not far away was a round metal service portal. There was no problem opening it; the clasps had been designed for large clumsy fingers. The portal was not designed for dwarfs and would admit creatures even larger than Valorius.

And suddenly he was back in the ancient world. The whole basement of the concrete palace looked like one of the computer nodes of the Black Ages. It was through the absolute control of all forms of information that Luther Beck and his successors had been able to control the entire planet for a thousand years. This was right out of the twentieth century, the golden age of authoritarianism.

The only lights came from the endless batteries of panels, consoles, video screens, and keyboards. Valorius had only a rudimentary knowledge of electronics. The science had not been evil in itself, but it had been put to evil purposes. Was this the real source of the dwarf's power? Could wizardry really be computerized? This

was all so typical of what he knew about the dwarf
wizard that he abandoned any idea of an even more
powerful wizard behind him. And yet he knew that
the dwarf had the ability to transport himself through
time. Unless that was done with machines too?

Valorius roamed through room after room of computer banks, all maintained at precise levels of temperature and humidity, and all deserted. Perhaps the
whole concrete palace was deserted. Perhaps Zenobia
was here alone, guarded electronically. But he could
not take that chance. The only means of getting to the
floor above was by elevator. If Zenobia was guarded
by wizards, like the dwarf child he had seen in ancient
Lhasa, they would be alerted the moment the elevator
started to move.

He found an elevator with open doors; its stage was
nearly as large as the one that had raised and lowered
Hannibal in the Flavian Amphitheater millions of years
ago. The service portal at the top of the car was like
the one in the foundation. He slid an empty packing
crate under it and prepared to climb. Then he noticed
the markings on the crate: MADE IN JAPAN. Had the
dwarf also gotten his equipment from the twentieth
century?

Hand over hand he ascended the elevator cable, his
Viking sword and scabbard banging against his shins
all the way up. There was just enough of a flange
inside the first door he reached to balance his weight.
He put his ear to the door and listened. Nothing.
Perhaps the concrete palace was deserted after all.
Cautiously he slipped the point of his sword between
the doors and pried them open a few inches. All he
could see was a deserted corridor.

By main force he spread the doors far enough apart
to slip through. There were some rather indifferent
pieces of art, indifferently dusted. The decorating
was in execrable taste, with tawdry arrangements and
clashing colors. The smell was all too human.

His Viking boots were of soft leather; he crept
without a sound down the corridor, sword drawn.

Behind a door he heard muffled voices speaking in a language he did not understand—if it was a language at all. After listening for several moments he realized that the voices were more garbled than muffled. It was not the door that was causing the distortion. The concrete palace was not deserted.

Most of the floor was mere space, without even tasteless art and tawdry decoration to fill it. He returned to the elevator and climbed hand over hand to the floor above. It was much the same, except that more of the rooms seemed to be occupied. He saw two people in electric blue uniforms with lime green stripes on the trousers moving away from him. They were huge and powerful-looking, but their oddly-shaped bodies were strangely awkward and clumsy. They reminded him of giant dwarfs.

His search was going slowly. The Vikings had ale and he had silver, but it would not be wise to make them wait too long.

There were more oddly-shaped people on the floor above; he finally got a look at their faces. All the normal features were there, but blurred and distorted. Garbled voices echoed up and down the corridors, and he could not search very thoroughly. There was no obvious clue to Zenobia's whereabouts.

On the top floor he ran across a whole troop of these strangely deformed people. He could not place them in history, unless they were something out of the Radiation Epoch. Scores of them hovered about the door to a suite of rooms in the southwest corner of the building; the art works and decorations were more elegant here, as if somebody had deliberately copied them from a manual of some kind. The smell was more human than ever.

It would have taken the whole fighting band of Odinkar the Good just to get past them. There were no stairs; these awkward creatures looked like they would have trouble using them. There were two elevators to the top floor, the only means of getting away. In any case, there was no way he could get the Vikings past the mirage, no matter how much silver he had. Somehow he had to get at least some of the dwarf's servitors away from the suite of rooms. He had no choice but to assume that it was Zenobia they were guarding.

Hand over hand he descended to the basement, pausing only once to rest his aching arms and shoulders. Fortunately nobody decided to use the elevator at that moment. He wandered from room to room, but could not figure out the purpose of any of the endless consoles and lighted panels. At last he gave up. Although his knowledge of electronics was rudimentary, he knew that there had to be an emergency alarm system of some kind. He just looked for the biggest switches he could find and started throwing them. That was bound to set off some kind of alarm.

It did. Bells and buzzers exploded all around him; lights flashed, gongs rattled. He raced for the elevator; the doors closed just behind him and it started to ascend. He kicked away the packing case as he leaped for the trapdoor in the ceiling; he closed it behind him, flattening himself against the top of the car. The elevator worked on exactly the same principles as the one at Club Sybaris in ancient New York.

Bells, buzzers, and gongs continued to sound all over the concrete palace. Valorius rolled over on his back; the top of the elevator shaft seemed to push down at him like a giant piston. But he had gauged his distance. The instant the elevator stopped he slid off it, supporting himself on the metal framework at the top of the shaft. The car trembled from the impact of people climbing into it. Despite the emergency the dwarf's servitors were slow and clumsy in boarding.

Then the car started downward. So did Valorius, hardly bothering to listen at the elevator doors before he wedged them open with his sword. This was no time for stealth or subtlety.

He charged straight down the corridor, ready for anything. There were two servitors standing guard outside the suite of rooms; they made some garbled noises as he rushed toward them. His sword was drawn, but their reaction time was so slow that he was past them before they could even raise their hands.

Everything in the suite was laid out with instruction-book elegance, although the dusting and sweeping were haphazard. He dashed past another person in an electric blue uniform with lime green stripes on the trousers. There were eight large rooms in the suite. Only one of the doors was locked.

He launched himself against it feet first, kicking out just as he hit the center panel. The whole jamb cracked and splintered. Regaining his balance, he threw his shoulder against the door. Zenobia was standing in the middle of the room, alone.

"The cabinet!" she cried. "Quickly!"

He stared dumbly at her for a moment, uncomprehending. Then he heard the garbled voices behind him. The dwarf's servitors were shuffling toward him out of the corridor. At last he realized that Zenobia meant for him to barricade the door.

"They're tremendously strong," she cried. "But it takes them a while to get moving."

Valorius got the heavy cabinet in front of the door just as a heavy body hit it from the outside. With Zenobia's help he began piling everything he could lay his hands on in front of the door. Still, he doubted that the barricade would last ten minutes.

He ran to the window. It was four storys to the rocks below but there were balconies on each floor.

"Sheets and drape-cords," Zenobia cried, disappearing into a small alcove. She reappeared a moment later with an armload of sheets torn from her bed. "The drape-cords! Quickly!"

Valorius hacked them down with his sword and kicked open the windows. Zenobia had already knotted the sheets together.

"This will get us to the balcony below," she said. "Wrap the cords around your waist. That's right. Give me a couple of them. I've been planning this for days, but I had no way of getting off the island."

"Do you think you can hold on to me while I climb

down to the balcony below?" asked Valorius, glancing
at the knots she had tied. "Just put your arms around
my neck and hold tight. I can hold both our weights."

She suppressed a smile. "I think it would be easier,
beloved, if I just climbed down myself. Close the
drapes behind you."

Before he could stop her she went over the railing.
It was a sheer drop to the rocks below, but Zenobia
went down the tied sheets like a sailor. She grinned up
at him from the balcony below.

"Remember the drapes," she whispered.

Heavy thumps rattled the door and pieces of furniture began to tumble down from the barricade. He
closed the drapes behind him and went over the railing.
Zenobia had already tied two drape-cords together
and fastened one end to the railing. From balcony to
balcony they descended to the ground.

"Oh, Valorius," she cried the moment they were safe.
"How glad I am to see you. I've been so frightened,
beloved."

She stood in such a way that he just naturally took
her into his arms and kissed her. She was warm and
yielding, trembling slightly at his touch. He tried to
comfort her.

At last, reluctantly, she gently disengaged herself.
Her eyes darted from balcony to balcony. They were
still empty.

"How did you get to the island?" she asked, giving
his hand a gentle squeeze.

He explained.

"I don't think we need worry about being seen," she
said thoughtfully. "They're rather slow, and they don't
react—"

The bells and buzzers and gongs suddenly ceased.
The eerie silence that followed was broken only by the
distant rush of the sea.

"We'd better get moving," said Valorius. "Do they
have weapons of any kind?"

"They're only dangerous if they get their hands on
you." She followed him around the corner of the

building, across the weed-choked gardens, and toward the shore. "With the drapes drawn upstairs it should be at least a few minutes yet before they think of the windows. It was you who set off the alarm, wasn't it?"

Valorius nodded.

She brushed against him as they walked, giving his hand another gentle squeeze. "I saw some strange lights in the sky, before it became so overcast. Was that Father?"

He explained everything that had happened, including Magus Rex's instructions to get her to a place of safety.

"I thought it must be." She nodded. "It was comical the way Bobo carried on."

"Bobo?"

She laughed. "That's what I call him. He calls himself Borimbo the Magnificent, and even tried to get me to address him as 'Magus Superbus.' He's terribly jealous of Father. Calling him *Bobo* and showing my contempt for him was the only way of keeping him in line. I think he'd be a little terror if he ever thought I was afraid of him."

They picked their way across a trench filled with transmission cables. The dwarf's servitors were starting to pour out of the concrete palace; their electric blue uniforms looked even more tawdry in daylight. They trotted at the speed of a fast walk.

"What in the world are they?" asked Valorius, glancing over his shoulder. "Radiation Epoch mutants?"

"I think Bobo made them," said Zenobia. "He tries to do everything Father does, but he's not very good at it. He dragged me around to see all the wonders he's created. Just for me, he said. That gave me a chance to taunt him with his inadequacy by telling him all about the really wonderful things Father's created. He gnashed his teeth for hours."

Valorius launched the coracle and helped her inside. The dwarf's servitors, plugging along with their slow-motion trot, were now less than a hundred yards

behind. For a few moments he had the same trouble
paddling the coracle: it tended to just rotate in the
water. Then he adjusted to Zenobia's added weight
and got them moving.

"Oh, Valorius," she cried. "Do you really think we
should leave the island? Somehow I feel—"

"It's an effect of the mirage," he said. "It discour-
ages people from approaching it. Just hold on. We'll
be through it in a few minutes." With short, choppy
strokes he paddled as hard as he could.

The Vikings had remained true to their trust (or
their ale). Odinkar wiped his lips with a corner of his
walrus mustache and looked on with bleary eyes as
the coracle was hoisted on deck. Most of the other
Vikings were looking at Zenobia; some of them were
also wiping their lips.

Valorius still had his sword, but he hoped he would
not have to use it. Zenobia's harem costume did little
to hide her gorgeous femininity. The Vikings did nothing at all to hide either their lust or the contempt they
felt for Valorius' slenderness.

Then Zenobia surprised him. She yanked her hand
out of his and glared angrily at him. Her words were
innocent enough, but she spat them in such a way
that anybody who did not speak the language would
think that she was cursing him.

The Vikings nodded approvingly, assuming now
that he had ravished her. He thereby rose several
notches in their esteem.

One husky young lout, however, still coveted Zenobia.
His tunic was cut off at the shoulders to display his
biceps; the tattoos on his arms were mostly martial in
nature. He leered drunkenly at Zenobia as she passed,
and even tried to paw her. Valorius thrust him aside,
clasping the pommel of his sword.

The effect was startling. Vikings grinned and shouted
at each other as they cleared away the benches and
casks from the center of the deck. The young lout
sneered and spat over the side. There was no avoiding
a fight now.

Odinkar broached another ale cask with his fist and gave the two combatants the first quaff. Then he led Zenobia to a bench near the steering oar and said something to reassure her, although his accompanying pat was not fatherly. The ship rolled slightly in the calm sea. The sails were furled.

Valorius knew that his only real danger lay in his opponent's first charge. But he did not underrate him. He was large and powerful, and probably a seasoned warrior. His own problem was adapting the techniques he had learned in the amphitheater to a long sword, which was most effectively used with two hands. The short sword of the Romans was a thrusting weapon; this one was for hacking and slashing. He braced himself for the charge.

Shouting his battle cry, the young Viking leaped straight at him, swinging his sword in a shining arc. Valorius skipped aside, thrust his own blade hilt to hilt against his opponent's, and ripped it out of his hands.

The flying blade caught the sandy-bearded old villain, Valorius' benchmate, square in the foot. There were howls of laughter as he hobbled about. Then he tore off his boot, smeared a handful of salt on the wound, and wrapped it with a dirty rag. His snaggle-toothed grin showed that there were no hard feelings. The joke was on him.

Meanwhile Valorius tried to soothe any hard feelings by his defeated opponent. He whacked him on the back, smiling as he pointed to the ale cask. The young lout nodded ruefully, although he was glad to believe that he had lost through drunkenness, and not lack of prowess. Swords were returned to their scabbards; benches and casks replaced.

All eyes were on Valorius as he swaggered back toward Zenobia. She now looked submissive. Again the Vikings nodded approvingly. That a beautiful young woman might at first feel somewhat vexed at being ravished from her homeland was understandable. They had seen it many times before. But a true woman should quickly submit herself to the doughtiest warrior. Their faith in womankind reaffirmed, the Vikings shuffled back to their oars.

Odinkar the Good could hardly be expected to turn aside from a trading voyage just because of an everyday ravishment. Valorius handed over the promised silver and returned to his bench. The sandy-bearded old villain next to him chuckled between strokes. He was probably crippled for life, but seemed to think it a wonderful joke.

Odinkar's bleary eyes grew crafty as they approached the stockade of his Viking neighbors. It stood on a small island of no more than ten acres just off shore. The cloud cover was at last beginning to break up, and beams of late afternoon sunlight slanted across the waves. There did not seem to be any openings in the stockade's defenses, and the Vikings resigned themselves to the role of peaceful traders.

They were not scheduled to return home for three days yet. Valorius did not care where he kept Zenobia, just so she was out of the clutches of the dwarf wizard. Only Magus Rex could overcome him, or make whatever deal had to be made. Besides, the dwarf's communications network would eventually locate them, no matter which fascicle they tried to hide in, and the Vikings would probably be least likely to tolerate spies.

There was a heroic feast that night to celebrate the arrival of the traders. Odinkar the Good and his crew were put on their mettle, matching their neighbors flagon for flagon, gobbet for gobbet. Valorius got away from the table as soon as he could. It was midnight, and dawn was only a few hours away.

Zenobia was the center of attention among the Viking women. Many of them had also been ravished in their time, and they laughed merrily over the good old days. They were not such mighty gorgers and swillers as their menfolk, but neither were they abstemious. Zenobia was now dressed in a thigh-length tunic and leather boots; her slender femininity made even the younger Viking women seem bovine by comparison. She smiled as Valorius entered the kitchen. His consumption of a gallon of ale and three pounds of roast beef made his entrance rather tentative.

He glanced nonchalantly into some of the vacant sleeping alcoves. On feast nights, Vikings usually slept wherever they stopped moving, or wherever they caught up with one of the women. Zenobia was gentle in her rebuff, but it seemed that her fathers' injunctions covered more things than just communication.

Valorius stepped outside for a breath of air while the women prepared a private alcove for Zenobia. He would sleep on a bench just outside the curtain. The Viking women thought this arrangement unusual, but apparently Zenobia was giving them some kind of explanation in sign language. Their peals of laughter rang through the night.

He stepped around the corner of the building, where he could get a good look at the southern sky. Only a few shreds of cloud skudded across the moon. But there were no atmospheric effects. Either the war of the wizards was over or it had entered a new dimension.

# CHAPTER XXV
## BORIMBO THE MAGNIFICENT

Magus Rex had warned him against any use of wizardry, and he had seen the network of transmission cables and the strange metal obelisks at the center of each fascicle. Nonetheless Valorius was tempted; his digestive system was rebelling against the Viking fare and needed a touch of wizardry to be put back in order.

Sleep was difficult. The hard wooden bench outside the curtains of Zenobia's alcove was not nearly as comfortable as sleeping on the floor. The Vikings were still carousing: gorging, swilling, shouting, singing and staggering about the smoky hearth. Most of the dogs were asleep by now but the pigs were still up and about, their beady little eyes alert for any chance table scraps within reach.

The Viking women were restless, getting up from time to time and sauntering into the main hall. Those who had not already been pounced upon by their drunken husbands or lovers could not get to sleep for the suspense of not knowing when the pounce would come. Valorius tried sleeping on his side.

Just before dawn he began to doze. His dreams were of pigs and Vikings, elephants, dwarfs and Chinamen. It was like the jazz-porn of ancient New York, only without the porn. Then he found himself once more in the basement of the concrete palace among a nightmare array of electronic equipment. Bells, buzzers, and gongs began to sound the alarm. Then he was falling through space. He awoke just as he hit the floor.

Odinkar the Good loomed above him, bleary eyed and grisly in the light of dawn. To wake Valorius he had simply kicked over his bench. It was effective: it did wake him up. He grunted something and ordered him to follow.

The whole barn-like dwelling was in an uproar. Vikings were stumbling about, buckling on their swords and plunging their heads into buckets of cold water. Valorius hurried after Odinkar. The alarm was being sounded by ram's horns, bleating from somewhere near the harbor.

The whole population was up by now. Dogs barked, pigs squealed, and Vikings shouted gleefully, running back and forth. Then Valorius saw what they were so pleased about. An armada of sleek galleys stood in battle formation far out to sea. They were not Viking ships. The Vikings did not care whose ships they were. It was a chance for glory, and they raced for the harbor shouting their battle cries.

Valorius raced back into the kitchen. Zenobia was already up and dressed; like the other Viking women she held a sword and scabbard in her hands. She helped Valorius buckle them on.

"It's Bobo, isn't it?" she asked.

"It must be. It looks like he's brought the whole Kalamandran fleet through the mirage to attack the Vikings."

"I wonder what's become of Father?"

"He can't be far behind. His greatest fear was that this Borimbo would destroy you out of spite the moment he thought he'd been beaten."

Zenobia frowned. "I never thought of that. But that's probably just what the little beast would have done."

"I wish there was a safer place I could take you," said Valorius. "But every place I've seen—"

"I've seen them all," Zenobia said. "That's the first thing Borimbo did after he abducted me, show off all his creations. He brought me here last of all, trying to show me how much superior he was to Vikings. I laughed in his face."

Odinkar reappeared in the kitchen door in full battle array. He glared at Valorius. Other Vikings stumbled past, encouraged by their wives and children. Dogs and pigs were under foot everywhere.

"We've got to stick together somehow," said Valorius. "But if I don't fight the Kalamandrans it looks like I'll have to fight Odinkar and his men."

Zenobia snatched a man's fur cloak from a bench and threw it over her head and shoulders.

"They'll never notice in this confusion," she said. "And once we're out at sea they won't turn back just to put me ashore."

"They might throw you overboard."

"Give me all the silver you have left." She grinned. "That should keep me out of the water."

Confusion or not, Odinkar did notice Zenobia as she scrambled aboard. But he just waved her to a corner of the stern. Evidently he considered her under his protection, since she had been ravished by a guest of his stockade. There were two other Viking girls aboard; their eyes flashed with excitement. They were eloping with two young men from the ship.

Valorius bent his back over his oar. He tried to remember what weapons the Kalamandrans had used in battle; they would certainly be more potent than the swords and spears of the Vikings. He thought he was wizard enough to protect at least this one ship. There was no longer any need to refrain from wizardry since Borimbo knew where he was. Although why so powerful a wizard should continue to attack only through agents was still a mystery. The whereabouts of Magus Rex was even more of a mystery.

All along the coast the dragon ships of the Vikings were rushing eagerly out to sea. Battle was even better than silver, and one usually led to the other. But they were too shrewd to plunge headlong into the ranks of the enemy. A disciplined flotilla was arrayed against them, and they wisely began to join forces. Zenobia stood to one side of the tiller, scanning the opposing fleet.

Valorius could not recall any exceptional weapons used by the Kalamandrans. They had electric lighting, and relatively sophisticated weaponry yet they went to battle in galleys. Machinery, he knew, did not flourish in societies based on slavery, and the Kalamandrans had enslaved half the world in the centuries following Balbek's Comet. In any case, it looked like the Vikings would be fatally outgunned. Perhaps he could save this one ship long enough to escape.

The sun was at their backs—that was one advantage. The Kalamandran galleys were less than a mile away. Their battle formation was in a quarter moon shape: thickest at the center with horns pointing forward. The Vikings also had the wind at their backs.

"There he is!" cried Zenobia, running forward between the banks of rowers. "The little coward is hanging back."

Valorius leaped up on his bench. Just behind the thickest part of the formation a galley stood alone. Even from this distance there was no mistaking the electric blue uniforms of Borimbo's servitors. They were probably strong rowers.

Odinkar shouted at him. The Vikings all around him grumbled—he was throwing off their rhythm. Instead of returning to his oar, Valorius pulled another man from his, the skald who spoke Latin. He dragged him back to the tiller and had him explain to Odinkar the importance of the lone galley behind the others.

Odinkar was angry over this breach of discipline, but he was too experienced a warrior not to realize the importance of the information. His bleary eyes narrowed with cunning. He barked something, and a man toward the center of the ship leaped to his feet and started blowing a ram's horn. The call was taken up all along the line. Sails were furled like magic, and the ships began to draw together. Odinkar bellowed right and left, and his information spread outward through the fleet.

Over a dozen reefing lines were held by members of the crew; the speed at which the sails could be adjusted was amazing. The Vikings maneuvered into a wedge, with the point taken by the ship of Odinkar the Good. They advanced on the Kalamandran line with sails furled, rowing at half speed.

Then fire began to arc toward them; patches of the sea burst into flames. The Kalamandran ships were using some kind of long-distance flamethrower. The Vikings were not fazed. Neither the gods nor men held any fear for them. Valorius, however, was afraid for them.

Once more he left his oar. This time he ran to the front of the ship. He leaped onto the neck of the dragon prow and summoned forth all the powers of wizardry at his command for the battle.

A cry from Odinkar. Instantly the sail was unfurled, and the men bent over their oars with all the strength they had. Valorius felt the wind quicken in his face. They were almost within range of the Kalamandran flamethrowers. Suddenly green fire-balls began to rain down on the enemy. It was a mere sorcerer's trick, but Valorius could think of nothing better.

The horns of the Kalamandran line began to sweep inward, attempting to engulf the enemy. But the Viking change of pace had thrown off their timing, their wedge bursting right through the center of the enemy formation. The Kalamandrans could no longer use their flamethrowers without incinerating each other. Valorius continued to send fire-balls shooting into the nearest ships, spreading panic and confusion among the Kalamandrans. A single galley stood alone right before Odinkar's ship.

Valorius hurled the biggest fire-ball he had ever attempted right at it. The fire-ball dissolved in midair. He tried another, but the same thing happened. He could now see Borimbo the Magnificent scurrying back and forth on deck with his stumpy little legs. The dwarf raised his hands and the mast of Odinkar's ship was shattered to sawdust; snippets of sail fluttered down like snow. Valorius was knocked off the dragon prow by the concussion.

The Viking ships kept coming. Nine of them had broken through the Kalamandran line and were bearing down on Borimbo's galley. His servitors were now at their oars, bending their oddly-shaped bodies with powerful strokes. The galley started to pull away. If it reached the mirage in time, Valorius knew that the Vikings would be too discouraged to follow. His own ship began to fall behind, demasted. The sails of the other Viking ships gave them an advantage over Borimbo's galley. It was a race for the mirage.

Valorius could do no more. He strode the length of the ship toward Zenobia. The sea was a turmoil of battle; the dragon ships of the Vikings that had not broken through the line were now ramming the Kalamandran galleys. The decks seethed with hand-to-hand combat. Odinkar the Good stood like an angry bear beside the tiller, furious that his demasted ship was falling behind. Zenobia had thrown aside her cloak. She smiled at him and held out her hand. The mirage was dead ahead.

No sooner did Valorius take her in his arms than they were in the midst of a ghost battle. All around them the dragon ships of the Vikings grew faint and hazy; the Kalamandran galleys slowly faded from sight. A sound like the crack of thunder rent the air, and they found themselves in the water. They were alone.

The barren Central Depression of Greenland rose

all about them, silent and lifeless. A quarter of a
mile ahead they could see a small island. The mirage
was gone, but the concrete palace of Borimbo the
Magnificent was still there. Borimbo himself was
splashing in the water just offshore. His servitors
were drowning.

Before Valorius could employ any lifesaving techniques, Zenobia had pulled off her boots and started
for shore. He admired her bravery. Pulling off his own
boots, he started after her, ready to come to her rescue
if the long swim should prove too much for her. But
she did not slow down. In fact, he had trouble keeping
up with her. She was sitting on the rocks, wringing
out her hair, when at last he stumbled, coughing and
sputtering, out of the water. There was a suspicious
twinkle in her eye.

"Oh, beloved," she said affectionately. "I'm so proud
of you. It was your wizardry that got us past the
enemy."

Valorius just naturally took her in his arms and
kissed her. Perhaps he had underrated his own abilities after all. But whose wizardry had dissolved the
whole computerized fairyland of Borimbo the Magnificent? A troop of his servitors was straggling across
the weed-choked gardens toward the palace; many
more were floating face down on the waves.

"What became of Borimbo?" he asked.

Zenobia continued to ring the water from her long
auburn tresses. Her wet woolen tunic clung to her
body like paint; it was obvious that she wore nothing
underneath. She grinned mischievously.

"He's looking at us right now," she said.

Then Valorius noticed a head peeking over the top
of a cable trench not fifty yards away. It disappeared
the instant he turned toward it. The trench ran straight
to the basement of the concrete palace.

"I think we'd better go after him," said Zenobia. "If
he thinks we're afraid of him he might do something
nasty. But there's no hurry. He can't run very fast."

The moment they started for the concrete palace,

so did Borimbo. His head peeked up out of the cable trench every few minutes, each time closer to the palace. Valorius began to suspect that the dwarf was actually afraid of him.

Borimbo's servitors, however, were afraid of nothing. Those that had survived drowning, reinforced by others from the palace, turned and began coming toward them. Valorius drew his sword and looked about for some place where he could defend Zenobia. They were within a hundred yards of the palace. He saw Borimbo scamper out of the cable trench and disappear into the basement.

"Just don't let them get hold of you," said Zenobia, as they backed away from the oncoming troop. "You can't believe how strong they are."

Their garbled voices and odd shuffling gait made them seem like the creatures of a nightmare. There were now at least fifty of them. Valorius gave up all hope of fighting them; he wondered aloud if there was a boat somewhere on the island.

"I've never seen one," said Zenobia. "But as long as we keep moving—"

Then a strange thing happened. The garbling voices stopped, and the whole troop came to a sudden halt. The afternoon sunlight dodged in and out of the skudding clouds. The soft slap of the waves against the shore and the murmur of the boreal wind were the only sounds. Fifty oddly-shaped beings, dressed in electric blue uniforms, stood like gargoyles in a garden of weeds.

Valorius and Zenobia looked at each other. These creatures were not computer phantoms; there was only one way they could have been turned off. Hand in hand they hurried toward the concrete palace.

If Borimbo's servitors were the creatures of a nightmare, the scene that met their eyes was an engineer's nightmare. The basement was saturated with ozone: consoles sputtered and flashed with shorted circuits, panels were scorched, cables spat electricity, and melted solder flowed like water. Borimbo scuttled from room to room in a panic of inadequacy; pushing buttons, pulling circuit-breakers, and throwing switches. Nothing seemed to help. His squalid little empire of computerized wizardry was melting before his eyes, literally melting.

Then all at once the electrical typhoon blew over, and a fresh wind whistled through the basement, carrying away the smoke and stink. Valorius and Zenobia, their eyes still smarting from the ozone, stood just inside the door. Borimbo turned to face them, but the sword in Valorius' hand seemed to unnerve him. For several moments they all just stared at each other.

A hum of machinery broke the silence. Somebody was descending in the elevator. It came to a halt at the basement level and its doors slid open. Out stepped— Magus Rex.

"So you did it all with machines, you little rascal." He sneered at Borimbo.

The dwarf whirled to meet him. "At last we meet face to face, Magus Rex."

"Not unless you stand on something. How dare you even presume to challenge the greatest wizard who has ever lived?" He glanced contemptuously at the batteries of electronic equipment. "Yes, the ancient twentieth century would appeal to a runt like you."

"These are the mere adjuncts of my power," Borimbo cried in a shrill voice. "My wizardry stands supreme in my own age. I dominate my world just as you did yours. I have creations of my own."

"If you're talking about these wretched gunks I see moping about, I wouldn't boast. Is that really the best you could do?"

"It was Valorius who set off the alarm, Father," said Zenobia. "That's how he rescued me from Bobo."

"Bobo?" Magus Rex grinned at the dwarf.

"I am Borimbo the Magnificent," he cried. "Many address me as Magus Superbus."

"But I shall address you as Bobo," said Magus Rex.

"And don't tell me about your powers. You couldn't charm a snake without some kind of machine." He shook his head in disgust. "To think that I, even I, Magus Rex, looked upon you as a worthy challenger. Bah!"

"Valorius led the attack against him in the sea battle, Father," said Zenobia. "That's what drove Bobo back to the island."

The dwarf sneered at Valorius, his eyes glittering with malice. Had Magus Rex not been present. . . .

"A Master Wizard capable of setting off an alarm and leading a sea battle would probably make your jolly old father an excellent personal secretary," said Magus Rex. "Is that what you're trying to tell me, Zenobia?"

"Yes, Father."

"Perhaps I have been hasty, Valorius," he said. "Your penchant for dumb luck has impressed me. But you really had no idea what you were doing when you set off the alarm, did you?"

"No, my lord," he had to admit. "My sole concern was rescuing Zenobia."

She brushed against him and took his hand.

"Nonetheless," said Magus Rex, "that was the turning point. Bobo had arrayed enormous powers against me, and I found myself questioning my own abilities for the first time in centuries. Then everything began to waver, and Bobo rushed from the battlefield. The reason is now obvious."

"This Viking swine could not have stopped me." Borimbo glared at Valorius. "Someday we shall meet again."

"That's just more of your presumption," said Magus Rex. "What makes you think you have a someday?"

"Would you kick a man when he's down?" Borimbo asked craftily. "A man so much smaller than yourself?"

Magus Rex smiled in appreciation. "That's rather cunning of you, Bobo. It seems that everybody wants to use my legendary equitableness as a weapon against me. Tell me, how did you get all these machines here from the twentieth century?"

"Other machines. I got the first one from a museum in the Brazilian Hegemony."

"Ah, the Technology Museum," said Magus Rex. "So you pilfered enough machinery to build yourself a time machine and then headed straight for the twentieth century? I'm surprised you didn't stay there. A sadistic dwarf would have felt right at home. But the trouble with relying on machines, Bobo, is that somebody might throw the switch. Then all you have left are gunks and concrete. And bad taste."

"You have defeated me, Magus Rex," said Borimbo, although he did not look penitent. "I ask only to be left in peace here on my island nome. I've learned my lesson."

"I doubt it," said Magus Rex. "But I fully intend to leave you here in peace. Your constituent elements shall peacefully enrich the island as they never did while still incorporated. Farewell, Bobo."

The basement of the concrete palace began to crackle with energy. Valorius could sense Borimbo using all his powers to resist, but it was like a squib against a tornado.

"Wait, Magus Rex!" cried Borimbo. "I have vital information. I know your fate."

The gathering storm subsided momentarily.

"Speak," ordered Magus Rex. "I am indeed curious to learn how I, Magus Rex, with perfect control of all my autonomic processes could ever perish from the earth."

"From the earth, yes," said Borimbo. "Perish, no."

"You crafty little rascal." Magus Rex grinned down at him. "You've hit upon the one thing that could save your cellular coherence. Speak, and if your words are true, I grant you your squalid little island, your gunks and concrete and bad taste."

"How do I know you will keep your word?"

"My legendary equitableness speaks for itself."

Borimbo thought this over for a moment, then

nodded. "Come," he said. "I will show you proof."

They started toward the elevator.

"Let me come with, Father," cried Zenobia. "My clothes are all wet, and this wool is beginning to shrink. Bobo has a whole wardrobe for me upstairs."

"Come along then," said Magus Rex. "You too, Valorius."

While Zenobia changed into dry clothes, Valorius dried off his own. When Magus Rex reappeared with Borimbo he was smiling.

"That answers something I've always been curious about," he said as he approached. "So dopplegangers can exist, even on different planets, in different solar systems. For so attractive a world I shall indeed be ready to leave earth, when the time comes."

"Then you will keep your promise, Magus Rex?" asked Borimbo nervously.

"That goes without saying."

"And I promise never to leave this island," said Borimbo. "You have my word."

"More important, I have your ancestor." He explained his removal of the dwarf child from ancient Lhasa, adding: "Should you ever attempt any skulduggery again, Bobo, I'll see to it that you never exist."

Borimbo's eyes narrowed in calculation. "The fact that I do exist," he said thoughtfully, "must prove that nothing can possibly happen to my ancestor. Time does not work like that, Magus Rex."

"Are you sure? You may be right, but then why did you secrete your ancestor in Lhasa in the first place? The machines you smuggled here from the twentieth century use electricity, sometimes with wonderful effect. But the builders of the machines had only the vaguest notions about the nature of electricity. We both can use time to a certain extent, but does either of us really know what it is? It would be an awful chance to take, Bobo. If you want to exist at all, you'd better behave yourself. Now go scuttle off and start cleaning up the mess. I've released control of your wretched gunks."

Borimbo bowed stiffly, but he could not refrain from a last malicious glance at Valorius. Then he took the elevator to the basement.

Zenobia no sooner stepped out of her dressing room than they were all engulfed in a maelstrom of psychic energy. Every piece of metal around them glowed with a blue aura. Then they were once more in the palace of Magus Rex.

The great wizard sat Indian-fashion on his musnud, stroking his black silky beard with his long violet fingernails. Valorius and Zenobia, both somewhat staggered by the transition, stood side by side before the ivory dais.

"I have gained new perspective," Magus Rex announced. "And yet there is still much to be learned here on earth."

"Remember what you said about giving Valorius the job of personal secretary, Father," said Zenobia. "You promised in Changan."

"But I had to go back in time and fetch him myself."

"All you said, Father, was that the job was his the moment he claimed it."

"And not granting him the job now would call my legendary equitableness into question? Is that what you're trying to tell me?"

"You promised, Father."

"All right, Valorius, the job is yours. And in all fairness you have displayed some degree of resourcefulness and dumb luck. Especially the latter. And so you've gotten around me after all, haven't you, Zenobia?"

"Yes, Father."

"And now I suppose you'll begin wheedling for my permission to become his consort?"

"Yes, Father."

"Then perhaps I'd better just grant that permission at once and have done with it."

"My lord—" Valorius began.

Magus Rex waved him to silence. "Don't start blatting, Valorius. You'd only cause me to change my mind. But I suppose every man of great ability must look upon his daughter's suitor with contempt. I don't look forward to teaching you your job."

"I've been thinking," said Zenobia. "Why don't Valorius and I go away for a long vacation before he settles down as your personal secretary? Say, a generation or two in one of the last dynasties of the California Islands."

"Do you really want to go off with Valorius before he's learned to control your aging processes?"

Zenobia turned to Valorius. "It really would be unfair to Father, to just run off before you've learned your new job."

Magus Rex said, "I thought you might see it like that, my darling daughter. But I'm still curious about something. You were contacting Valorius against my strict injunctions. Could you really have so convinced yourself that you were only writing poetry that even my powers couldn't detect a lie?"

"Yes, Father."

A sardonic twinkle appeared in his eye. "Well, good luck to you, Valorius. But now I shall be leaving you for a few days. Where or why I'm going does not concern you."

"Would I be correct, my lord," said Valorius, "in assuming that you are returning to ancient Rome, to the time of Marcus Aurelius? And that you intend to spend ten years studying among the great libraries of antiquity?"

Magus Rex looked astonished. "But how could you possibly have known that?"

"There is nothing more mysterious than time, my lord."

Magus Rex looked at him for a moment through his heavy-lidded eyes. "You must explain that to me when I get back, Valorius. In the meantime I grant the pair of you the run of the palace. Injunctions of any kind are pointless in matters of the heart, or whatever organ happens to be involved. You'd only get around them somehow, wouldn't you, my darling daughter?"

"Yes, Father," said Zenobia.

"How like your mother you are, in so many ways."

He waved his long violet fingernails and a surge of psychic energy rushed toward the ivory dais. The great bronze doors clanged shut. Valorius and Zenobia were hit by a strong wind; they blinked and staggered. When the storm had subsided there was nothing but overstuffed purple cushions on the musnud of Magus Rex.